LINCOLN FRIDAY

A Novel

William Stuart Gould M.D.

WMG LTD.
New York

WMG
WMG Ltd. Publishers
288 Lexington Avenue
Suite 6-F
New York, New York
10016
wmg.ltd.publishing@gmail.com

For information about WMG Ltd.'s Speakers Bureau or discounts for bulk purchases, please email: wmg.ltd.publishing@gmail.com

ISBN 0991223780
ISBN 9780991223787 (pbk)
ISBN 978-0-9912237-7-0 (ebook)

ALSO BY BILL GOULD

At Yonah Mountain
Captain Iron Mustache
In Black Granite
C.O.L.A.
A Heart Wind from the Desert
Raphael's Blanket

ACKNOWLEDGMENTS

For reviewing my understanding of prostate cancer, I thank Michael Y. Han, M.D. For correcting my Spanish, Martha V. Zamora.

And, most of all, for sticking with me through the endless hours of editing and discussions, my best friend of all in this world, my beautiful wife, Marlene Ann Gould.

To the women and men who served in Viet Nam and were then forgotten by Congress and the VA.

Dear Senator Kozub,

I am sorry to bother you, but I am writing to ask for your help. My husband is a Viet Nam veteran and has prostate cancer. The VA says it could be two months before they can even give us the results of his biopsy. His doctor told us it doesn't matter because prostate cancer is not serious, and we can safely wait for a long time.

He was a helicopter pilot in Vietnam and sprayed Agent Orange. The VA doesn't think that caused his cancer. That is what his VA doctor told us, but I read on your website that you have been fighting to take care of the men who were exposed.

I must tell you that he earned the Medal of Honor. I know that doesn't mean he should get special treatment, but what kind of care are the privates and corporals getting?

Please help us. We have been married for 47 years. I love him so much.

Thank you.

Isabelle Friday

Dear Ms. Friday,

Thank you for contacting my Philadelphia office regarding the difficulties you are experiencing with your combat-related claim. I am happy to look into this matter for you.

A member of my staff has forwarded your letter to the Department of Veterans Affairs seeking further information regarding the issue at hand, and she will notify you as soon as a response is received. If you have any questions or concerns in the meantime, please do not hesitate to contact Cindy Startup in my Philadelphia office.

Sincerely,
Francie
Francine Kozub
United States Senator

Dear Ms. Friday,

I have now heard back from the Veterans Administration regarding the request for treatment of prostate cancer. They remind us that there are many men being treated for acute wounds received in Iraq and Afghanistan. We must wait our turn.

If the subject is terminal, please let me know, and I will see what I can do to help you expedite the process. In the meantime, please follow up with the Veterans Administration directly. Their hotline number is 542-569-2548.

Sincerely,
Francie
Francine Kozub
United States Senator

BOOK I

PART I

CHAPTER ONE

Friday Brothers Farms
Wilkes Barre, Pennsylvania
1953

"Papa! Papa!"

Parnell Friday tore through the screen door. Despite a limp, the cadaverous man moved nearly at a run. When he turned the corner and found his son behind the weathered barn, Parnell pulled to a stop and demanded, though feebly, "What is it, Lincoln, what's wrong?"

"Papa, look! Look up there!"

Parnell puffed weakly. "Oh…that. Why, that's just a blimp, son."

"What's a blimp, Papa?"

Parnell's back straightened a few degrees. "It's like an airplane, Linc."

"But, Papa, it ain't got no wings."

"No, it ain't. Just gas holds it up, like that balloon I got you at the Luzerne Fair. You see that tube on the bottom?" Parnell knelt and rested his forearm on his son's shoulder then pointed with an unsteady hand.

"I think I can."

"There's people inside there, Linc. Maybe ten. Sometimes even fifteen of 'em." He paused and drew a few more labored breaths. "They's takin' a hop, flyin', that's all. Just like your papa did in the war."

Lincoln jumped into the air. When his tattered leather shoes touched back on the dust of the barnyard, he groaned, "Papa, why can't I stay up in the air like them people? I want to fly."

"Son, people ain't birds. A man has to learn to fly. Learnin' flyin's hard, and it's a long way off...please, Jesus."

"Well, Papa, then let me drive the tractor. It's just like flyin'. That's what the other boys say."

Parnell's voice hardened. "Boy, you stay away from that goddamned tractor, you hear?" His voice rose to a weak screech. "Just stay the hell away from that cursed thing!"

"Papa, I'm six years old. All the other boys are drivin'."

"Well, they shouldn't be. You hear me, damnit? And stop your lying. You're only five."

Parnell's head sagged, and his wasted body wavered like a stalk of dying corn in the field just behind the barn, a patch of earth he had sown with hope in his heart but not set foot in for two months, ever since the accident. He pivoted crossly for the house, but it was only steps before he dropped to his knees then collapsed onto his back. The front of his coveralls slowly darkened, and his eyes reddened.

Lincoln screamed, "Papa, Papa, I'm sorry. I'm sorry, Papa."

A once-handsome woman, her raven hair dry and streaked with wild strands of gray, ran from the kitchen and knelt at Parnell's side. Her face, long furrowed with worry lines, hardened in panic as her husband rolled his head to the side to stare into the endless pastures and woodlands.

She spoke tremulously in a thick, Southern drawl, "That's the last straw, Parnell. We're going to the doctor right this very minute. Look at you. You're like a scarecrow. No more excuses."

Lincoln watched from a squat, motionless, as his mother helped Parnell to his feet. He grumbled incoherently, and Lincoln's eyes dropped in contrition. He picked up a stick and scratched mechanically at the dirt, but as his parents turned toward the house, he jumped up and began to sob. "I'm sorry, Mama. I didn't mean to hurt Papa."

"Lincoln," she spoke shortly, "you listen to me. You didn't do nothin'. I've told you that over and over. Do you hear me? Your father don't feel good. He's not angry at you. He's scared, Lincoln, that's all. We're all scared. He just wants you to be safe more than anything in the world."

She guided Parnell into the house, where he slumped into a chair at the cluttered kitchen table. When his breathing slowed, he lifted his head and stared out the torn screen door. Miriam's shoulders relaxed as she reckoned he was watching his son, but not a single muscle twitched, and she bent forward to look into his face. His soul was, though, absorbed far, far in the past.

She wiped her hands on her calico apron and slid them tenderly onto his shoulders. "Parnell, it's going to be okay. The Lord gives us strength. All he asks in return is that we have faith. I had conviction in God's love, and he brought you home to me from that damn curse of a war, and he will deliver us again." She heaved out a deep breath "And please, Parnell, don't be so hard on the boy. He worships you. He and the Lord are all we have left."

He grunted, "Yeah, well, Lanny worshipped me, and look what the hell I let happen to him."

"*You* did nothing to harm that child. And you need to stop blamin' yourself. I'm sorry the Lord didn't grant us a simple life. We have to work hard to live. But we're better off than them lazy, highfalutin ones in the city." Her head dropped, and she went on in a whisper. "Parnell, things happen along the way. It's God's will. We ain't the first." She paused and ran her fingers over the bony lumps of her husband's shoulders. "You're losing too much weight. How many times do I have to tell you to start eatin'?"

"I ain't hungry."

"You better get hungry. You still have Lincoln and me." Her hands began to tremble. "I'm sorry, but you're goin' to the doctor's right now."

She packed Parnell and Lincoln into the Nash. Her first stop was at Schroeder's, the horse farm that raised trotters, pacers, and a few thoroughbreds on the next scrap of land along Lebanon Road. Della Schroeder agreed to take Lincoln, "…but not for too long. You know how Dieter is. But we're happy to have him for a couplea hours."

Miriam went back out to the car. "Lincoln, come on. Let's have you stay here until your daddy and I get back. You just be quiet and sit down in the corner or wherever they put you." She drew a breath to tell him to say goodbye to Parnell, but worried it would only frighten both of them.

Lincoln Friday never saw his father again.

She drove into Wilkes Barre to the tiny hospital in which both Lanny and Lincoln had been born. The emergency room doctor called the local GP, Arthur Heldman, for help. The man spent a just a few minutes examining Parnell before asking a nurse to inject his new patient with a sedative. While he waited for the shot to work, Heldman asked softly, "You serve, Mr. Friday?"

There was a pause, and Parnell whispered, “Yes, sir, Red Arrow Division.”

Heldman nodded, patted Parnell on the shoulder, and smiled. “We’re gonna take good care of you, GI. Don’t you fret one little bit. We got your back covered.” Parnell grasped the man’s hand, and they remained like that for some seconds, silent, both staring into their own worlds.

As Parnell’s eyes fluttered shut, Dr. Heldman placed the man’s hand under the blanket, patted it, then wrote orders for his patient to be sent to a private room on a quiet floor. When Parnell was settled and asleep, Heldman guided Miriam into the hallway. He looked her directly in the eye. “Now, Mrs. Friday, your husband was a soldier—Thirty Second Infantry Division, he told me. They were in Japan right after the war, if I remember correctly.”

Her face tightened, and she nodded. “Wasn’t ever the same after he came back from Japan. Always starin’ into the future. Well, at first I thought it was the future. Before he went off to the war, he had such plans for us, a house full of kids, a payin’ job as a carpenter. Oh, he did so fine with wood.” She stopped and caught her breath. “Lately, makes me think I was wrong, I mean about his lookin’ into the future. I do believe his heart’s mired in the past, Doctor. I don’t know what to do.”

“Mrs. Friday, he was part of the occupation force. Do you know if he was sent to Hiroshima to assess the damage? They did that with some of the 32nd.”

“Yeah, he told me that.”

“How long was he there? Do you know?”

“Doctor, you need to ask him. He don’t talk about it much.”

“But you’re saying he was actually *in* Hiroshima after the bomb?”

“Yes, he was. I’m sure about that much.”

"Well, I think that may help us get to the bottom of what's going on, Mrs. Friday. I do believe your husband has prostate problems. I'm afraid it looks like cancer." Her head turned in confusion. "That's a little gland down in the crotch. Lotta men get cancer there."

"Cancer? I can't believe it. He's so strong. Still works from before the sun. How did he get it? He was healthy as a horse until our boy died. You think that had something to do with it?"

"Mrs. Friday, I don't know how cancer happens. Nobody does, but there's a lot of returnees with it. The men from Japan, especially. The ones they sent to dig around where the bomb dropped." He fell silent for a moment and turned to stare out a smudged window. She stood tensely until he turned back. "Mrs. Friday, your husband is a veteran. I think it's best we send him to the VA Hospital in Philadelphia. He'll be treated for free. And I will make sure he sees one of the good cancer doctors down there. I know just the right man. Let me give him a call."

Her eyes reddened. "Doctor, we don't have money to pay today's bill, and surely not for a bus to Philadelphia."

Dr. Heldman put a hand on her shoulder. "We'll take care of that. And you don't need to fret about today's bill, Mrs. Friday. I was in Japan, too."

Miriam called the Schroeders. The old man grumbled he wasn't running a hotel, but Della took the phone from him and agreed to take Lincoln until morning if she paid for his food. She heard Schroeder hiss, "Put him out there in the barn. He can sleep on the floor for all I care."

Lincoln was led from the house by a groom. When they were out of earshot, the man whispered, "I am Domenico. We take good care of you. You do as I say and do not talk. Everything be okay." He had Lincoln sit on a bale of hay in the barn until Mrs.

Schroeder stuck her head in, glared, and left without a word. Domenico whispered, "After dinner, we sneak you into the tack room. Much nicer. We put bags of oats on the floor. Then we cover them with a couplea horse blankets. We gonna roll one more for a pillow, and then I put one on top of you to stay warm." He glanced surreptitiously out the door. "You don't tell Schroeder where I put you."

He brought a bucket of water, a shard of brown soap, and a slip of cloth for Lincoln to wash himself. At six, Mrs. Schroeder came to the barn with a tin plate of boiled cabbage and a strip of fatty ham. She placed it on the floor, took a slip of paper and a pencil out of her apron pocket, and started a food list.

As the sun set, Lincoln came out of the barn and approached Mr. Schroeder to ask for a toothbrush and a bit of baking soda. The old man growled, "You're too young to brush your teeth."

Parnell Friday was transported by ambulance to the Philadelphia Veterans Hospital the next morning. The urologist told them a number of soldiers who had been sent to Hiroshima and Nagasaki after the bombs had developed cancer. While some of them had prostate cancer, many more suffered from leukemia, and at the same frequency as the Japanese who survived the actual blasts.

The doctor stood and peered into the hallway, looked left and right, then spoke in a hushed voice. "But I have to be up front and tell you that the government and the VA deny the connection. They don't want to pay the millions to care for the GIs who got sick." Miriam gasped, but the doctor smiled and raised a palm toward her. "Now, now, don't worry. I didn't mean that Mr. Friday won't be cared for here at the VA. He will, and there will be no charge. What I meant was, there are, unfortunately, no grounds to file a claim against the government for war-related damages, you know, no disability pay."

Miriam remained in Philadelphia that night. She drew the last of the money from her purse for a tiny room at the YWCA, but when she got back to the hospital, Parnell's nurse, who had been in the Army in Europe, allowed her to sit by her husband's bed after visiting hours. Nearing midnight, and the change in nursing shifts, Miriam was told she'd have to leave until morning, but as she rose, Parnell became confused. He strained to lift himself, then mumbled to the ceiling about walking through the rubble of Hiroshima, about the children huddled against the rain. He suddenly spoke very clearly, the grittiness in his voice gone. "There was this little girl. Why, she pointed right at herself and said, 'Fumiko, Fumiko Matsukawa.' And I said, 'Uncle Parnell,' and I pointed right at *my*self. Then I said, 'Fumiko San, you're so pretty and smart'. You see, you say *San* in their tongue to show respect. Then I said, 'Don't you move a muscle. You stay right here, child. Uncle Parnell gonna bring you and your sisters some *good* American grub. Straight from that ole mess hall.'" He paused for a moment then smiled, and the two women's shoulders slackened. "Your old papa did good, didn't he, Lanny? That's why God gave us you." There was another pause until his face tensed, and he wailed, "Lanny!" He sucked in a deep breath as if to go on, but his head abruptly collapsed onto the pillow, his eyes closed, and his breathing became uneven.

The nurse took Miriam by the elbow. "Honey, let me put you in this closet out here in the hall. Soon as the coast's clear, I'll get you back with your husband."

After report, the nurse went straight to Parnell's room. His breathing had become impossibly labored. As she straightened the blankets before fetching Miriam, he mumbled a few words, his head lolled, and he passed.

Miriam sat quietly holding her husband's waxy, skeletal hand. She whispered to the nurse, "Did my Parnell say anything before he left on his journey?"

"Something about losing his son. Sounded to me like he died of a broken heart more than the cancer."

CHAPTER TWO

Several weeks later, a social worker from the Veterans Administration came out to the farm. VA legal services had made an appointment for Miriam to see a private lawyer on Franklin Square in downtown Philadelphia. She was granted fifteen dollars to cover bus fare and meals. At the 30th Street Station in Philly, Miriam counted the change left over and considered taking a taxi to the office, but, hours early for her appointment, she stuffed the coins back into her faded purse and set out walking. It was not three blocks before she was so hopelessly lost, she gathered her nerve and stopped a man for directions. He spoke so fast, though, she understood not a single word, and by the time she happened upon Franklin Square, her frock was moist with sweat.

She knocked obsequiously on the opaque, glass door, and when there was no answer, she opened it slowly and peered around the edge. A blast of frigid air bewildered her, and she stepped back out, pulling the door closed with a bang. In the hallway, she stepped away from the door but nodded to herself, remembering Parnell's tale about cold air blowing out of noisy contraptions in the windows at General MacArthur's headquarters in Tokyo. She knocked again, reopened the door, and took a hesitant step into the office. A young woman at the mahogany reception desk looked up and stared at Miriam's faded dress. She crooked a finger for Miriam to approach. "You must be Mrs. Friday. VA, right?"

"Uh huh."

"Why don't you have a seat and fill these out." She poked a sheath of papers at Miriam and pointed to a plush, leather sofa in the corner.

Miriam craned her neck forward. "What are these?"

"It's paperwork. You know, just so we can get paid."

Miriam took the pile with quavering hands but remained at the desk and squinted to read the tiny print. She tried to form the words in her mouth, but there were so many syllables in each, she gave up. The one thing she saw clearly, though, was Miriam I. Friday typed under a straight line at the bottom of the top form. She pointed at it. "Does this mean I have to sign?"

"Why, yes, of course. It's a legal and binding contract between you and the Law Offices of A.B. Highbridge, Esq. I'm sure you can understand that Mr. Highbridge has a lot of expenses running this office."

Miriam froze. "I can't do this. I can't promise you money I don't have."

"Well, Madam, if you don't sign it, we can't give you legal advice, now can we?"

"Well, my name's already on the paper, down here at the bottom. Does that mean I already owe you?"

"No. There's no charge for the first consultation. The rest of it, well, you'll have to discuss it with Mr. Highbridge's legal assistant. She's the one who's going to see you today. Look, Mrs. Friday, why don't you just take a seat over there in the corner and fill out the forms. Then we can get you in with her. I'm sure she'll get everything straightened out."

Miriam retreated to the couch, hands clutching a dozen legal-length documents, a pencil, a primitive ballpoint, and her tatty purse. Eyes on the papers, still mouthing the letters, she turned and lowered herself reflexively onto the puffy, leather sofa but sank past the point at which she'd expected to stop. Her arms flew up over her head, and when she hit bottom, the papers sailed out of her right fist, the purse out of her left. The latter thumped an ersatz blue and white Ming vase on the end table. Though an explosion of ceramic shards showered the room, Miriam saw only the puff of dried insect carcasses and dust bunnies that had dwelt inside the urn since the Hoover administration.

The secretary yelped and sprang from behind her desk, coming to exasperated attention, fists on hips, in front of Miriam. The woman drew in a deep breath to begin her harangue, but the lungful of the detritus-laden air triggered a wave of boisterous coughing.

The commotion drew a man in an elegant, double-breasted suit from the bowels of the office, though all Miriam saw of him before her eyes plummeted in disgrace was a bulbous, silk handkerchief and fresh boutonniere. Staring at the floor, she guessed at the cost of the vase and imagined that added to the tariff for the coming jurisprudence. The man, though, spoke cordially. "Mrs. Friday, I presume. Please be so kind as to follow me."

They entered a room bare of decoration save dozens of yellow and green, leather-bound law books on dusty shelves. He nodded toward a seat at the mahogany conference table. Miriam glanced sideways at the pot of brewed coffee next to china cups and saucers; the sterling cream and sugar service glittered. A pudgy woman entered the room without knocking. She lifted a cup. Miriam smiled and took a breath to ask for just a bit of sugar and cream, but the woman did not look up. She filled half the cup with cream and sugar, added a splash of coffee, dropped with a thud into a corner seat, and opened a stenographer's pad.

The man cleared his throat. "Mrs. Friday, good afternoon. I am Arlington Byrd Highbridge. I understand you are here to effect the sale of the real property in your deceased husband's estate." Her head rotated slightly. He cleared his throat again. "You want us to sell your farm. Is that correct?"

Her voice quavered as she spoke in an undertone. "Yes, but could you tell me, mister, how much do I have to pay?"

He leaned forward and patted her forearm. "Madam, I am on contract with the Veterans Administration. There is no direct charge to you. We keep a small percentage of the sale of the house, but it is less than that extracted by those unscrupulous real estate agents that have taken over the market around…," he stopped, opened a chart, and shifted through a few pages. "Wilkes Barre. Yes, Wilkes Barre. The VA remits to us the difference between our small percentage of the proceeds on the property and our usual fee."

She sat without expression. "Now, Madam, may I see the deed and your husband's death certificate?" He glanced at the documents, made a note on a legal pad, then asked, "Who is Wallace Friday? Is that your husband's legal name?"

"No. Wally was my brother-in-law. He bought the farm first, then we took over when he died. It was right after the war."

"I'm sorry to hear that." Without a pause, he went on. "Do you have the transfer of title?"

"We started to do all that paperwork, but it cost too much. It was my husband's brother. Parnell said it came to us automatic. Is there a problem?"

"Have you paid the taxes on it since…," he searched the deed, "Wallace died?"

"Oh, yes. We never missed."

"Well, in that case, we're going to have to establish Intestate Succession. Let's see, that's 20 Pa. C.S.A.; I believe it's section 2101. I'm going to need to do some work here to get this straightened out."

"Mister, do I have to pay for that, you know, what was it you said?"

"Mrs. Friday, this should have been done years ago."

"But, like I said, we didn't have the money. And why don't the VA pay for it?"

"Madam, the VA can't be paying for all your legal expenses in life, now can they? This is one of those pay me now or pay me later deals." He stopped and stared at her. "Madam, you're going to have to decide if you want us to help you."

"Oh, I want you to help me, somebody has to, but I need time to think about how much it's gonna cost. Can I come back in a few days?"

He agreed, and the VA sent another few dollars for car fare.

With the mortgage and property taxes due in two weeks, Miriam wrote to her kin in Oklahoma begging for a loan and hinting that she'd like to come home to make amends. She had not been back to Enid or been in contact with her family since she'd left to work at the Fort Sill PX in 1942. And it was just six weeks later that she and Parnell eloped, and only a few days after that he left for the Pacific Islands.

After the war, the very day he was discharged, he bought a '32 Plymouth, and the two drove north to Wilkes Barre, where the VA had helped Parnell's brother secure a loan on a patch of fallow farmland. In '48, though, Wallace became very sick with a bone infection in his leg. The VA doctor told him it was from a wound he had sustained when his unit, the First Infantry Division, stormed Omaha Beach on D-Day. He was hospitalized, but faded when the antibiotics were ineffective. The doctors could not understand the lack of success, and they loaded him with larger and larger doses. When that failed to curb the infection, they tried a new antimicrobial, streptomycin, as a last ditch effort, for if that failed, the only alternative was amputation. Immediately after the first dose was administered, though, Wallace went into anaphylactic shock and was gone in minutes.

So there had not been time to draw up a will to deal with the large mortgage solely in his name at the Wilkes Barre Mundy Community Bank. Since Parnell and Miriam had paid the bill in Wallace's name precisely on the first of the month for more than five years, no questions had ever been raised.

She went back to Philadelphia at the end of the month after the bank wrote her a threatening note, and the county assessor added a late fee. Highbridge sat in front of her lost in thought. He looked up finally and roared, "I know what to do!"

He arranged a meeting between a superior court judge from Luzerne County and the bank manager, his son-in-law, and a title of sorts was drawn up by Attorney Highbridge. He charged one hundred dollars.

The farm sold quickly to a developer, the bank manager's brother, but for so little, there was nothing left after Highbridge was paid and the mortgage satisfied—not even enough to take a bus to Enid and rejoin her family, from whom she hadn't heard a word.

CHAPTER THREE

Lincoln and his mother took a room in a seamy motel while she looked for work. The rancher, Schroeder, who had taken Lincoln in the day of Parnell's death, offered a leaky, two-room bungalow on the grounds of the horse farm, willing to forgive the rent if Miriam agreed to do the cooking and cleaning in the main house. He paid her less than minimum wage, but it was enough for basic groceries and hand-me-downs from the St. Vincent DePaul.

Lincoln's bed was squeezed into a shed linked to the bungalow by nothing more than a few missing planks in the back wall. His warren abutted the woodstove's exhaust pipe, and his bed was warmer than the twelve-by-fifteen main room in which Miriam slept on a fusty couch.

On a Sunday morning a few weeks later, with the Schroeders gone to church, she coaxed the groom, Domenico, to cut a proper hole in the wall, sneak back to the old farm, filch a closet door, and hang it to separate Lincoln's bed from the main room.

After a month in the bungalow, there began nights when Lincoln was woken by hushed voices and muted rustling on his mother's side of the planks. Sometimes, he'd fall back to sleep only to be startled by sharp cries, the thud of a closing door minutes later, and then an hour of sobbing. Though Miriam would be subdued after the episodes, Lincoln didn't mind, for fresh vegetables and, occasionally, a piece of beef found their way to their dinner table. But a few days would pass, and it was back to day-old bread, macaroni, sardines, bruised cucumbers, and mushy potatoes. The cycle, it seemed to Lincoln, repeated itself every couple of weeks.

There were also nights a car would pull up to the bungalow after Lincoln had gone to bed. He'd watch through a rent in the boards next to his bed as his mother hopped into the passenger side and the car drove off, sometimes only as far as the copse of trees at the end of the dirt road. Occasionally, on those nights when she was gone, Lincoln heard prowling about the cottage and soon a man's voice hissing Miriam's name in a whisper. With no answer, the voice became progressively louder, until Lincoln trembled in cadence with the staccato waves of wrathful cursing.

While Miriam began to leave for work at the main house later and later in the mornings, she usually dragged herself out of bed to make a sandwich for Lincoln and walk him down the winding, muddy driveway to the school bus. Though Schroeder refused her time off during the day, she often managed to sneak to the bus stop and meet Lincoln. There were also times that the old man caught her, and he rebuked her in front of the boy, his enraged bellowing an echo of the nocturnal fury outside the bungalow that had so frightened Lincoln.

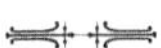

Just days after his ninth birthday, Lincoln came home from school to find his mother curled under her threadbare blanket crying and moaning. As he approached her bed, he stopped short, terrified by her pallor and the sweat pouring from her face. He ran to the main house to fetch Mr. Schroeder. When they got back to the cabin, the blanket around Miriam's middle had become soaked in red. The old man glared down furiously and snarled, "Goddamnit! Can't you get anything right?" He shoved past Lincoln and limped to the garage, threw a couple of dirty horse blankets into the LaSalle, then drove back to the bungalow. He lifted Miriam gruffly from the bed and dumped her onto the back seat.

He barked over his shoulder at Lincoln, "You get yourself back in your room and stay there. You don't come out for nothin'. You hear, boy?" Schroeder jammed the gas pedal so hard, gravel sprayed over the bungalow, and while it stung Lincoln's face, he didn't take his eyes off the car as it raced down the drive and onto the main road toward Wilkes Barre.

When Schroeder returned alone several hours later, his wife came to the bungalow. She told Lincoln to fetch his toothbrush and bedding and carry it to the main house. As he tried to fall asleep on a pile of blankets in a back pantry, he heard Schroeder grumbling to his wife, "Looks like the harlot got herself knocked up good by one of them whore-chasers been sniffin' 'round."

A couple of days later, Miriam returned in a taxi. She was thin and pale and far quieter than she'd been even after the stormy evenings. She stopped walking Lincoln to the school bus and wasn't there when it dropped him off. Even though there was more food for a while, it was a long time before the midnight rustling began again.

A year later, Lincoln was put to work cleaning stalls. By twelve, he was allowed to curry the horses and often snuck sugar cubes from the teachers' table in the cafeteria to indulge the barnyard creatures. The animals came to know him so well, he was greeted with a cacophony of braying, whinnying, oinking, and clucking as he opened the bungalow door on his way to school. On sunny mornings, the racket drew Schroeder from the main house. He'd skulk into the barn and stand hidden deep in back, staring out as the noise built. When Miriam came to the door to watch the animals push and shove, trying to get to Lincoln, she often took a step into the yard to scratch their heads. As the brightness of the new sun shimmered through her threadbare nightgown, Schroeder would step deeper into the barn's darkness and touch himself.

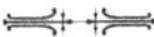

When Lincoln was thirteen, Miriam began to take more and more days off from the main house. She'd send Lincoln to tell them she was ill with a headache or back pain. On those mornings, Lincoln made his own lunch, for Miriam remained in bed, facing the wall, and it seemed she had not moved from that pose when he got home from school.

In mid-autumn, he came home early on a parent-teacher conference afternoon. Miriam had promised to go, and even filled out a request for the last time slot at five-thirty. Lincoln was stunned and then frightened to find her asleep, snoring deeply. He took a step toward the bed and stood over her, watching silently. He was, though, soon shocked from his confusion by a repulsive, pungent odor that wafted from her bed. He stumbled backward.

That woke her, and she sat up quickly. "Lincoln, for Christ's sake, what are you doing home? Why aren't you in school?" She followed his eyes to a tumbler of brown liquid that sat precariously on the edge of an up-turned produce crate next to her bed. Her hand shot forward to hide the evidence, but it struck the crate, and the glass hurtled to the floor. As Lincoln reflexively bent forward to clean up the slivers, Miriam shrieked, "Now look what you caused. Just get the hell outta the house. Do you hear me?" He slithered backward through the door and played with the animals until Miriam called him for dinner at sunset. Though she was washed and dressed, they ate in silence.

For a while, Miriam took fewer days off. If Lincoln got home from school before his mother was back from the main house, he'd search for a bottle but never found one. And while she was a little more talkative during the skimpy dinners, after a month or two, the headaches and back pain returned, and she took refuge in her sickbed several days a week.

Lincoln and his friend, George Wentlandt, often played after school. On a blustery November afternoon, George invited him home. His mother made bologna and lettuce sandwiches on Wonder Bread, spreading them thick with mayonnaise. Lincoln wolfed his, and she made a second. When he finished, she dropped sideways into a seat at the table with a platter of cookies but kept it next to her, out of the boys' reach.

She yawned and asked with a thin smile, "By the way, Lincoln, how's your mom doin'?"

"Fine, Mrs. Wentlandt."

"Feelin' better?"

"Yes, ma'am, mostly. Back to work. Also fixin' up our house. New curtains. Really looks good."

"Those friends of hers still comin' 'round?"

"Oh, I don't really know, Mrs. Wentlandt. Been workin' in the yard and all."

"You know any of their names?"

"No, ma'am."

"Maybe you seen 'em in town?"

"No, ma'am."

She glared at him until he took his eyes off the cookies and dropped his head to stare at the floor. She clucked as she rose and pushed the cookie plate across the table.

It was dark when he got to the bungalow and, as usual, found Miriam curled in a fetal ball facing the wall. His eyes shot to the bedside fruit crate, and while there was never again a glass of whiskey, the tiny room always reeked of stale alcohol. It was a spoor he recognized from the bars he passed on South Main as he paced away the afternoons downtown, too ashamed to go home or to George's.

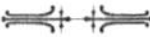

When Lincoln was almost fifteen, he and George went to Schroeder and asked for paying jobs. The old man grumbled, "You two? Why, I don't have time for no lazy kids. I need good workers, boys I can count on." He started to walk away, but turned back and bellowed, "I'll pay you two dollars a week, and let me tell you, there ain't gonna be a penny more, no matter what I have you two do. You understand?"

George started a bank account for college, but Lincoln used his first month's pay to buy lunch, and sometimes two, in the school cafeteria. Eventually, there was enough left over to buy a pair of black chinos and white bucks. When he'd scuffed the shoes to a fare-thee-well, he wore them to breakfast on a morning Miriam was out of bed and dressing to go to the main house for work.

She remarked gently, "My, my, ain't we all gussied up? You turned into quite the man, Lincoln Friday, ain't ya?"

But that afternoon, when he got home, she was back in bed facing the wall, worn-out blankets drawn up nearly all the way over her head. The tiny cabin reeked of fresh alcohol, and her breath was repulsive as he took a step toward her to say hello. She rolled partway over and stared down at his feet. "Oh, look who's home. Mr. Fancy Dancy. Tryin' to impress the girls. Get some, huh?" She rolled back toward the wall and mumbled indignantly, "Only thing a girl understands is money and class. And you ain't got neither one."

If he got home while it was still light, he'd first sneak a look through the bungalow's one, dirty window. If his mother was in bed, he'd tiptoe to the stables and play with the horses, especially Honey Barre, a retired, chestnut mare who loved to nuzzle him as he cleaned her stall. Eventually, old man Schroeder caught him slipping her sugar. "What you got goin' on with that mare, boy?"

"She just likes a clean stall, that's all, sir."

The man looked at him skeptically. "You listen, boy. 'Cept when you're workin', you keep your distance from them horses. They cost a lotta money. Each one, they's worth tena you."

When she did work, Miriam often didn't leave the main house until after dark, stalling so she could spirit away a bit of meat under her smock. Lincoln knew he was safe until seven or so, and he spent the time learning to drive the tractor. Schroeder often sent him out to the far reaches of the property to collect stray colts and confused old mares.

One mid-afternoon, though, Miriam left work early complaining of back pain. As she approached the bungalow, a grinding clatter caught her attention, and she looked up to see a stick-thin creature on a tractor hurtling in from the far pasture. She froze for a moment, neck craned, gaping to see which of the hired hands had the bravado to drive Schroeder's equipment so recklessly. When she realized it was Lincoln, her shriek was so piercing, it drew the old man from the barn. Miriam darted up to him and began pounding his chest, yelping, "You keep that boy off the machinery. You hear? If I ever see him on a tractor again, you sonofabitch, I'll quit this here job and everybody'll know. I'll tell 'em all, every last one of 'em." Her head dropped for a moment, and she became silent. Schroeder's face relaxed, but she began to bawl, gasped for breath, and shrieked, "You sonofabitch, now you want to murder him, too? I'll kill you first, you bastard!"

CHAPTER FOUR

On Sundays mornings, the Schroeders left the farm early to attend the church at which the old man had been a volunteer assistant pastor for decades. Lincoln was expected to have the stalls cleaned before they returned. With the quiet, Miriam liked to sit in the bungalow by the window, drink powdered coffee, and stare into the hills, pretending she could go back twenty years and start over again. She fantasized about finishing high school and becoming a stewardess for TWA or Pan Am. Her eyes filled with the image of a lithesome, raven-haired beauty in a trim, blue uniform and heels flying to New York and London and Paris. Men would stare at her and drool but never dare touch. Maybe she'd let the pilots get close, but only if they begged and pleaded and, first, took her to champagne dinners. And if she felt like it, she'd let the occasional captain take her to an exotic hotel where tuxedoed men behind reception desks quavered as the pilot and his magnificent lady waited hand-in-hand for the elevator. She imagined she'd turn her head before the doors closed and laugh down her nose at them. The peasants would never again have her. Never again. That is what she dreamed every desolate Sunday morning.

Her fortieth birthday fell on one of those quiet Sabbaths, and she looked about her surroundings, her eyes soon fixing, as they always did, on the five-by-eight Woolworth photo in the cardboard frame. Parnell, though as unsmiling as always, sat straighter than usual, his eyes fastened on the toddler he held so solidly in his arms. Miriam, sitting, had her arms tight about an infant cradled in her lap. Her eyes reddened, but before the tears came, she drew a deep breath, slammed her fist on the rickety table, and shoved it aside. She pried loose a floorboard and snatched a quart of rye from a towel-lined hollow. Holding it behind her, she marched outside and smashed it against one of the crumbling cinder blocks that held her hovel barely erect. Drops of the cheap whiskey flew into her face and dribbled onto her lips. She paused at the whisper of what she was surrendering, but her mouth drew into a snarl, and she flung the shattered neck into the pile of trash Schroeder cleared once a month. She turned on her heels as if a soldier and tramped back inside to stand above the void in the floor. Her face twisted in disgust as she reached down, snatched the towel free, and hurled it into the corner, onto the pile of dirty laundry.

She went back to the table and dropped into her chair, the knot in her chest slackening with the joy of knowing the nightmare was finally over. All that was left to do now was wait, perhaps for the Lord's hand to touch her shoulder in approval—that would suffice—or, please God, a windfall of money for having straightened her path. But after thirty minutes, there was no voice or touch or cash, so she went to the kerosene stove and boiled water for another cup of coffee. An hour later, there was still only the loneliness and a few cold sips at the bottom of her mug. When Miriam Friday eventually admitted she had not a single notion of what one did to stop a life charging toward ruin, a flood of despondency overcame her. Her eyes dropped back to the loose board in the dirty floor.

Lincoln flew into the cottage and pecked her cheek. She looked up as he pulled a spiral notebook from his schoolbag on the floor. That was it, she rejoiced inwardly. "Hey, Lincoln, can I have a piece of your paper? Need to make a shopping list." He pulled five sheets free, handed them to her, then placed two sharpened pencils by her other hand.

As he darted out, she scribbled the date on the first sheet then, "Happy Birthday to me." With a fresh cup of coffee by her hand, she waited for remedies to flow from the tip of the pencil. It was all in there, she was sure, her new life, the answers locked in the pencil lead, just waiting to be freed.

Still nothing happened, but the notion of a windfall of cash piqued her imagination, and she set about thinking of jobs that would make her rich. Could she do it without a high school certificate? Yes, she had to start somewhere, and her pencil began to move slowly, then faster. Soon it was flying, not pausing as the tip crossed over the tears pooling on the composition. She wrote furiously for twenty minutes then folded the paper and placed it with both hands into the hollow in the floor.

She bathed, put on a flowery dress, the same one she'd worn in the family picture, and covered a tear in the lace above her left breast with the brooch Parnell had bought for her from the PX in Oklahoma. She'd worn the trinket in that spot after they married, for she wanted Parnell to know he was the guardian of her heart. It sat there, years later, on the drive north to Pennsylvania after the war, and on that same dress every Sunday for church, until they stopped going after the accident. The dress was scarcely snugger than it had been fifteen years before, still falling quite agreeably on her slender figure.

Miriam drove her '39 DeSoto into Wilkes Barre. At the A&P, she sat in the parking lot for fifteen minutes, steeling herself, then marched in and asked firmly for the manager. She stood erect, seemingly arrogant, but the façade of poise perished as the swinging doors flew open. By the time the man halted in front of her, she stood frozen, her demeanor deferential, instantly paralyzed by the mien of impatience swathing the man, who had armed himself for the latest customer grievance.

She did not, though, wait for him to speak. "Mister, I'd like a job. I'm a very good worker."

His eyes dropped immediately to her left hand, then up along her tummy to her breasts, where they lingered. He smiled unctuously and eventually looked into her eyes. "Well, *Miss* Friday, is it?"

"Yes, I lost my husband."

"Oh, that's too bad. Look, there's nothing available now, but let's see what comes along. Why don't you check back sometime this week? Always better to come at the end of the day. That's when I'm free to spend some time." He reached out and took her hand softly, then covered it with his other.

Her face hardened, and she turned on her heels. Next, the Safeway, though there was no joy there either. She drove by the other food markets. All were closed for the Sabbath, and it wasn't until Wednesday that she mustered the nerve to leave work early and drive back to the A&P. The manager glowed when he noticed that she had put on a bit of makeup and cheap perfume. He led her up the stairs to the shabby office that sat propped over the cash registers.

He closed the door. "Now, Miss Friday, we still don't have anything open, but I'm sure we could speed things up. Let me ask, are you free to take a little ride after I get off tonight? I mean, we could just talk about what we could have you do here."

He stood, and she stood, and he took her hand. She shook it. But then he let his left hand stroke her forearm, and soon the tips of those fingers reached across her chest to brush the silver-plated brooch. When she froze, his hand slid over both breasts, finally cuddling the right. Still she did not move. He grinned and he pinched it playfully.

"Don't you touch that pin, you bastard!" She ripped her hand free and slapped him. He cuffed her face. She kicked at his groin, but he jinked and twisted and bellowed, "Get the hell outta my store before I call the cops. Git!"

As she ran down the stairs, stumbling in her heels on the rickety wood, sobs and tears exploded. One of the female cashiers looked up and cackled as a broad smile ripened on her porcine face. "Looks like old George's never goin' to learn to keep it in his pants." Hoots of laughter trailed her out of the market.

She bought a fifth of cheap whisky on the drive back to Schroeder's farm and guzzled three fingers before falling onto her bed. She passed out without having slipped from her one dress.

CHAPTER FIVE

The next Sunday morning, with his mother asleep and snoring so raucously the slats on the bungalow's walls shivered, Lincoln tiptoed to the cupboard and grabbed a handful of saltines, a soft tomato, and a few cubes of sugar. He stole from the house to hide behind the stables until Schroeder and his wife drove off to church. When the car turned onto the highway, he crawled into the locked tack shed through a trench excavated by generations of terriers. He chose a pretty thoroughbred racing saddle and harness, snuck into the stable, and gave Honey Barre a lump of sugar. He whispered as he slipped the bridle over her head, led her through the doors, pitched the saddle over her back, then fixed the girth as he'd seen the grooms do a thousand times. He marched slowly by her side until they neared the half-mile exercise track. She suddenly tossed her head and began to prance, but calmed when he stroked her withers, and she remained quiet as he pulled himself into the saddle. It was the first time he'd ever been on a horse.

When he settled, Honey moved forward on her own, but slowly, regally, head and neck held feet higher than her fifteen hands. Lincoln leaned far forward and slipped her another hunk of sugar. Her head bobbed several times. She whinnied as if laughing passionately, and abruptly broke into a gallop, immediately moving to the rail as if drawn by a celestial force. At first, he was stunned at the pace with which the rail was tearing by, and his hands locked the gullet in a death grip. In seconds, though, he realized her stride was beautifully fluid. His hands relaxed, and he let go of the saddle completely. Then he discovered that if he leaned forward and let his body glide back and forth in the seat, he could whisper for her to go even faster.

With the thunder of her hooves embracing him, Lincoln did not hear the drone of a tiny airplane until it descended to turn lazy circles over the racetrack. When he spotted the Cessna coming toward him, he waved wildly and murmured into the horse's ear, "Girl, look up. You see that? There's people in there, but we're faster than some old airplane, ain't we? Show 'em girl, show 'em just how fast."

Now the ground soared past in such a blur, he believed he was hurtling through space, faster even than the little aircraft. He shook a fist at the plane in victory, as he'd seen jockeys rejoice all the years he'd lived on the horse farm. The plane turned back and descended, turning tighter and tighter circles, until the pilot slowed to a crawl and waved out his window.

The boy was astonished by the power he controlled in Honey Barre, and by the nearness of a great flying machine. A real live pilot had taken notice of Lincoln Friday and hailed his competence. These were the first free moments of his life, ones that would, he could not know at the time, drive him forever.

When the plane made a final swoop at less than fifty feet, Lincoln saluted the aviator with both arms raised. But with the noise, the vibration, and the unexpected gymnastics in her saddle, Honey Barre, who had begun to shiver several passes before, threw her head back, jammed her hooves into the soft earth, twirled sharply, and reared. Lincoln fought to grab the flimsy racing saddle, but he had not tied the strap well under her, and when the arched angle of Honey's back lessened her girth, both the saddle and its rider rolled violently to the side.

At first, he sensed only weightlessness, but the back of his head soon slammed into the rail. Then came a terrifically loud explosion, an intense burst of light, and finally, a flare of agonizing pain. An instant later, though, the suffering strangely faded, and Lincoln Friday was comfortable, trouble-free. That pleasantness lasted but a trice before his world dimmed into nothingness. He did not feel his left forearm being crushed between his back and the ground.

Several seconds passed before he stirred. The pleasantness was gone, replaced by a throbbing that billowed from his wrist, passed through his elbow, and massed, finally, in his shoulder. He tried to stand but became nauseous, dropped to his knees, and fell back to the ground. He remained motionless, all sense of time obliterated.

He lifted his neck after a few seconds to make out the hazy image of Honey Barre galloping madly for the pasture. His head dropped back to the turf as the Cessna turned several tight revolutions over him until the wings righted, and it passed above the main house, wheels nearly brushing the roof. The plane came about and flew the same course twice more until Lincoln's mother staggered into the yard. The pilot thrust his arm out of his window and pointed wildly to the track. Miriam looked into the distance and saw Honey Barre bucking, saddle flapping below her belly, the creature's magnificent chestnut coat glistening with sweat in the early morning light. Miriam ran to the main house, but it was locked, the LaSalle gone from the garage.

Lincoln had crawled fifty meters toward the bungalow but collapsed again when he saw his mother sprinting unsteadily toward him. He was shivering and crying, mumbling to Miriam, "Mom, I'm sorry. I'm sorry. I don't mean to be any trouble. Don't let Mr. Schroeder hurt Honey. It was my fault, mom."

She helped Lincoln to the bungalow, put him on his bed, and went to the sink for wet towels to cleanse the blood from his head. She came to a gash in his scalp and studied it carefully. It was quite shallow, and she sighed in relief. "Ain't nothin', Lincoln. Don't need no stiches, thank God."

Lincoln's left forearm dropped from the bed, and she grasped his wrist to lift it back onto the mattress. He screeched in pain and jammed the pillow into his mouth, then cried even harder. Miriam rolled up his sleeve and became woozy as she uncovered the misshapen arm.

She quivered, "Lincoln, we need to get you to the hospital."

"Mama, I'm okay, really. I don't want you to spend your money on a doctor."

She was silent for a moment, then snapped, "We'll worry 'bout the damn money later. I'm your mother. I'm here to take care of you. Don't say another word." She eased Lincoln off the bed and guided him to the garage, then placed him gently on the back seat of the DeSoto. As they turned onto the main road, he heard the drone of a plane and lifted his head just high enough to see the Cessna turn in the direction in which they had set out. The aircraft made a few sweeping circles until the DeSoto pulled into the parking lot of the hospital in Wilkes Barre then banked north and was gone.

Miriam helped Lincoln into the emergency department of the dingy, rural clinic that served the entire county. The waiting room was teeming with the wounded and ill. An old man in overalls stood and grunted at Miriam, tipping his head toward his rusting folding chair. She folded Lincoln's distorted wrist to his belly and placed his good hand there to protect the wound. She kissed the top of his head, then joined the serpentine queue of farmers for the intake desk. Many were holding bloody towels to their faces; some had arms in splints fashioned from tree branches. An elderly, gray-haired woman jumped in and out of line, circulating around the room, grasping her belly, and screeching, "The baby's comin', it's comin'! Somebody, do somethin'!"

The spectators were laughing, and Miriam couldn't suppress a smile, though when she stole a glance back at Lincoln, she became light-headed. His eyes were glassy and distant, like Parnell's after Lanny.

When she reached the desk, she told her story. The clerk nodded in gentle understanding, smiled, and asked how Miriam intended to pay for her son's treatment. Miriam opened her purse, drew out a ten-dollar bill, and placed it shakily on the table.

"Oh, no, you don't pay now. You pay at the end."

"How much is it gonna be?"

The woman stared at the bill for a moment and looked up. "Well, we're going to have to see what all is done for your son. I mean, there will be x-rays, and we don't know yet how many..." She stopped abruptly and lifted her eyes. A man had come to stand just beyond Miriam's shoulder, his head crooked to better hear their conversation. The clerk cleared her throat coarsely, and the man took a step away. Her eyes dropped back to Miriam's. "And then, of course, there's a cast, and we don't know how many layers of plaster doctor will put on, and how many aspirins your son is going to need. It's all..."

The clerk stopped again as the man came closer and touched Miriam's shoulder. Before Miriam turned, he took a broad step back. "Ma'am, I'm the pilot of the plane back there at the farm. Don't worry, I'm going to pay the medical bills. Why don't you go back and sit with your son? Please. I'm going to take care of this."

Miriam gasped, but the man's gentle manner and subtle, warm smile disarmed her, especially when he stepped aside to clear her way back to Lincoln. He reached into his jacket pocket, pulled a folded check from his wallet, scribbled only the date and his signature, then placed it on the desk with his driver's license. The clerk froze.

The man walked slowly to Lincoln and squatted, but not too closely. "Son, what's your name?"

The boy murmured, "Lincoln Friday, sir." Lincoln's expression tightened as if he recognized the face. Then a wave of throbbing from his wrist gripped him, and his head dropped.

The man asked Miriam, "Ma'am, are you his mother?" She nodded. "Has the boy been given anything for pain?"

Miriam shook her head. He grunted and walked back to the clerk. He retrieved his driver's license and forced a smile. "Ma'am, could you get a doctor out here to give that boy some pain medicine? It isn't right to let him suffer like that."

She rustled in her chair uncomfortably, gathered the documents on her desk into a disordered pile, and swept them into a drawer. She fumbled with a key to lock it then pushed through the swinging doors. She was back in a few seconds to unlock the drawer and rearrange her papers, though she did not look up at the man. There was whirling in the bowels of the emergency room, and a portly woman in a stained, white nurse's smock waddled through the swinging doors toward Lincoln. She announced forcefully, "The boy can have nothing by mouth in case we need to do surgery on him."

Miriam wheezed, "Surgery?"

The nurse didn't answer, but bent forward and rolled the sleeve up over the fracture. Her face reddened. She spun about and marched off.

The man kneeled again in front of Lincoln. "Son, my name is Harlan Hettmans. I'm a football coach over at Penn State." He put his hand on the boy's knee. "I was the one flying the airplane that caused your horse to spook. I'm really sorry; I shouldn't have done that."

Both Miriam and Lincoln stared mutely at the man until the nurse returned wielding a syringe in her right hand, business end thrusting forward with each step. As she pushed up the sleeve on Lincoln's good arm, the glistening drop of fluid that had hung from the tip dripped onto his thigh. With Lincoln distracted watching the fluid soak into his filthy pants, the nurse jammed the needle into his deltoid and squeezed so hard, her thumb blanched. Neither Lincoln, his mother, nor the stranger had had time to draw a breath before the nurse took a half-hearted swipe at the sleeve to roll it down, turned on her heels, and trundled back through the swinging doors.

Hettmans nodded and murmured, "It shouldn't take too long before it starts to work. You're going to be fine, son."

They sat quietly for nearly an hour before Lincoln's turn came at the only x-ray machine in a twenty-mile radius. Both bones of the forearm were broken right above the wrist, and there was some question about one of the bones right below the thumb. The emergency room doctor shook his head as he pointed to the x-rays. "Generally, one breaks this bone down here at the wrist and this other one up by the elbow, and usually, this one here, the scaphoid, in the wrist itself, it doesn't break in kids. I'm going to need to call a bone man for consultation."

Miriam's eyes swept downward as if the last glimmer of life had seeped out of her, but Coach Hettmans put his hand on her arm and spoke softly. "Don't you worry, ma'am. Everything's going to be taken care of. I promise."

Hours later, an unshaven bull of a man pushed his way through the crowds of Sunday afternoon's infirm. He stopped at the x-ray box, glanced casually at the films, then across the room at Lincoln. He commanded above the din, "Get a nurse out here to prepare that kid," he pointed gruffly with his thumb, "for surgery." He turned on his heels and strode toward the elevator.

Before Lincoln was wheeled away, Hettmans leaned over the boy's gurney and squeezed his shoulder. "When this is all done, son, you let me know. I'll fly over from Penn State and give you a hop in the plane. Let you fly and all. We'll just stay away from horses. Whata you say, Champ?"

Lincoln looked up. In his medicated stare, he garbled, "I'd sure like that, mister."

Miriam, though, gasped and wedged herself between the man and Lincoln's gurney. "You're not taking my son in that damned machine. He's all I have left. You've done enough, mister, don't you think?"

Hettmans nodded and stepped back. When Lincoln was wheeled away, he took a seat next to Miriam, but she stood and marched indignantly to the far end of the waiting room. They remained like that for two hours until the surgeon's nurse-assistant came to the waiting room. "Doctor wants me to tell you that your son really broke his arm bad. He fixed it best as he could, but it's never going to be like new. He won't be able to move it too good. But at least it'll be almost straight. Good thing is, he'll never have to go into army, or anything like that, unless there's World War III." She laughed. "And doctor said, 'Stay off horses.'"

CHAPTER SIX

At first, Schroeder said nothing directly to Lincoln but glared at him as the boy left for school. He confined his comments to Miriam, warning that Lincoln was not allowed near the stables. He would not be paid while the cast was on, and when it came off, his pay would drop to fifty cents a week, to cover the vet bills he alleged Honey Barre had amassed. He threatened that if Lincoln was caught near a horse again, he'd make sure the cops put him in Juvenile Hall until he turned eighteen.

Miriam hovered over Lincoln, barely allowing him out of the house for school, fearful Schroeder would get a glimpse of the boy and call the police just for spite, but after eight weeks, when the cast was removed, Schroeder came to the bungalow and ordered Lincoln back to the stalls. His duties, though, were limited to shoveling manure, and that was only if all the horses were on the track or in the pastures.

Coach Hettmans had come down every two weeks while the cast was on, and a few times over the months after it had been removed, though Miriam had not let Lincoln leave the farm with him. Lincoln finally sent Hettmans a secret letter. They agreed to meet on Saturday afternoon at the crossroads near the horse farm. The man flew to Wilkes Barre, took a cab from the airport, and found the boy hiding behind a hedgerow. At a restaurant in town, they sat together at a table in the corner for nearly two hours. Hettmans gave Lincoln a primer on what made a plane go up, what sent it down, and how to make a simple turn.

Lincoln was quiet as they rode out in another cab to the airport, then absolutely silent and rigid as they flew high above the Susquehanna River. Coach Hettmans asked, “Hey, Lincoln, what do you call a boomerang that doesn’t come back?”

“I don’t know, sir.”

“A stick.” Lincoln smiled. “Hey, Lincoln, What’s the last thing that goes through a bug’s mind as he hits the windshield?”

“I don’t know, sir.”

“His butt.” There was a giggle, and Coach Hettmans directed Lincoln to place his feet on the pedals and then his hands softly on the wheel. “Keep the plane pointed south, toward that hill. Just like driving a tractor.”

Slowly, the coach loosened his fingers on the yoke, but kept them so close, Lincoln could not tell who was in control. For the first minutes, the aircraft jerked in resonance with the trembling of Lincoln’s hands, but they soon steadied, and he flew as straight as an arrow. That was because Lincoln saw the man’s hands were actually free of the yoke, and when he accepted he was really flying, Lincoln fell into a rigid, nearly catatonic state, half in fear, half in astonishment.

Hettmans spoke to him soothingly. “Now, Lincoln, I can’t believe how good you’re doing. And it’s just your first flight. Okay, let’s loosen up those hands a little. That’s it. Don’t have to hold on hard. Real light. That’s the mark of a good pilot.” With the coach’s soft words, Lincoln slowly relaxed his knotted fingers, and while the plane began undulating again, the change in altitude was so placid, Hettmans smiled, leaned back in his seat, and pretended to be gazing at the rolling farmland. After ten minutes, Lincoln burned through his ability to concentrate, and his hands retightened on the controls. The plane soon began swooping up and down in great arcs. Hettmans sat up straight and spoke authoritatively, “Okay, Flight Cadet, I got it.”

Lincoln’s hands flew off the controls. The plane jerked up. Hettmans waited a couple of seconds and spoke firmly. “Okay, now *there’s* a good lesson for us pilots. When I say, ‘I got it,’ you keep your hands on the controls and you say, ‘You got it,’ and *then* you slowly lighten your fingers on the wheel, but you don’t let go completely until I say, ‘I got it,’ one more time. That way there isn’t a minute, not one second, when no one’s in control. Let’s practice.”

After three transfers, Hettmans took the wheel and headed west over the emerald fields of northeast Pennsylvania. Lincoln was not sure what was passing beneath, for none of it looked familiar from three-quarters of a mile in the air, but when Coach Hettmans pointed out a racing oval, Lincoln gasped. Coach had him put his hands back on the controls and make a couple of lazy turns over the horse farm. Lincoln was mesmerized by the images of buildings and landmarks that had been his entire life but were now no more imposing than miniature toys. Even the main house was minuscule and insignificant, not at all noticeably superior to the bungalow. All that had been so vital and critical on the ground was really quite trivial.

Hettmans felt Lincoln’s contemplation and said nothing for a few minutes, but he noticed clouds closing in from the west, and they flew back toward the airport. Lincoln kept his hands lightly on the controls for the rest of the trip north, through the approach, and even as they were about to touch down. When they were gliding just three or four feet above the runway, Coach ordered, "Okay, Lincoln, now real, real slow, I want you to pull back on the wheel a little bit at a time, just use your fingers, *slowly*, that's it, keep pullin', you're doin' good, just a little more, don't let 'er land, pull back just a little more, almost there."

To Lincoln's eyes, the landing was going on longer than an algebra test. Worse, the plane's nose was now aimed, he was sure, straight up into the graying sky. His entire body tightened waiting for the crash, but an instant later there was a gentle thump, and the nose lowered gradually until it was level with the runway. Coach Hettmans turned to Lincoln and grinned, "Ain't that a kick in the pants!"

Lincoln heaved an enormous breath, wiped the sweat from his palms, and forced a smile. As they rolled in a crawl toward the hangars, Coach pushed a few buttons before laughing aloud. "You just landed a plane, son. You got the touch. Congratulations."

CHAPTER SEVEN

After school the next day, Lincoln stopped at the public library and borrowed a book on flying. In the shed behind their bungalow, he built a cockpit out of wood scraps, a yoke from the rusted wheel of his first bicycle, then cut shoulder seatbelts from a burlap feed bag. He fashioned a wooden frame the size of an airplane windshield, hung it over the front of the cockpit, and blocked the space around it with strips of a moldy tarpaulin.

He copied the pre-flight checklist from the book and read it aloud before pretending to turn the key to start the engine. He practiced pushing the pedals and turning the wheel at the same time, leaning far to the side, as if banking his plane. He pictured sweeping turns over the pastures of Wilkes Barre, then imagined righting his aircraft, checking his fuel, and making for the airport. As the runway emerged from the haze, he radioed that he was inbound. Then he read aloud the pre-landing checklist, just as he had been instructed in his flying manual. On his fantasy approaches, he pulled back slowly on the wheel as he envisioned the main gear about to touch down, then spoke aloud to himself. "Don't let it land, don't let it land." He bounced in his seat as the make-believe wheels touched down. "You can do better than that."

Coach Hettmans wrote to Lincoln that varsity football was in full swing, and he couldn't get away to visit, but assured he would be back, and they would get together when the season was over. Though he did not mention flying, Lincoln understood and redoubled his shed simulator lessons. At Christmas, Hettmans sent a card to Lincoln and his mother wishing them a happy holiday and explaining that Penn State was going to the Gator Bowl. He would be out of town until after the new year, but would write as soon as he was home. Lincoln waited by the mailbox for days after the holiday, but it wasn't until mid-January that a letter arrived. Hettmans had been recruited to coach at Notre Dame, had sold the plane, and would be moving his family before the end of the month. He promised to write again when he was settled in South Bend. He asked Lincoln to study hard and make school the most important thing in his life, "…beside your mom, of course." He also said he would count on Lincoln to write to him when he was ready to apply to college.

Lincoln pinned the letter to the wall in his room. He spent more and more time after school doing homework in the library, and when he got home, he gave his mom a peck on the cheek and dashed directly to his simulator. Slowly, he improved it, adding an instrument panel and a lever for flaps. He performed stalls, chandelles, and steep turns over and over in the shed, then imagined doing them before he fell asleep.

Late on a Sunday afternoon, Domenico Sanchez, now head groom, came to the bungalow and ordered Lincoln to the barn. It was Lincoln's sixteenth birthday, though Miriam had barely mentioned it at breakfast. In a torn housedress, hair scarcely combed, she followed and stood behind Domenico as the groom wheeled a three-speed Raleigh bicycle into the barnyard. "*Amigo,*" he laughed, "you ride this, not them horses, *¿entiende lo que le digo?*" He clapped the boy on the shoulder and shoved a dollar bill into his hand. Miriam waved two more in his face.

That week, Lincoln did not buy lunch at school but took the bills and added them to the two dollars he'd hidden under his bed, money earmarked to buy a book of World War Two fighters. On the next Sunday morning, just a moment after the Schroeders drove off, Lincoln packed two peanut butter and jelly sandwiches, ran to the barn, slipped Honey Barre three lumps of sugar, and set off on his bicycle, north along the Susquehanna River and through Forty Fort. After twelve miles, he coasted into the airfield's gravel parking lot.

He was scared, and then surprised, when no one stopped him as he pushed the bike through the gate of an Anchor fence to find himself standing amid half a dozen tiny aircraft. In the distance, he scrutinized a puddle jumper as it touched down. He stood in awe as the plane taxied up and stopped just feet from him. The pilot jumped out, dropped into a clumsy squat, and affixed a tow bar to the tail wheel. When he did not glance up, Lincoln took a few terrified steps toward the man, stood bolt upright, and stammered, "Hey, Mister, could you give me a ride?"

The man's lips pursed as he barely raised his face. "Ain't got the time." He lowered his eyes to finish his work.

Despite the fluttering in his stomach, Lincoln reached into a pocket and drew out the birthday, lunch, and book money. "Sir, could you give me a ride for this here five dollars, please?"

The old man's head turned abruptly, eyes locking on the cash. He was scarcely halfway out of his squat before his gnarled fingers shot forward to snatch the bills. He nodded toward the passenger door, and without a word, placed the seatbelt carelessly about Lincoln, started the engine without consulting a checklist, made no radio calls to announce his intentions, and sped along the taxiway nearly fast enough to fly. As he turned onto the runway, long before lining up on the center line, he jammed the throttle forward. The plane skidded to the left and began to roll counter-clockwise but became airborne before it could flip over. The nose bobbed up and down for a bit; they entered a sloppy, 180 degree turn, and just that fast were pointed back toward the airport. Lincoln yelled over the engine noise that he'd like to touch the stick for just a second, but the pilot grumbled and shook his head petulantly. After a final, squidgy turn, the plane was over the runway in the direction opposite from which it had just taken off. Lincoln expected the drawn out landing, going over in his head the steps of controlling the final seconds of flying, imagining coming back on the stick slowly and keeping the main gear off the ground as long as possible, but the wheels hit with a wallop, the plane porpoised a few times, then finally settled on the ground. A moment later, they were racing for the line of parked aircraft. The man flipped the buckle open on Lincoln's belt and pointed to the door. The boy stood by for a minute, hoping the pilot would give back a dollar, or something, for not letting him touch the controls, but the man ignored him, so Lincoln pushed the bike away, head down, not looking back as the plane was rolled into its parking spot.

At school the next morning, his third period music teacher, Miss Kola, greeted the class with a record booming on the 78. It was the theme from *Victory at Sea.* As the students filtered in and caught the music, the boys' postures straightened a dash—the girls giggled at them. They soon, though, all became very serious as the music built to a crescendo, and Miss Kola took her place in front of the room. With the class hushed, most of her students vertical in their seats, she lifted the needle. "Can any of you guess what I did this weekend?"

Brian Besozzi blurted, "Got married?" As the chortles trailed off, she stared at him for a moment, hiding a smile, "No, Brian. And please be good enough to raise your hand in the future before answering. Thank you."

Renate Harman's arm flew into the air. "I know. Your husband bought you those airplane earrings!"

"Ah, no, Renate. You know I'm not married. It just so happens, I bought them for myself, but the earrings have something to do with it. And, Renate, I know your arm was up waving in the air, but would you please wait to be called on even *after* you raise your hand? Okay, I'll tell you. I started to learn how to fly! It was really scary, but I can't wait for the next lesson."

The kids gasped, and a hum of excited natter laced the room. Lincoln, though, was struck silent. He could not take his eyes off of her for the rest of the period and after class rushed up to the front of the room. He stuttered, "Miss Kola, I'm studying to become a pilot, too." He paused and looked down. "But the man who took me for a ride didn't let me touch the stick."

She looked at him sideways. "When was that?"

"Yesterday."

"Where was this? Up at Wilkes Barre?"

"Yes, ma'am."

"Was he short and stubby, didn't shave for a few days, white hair? Half a cigar in his mouth?"

"Do you know him, Miss Kola?"

"Was this kinda late in the afternoon?"

"Yes, ma'am."

"Oh, Lincoln," she laughed cynically, "I thought that was you. Old Man Spehl. He's angry all the time. They say he tried to become a pilot during the war. Washed out of flight school, or so the story goes. Nobody'll fly with him. Too dangerous and too mean. I'm surprised he even took you up."

"Well, he wasn't going to, but I gave him my birthday money."

She huffed, "*Birthday money*? Oh, my, you didn't. How much did he take?"

"Five dollars."

"Oh, my gosh. So that's why he was parading around, talking about filling up the plane with the good gas." She touched his shoulder. "You stay away from him, Lincoln Friday. Do you hear me? You're too precious to lose."

The bell rang, and as Lincoln turned toward the door, he nearly knocked into Isabelle Dalton, who had been standing just a foot behind him, listening. Her eyes dropped shyly, but as Lincoln took a step to walk around her, her head rose. "Lincoln, you're going to be a pilot?"

He stopped and stared at her for a moment. "I don't know. Takes a lot of money, I guess."

"Well, Lincoln, did you know my father was a pilot in the war?" Her eyes widened. "He was in the *Marines.* He told us about going off carriers." She asked with a quaver, "Would you like to meet him?"

She held his gaze for a twinkling longer than any girl ever had. His chest felt funny, and his face reddened. "I donno," he mumbled and marched from the room. Miss Kola put her arm on Isabelle's shoulder and smiled, "You ask him again. I think he's just a little shy. I bet he really wants to meet your dad and talk flying. Guys love that sort of thing."

CHAPTER EIGHT

Occasionally, first thing on Monday mornings in music class, Miss Kola would mention what she had learned in the cockpit over the weekend, and Lincoln would stop at the city library to research that maneuver. Then he'd practice it for hours, and when it was perfected, he'd tell Miss Kola what he was doing. In early April, with the snow gone, he was back on the road to the airport on Sundays, where he'd watch planes take off and land. He'd also sidle up to gaggles of pilots and listen from the periphery as they stood bragging, "Shoot, I just crossed the Pokies at darn near hundred-and-eighty knots." The old man next to him would counter, "Well, just yesterday, got up to seventeen-five, and that was without that useless supplemental oh-two."

On the Saturday before Easter, he saw Miss Kola climbing out of a Cessna, so he rode over to ask what she had practiced that day. She rolled her eyes in mock fear and squeaked, "Departure stalls. You know, when you lose airspeed just after you've taken off." He smiled and listed with military precision, ticking off on his fingers, the steps a seasoned pilot employed to avoid disaster as the wheels lifted off the ground. She was silent until he finished then shook her head, leaned forward, and hugged him. As she pulled away, her eyes reddened. "I'll never forget you, Lincoln Friday." She turned and stared into the sky.

Lincoln rode home, his chest burning, pondering what he'd done to make her so sad. He did not sleep well that night, or the next, waiting for school to begin on Monday morning, the first day back after Spring Break. He spent Periods One and Two nauseous, dreading music at ten. As he edged to Miss Kola's room, he prayed for scratchy, cheery music blasting from the Victrola, but the room was eerily still as he made his way, head drooping, to his seat.

Lincoln finally gathered the nerve to look up. A young male teacher was at Miss Kola's desk, and Lincoln assumed instantly that she had resigned because he had been such a know-it-all. His gut cramped, and he sprang from his desk, praying he would make it to the boy's room in time. That culled waves of chatter, and even more when Lincoln slid back into his seat just before class started. With the bell, the class instigators began issuing whispered tactical orders to drop pencils on the ground every five minutes by the clock. They would torment the substitute until he cried uncle and left the room in tears. Though not above joining his classmates in the fun, Lincoln was slouched so far down in his seat, his neighbors ignored him and whispered over his head.

The new teacher marched to the front of the class and stood at near attention as he waited for silence and the eyes of his pubescent scholars. He finally spoke with terse authority. "I am Mr. Gallotti, your new music teacher. Please take out notebooks and let's get started." Lincoln slithered deeper in his seat. The man snatched a roll of Scotch Tape off the desk, grabbed a sheet of paper from the wastebasket, and slid a chair to the wall upon which the clock hung. He climbed up and taped the paper over the face.

"Now, not that long ago, I was a soldier in Korea—during the war. You might have heard of the place. Those kids over there didn't have anything. In school, they had to share. Two kids to a desk, three to a pencil, six or seven students to one book. So pencils were precious—like gold—and a smart person doesn't let gold fall on the ground, right? Have I made myself clear?"

The kids looked about quizzically, but, one by one, rolled their eyes. He smiled and spoke gently. "Well, glad we're all on the same page. Now let's get started."

Mr. Gallotti took a breath to go on, but one of the boys hollered, "Hey, wait, where's Miss Kola?"

The man's lips tightened. "Let me guess. You're Brian Besozzi. Like I said, let's get started. If you act like adults, I will treat you as such. Now, today, we are going to discuss the woodwind instruments in the modern orchestra."

Just before the bell, Gallotti had them close their notebooks. "Thank you for acting so maturely, even you, Brian." The boy dipped deeper in his seat than Lincoln. "Now I will tell you. Miss Kola got married a few days ago. She has moved to New York City with her new husband." The bell rang, and he turned to erase the board.

After school, Lincoln went to the principal. He asked for permission to write to Miss Kola. "Okay, Lincoln. Tell you what. You give me the letter. If the grammar is perfect, and don't forget your spelling, I'll send it along."

Miss Kola and Lincoln wrote twice, but after she became pregnant, she stopped flying, and he did not hear from her again.

CHAPTER NINE

At the end of that summer, Lincoln told Schroeder he had taken an after school job as a dishwasher at a nursing home in Wilkes Barre and couldn't work at the farm anymore. Schroeder howled he hadn't yet paid off his debt and made him quit his job at the home. The old man, though, raised his pay back to two dollars, and for a couple of days, issued orders in a tenor a decibel or two lower than a screech. That lasted until the afternoon Lincoln was ordered to dig a series of postholes in the barnyard. He spent hours making sure they were exactly two-and-a-half feet deep and spaced perfectly, six feet on center. At the end of the afternoon, he looked up from his shovel to see Honey Barre being led back to the stable by one of the lesser grooms. Lincoln clicked his tongue and called out, "Hey, girl."

With ears perked, she swung her head toward Lincoln, eyes as wide as the holes he was digging. She bolted toward the boy, but got only a few feet before her right forelimb dropped into a posthole. The crack was as deafening as a flash of lightning, and the grand thud as she collapsed reverberated across the farm.

Honey Barre writhed wildly, trying to pull the bottom half of her leg from the hole. She cried in a high-pitched, ear-piercing squeal that carried so far, Schroeder sped in from the far pasture on his tractor. His wife and Miriam sprinted from the main house.

The old man's face smoldered an apoplectic crimson for a few seconds as he watched Honey Barre thrash. When he realized the creature's leg was pointing in two directions, he whirled about to face Lincoln. "Now what the fuck did you do?" He was silent for a moment, gasped, took a giant step toward Lincoln, and swung wildly. Though Lincoln arched his back and escaped the full force of the punch, it was enough to drop him to his knees. Schroeder lunged forward and cocked his leg to kick Lincoln in the head, but Miriam jumped between them. Schroeder slapped her so hard, she fell backward over her son.

Schroeder lifted his leg again, but Eunice shoved him fiercely and screamed, "*Dieter, ihn nicht kicken! Bist du bescheuert?*"

"No, I am not crazy. Look what the little bastard did to this animal! Shut your mouth and get my Winchester from behind the door."

When she did not move, Schroeder hissed, "Okay, goddamnit, you'll see," then marched back to the house. The screen door managed to bang only once before he was marching back, the thirty-aught-six waving in his hands, jerking to a fractional stop as its barrel arched past each living creature on his horizon. The man's body puffed when he skidded to a stop and jammed the rifle against the bone between Honey's tearing eyes. He charged the weapon and turned to Lincoln; the knuckles of his trigger hand blanched. "I ought to make you do this, but that would just make your mommy start sniveling and beg..."

The shot came before he'd finished his sentence. It surprised even him. When everyone stopped gasping, he turned to the groom. "Call that guy at the rendering plant and get the carcass the hell out of here." He started for the house, but stopped and took a step toward Lincoln. "Neither of you's worth a tinker's damn. I want both of you outta here in two days. Not worth a pint of weasel piss." He screamed at the top of his lungs toward the heavens, "And don't you's ever come back. You hear me?!"

Lincoln straightened. It was the first time he realized he was seven or eight inches taller than Schroeder. His face tightened, and his fists followed suit. He took a step toward the old man, but the groom reached up and grabbed him by the shoulder.

Fall semester began the next morning. Miriam wanted to walk him to the bus, but he prevailed upon her to stay in the bungalow and pack. She kissed him goodbye, then pulled him back and held him for several seconds. "Don't worry, Lincoln. Everything is going to be okay. I promise. This starts a new life for us. We shoulda never come here in the first place, but we're gonna fix that right now. I heard this guy on the radio—Earl Nightingale. He's so smart, like you. He said, where is it? I wrote it down just a couple of days ago. Here it is. 'Believe you can and you're halfway there.' Ain't that beautiful?" Lincoln nodded. "It's gonna be a new life for us. We're halfway there. I promise."

He gave her another peck on the cheek and started through the door. "Mom, don't worry about me. And, please, Mom, you don't need to come and meet me at the bus. I'm fine." A slight beam crossed her lips as she waved him away with a flick of her hand. It was the first smile Lincoln had seen on her in years. He turned back and hugged her, his heart flooded with relief.

That afternoon, while Miriam was not at the stop, Eunice Schroeder happened to be driving off the farm just as the bus pulled up. She stopped the car barely two feet from him and rolled the window down. Lincoln took a pace backward, and while he was aware of a surge of taunts coming from the bus, the buzzing in his ears having to face Schroeder's wife was so thunderous, the jeers were but a garble.

"Lincoln, I am so sorry for what happened yesterday. I'm sure you can understand that Mr. Schroeder was very upset. He loved that horse. The groom told him you didn't do anything directly to hurt her. Tell your mom I'm going to talk to him and see if we can't get him to let you stay. How's that?"

Lincoln nodded and turned brusquely. She called to him once more, but he ignored the raised voice and started up the driveway. As he walked, the teasing began to echo in his head, and he muttered to himself, his rage building. By the time he reached the bungalow, he was shouting, and bashed his body into the front door so brutally, a hinge came loose. The cabin was nearly bare, dozens of paper bags piled near the door. Miriam was sitting on the edge of the bed. Lincoln sniffed for alcohol, but there was only the musty odor of years of grime that had not been disturbed since they'd moved in.

He walked to his mother stiffly and gave her cheek a distant kiss. "Mrs. Schroeder said she was going to talk to Mr. Schroeder about us staying."

Miriam said nothing then, nor while Lincoln changed into his work clothes. As he started out the door, head down, she spoke forcefully. "What I tell you this morning? We ain't givin' up. Not you, not me. I *believe* we can, and we will. Now you start believin', and everything's gonna be fine."

"Uh huh."

Lincoln was leaning on his rake in Honey's stall, eyes moist, when Domenico walked up behind him and asked softly, "Why so glum, *mi amigo*? You should be happy to finally get out of this damn place." He handed Lincoln a stick of gum.

"Hi, Domenico. You heard, huh?"

"Of course. I'm gonna miss you, *amigo.* You're the best there is around here. The old man is *muy loco.*"

"He's not crazy. I shoulda never called out to Honey. It's all my fault. Mr. Schroeder was right."

"The hell he was. Honey was a fine lady, but she was a big gal, over 500 kilos. She goes where she wants, when she wants. Nobody could stop her if she made up her mind. She saw you, and if you called her or not, she wanted to come to you. She knew good from bad. Never went near the old man if she wasn't forced, did she?"

"I guess not."

"Like I said, you and your mama are lucky to be going away from this shit farm."

Lincoln looked up from the ground. "Domenico, why do you stay if you hate it so much?"

"I hate it, yes, but I am happy to be here." He laughed sourly and stared out into the pasture.

Lincoln thought for a moment. "How can you be angry and happy at the same time?"

"I have no choice but to be happy. See, you are American. You know how lucky that is? If I try to quit, the old man, he turn me in to immigration. Then I go to jail, and when that's done, do you know what they do to nothing-*hombres* like Domenico?" Lincoln shrugged. "You get deported without a peso to your name. Then what happens to my family? No, it is a different condition for me. You can take control of your life. But I tell you, you must not let a bastard like Schroeder ever touch you again. You are a man now, Lincoln."

"You sound like my mother."

"And maybe she knows something you don't."

Lincoln's mumbled, "I don't feel much like a man. Seems like everything I do gets screwed up. I get my arm broken. I get a good horse killed. I get my mother thrown out of her house *and* her job. I get on the bus, and the other kids don't give me a minute of peace. It wasn't even my mother they were goin' on about today."

The man plunked himself down on a bale of hay, then pointed to one a few feet away. "Lincoln, it is sounding like you are feeling sorry for yourself. I won't have that." Domenico pulled a pack of cigarettes from his shirt and held it out to Lincoln.

He groaned, "My mother'll kill me," but he reached for one, stuck it clumsily between his lips, and leaned forward for a light. He took a tiny puff, coughed, then just sat holding it in his hand, soothed as he watched the smoke curl into the still air.

Domenico savored the first few puffs of his cigarette and relaxed. "Tell you what. I have an idea. You work so dang hard, you got more muscles than the rest of them fools at school. And you're tall, too. Why don't you go out for football? Get a college scholarship. When I played soccer in Guadalajara, those were the best friends I ever had. And the rest of them losers on the bus, well, *amigo*, they won't mess with a football player. See, the loudest ones are all *cobarde*, cowards, chickens, when you stand up to them."

CHAPTER TEN

After school the next afternoon, Lincoln found himself in his drawers at attention in front of the football coach, Jack Knox. The man looked him up and down critically and broke into a grin. "You're so stretchy, I don't know if we have pants skinny enough for you, son, but I bet we can put some pounds on you."

Lincoln was handed a tattered jersey, a faded number 76 barely visible. He turned to a kid dressing next to him. "Seventy-six, ain't that a lineman's number?"

The boy laughed, "Yeah, you're a tackle."

Another boy, his head buried in a locker, grunted, "That's where coach starts all the mama's boys."

But in the weight room later that afternoon, Lincoln threw dumbbells around with such ease, even the toughs backed off. That left the smaller, weaker boys to stand in a corner, shoulder to shoulder, snickering. One ducked behind his pals and snorted, "Hey, Farmer Brown, clean them stalls, lift them hay bales."

On the practice field, coach yelled to Lincoln, "Stand over here, one guy away from the middle. Now, I don't want you rushin' the passer. Too skinny. You'll get steamrolled. I want you to make like a scarecrow out there, arms up in the air. When the quarterback throws a pass, knock it down. You're gonna be the China Wall of Wilkes Barre."

On the first day of practice with pads, though, Coach barked, "Seventy-Six, changea plans. All of a sudden, you look more like a receiver. Let's get you over here on this side of the ball." When Lincoln didn't move, Coach Knox marched up to Lincoln and dragged him by the jersey to the end of the offensive line. "Stand here until the ball's snapped. Then I want you to sprint out five yards, turn hard right, and run across the field. When the quarterback, Ricky here, throws you the ball, I want you to catch it. Now, you'll need to wait 'till it's in your hands good and tight; that's the most important thing you need to remember. And when you're sure you got it, but don't wait too long, I want you to turn left, hard left, and run down the field toward them goal posts. Easy as pie. Got that?"

"Yes, Coach, I'll try."

"Boys, did you hear what he said? 'I'll try.' Try is for losers. What should he have said?"

In a weak chorus, they sang, "Don't just try. Do it."

Lincoln covered the ground in a flash, easily beating the defender, but when he and the pigskin came together, while his right hand drew the ball toward his chest, his rigid left wrist remained locked in neutral. The fingers of that hand, also stiff from scar tissue, gained no purchase, and the ball bounced off his pads into the air. One of the boys smirked, "Hey, Farmer Jones, you're supposed to hang onto it, you know, just like it's a cow's tit."

He tried again and again, until his wrist throbbed and several of his fingers were swollen from passes thrown with increasing irritation each time he bobbled the ball. Coach finally sent Lincoln and the third string quarterback into the teachers' parking lot to practice throwing and catching. As long as Lincoln was directly in front of the pass, he had no problem drawing the ball to his gut, but when he turned to his left, the ball flew off his chest, high into the air, easy pickings for an interception.

Coach drifted into the parking lot and hid behind Mr. Gallotti's pickup, watching. He called Lincoln aside. "Son, what's wrong with your hand?"

"It's okay, sir."

"No, it isn't. Lemme take a look." He pushed up the sleeve of Lincoln's jersey and winced at the broad, meandering, surgical scar. "You hurt your arm son. What's going on?" When Lincoln related the story, coach ordered him to see the school nurse in the morning.

She declared Lincoln's left hand paralyzed and warned that if he was hurt on the field, the school would be held responsible. She refused to sign the paper releasing him for sports. Coach Knox cut him that afternoon.

Lincoln rode his bicycle home in tears. Though he ran his sleeve over his eyes before pushing through the bungalow door, he dropped his books and went straight to his simulator with neither a word of greeting nor a glance at his mother. She followed him out to the shed.

"Lincoln, I know you better than you know yourself. What happened at school today?"

He told her, then added, "It doesn't matter. When we move, I'll probably be in another school. I can try again."

She took a hanky from her sleeve and dabbed at a tear on her cheek. "No. You like that school, and you're going to stay right there."

Lincoln started to answer, "Mom, you don't understand how it is out there..."

She cut him off, “What I wanted to tell you before you ran out of the house was that we *are* moving. But we’re not going ’till Saturday. I just went in and told Schroeder that was the way it was going to be. I learned that from Mr. Nightingale. Then I zoomed right down to Mr. Grollier at the hardware store and told him I wanted a job. Just like that. And he didn’t even blink and said he was looking for a good counterman. I told him I used to clerk at the PX in Oklahoma at Fort Sill, when your papa and me met. Got the job on the spot. He even gave me money for clothes. I bought two dresses at the St. Vincent DePaul’s this afternoon. Good as new. Wait ’till you see ’em! And best of all, you know that apartment above Grollier’s store, well that’s ours for as long as I work there. He needed somebody to live in it and keep it clean. God is good, Lincoln Friday. Don’t you ever forget that.”

She put on one of her three dresses, pinned the broach above her left breast, trooped into the school office the next morning, and demanded to see the new principal. “Well, Mrs. Friday, it’s not my decision to make.”

“Well, you let the nurse make it, and she’s not a real nurse.”

“Tell you what, Mrs. Friday, we’ll let a real doctor make the decision.”

“How ’bout Dr. Heldman? He sure was a nice man.”

“Heldman? He’s long dead—leukemia. Son’s in medical school, but that’s not going to help us. Look, I’ve got a friend in town. Let me give him a call.”

The man agreed to see the boy for free as a favor, but when the doctor took one look, he shook his head and phoned the principal. “George, this case is too complicated for a GP like me to diagnose. Can’t do it.”

The principal was dumbfounded. “Doc, look, this is a good kid. Let him play. If he gets hurt, that’s the knocks of the game. His mother knows that. Everybody knows that.”

The doctor laughed cynically. "George, this isn't the 50s anymore. Things are changing, and fast. Didn't you hear about the kid at Bristol High, up north of Philly? Died on the basketball court right in the middle of the first game. Enlarged heart. They said the doctor who did the sports physical should've discovered it. But there was no way some family doctor like me could have known. No way. Breaks of the game, you say, but they sued the doctor, both the school and the family did. Man lost his practice."

"Never heard of such a thing."

"Wave of the future, George. Not who we were a dozen or so years ago, right after the war. New generation on our hands. Everybody owes you something. So, my friend, I, myself, can't pass this kid, but I'll tell what I'll do. I'll send the boy to a specialist over at the hospital. Mean old bastard, but he's the only bone man in the area. If *he* says okay, and writes it down, that's the word of God, as far as I'm concerned."

The orthopedist was the same surgeon who had fixed Lincoln's arm years before. He spoke quickly to Miriam. "It's a good job. But like I told you at the time, he's lucky to be able to move his fingers at all. He can't be playing sports or go in the army, nothing like that. He needs to be easy on it. Don't want it to wear out too soon, do we?

"Doctor, what do you mean wear out?"

"If he takes care of it, it might last 'til he's thirty."

"Thirty? Then what?"

"Then he learns to live with the pain, or, if he can't, we do another operation to fuse all the bones in the wrist together so that nothing moves. Joint can't hurt if it doesn't move, now can it?"

Miriam looked down, thought for a moment, then rose. She bowed slightly to the doctor and pulled Lincoln by the good arm. She stopped as they walked out the door and looked her son straight in the eyes. "Lincoln, I hope you never turn out like that man." She paused and smiled at him. "No, you never will."

For dinner that night, she made Lincoln's favorite, hamburgers with bacon, and sat with him after the meal. "Lincoln, you're the last Friday. I want something better for you, for your father's name, than you winding up on a dirt farm for the rest of your life. You've got a good noodle up there like your father, may his soul be resting in peace. I looked in the school booklet. There's a science club in the afternoon. It's ten dollars for the year. I'll stake ya. How 'bout that?"

CHAPTER ELEVEN

The science club teacher, Carl Wick, had each new member come up with a two minute talk about his life's dream. Lincoln spoke for five—about aeronautics and how he had created his own cockpit, about coordinated turns in an airplane and stall recovery. The teacher bullied the Better Business Bureau into donating money for a used model airplane. Lincoln was in charge of the refurbishing. He sanded the hull to a silky, frictionless finish, painted it with the school's colors, then stenciled 'Tiger Barre' across the top of the wings, and BBB on the fuselage. Mr. Wick also found a volunteer from the Air National Guard to come and teach them to fly it. When Lincoln was able to control Tiger as easily as he did his bike, the man donated a second plane. By spring, the boys were tying ribbons to the tails of their planes and flying dogfights in the teachers' parking lot while the jocks hollered catcalls from the goal post.

By the end of his junior year, Lincoln had become a master at maneuvering model planes. What impressed Wick more was that even when Lincoln drew the slowest, clumsiest, of the club's now fleet of four tiny aircraft, he outsmarted his opponents, waiting and waiting off to the side, turning lazy circles high and away from the enemy aircraft, refusing to engage, stalling until the other boys became impatient and executed heavy-handed maneuvers to close on him. He'd pull away when they chased, using the seconds to gain small sums of altitude, never executing wild, fuel-inefficient climbs as did the others. It was not long before the engines of the enemy aircraft began spluttering, fuel tanks running dry as their exasperated pilots climbed madly to reach him. That was the moment Lincoln tipped the nose forward and dove like a dart into the attack.

"He who has the most energy wins!" shouted Mr. Wick as Lincoln smoothly cut the other pilot's tail ribbon with his propeller. "See, this is a lesson in flying, but also in life, boys. First, you must learn patience. Then, remember fighting uphill isn't as easy as fighting from above. Plan ahead, make sure you've got the high ground before you tackle a problem. Develop a strategy—you know what that means, all of you?" The boys nodded, and he went on. "You assess the situation then make a detailed plan and stick to it, even when the going gets rough. Gentlemen, you just don't give up on something you really want. It's a law of life. I hope it's the one you fellas remember a hundred years from now, when I'm long gone, and you say to your great-grandkids, 'Hey, did I ever tell you about Old Man Wick, the guy who showed us kids how to win in life?'"

After Science Club that afternoon, Mr. Wick told Lincoln to throw his bike in the back of the station wagon. "I'll give you a ride home. I want to talk to you." He stopped by the ice cream shop and bought two cones. They sat at a table. "Lincoln, you love flying, don't you?"

"Yes, sir."

"I never told any of you this, but I was a pilot in Korea. Flew PBMs, flying boats, in the Navy. I've been watching you. I think you'd make a fine pilot. Now, Lincoln, you're an adult, so let's talk like men. Why, in one year, you'll be old enough to get drafted. Things are heating up in Viet Nam. I don't like it, not one bit." He looked into Lincoln's eyes. "I don't imagine you have a lot of money saved up for college."

"I don't, sir."

"Okay, then I want you to listen to something I have to say. You know about Annapolis, don't you?"

"Yes, sir, heard of it."

"You want to go to college, learn to fly real planes?"

Lincoln's back straightened, and his pupils narrowed. "Yes, sir!"

"Good, then you think about going to college there. I guess I also have to mention the new Air Force Academy out in Colorado. Not the same as the Navy, you can be sure, but it's okay, too. Best thing is, education's free at both places—U.S. government pays the tuition, room and board, free uniforms, even travel. When you graduate, you have a fine degree in science, and you get to go to flight school, if you do well in your classes, and if that's what you decide you really want. Flight school's a bear, but not after you've been through the Academy. Worst thing is, it's hard as the dickens to get in, and the courses are really tough once you get there. But you can do it."

"Yes, sir, I'll try. No, sir, excuse me, *I can do it.*"

"Coach Knox, huh?"

"Yes, sir."

"Good man. He was a Marine during the war. Comes from a football family. Okay, now, first, you have to wangle an appointment to the Academy. That has to come from your senator or congressman. I'll write you a letter, but there's a list as long as your arm of guys who would die to get into Annapolis, or even the Air Force Academy. And they're just as good as you, smart kids, kids with a future. But you listen to me. They are *not* better than you.

"Now, I want you to go to the library and look up both academies. Tell me in a few days if you're interested. If you are, I'll help you. I think you're worth it."

That summer, Lincoln wrote to his congressman and to the U.S. senators for Pennsylvania. He got only one reply, from Senator Hugh Scott, who offered an interview. Mr. Wick sent Lincoln back to the library to look up Scott's biography. The senator had been in the Navy during the War, and Wick told Lincoln to mention that he wanted the Navy and nothing else. He bought Lincoln a white shirt, tie, and jacket; showed him how to spit shine his shoes; then drove him to Philadelphia for the meeting. Scott, a hefty man with a bushy, black mustache, pulled the pipe from his mouth and growled down at Lincoln, "You think you can make it through the Academy?

"Yes, sir."

"Hard place to live, son. Great education, but they jam it up your behind a nickel at a time. You sure you're ready for it?"

A week later, Lincoln received a letter, signed by the senator, offering him an appointment to the Air Force Academy. He had scribbled on the side that he had spoken with Carl Wick, the famous, highly decorated, Korean War pilot. "You're lucky to have had him as a teacher."

CHAPTER TWELVE

Lincoln received all manner of packets over the next weeks, the thickest, an admission questionnaire that was to be returned within ten days. Included was a preliminary medical form that requested a list of doctors the candidate had seen in the past five years. It asked if the candidate had ever been admitted to a hospital or undergone surgery, no matter how minor. Lincoln went to his mother. She patted him on the shoulder. "Lincoln, you be honest. It's the best policy. The truth can't hurt you. God tells us that."

A week later, the Department of Defense sent Lincoln a bus ticket to Indiantown Gap Military Reservation for a formal, two-day physical examination. The candidates were to follow the enclosed instructions to the letter, lest they run afoul of the DOD. On top of the list was an order to bring two changes of clean clothing. Farther down was a line noting the need for soap, shaving cream, and a razor.

At the first station, the candidates were ordered to strip down to their drawers, put all their possessions—save a pair of pants, a shirt, and shoes—in big paper bags, write their names on the outside, and line them up on the floor—dress right dress—in alphabetical order. A sergeant demonstrated how they were to fold the pants and shirt and put the shoes on top, laces tied, toes pointing forward. "Candidates, situate the clothing bundle under your left arm, as is being demonstrated by Private Calhoun, here. And, probably most important is to make sure the tips of those shoes are pointing forward—just like if they were walking." They were marched out of the room, the door was locked, and they did not see the rest of their belongings for the next forty-eight hours.

As the sergeant hustled them, not quietly or gently, to one station after another, a growing number forgot their shirts, pants, and shoes. The sergeant followed, kicking left behinds into a meandering ridge along the hallway.

After each exam, Lincoln asked, "Am I passing?"

The sergeant glared at him and grunted, "Just move your butt."

Sandwiches of a slice of bologna on dry bread were handed out at noon and again at eight that night. For each twenty-five examinees, one man was pulled aside and issued a single razor, a tube of toothpaste, two bars of Ivory soap, and a roll of brown paper. "Bath towels," the sergeant snarled, "for those of you who take showers."

They were told to dress quickly, but it took an hour to get through the pile of abandoned clothing. At nine, they were herded into an ancient barracks, and the sergeant hissed at them to sit on any open rack. He warned, "Every man will be showered and freshly shaven in the morning. You will not pass your physical if you do not follow my orders." The lights were extinguished before he finished his sentence.

Long before sunrise, the barrack lights burst to life, flipped on by the sergeant, who bellowed orders to get out of bed, wash, shave, and appear in formation outside, in the rain, in eight minutes. They splashed cold water on their faces, ran the shard of soap over their cheeks, passed the razors from man to man, and fell in. After breakfast, they were back in the exam quonsets, again stripped down to their drawers, crawling from station to station. At 8 P.M., Lincoln came to the last door along the final hallway. As he stood outside waiting his turn, it dawned upon him not a single doctor had assessed, or even noticed, his arms. He assumed this was the orthopedic station, and that his infirmity was finally to be exposed. His anxious musing, though, was suspended by the shove of the sergeant's palm in his back. Lincoln did manage to swing his arms behind him and walked in as if he was considering a momentous decision. His first impression was that there were no medical instruments in the room. It was, in fact, bare, aside from a small, olive drab field desk, an olive drab folding chair, and an old man in a fancy, green uniform sitting behind the table.

He spoke gruffly. "Sit down, Candidate. You get in any trouble when you were a kid?"

"No, sir."

"How do you and your father get along?"

"It's only my mother and me. My father died when I was very little."

"What was the cause of his demise?" Lincoln squinted. The man rephrased. "What did he die from?"

"My mother told me it was either prostrate cancer or a broken heart. She didn't know which one."

"That's pro*state,* and tell me what supposedly broke his heart?"

"I don't know for sure, but I guess I had a brother and he died, and I must have had something to do with it."

"Why do you say that?"

"'Cause she would never tell me."

"Did you physically hit your brother? Was there a gun in the house, something like that? What *do* you remember of it?"

"The last thing I remember is that my dad, he yelled at me real hard, and she told him to leave me alone."

"What happened then?"

"She took him away, to the hospital, I guess."

"What happened the next time you talked to him?"

"I never saw him again. His casket was in the next room. I told my mother I wanted to say I'm sorry, but they wouldn't let me into the room. That's all I remember."

"How do you feel about that?"

"I don't think about it."

"Have you talked about it with your mother?"

"She has enough problems. And, anyway, we don't talk about much."

The interviewer searched Lincoln's eyes. "Do you feel guilt for…" Lincoln's hands began to tremble, and his face reddened. The man's eyes dropped to Lincoln's left arm. "That scar," he pointed, "does it have anything to do with your brother's death?"

Lincoln mumbled, "No, sir. I fell from a racehorse."

"Huh. A racehorse, you say." The doctor shook his head cynically and started writing on a form, but looked up when there was a rustling at the doorway. The sergeant was prodding another candidate into the room. The doctor muttered crossly to Lincoln, "You can go."

Before he left Indiantown Gap, Lincoln spied a soldier with two stripes sewn to his sleeve. The man was sitting on a curb smoking a cigarette, just outside the medical building. Lincoln went up to him and asked politely, "Excuse me, sir, but do you know how long it takes before they send you the results?"

"Results?"

"Yes, sir. You know, how did you do on the tests."

"Oh, that, well, the *results'll* probably be there before you get home."

When nothing came by the end of that week, Lincoln drove to Schroeder's, parked outside the gates, and slipped to the barn to ask Domenico to ask the maid if a letter had come for him. Then he went to the post office and was reassured that the change of address form was current, and that it was impossible a piece of mail addressed to a Friday could have been mistakenly delivered to the Schroeder farm. Late that afternoon, Domenico called Lincoln and told him that there was, indeed, a letter, and that the maid had found it when she was emptying the trash cans.

"Who's it from?!"

"Department of Defense."

"I'll be right out."

The maid snuck to the barn, handed him the envelope, and as Lincoln was tearing at it, she huffed, "You ought to call the poh-leece on Schroeder. They gotta be some law 'genst one man throwin' way 'nother man's mail." Lincoln listened until she was done, then unfolded the single sheet. It was a letter ordering him to report to the United States Air Force Academy on July First, Induction Day, I Day, for he had been chosen to join the Class of 1970, pending the outcome of his physical exam.

CHAPTER THIRTEEN

On his seventeenth birthday, Lincoln rode his bicycle to the Sterling Hotel and stepped up to the desk man. "Sir, I'm going to be a cadet at the Air Force Academy startin' in July. Gonna be a fighter pilot. Can I have a job until I leave?"

The man picked up the phone, and in seconds, Chef Gunther Radicchio burst into the lobby, a carving knife brandished in his right hand. When the clerk jerked his head toward Lincoln, Radicchio clutched the boy's elbow and tugged him through the lobby past astonished guests, through the rear door of the main kitchen, and into a steamy, walled–off alcove. At a row of rusted, porcelain sinks, he looked the boy up and down, snatched a soiled rubber apron from a peg on the wall, tossed it at Lincoln, and ordered with a grunt, "You vill do ze pots, goddamnit."

A week later, Chef Radicchio popped into to the dreary niche, a dark-skinned man in tow. To Lincoln, the chef declared, "Now you vill do dishes, goddamnit," and to the new man, "You verk here'a, goddamnit."

Radicchio flipped a soiled apron at the new man and pointed to the heap of pots, then turned on his heels, seized Lincoln's elbow, and drew him to a massive, boiling, industrial dishwasher. The chef pointed at the mountain of last night's dishes and left without a word.

As Lincoln gaped at the control panel, the new man walked over and mumbled an unintelligible question, though Lincoln recognized the accent as very similar to Domenico's. But Lincoln just shrugged, so the man nudged him out of the way, loaded the machine methodically, pulled a pair of rickety eye glasses from his pants pocket, and stepped slightly to the side so Lincoln could watch as he worked the switches and dials. Finally, he pointed at a red button, waited for Lincoln to push it, then went back to his station and commenced picking away at crusts of scorched carbon. As one pot was done, two more were dropped arrogantly and noisily by the lesser cooks.

At 5 P.M., Lincoln put the last of the dishes in place for dinner and hung his apron on the wall. The new man was still at the sinks, sweating, his arms deep in a pot, scrubbing sluggishly. Lincoln smiled at him, but he remained expressionless.

The next morning, the new man was at work before Lincoln dragged in at seven. He did not look up from the heap of pots then, or during the morning, his eyes locked perpetually on his pool of greasy water. At noon, he left the kitchen for the parking lot, where he stood in a corner, facing away, as if hiding. While the other workers took out bits of food filched when Radicchio had turned his back, the new man ate nothing, said nothing, smoked a cigarette, then crept back to his sink.

After work, Lincoln borrowed his mother's car and drove out to the horse farm. He slipped through the woods that flanked the driveway and dashed across the field to Domenico's shack. He told the groom of the cold, new pot washer, and asked, "Do you think there's anything I can do to talk to him? I think he's Spanish, like you."

Domenico lit two cigarettes and handed one to Lincoln. "*Amigo,* probably this *hombre,* he doesn't speak English." He put his hand on the boy's shoulder. "Maybe he is like me and does not want to be kicked out of your country. Maybe he is hiding. It is very dangerous for us here, *amigo.* Every minute of the day could be our last."

"Yeah, you're right. I probably should just leave him alone, right?"

"I didn't say that, Lincoln, but you must understand how we live every day afraid." They were silent until Domenico looked up. "Maybe, he does need a friend here. Just like if you were trapped in another land."

"Domenico, he's not trapped. He can go home if he wants."

"But he is trapped, my friend. If he goes back to Mexico, or Puerto Rico, or Cuba, then his children don't eat. Just like I told you before, any road he walks leads to sour. Do you think it is nice every time you go into town to be stared at like a freak? Like we are going to rape your daughter or your mother?"

"Domenico, who says that?"

"No one *says* the words, but it is in their hearts. Tomorrow, you look when your friend comes and goes. Watch them, the Americans. You will see it in their faces. You see their eyes; they get tight, don't blink so much as he passes. Watch how they turn their bodies a little away, so they can run if this dangerous, foreign animal lashes out."

"People don't see *you* that way, Domenico. Everyone likes you."

"*Amigo,* this is on the top they like me. You just have to dig down a few shovelfuls."

"Man, I don't think so, but I don't live in your skin. I'm sorry to bother you. I wish it wasn't this way."

"Always has been—always will be. Not good news, but you're a man now, and you need always to think what others see through *their* eyes." He crushed his cigarette into the dirt with his boot. Lincoln looked down at his and laughed nervously at the ash that had grown an inch long. He took a meek puff, dropped it to the ground, patted his thighs and started to rise, but Domenico leaned forward and gently pushed him back onto the bale.

"One more minute, Lincoln. You know, *amigo,* every man lives with some good and some bad. Even the millionaire has problems you cannot believe. Right now, your life is mostly *very* good. Maybe you can share that with your friend at the hotel."

"He won't even look at me."

"He is your guest. *¿Si?*" Domenico smiled, though not warmly. Lincoln shrugged. "Did you welcome him to your country? You were working there before he came. Did you welcome him to *your* kitchen?"

"How could I do that? I mean, it's not normal. What if he got angry at me for talking to him?"

"Lincoln, when did a man ever get angry when another soul welcomed him? Here is an opportunity to help this man."

Domenico let Lincoln think about that for a moment, then pulled another cigarette from his pack and tilted it toward Lincoln. This time, Lincoln didn't even take a first puff, and Domenico watched, suppressing a smile when Lincoln's thumb very intentionally flicked the filter every few seconds.

"Okay, this is what we do. I teach you to say a few words in Spanish. He will be so happy, he might greet you with a kiss. It is called *besitos.*" Lincoln's eyes flashed, and Domenico chuckled. "You know, Lincoln, not in my Mexico, but in Cuba and Spain, it is the way they greet each other, even the men, with a kiss on the cheek. There is a whole world out there you don't know about yet, my friend. I hope you can see it someday." He was quiet for a moment. "You are a good man, Lincoln Friday. What you do today, it will come back to you. One day, someone will welcome you when it is your turn to be the stranger."

In the morning, Lincoln glanced at the new pot washer several times, but the man hastily dropped his head, and Lincoln spun around uneasily to start on last night's dishes. At ten, the man walked past Lincoln's work station, headed outside for a smoke break. Lincoln girded himself and drew a breath, but lost his nerve and buried his head deeper in the interminable flow of dishes and silver. At the end of the day, he followed the pot washer outside, but the man dragged himself aboard a city bus before Lincoln could stop him.

The next morning, Lincoln arrived an hour early. Chef Radicchio was already at his cooking table, pushing cloves of garlic into an enormous steamboat roast for the wedding reception late that afternoon. He looked up and shouted at Lincoln, "Vat is dis, goddamnit? Now you vant extra money for come in early to sit around?"

Lincoln stuttered, "No, sir. I just wanted to take care of the leftover dishes from last night. You know, sir, so I don't get behind before the party."

Radicchio stared at him for a long minute. "No more dishes. Now you are vegetable man, goddamnit." He snatched a relatively clean apron from the food prep area, tossed it at Lincoln, and pulled him by the wrist to the salad table. "Now you cut tomato so lean, blind man can see through."

The chef held a tomato up to the light. He washed it, plunked it down in front of Lincoln, then slid a great knife across the table. "Slice him." Radicchio stepped back to observe as Lincoln hacked a few strokes. Lincoln heard the gurgle of disgust at the same instant the chef knocked him out of the way and grabbed the knife back. "No, goddamnit, you cut off finger. I show you one time." Radicchio treated the knife with a hone, holding both just inches from Lincoln's eyes. He adjusted the angle of the blade, chattering in theatrical German when the slope was too steep or too shallow. He came to a midpoint and burped, "*Ya vol*! Tventy-two-and-half degree is goot." He shook his head sadly at the confusion on Lincoln's face. He clucked his tongue, "Best for cutting is forty-five degree, *ya*? Less, edge too thin. *Ya*, cut good, but become dull right away. More than forty-five degree, blade never dull, but cut nothing. So each side of blade must be half forty-five degree—tventy-two-and-half degree each side. You hone this angle for sharp blade. You vill remember for whole life."

Radicchio pulled several tomatoes from the basket, eyed them in the light, ran a sprinkle of water over each, and lined them up within hand's reach. He turned to face Lincoln. "You vatch hard." The knife flipped into the air, Radicchio caught it by the handle and, without having taken his eyes off the boy, curled the ends of his fingers melodramatically into his palm to demonstrate the tips were nowhere near the blade. Still staring at Lincoln, he began slicing very slowly. When half of the first tomato was carved, the man's head dropped abruptly to the cutting board and the knife quivered faster than Lincoln's eyes could follow. In less than thirty seconds, five tomatoes had been sliced so microscopically thin, it appeared as if mounds of red tissue paper had fluttered onto the cutting board.

He turned and handed the knife to Lincoln, who thumped the last tomato so hard with the blade, it squashed. Radicchio shook his head and growled, "Maybe five year, goddamnit." He spun around and went back to trussing the massive roast.

When the new pot washer came in the back door, he did not see Lincoln at the machine and turned to his sink, eyes cast down. Lincoln, though, thought he heard the door, and when no one appeared in the kitchen proper, he walked around the corner and went up to the man. He quavered, "*Disculpe señor. ¿Hablas Español?*" The man's head swiveled sharply, and Lincoln took a step back, but the dark eyes sparkled and Lincoln wheezed, "You speak Spanish?"

"*Si, si!*"

"Well, then, *bienvenido a mi país.*"

The man jumped forward and placed his barely shaven cheek against Lincoln's and made a kissing sound. Lincoln stiffened, though managed to squeak, "*Besitos.*"

"*Si, si, amigo, besitos.* I am from Cuba."

As the color returned to Lincoln's face, the man began a soliloquy that went on, Lincoln was sure, for half-an-hour. Lincoln nodded politely every few seconds, and the man finally stopped. "*¿Entiendes?*"

"*No, señor. No hablo Español.*"

"No problem. I teach you. You like that?"

"Yes, sir, that'd be great."

"So, *¿Cómo se llama?*" Lincoln stared at the man, whose face twisted in surprise. "Well, that means in Spanish, 'What is your name?'"

"Oh, it's Lincoln."

He laughed, "Lincoln? Lincoln?" He waved an index finger in the air and grinned, "I will call you 'Mr. President.' I am…," but Chef Radicchio rounded the corner of the dividing wall that separated the washing area from the kitchen.

"Vat goes on here'a, goddamnit?" Lincoln skulked to his station, and the new man turned to the sinks. Radicchio paced back to his oven, muttering, shaking his head crossly.

At noon, the chef pushed through the swinging doors from the dining room into the kitchen. He bellowed, "Vat is zis shit?" Lincoln looked up from his cucumbers, but averted his eyes when the man looked directly at him. "You, you come here, goddamnit!" Lincoln froze, but Radicchio took several giant steps toward him. "You are now busboy. Other busboy drunk. Get on white shirt, tie, black pants, shine shoes."

"Mr. Radicchio, sir, I don't have any clothes here."

"Goddamnit. Vhere are clozings?"

"At home, sir."

"Get zem now!"

"Sir, I don't have a car. I only got a bicycle."

"You have license?"

"Yes, sir."

The chef reached down to his belt and unhooked a ring of keys. He thumbed through them, pulled one off the clasp, and handed it to Lincoln. "Red Audi in parking lot. You be careful, goddamnit." He pivoted and disappeared into his office.

Lincoln drove to the apartment at fifteen miles per hour. His one white shirt, one tie, and black chinos were at the bottom of a pile in a corner of his closet. They had not been washed since his interview with Senator Scott. The shoes, though, when he blew off the patina of dust, were still glistening. He jumped into the clothes and sped back to the Sterling Hotel. The instant he burst into the kitchen, Radicchio descended, grumbling, hissing, and smacking a fist into his palm. "You look like no-home man." He swept his arm and pointed down the hall. "To office." Inside the space, no larger than a walk-in cooler, he roared, "Take off clozings, goddamnit."

Lincoln froze, but Radicchio reached forward gruffly and tugged at the tie, then began to unbutton the boy's shirt. "Now pants." Lincoln shook his head. Radicchio lunged toward the boy's belt, and Lincoln jumped back, but his trousers soon dropped to the peeling, linoleum floor. He struggled to get them past the shoes and scuffed the shine in several places. Chef Radicchio pushed Lincoln into the desk chair, pried the shoes from the boy's feet, and rolled the shirt, tie, and pants into a ball. He opened the door and yelled, "Matilda! Now!"

A corpulent, older woman peered into the room, glanced at Lincoln's face for an instant, then dropped her eyes to his crotch.

Radicchio tsooked and shook his head in disgust. As he jammed the bundle into the woman's chest he bellowed, "*Schnell*! Be fast."

In ten minutes, the door opened without a knock. The woman shuffled in, handed Lincoln the pile of clothes, leered at his privates again, and was gone. The shirt and pants were pressed hard and flat. Bits of spray starch flaked off the board-like tie. Radicchio rushed in with a bottle of olive oil. He growled, "Dress," then snatched the shoes and rubbed a coat of the oil on them with his fingers, waited impatiently as it soaked in, then buffed the leather with a dry corner of his apron. "Ve go now."

Radicchio dragged Lincoln by the elbow into the dining area. He called to Matilda, "You teach him to be busboy right now, goddamnit."

When she smiled up at Lincoln, he could not wrench his eyes off the gaps in her yellow, chipped teeth. She cackled in a whisper, "You do good job for Matilda, we go for ride in elevator tonight." She winked and began the course on dining room etiquette.

CHAPTER FOURTEEN

At 6 P.M., wedding guests began filtering into the hotel. Lincoln stood ramrod straight in a corner, a white towel draped over his left forearm. He stared at the far wall, avoiding eye contact with the guests as they took seats filling two dozen tables. With a subtle snap of the chef's fingers, a platoon of crisply dressed waiters flowed from the kitchen to descend upon the guests with soup and salad. Lincoln remained at attention until he saw, in his peripheral vision, guests beginning to lean back from the table. He lunged forward and flew about clearing dishes—once or twice snatching them up before the guests had finished.

Radicchio was watching through the window in the swinging doors between the kitchen and the dining room. He howled over his shoulder to Matilda, "He is not professional, goddamnit. Instruct him!" It was so loud, Lincoln heard it.

When Lincoln brought a half-full tray of dishes into the kitchen, Matilda ran to him and counted off on her pudgy, arthritic fingers the litany of his sins. She finished by warning, "I tell you, no good vork, no elevator."

A waiter, Barry Abada, passed by just as Matilda issued her ultimatum. His shoulder brushed Lincoln's, and the nascent busboy took an edgy step closer to Matilda, turned, and mumbled, "Excuse me, sir."

An air of disapproval masked Matilda's face. "You do not say sorry to zat vun."

Lincoln bowed slightly, and she forgave him with an unctuous grin. He slid to his side, rounded the dishwashing partition, and unloaded his tray. As he turned the corner, headed back to the dining room, Abada blocked his exit. "The elevator, huh? Look, let me lay it on the line for you. You need your pipes cleaned, you let *me* know." He grinned with his lips pulled tight to expose a set of very straight, very white, teeth. His face hardened. "Take your pick. You want to die of the syph or some other silly Nazi sickness, go and have your fun."

On his third circuit collecting dirty dishes, Lincoln eyed a table that was still cluttered. The busboy assigned there had dropped a tray and was on his knees scooping up lettuce and wiping ranch dressing from the rug. Lincoln dashed over. As he rounded the table, eyes down, snatching plates mechanically, he heard a shocked gasp. Surely, it was the woman from whom he had just pulled a salad plate. Lincoln looked up reflexively, preparing to apologize for the blue cheese dressing he imagined having slopped into her lap.

"Lincoln, is that you?" He looked uneasily toward the voice, his mind a jumble of directives, not one of which addressed speaking when spoken to by a guest at a Sterling Hotel banquet. A young woman waited for a moment, and when Lincoln remained mute, she turned to a handsome, older man seated to her left. "Poppy, that's Lincoln Friday. I told you about him. You know, the boy at school that's already a pilot."

The man nodded in recognition and stood. His blue eyes were set off by lightly silvered, though still mostly ebony, hair. He extended his hand to Lincoln, who turned toward the window in the kitchen door, his attention seized by the blaze of an enraged, Teutonic face. Lincoln half-turned back to the guest, stiffened, and bowed slightly as he took the man's hand.

"Bob Dalton. Isabelle tells me you're going to the Air Force Academy. That's quite an honor." Lincoln's head dropped a few more submissive degrees, but the pressure in his chest forced his eyes up, where they fixed over the man's shoulder on the burning face behind the window. Isabelle's father smiled. "Well, I better not keep you from your work. Nice to meet you."

"Yes, sir, Mr. Dalton."

Lincoln loaded a tray and wobbled toward kitchen as if headed to his own crucifixion. Radicchio waited until the door swung nearly shut. "So you are Vilkes Barre high society, ze guest of honor?"

"No, sir."

"Vell, you are a special vun, aren't you? You see how zey look at you? Especially ze girl? Now, Mr. President Lincoln, Your Royal Highness, back to vork, goddamnit." As Lincoln turned to drop his tray at the sink, he caught Matilda shaking her head in rebuke.

After the last dish was cleared, the tables broken down, and the carpet swept, Lincoln took off his apron, barely able to lift his arms to hang it on the rack. As he paced wearily toward the kitchen's delivery entrance to fetch his bicycle, Matilda stepped from behind a walk-in freezer and stopped just inches from him. "Zo, you do goot?" Lincoln shrugged his shoulders. "Vell, chef say 'okay'. Zo, it is time for Matilda to give reward, *ya*?" Lincoln's mind was too muddled to resist as she jerked him back into the corridor and pushed the button on the service elevator. The doors parted instantly. The steel grating was already open, and she maneuvered him into the car with her belly, as if herding a calf. Her flabby arms yanked the grating closed, and the elevator lifted.

Lincoln eyed a fire extinguisher hanging by a single nail. It swayed precariously as the car moved upward. He put his hand out to steady it. Matilda grunted, "Zat is for us if ve get too hot, *ya*?"

As the peeling "3" painted on the doors outside the car passed below them, she hove up on the grating ferociously. The elevator stopped short. Lincoln grabbed at her to steady himself. She patted his hand. "Vell, just a minute, if you please."

She opened the first two buttons on her blouse and put his hand on her sweaty bra. He pulled away to stand bolt upright in the corner, fists clinched. "Zo, you are shy?" She took a step toward him and leered in his face, then reached forward slowly to open his belt. He did not flinch. And still he did not when she jerked at his zipper, nor when she yanked his pants down.

"Vell,' she laughed throatily, "ve need to get you started, *ya*?" She massaged him gruffly, and he pulled farther back into his corner. She cackled even more gutturally, "Zo, you are ze soft man, *ya*?" As her fingers lightened, a thin whimper escaped him, and with that, she worked herself rheumatically onto her knees. Soon, it no longer mattered that he sensed the gap in her teeth or once or twice felt the raggedness of the chipped, yellowed enamel. After a minute, his eyes opened ever so briefly, though all he perceived in his building frenzy was the bottom half of the number "4" painted on the wall outside the elevator door. Seconds later, he heard himself moan, then felt his legs go pleasantly rubbery. A quiet descended over them, but Matilda soon pulled away. She snorted, "You see vhy you should be goot boy at vork?" She pulled the grating down with a vicious swipe. The elevator jumped up to four, then dropped back down to the kitchen. Matilda was gone before Lincoln realized they had landed.

On his bicycle home, he was seized with a guilt deeper even than the day Honey Barre died. On the hill near the Friday's apartment, his legs weakened again, and he had to stop to sit on the curb. It was midnight. A cop rolled to a stop and ordered Lincoln to his feet. "Why you sittin' there? You do something you shouldn't?"

"No, sir."

"Well, then, move along before I run you in for vagrancy."

Lincoln could not fall asleep, worried more about losing his appointment to the Air Force Academy than the devastating venereal disease surely percolating in his loins. He found one of his mother's bottles of cheap rye and after two guzzled swigs, fell asleep, though woke a couple of hours later, the room spinning and his heart thrumming. He couldn't fall back to sleep and dragged himself out of bed at five and left for work.

CHAPTER FIFTEEN

He planned to hide until it was time to show himself at the vegetable bench, but Radicchio caught him in a storeroom and grumbled, "Vell, ze social boy. Vat goes on here'a, goddamnit?"

"Nothing, sir, just looking around at what a real restaurant keeps on hand."

Radicchio eyed him suspiciously. "Vell, ve need sandwich man today. I fire the old for putting too much ham." He drew Lincoln to the short order station and pointed at a food-stained sheet of paper hanging from the counter. "Look at ze menu, ze sandvich." He paused for three seconds and laughed, "No questions? Goot."

As Lincoln inspected the drawers and cabinets of his new work space, Barry minced past. When Lincoln looked up, the waiter turned his head away and made a barely muted spitting sound. Lincoln's chest clutched. Everyone in the restaurant, the hotel, and likely the city of Wilkes Barre, already knew. The next time Abada swayed past, he looked Lincoln straight in the eye, bared his teeth, and spit again. Several of the waiters pinned orders on the sandwich board, most smiling crudely, one quipping with a grin, "Welcome to the club!"

During morning break, he was too anxious to drink coffee in the backroom and walked outside into the staff parking lot to be by himself. His friend the pot washer was standing at the dumpster smoking. When he saw Lincoln, he raised his arms in welcome. They stood quietly for a moment until the man offered, "*Senior* Mr. President Lincoln, still I have not said my name. It is Rico. Do you know what that is in Spanish?"

"It sounds like it means a man who is very strong and tough."

"No, no, that is *bronco.* No, *rico* is rich! As you can see." They laughed, but the man stopped unexpectedly and spoke softly. "Mr. Lincoln, you need to be careful here. There are many holes to fall into." When Lincoln only stared, he went on. "The *señiors* and *señioritas* here are not too, what to say?" He gazed at the ground. "Maybe not too clean." Lincoln was silent, but the vise closed even more tightly about his chest. Rico watched his face and shook his head. "Not to worry. Just one time. It is no problem."

At lunch the next day, Barry Abada placed an order for a sandwich on Lincoln's board. Along the bottom of the slip was a scrawled note. "Hey, let's you and me talk, okay? Clear the air. How 'bout it?" Lincoln's hands froze, and he gazed blankly at his cutting board, avoiding Abada's expectant stare.

Chef Radicchio appeared from behind the walk-in refrigerator. He placed his lips inches from Lincoln's nose. "Vhat is zis? Too vorn out?" Lincoln's mind cleared, and he fell back into his rhythm of snatching bread from the toaster, slapping on the dollop of mayo, three thin slices of turkey breast, four wafers of tomato, and finally, the lettuce leaf. The backward swipe of the knife divided the sandwich diagonally—the forward thrust lifted the halves. A twirl of the fingers settled them on a spotless, porcelain dinner plate. Less than a second after the scoop of potato salad hit the plate, the dish was on its way to the serving shelf, the garnish meeting it on the fly.

Lincoln had the process down to eleven seconds, but Radicchio shook his head and growled, "Too long. Customer starve to death vaiting for ze president to make lunch." He turned away from Lincoln and stomped to a spot in the middle of the kitchen floor, planted his feet shoulder-width apart, and jammed his fists to his hips. The waiters, waitresses, and busboys flowed around him in efficient waves, like air over a wing. Radicchio turned left and right with crisp precision, as if an actor accepting accolades from the corners of his audience, then drifted to various worktables and took a bow. It was not, though, in humble appreciation. He bent forward to drop his eyes closer to the hands of his soldiers, evaluating the fluency with which they carved roast beef left over from the night before, appraising the girth of hamburger patties and the generosity of apple pie wedges. Eventually, he nodded, drew to Prussian attention, about-faced, and marched to his office. Before the strings of his apron had passed out of sight, the flow of industry succumbed to the law of entropy, the surge decaying into a muddle of Brownian motion as waiters and busboys drifted off course to take up interrupted conversations with countermen.

Barry sidled up to Lincoln. "Say, I just wanted to tell you, I heard that you don't have a car. That's a shame for a guy like you." Lincoln stared at him. "Hey, I've got this Pontiac I been thinking about letting go. You want to take a look?"

Lincoln's mouth finally opened. "Jeez, I don't have that kind of money, sir."

"Nah, don't worry. We'll give you a good deal. I'd like to get to know you anyway."

Radicchio suddenly reappeared. He bellowed, "Vat goes on here'a, goddamnit?" and the troops whooshed back into laminar flow. Lincoln created his cold sandwiches as fast as his fingers could separate slices of ham, but the chef watched him out of the corner of his eye for a moment and turned abruptly. "You keep mind on vork."

Lincoln was done at two-thirty. Barry was waiting for him outside by the dumpsters, next to a faded, rusting, grey '52 Pontiac Chieftain. Barry put his hand on the fender. "Nice, huh?"

Lincoln's eyes welded to the vehicle, and his jaw dropped. "But I don't think I can afford it."

"Look, it needs some work, a radiator, but that's cheap. You can pick one up at a *bone*yard." He peered into Lincoln's face. "Speaking of *bones*, let's let bygones be bygones. You stay away from that panzer division, and I'll let you have the car for twenty-five bucks. Keep you healthy *and* make you mobile at the same time. How's that sound?"

"Twenty-five? Wow. You really mean it?"

"Of course." His face hardened. "But I mean both things. Do I have your promise?"

"Yeah, sure," Lincoln squeaked without a second thought, though his attention was glued to the car, not on Barry's entreaty. He mumbled, "Let me run home on my bike and get some cash."

"Nah, just put your bike in the trunk and bring the money tomorrow." He paused and looked harder in Lincoln's face. "Hey, maybe we can go for a ride in the country next Tuesday."

"That's my day off. How did you know?"

"Oh, I just guessed."

CHAPTER SIXTEEN

Lincoln parked behind the apartment in a corner of the hardware store lot and tried to open the hood. His fingers could not find the latch, and it was minutes on his knees before he spotted a slip of hanger wire poking from the grill. He pulled it out of curiosity and the hood popped. He found several clean holes, the size of his pinky, in the radiator and a few in the fan. He followed their trajectory and discovered two crushed bullets jammed into the engine block. He detached the fan and radiator and borrowed his mother's DeSoto to search junkyards for replacements. At Rick the Wrecker's, he pulled parts from a rusting hulk that was in better shape than his car. When Lincoln carried them to the yard office, Rick wiped sludge-caked hands on his overalls, pulled a stub of pencil from the breast pocket, licked the tip, and screwed up his face in deep thought. "Now, let's see what that's going to cost ya." He stopped for a moment and looked up at Lincoln. "Son, you seem like a good, strong kid. You mind givin' me a hand gittin' this transmission off the floor and back out to the shop?"

Lincoln smiled, "Why, sure, sir."

As both men bent forward, the owner grabbed the heavy side and jerked before Lincoln had tightened his hands on the shaft. There was an audible snap; Rick groaned piercingly and dropped to his knees. Lincoln blurted, "I'm sorry, sir."

The man made no sound as he curled into a fetal position on the grease-obscured, concrete floor. Lincoln bolted to attention and began to tremble. He turned to the door and took a step to run, but an invisible hand clutched his shoulder. He turned back and bent over the man. "Are you okay, sir? Can I help you?"

There was a panted, "I can't breathe. My back."

"You need to go to the hospital, mister?"

The owner barely moaned, "It's too late. They told me to stop..." A tear ran down his cheek, and his eyes peered distantly, though pleadingly, into Lincoln's.

Lincoln ran to his car, fumbled for the keys, dropped them in the oily mud, found them, then tried to jam the wrong one into the ignition. The quaking of his hands amplified, and the keys dropped again. As he shot forward to retrieve them, his head hit the steering wheel. The shock slowed time. In the black mist of his fear, the image of his flight simulator formed, and he was suddenly practicing spin recoveries, recalling how his flying books had stressed, time after time, page after page, that during an emergency, one stopped and thought of nothing other than 'flying the plane. First, fly the plane.'

He had read about World War Two pilots in damaged P-51s, freezing when they saw the Earth coming up at them at three hundred miles an hour, and how the ones who survived forced themselves to cull their training and, somehow, ignore the vision of death looming only seconds away. Going back to basic flying maneuvers, they just flew the plane. Some lived.

Lincoln's world cleared. The right key found its way into the ignition, and the DeSoto came to a stop in front of the junkyard office. In fits and starts, he lugged the man outside, then folded him onto the back seat, body part by body part.

Lincoln stayed in the emergency room waiting area until a nurse came out and sat next to him. She put her hand on Lincoln's shoulder. "Your father is very sick—pancreatitis." Her voice dropped to a whisper, and she spoke behind her hand. "Pretty heavy drinker, huh? Good lesson for you, young man."

"Don't know, ma'am."

"Well, it should be a good lesson," she huffed and stood. "And your father said to make sure you took the radiator, or something like that. I asked him what he meant, but that's when he just stopped talking."

Lincoln drove back to the junkyard, put ten dollars under a coffee cup on the man's desk, wrote, "For the radiator," locked the door from the inside, closed the front gate, and draped the chain around the latch.

He went by the hospital the next day to check on the man, but the nurses were mum. As he walked through the lobby to leave, a Candy Striper looked up from her desk and gasped, "Lincoln, is that you?"

She came around the desk and walked quickly toward him. His eyes ran from her face to her white shoes. "Isabelle! Wow, you're a nurse?"

"Well, not yet, but that's what I want to be. Hey, it was real good to see you at the wedding the other night. My father says you look like a pilot. He should know, huh?" She became serious, "Why are you here? Everything okay?"

"Yeah. Oh, I don't know. I brought this guy here yesterday. Nurse said he drinks too much. But he was pretty nice to me. Maybe I shouldn't ask, but do you think you could snoop around and find out how he's doing?"

She shook her head and followed that loudly with, "I'm very sorry, but I'm not permitted to give out information on patients." She spun about, took two brusque steps back toward her information desk, stopped abruptly, and whispered, "You stay here for a minute, Lincoln. I'll be right back." He watched her climb the stairs, his eyes stuck on her just slightly swaying hips. When she disappeared around a corner, he found himself wringing his hands, impatient for her return.

She was expressionless as she came back down, and he unconsciously averted his eyes. This time, though, she touched his arm. "I'm afraid Mr. Kelleher is in a coma, Lincoln. The nurse didn't know if he was going to be okay. I'm sorry."

Lincoln barely looked at her as he mumbled. "Hey, thanks. I didn't really know him. Just gave him a ride in."

"That was sure nice of you. That's what I told my dad, that you're not like the rest of the boys. You know, he would still like to meet you."

Lincoln turned a few degrees toward her. "Isabelle, would you like to go to the show Saturday night? I could pick you up in my new car, and I could meet your dad, too."

"You mean go out on a date?" He nodded. "Oh, oh, I don't know if my parents'll let me." She looked up, smiled softly, and took a breath but swallowed her first words. A second later, she stammered, "Let me think about it."

Lincoln squeaked, "Well, can I call you, then?"

She went back to the desk, wrote on a slip of paper, and handed it to him.

As Lincoln turned to leave, she called out more loudly than she'd intended. "Yes!"

The next morning, Lincoln worked much more slowly than usual. Radicchio assailed him several times before he was able to put Isabelle's image behind him. Time moved at a drudge until noon, when the maître d' flew into the kitchen from the dining room. He spoke in flurry to the cooks. The men left their ovens for the door, following the maître d' so closely, one tripped on the man's shoe. It flipped off and there was scuffling and cursing, but the gaggle soon came together and peered through the window into the dining room.

One giggled childishly, "Sure looks like her."

"I don't know," the other cook muttered. "She looks fatter than in the movies."

That brought the staff tearing for the door, and Lincoln considered abandoning his station to join them but caught sight of Radicchio rounding the corner from his office. He covered his ears to mute the coming diatribe. The crew, though, sensing the chef's arrival, surged back to their work stations before the blast. Without expression, Radicchio stomped to the door and nodded, "*Ya*, it is her. Now, back to your production."

Seconds after the chef left for his office, several of the waitresses coalesced into a pulsing throng until one stepped forward as spokesperson. She ordered the maître d', "You go out there and ask if it's really her. Then you come back and tell us."

He stepped obsequiously through the door and approached an attractive blond who looked up, her lips taut. She whispered, "If you promise not to say anything, I'll tell you." He clicked his heels and nodded. She muttered, "Yes, I am. And this hamburger is overcooked. Please take it back and bring me a club sandwich." The maître d' bowed, lifted the plate fawningly, and ran to the kitchen. Before the swinging door commenced its closing arc, he thundered, "Yeah, it's her, it's Doris Day all right!"

He threw the burger into the meat barrel and barked at Lincoln. "She wants a club sandwich. Think you can do that?"

The maître d' personally delivered it. She commented, "This is very good. Please thank the chef." He ran directly to Radicchio's office to deliver the kudo.

Radicchio gave Lincoln Saturday afternoon off. Lincoln spent the time washing and waxing the Pontiac for his date with Isabelle. He also scrubbed the engine compartment and discovered the linkage to the antediluvian transmission had come apart in the spray from the hose. He pushed the rods together in what seemed a logical sequence, showered, dressed in his white shirt and tie, rubbed a bit of olive oil into his shoes, and left for Isabelle's house. The car would not shift out of first gear. He watched the temperature rise and finally had to pull over when steam puffing from under the hood clouded his windshield. He poked around but did not have tools to adjust the linkage and limped at two or three miles per hour to her house. With a metal on metal screech, a shudder, and a hiss of steam, the engine quit.

Mr. Dalton opened the door and stuck out his hand. Lincoln was mortified and started to extend his but pulled back sharply. The man's head cocked in uncertainty until Lincoln held up his greasy palm. "My car's on the blink, sir. I think it's the transmission."

"Well, let's take a look, son."

He brought out a shop light and tools. They went over the linkage piece by piece. Mr. Dalton groaned, "These old trannies are impossible. Look, this is going to take some time. Here." He reached in his pocket and handed Lincoln the keys to the family's Olds 98. "Wash your hands in the garage, then you two go on your way before you miss the movie. And I want you back before midnight, young lady. And I know you guys won't do any drinking. Go on. I'll get this thing going."

"I couldn't do that, Mr. Dalton."

"Just go on. Have fun."

The Thrill of It All had already started. As they settled into seats at the back of the theater, the first face they saw on the screen was Doris Day's. Lincoln's chest tingled, and he whispered to Isabelle, "Oh, I got a great story for ya," but the man to their front turned and shushed him. Isabelle shook her shoulders, made a taunting face as the man's head turned forward, then opened and closed her mouth in silent derision.

Lincoln laughed, "You look like Mr. Bluster," and the man half-turned again. Isabelle stuck out her tongue several times, scrunched in her seat, and apologized when her arm accidently brushed Lincoln's. Two seconds later, their hands touched, and her head came to rest on his shoulder. Lincoln felt a prickle in his middle, and though it was at first pleasant, it soon culled memories of his elevator ride, and the muscles in his chest tightened with the dread of what was growing inside him. He agonized that if anything happened with Isabelle, it would be passed on, and Mr. Dalton would have him sent to jail. He pulled his shoulder away.

By the end of the movie, though, they were holding each other so closely, Lincoln's anxiety vaporized, and he was aware of little else beside his heart and his privates. As they walked to her father's car, she stopped, stood on her tiptoes, and kissed him. His lips were drawn so tightly sealed, she pulled back and touched his face. "Lincoln, I'm sorry. Are you angry with me?"

He put his arms around her and bent forward to let their cheeks touch. The tingle was back, and he slid his lips to hers. Slowly, he let his mouth open. They made out in the car for a bit, but he pulled away and whispered nearly out of breath, "Don't want to upset your dad. He's a great guy." She pulled him to her lips a last time, and they drove home talking about worms and snakes to slow their breathing.

CHAPTER SEVENTEEN

Lincoln found a letter from Senator Scott's office on Monday before he left for work. He ripped at it, though it only asked if Lincoln had heard from the Department of Defense about the results of his physical examination. Miriam shook her head. "As usual, government's left hand don't know what the right's up to. Go ahead and call his office, but make it short."

The senator's secretary paused. Her voice hardened. "That's strange. Did you have trouble with any of the tests? May mean that you didn't pass. I'll have our office look into it."

Lincoln drove to work, his mind cluttered with notions of failure, of Isabelle, of never becoming a pilot, and the lingering, sour guilt over his liaison with Matilda. Just when he thought he'd carved a future, he had to face that the Academy had found out about Matilda, or his arm, or, perhaps, a psychiatric report that he'd murdered his brother.

A channel of gloom wrapped itself around him as he parked at the hotel. He sat at the wheel for five minutes, steeling himself to face another day in the kitchen. As he opened his door to report to work, Barry Abada flounced up to within a foot of the car. "Hey, Lincoln, good to see you. You as excited about tomorrow as I am? We should talk and decide where we want to go. Let's choose a place that's soft and quiet, yes? We ought to talk about it now, you know, before the day starts."

"Yeah, yeah, sure."

Barry smiled. "Let's talk in the car."

"Ah, I don't know. Ya know, I had kind of a bad morning. I need to get into work."

He lifted himself from the car, but Barry took a step closer, pushing his groin against Lincoln's door, forcing it closed. "Well, you know, a promise is a promise."

"Yeah, sure, I know. But, ah, how 'bout later? Okay?"

"Okay, but you promised. I trusted you. I'd hate to have to take the car back."

Inside the kitchen, Matilda eyed Lincoln as he put on his apron. She waddled to the sandwich counter. "Zo, you are vork hard?" Her bellowed laughter had the resonance of an oompah horn, and several of the kitchen staff looked up. She chortled again, winked at Lincoln, and trundled off. His face burned red, and he unconsciously lifted the hone to sharpen his knife, though swiped without watching his hands. The blade sliced over the back of his thumb, and while it was not painful at first, the sight of his hand disappearing in a fountain of red dragged his mind back to the kitchen. "Shit!"

Barry spun around. He stared at the spurting blood. "Jesus, Mary, and Joseph!" He reeled backward toward the ovens, his eyes rolled up in his head, and he collapsed against the sous chef, who was searing the outside of a breakfast steak with a propane torch. The flaming canister sailed from the man's hand, bounced off the stove, and dropped into the deep fryer. The second cook made a move toward the torch, but the oil had already exploded in flames, and the hair on his arms singed before he got near the fire. He ran out the back door rubbing his arm and cursing.

In seconds, the kitchen was filled with a brightness three times that of the normal gloom. The change in ambient light was so drastic, it wrested even the attention of the busboys, one of whom tore out of the kitchen into the dining room, past the patrons, and out the front door. When he was halfway down the block, he stopped and screamed, "Fire!" The door to the hotel had already swung shut and no one heard.

Lincoln snatched a cloth napkin and wrapped his thumb. He pulled a fire extinguisher from a pillar in the middle of the kitchen, pointed it at the base of the flames, and clamped down hard on the handles. A single, languid puff of white powder dribbled from the nozzle. He looked at the gauge—the pointer was deep in the red. He grabbed the next bottle, glancing at the gauge before squashing the handles. It was even further in the empty arc. He tried anyway. Not a wisp of chemical was produced.

The aluminum pots hanging above the fire began to deform in the heat. One dropped from its hook, hit the stainless steel cook's table, and rebounded into the second deep fryer. Blazing oil splashed over the ovens, and the room filled with greasy, shrimp-and-chicken-and-fish-and-potato-scented, blue smoke. Lincoln remembered the fire extinguisher in the elevator and ran to get it, but the car was stopped on an upper floor. He went to the chef's office but nearly tripped on Barry Abada, who was outstretched on the floor, head flopping left and right. Lincoln dragged him into the parking lot and left him next to the sous chef, who was trembling so helplessly, he was barely able to hold his cigarette.

Lincoln ran back in. His jaw dropped when he saw the maître d' peering into the kitchen through the window in the swinging doors. Lincoln pushed through the door and ordered, “Get the guests out, but do it slow.”

The man turned and shrieked, “Fire, get out, but don’t be in a hurry!”

Inside, flames were licking the wooden webbing that buttressed the plaster ceiling of the Nineteenth Century structure. Lincoln heard wild screaming from the service elevator in which he had had his tryst with Matilda. He pried the doors open with his fingers. She and a waiter were flat on the floor in the shallow pocket of air left in the smoke-choked car. They crawled past him, jumped to their feet, and sprang for the parking lot. They were, though, nearly run down by the spearhead of the Wilkes Barre Fire Department. Several men in smoke suits and gas masks burst past the elevator into the kitchen. One shoved Lincoln toward the door and yelled, “Get the hell outta here, asshole.”

A sputtering gaggle of hotel workers came together into the middle of the parking lot but soon juddered en masse into the street, away from the sparks and burgeoning smoke. As the maître d’ chased behind trying to count heads, an Audi skidded to a stop. Chef Radicchio exploded from the car. “Vat goes on here’a, goddamnit?” Without waiting for an answer, he ran into the kitchen, though two firemen heaved him out the door so hard, he fell backward and slammed his head against the macadam. The staff, now shoulder to shoulder, vibrated away even further down North River Street, the fear of God contorting their faces. When no one approached the chef, Lincoln walked back and extended his hand.

Radicchio said nothing to Lincoln or to the cowering staff. He wobbled to the maître d’, grabbed him by the tux lapels, and dragged him through the front doors of the hotel and up the stairs to the auxiliary half-kitchen that served the ballroom on the mezzanine. They spoke a few sentences, came back down to the parking lot, and shouted commands, one over the other, for the staff to shape up. Radicchio walked the ranks pointing at those he wanted for the evening meal.

Lincoln was amongst the skeleton crew. Chef Radicchio growled, "Now, you are a cook. You vill vork every day zis veek."

Though Barry Abada was still on the ground, he had lifted himself into a sitting position against a car tire. Lincoln half-turned to see the rage in the man's face. He turned away quickly, only to meet Matilda's blank eyes.

Two days later, the Sterling's parent company sent two high level managers to the hotel to assess the damage. They arrived by train from Washington, D.C. The staff was summoned to the ballroom kitchen. The top man stood before the crew. "There will be no time off or vacation until this hotel has been restored to its full working capacity. And there will be no overtime paid, as this fire was caused by the carelessness of several staff members. If you have any complaints, take it up with the instigators."

Lincoln had been standing next to the scrap meat and oil barrel. The employees were packed so closely, one of the waiters nudged the barrel. Slowly, a few bubbles of putrefied gas were knocked free from the bottom and shimmied to the surface. They oozed around for a few seconds, fused into one enormous, greasy orb, and, with a final jolt from Matilda, who was trying to get close to Lincoln, ruptured. Lincoln was the first to suffer a lungful of the pernicious gas. His face twisted in disgust. "Jees, that is unbe*lievable*!"

The manager at the center of the half-moon stopped speaking. He glowered at Lincoln, pointed at him, and hissed, "Don't like the new rules? Good. Pack your stuff and get the hell out of here. Anyone else dissatisfied with my directives?" He peered at the sea of shocked faces. "If you don't want to be here, we don't want you. This is a team, and this team is going to work around the clock until the job gets done."

Chef Radicchio took a short step forward. "Mr. Smith, he is new cook, that vun. He vas good in ze fire."

"You know, Chef, I don't give a shit about yesterday. He's no good to me today."

CHAPTER EIGHTEEN

Lincoln drove to a park and sat peering into the Susquehanna. He thought about going home and talking to his mom, but he worried she might ask Mr. Grollier for the afternoon off and then get into bed and start drinking because her son was such a disappointment. If he snuck onto the farm and found Domenico, Schroeder would surely discover them, and it might cost the man his job. He got back into the car and drove slowly to the hospital. Isabelle's back was turned toward him. She was guiding an ancient woman, step by step, toward the doors of the intensive care unit. A nurse met them and took the woman by the arm into the patient area.

Isabelle turned and walked, head down, back to her desk in the lobby. After a few paces, she stopped abruptly and looked up, aware she was being watched. She gasped as she met Lincoln's gaze. He took a step forward but halted when he saw the despondency in her face. She exploded in tears. An older woman at the volunteers' desk creaked out of her chair, took a cane, and shuffled toward them. She studied Isabelle's face. "Oh, dear. Isabelle.

Are you okay?" Isabelle barely nodded. "Well, then, why don't you take your break now? You two just go out and sit in the courtyard. It's a beautiful spring day."

"I can't leave you alone, Mrs. Rhodes, what with your foot and all."

"Oh, good gravy, I'm a big girl now. I'll be just fine. Off you two go."

They sat on a picnic bench amongst the forsythia in full bloom and maples just beginning to bud. A robin landed on the birdbath and pecked away at the detritus left by the winter. Isabelle exhaled slowly. "The first robin of the season. I guess there really will be a spring—at least for us."

Lincoln let his forearm touch hers. "Did I do something wrong?"

"No, of course not. It's the lady I was taking to the unit. They told me to get her from the chapel so she could say goodbye to her husband." Isabelle began to cry softly, and Lincoln looked around surreptitiously before taking her hand. "They've been together for fifty-eight years. She told me, 'I breathe for him, and he breathes for me. How will I live without him? We're one soul, one breath.'"

Lincoln tightened his fingers around hers. "I guess I can't imagine."

"I hope I never have to." She paused for a second and whispered, "Thank you for coming here. How did you know I needed you?"

He drew a breath to start his litany of sad failures but just shook his head. "What time do you get off work? Could I see you tonight?"

Without looking to see if the coast was clear, she threw her arms around him.

They met at the Carvel on Sans Souci. She drove her father's 98 Olds. Lincoln told her he wanted to sit in her car because the Pontiac had sprung a gas leak. "The inside, it smells like those refineries outside Philadelphia."

So they sat in her car and stared through the windshield for a few minutes until Lincoln stoked his courage and took her hand. He told her everything—though still not about the ride in the elevator.

She thought for a moment and laughed. "Lincoln you don't belong in that crummy kitchen. You belong at the Air Force Academy. My daddy tells me that's where the best of the best go. So, that's why you're going there."

"I know, but it means I'll be away for four years."

"It'll be a lot longer than that. It's forever, Lincoln. My Papa said you'll never live back here, never, ever again."

"Then what about seeing you?"

"Well, like he always says, 'What will be, will be.' And when your head drops and you feel like dying, he always laughs and says, 'But what will be is what you make happen.'" She squeezed his hand in both of hers and pulled them to a spot just below her breasts. He was not sure if she had let his fingers brush them. "Lincoln, I know you have a lot of experience. But I'm different. You may not believe this. You are the first boy I ever kissed. I mean, like we kissed that night. I did it because I know who you are."

Lincoln's face reddened. "Isabelle, you know what, you want the truth?"

She gasped, "Oh, my God. Did you get a girl pregnant?"

He laughed. "No, no way. I just wanted to tell you that you are the first girl I ever kissed. And now, I don't want to kiss anybody else."

She tightened her arms around him and brought her lips to his. Their kisses were soon far deeper than on the first night. In minutes, the windows fogged and their breathing quickened.

Then their hands began exploring. Lincoln felt himself begin to lose control, just as he had in the elevator, though this time he wasn't as shocked at the feeling, nor was he as vulnerable. He pulled away and sat rigidly, but quietly.

When their breathing slowed, Isabelle asked in a throaty voice. "Did I do something wrong? Did it hurt when I touched you?"

"No, it was perfect. That's the problem. I know what's going to happen. If we don't stop, you'll be miserable in the morning. Look, I'm going to be gone soon." He became silent, and she began crying softly. "Isabelle, I don't know what to do." He was still for another minute then kissed her cheek, struck by the salty taste of her tears. He gasped, "I'll call you tomorrow," then ran to the Pontiac.

As he opened the door, he was surprised at how dim the dome light was. There was also the most distant tinkle of music, and he looked down to realize he had forgotten to turn off the radio when he'd gone into the Carvel hours before. He was still shaking and waited until he felt ready to drive, but when the key turned, there was but a click in the engine compartment, a feeble groan, then nothing. He tried several times, until even the click disappeared.

He went back to Isabelle's car. "You're not going to believe this, but my battery is dead. Do you have jumper cables?"

"Have jumper, what did you say?"

"Let's look in the trunk." There were none. "Isabelle, can you push me to the top of the hill right over there? If I get it coasting fast enough in neutral, I'll drop it into low and jump start it. You know what I mean?"

"Oh, yes. Just drop 'er into low, and it'll jump right up, or something."

Lincoln kissed her cheek and laughed. He pulled his mildewed backseat free and tied it to his bumper to protect the Olds.

She pushed very slowly, and Lincoln soon crested the hill, waved at her to stop, and let the Pontiac gather speed. Halfway down, he jammed the transmission into low—nothing happened. The speedometer passed twenty-five. When he understood the engine simply wasn't going to start, his concentration shifted to the T-intersection at the bottom of the hill. Disgustedly, he pushed on the brakes. Though they responded briefly, and the car slowed a few miles per hour, the brake pedal coarsened on the next push, and on the third, it felt as if he was ramming his feet against a brick. The Pontiac was doing nearly thirty, and Lincoln grabbed the steering wheel for purchase as he mashed both feet on the brake. The Pontiac slowed slightly, but the end of the road was now less than fifty yards away. He tried rotating the wheel to start a turn before the intersection, but without the engine to drive the primitive power steering, he was able to move the wheel only a few degrees at a time. By the end of the hill, he had forced the wheel ninety degrees, enough to send the tires into a skid. While the car's nose was facing left, the two-ton machine continued its slide toward the telephone pole at the T. He threw his arms over his face to wait for the crash. When it came, the car lifted off the ground, and Lincoln's body smashed into the tattered headliner. He felt an electric jolt radiate into both arms, then no pain, for he had lost consciousness that quickly.

Isabelle jammed the brakes of her car at the end of the hill and sprinted to the Pontiac, which had run up one of the pole's guy wires and come to rest on its side, rocking slowly, perpendicular to the ground. All manner of fluids were dripping and spurting from the underside. She tried to climb up along the roof to get to the passenger door, though when she found it impossible to scale with nothing to hold onto, she ran to a payphone and called the police. The fire department came as well, but neither they nor the cops approached the car. She screamed at them that Lincoln was inside, but they answered in concert that they weren't getting near it until the foam truck came to neutralize the gas leak. "I ain't sendin' my men up to get blown to pieces for no drunk," the lieutenant shouted at her.

When the seepage of gas was contained, and the underside of the car foamed, two firemen climbed to the driver's side, fought to lift the door, then crawled inside. One called for a stretcher and two more men. Another fireman placed a ladder against the side of the Pontiac for the stretcher bearers, but Isabelle ran ahead of the men and managed to climb two steps before a cop grabbed her skirt and hauled her to the ground. She tried to get up, but he put his boot on her back and snarled, "You move a muscle, girl, and your skinny ass'll be goin' for the ride tonight. Both of you be goin'. Drunk in public, interfering with a police investigation, and I'll come up with a few more items. So go stand over there like a good little girl."

When Lincoln was lifted out of the car, his forehead was adhesive-taped to the stretcher. Isabelle cried, "Oh, my God, Lincoln," and ran toward him.

His eyes flickered open and he tried to turn his head, but when he couldn't, he moaned, "Isabelle, don't leave me."

One of the firemen growled, "Close your eyes and keep your mouth shut."

Isabelle drove to the hospital and stood at the door of the emergency department. When Lincoln was taken to the back, she sped home, woke her dad, told him the story, dressed in her candy stripe uniform, and dashed with her father to the hospital.

As they ran through the doors of the ER, the officer who had thrown Isabelle to the ground looked up from his paperwork. When he recognized Isabelle's father, he came to semi-attention and bowed slightly. "Good evening, Councilman Dalton. Hope you're not here for something bad."

Isabelle gasped, "Daddy, that's the man who threw me on the ground."

The officer stiffened, puffed his chest, and swaggered a step forward. "Didn't happen like that, sir. She was interfering with police work. We can't have that. Lucky I didn't run her in for drunk and disorderly, and the boy for drunk driving. Still may if we hear any more about this. I'm not one to play favorites."

"Poppy, that's not true at all. We didn't touch any alcohol. I swear we didn't. I just went to help Lincoln."

Dalton put his arm around his daughter. "I know, Sweetheart. Okay, first things first. Let's make sure Lincoln's taken care of. We'll look into the police in the morning." He had Isabelle seen in the ER and convinced the doctor to take her blood for an alcohol level, and Lincoln's as well. Then he called Miriam. She answered after nearly ten rings, her tongue so thick, he barely understood her. He explained matter-of-factly that Lincoln had sprained his neck and was being looked at, just to be safe.

She screamed into the phone what Dalton thought sounded like, "He's gonna die, ain't he? I'm comin' down there."

"No, you're not, Mrs. Friday. I don't want you driving. Look, Lincoln's going to be fine. Here's what we're going to do. You get dressed and fixed up, and I'll come over and pick you up."

When Isabelle's father got to the apartment, Miriam was weaving down the stairs. She held an envelope but was gripping the handrail so hard, the paper crumpled. When Dalton took her arm, she shoved the paper into her pocket.

At 1 A.M., the x-rays were brought to the ER doctor. He gave the films a cursory glance, pronounced them normal, and ordered the adhesive tape loosened. "Oh, and there was no trace of alcohol in their blood, either one of them."

Lincoln's gurney was moved to a non-emergent cubicle where Miriam, Dalton, and Isabelle were allowed to sit with him. Isabelle took his hand and touched his face. Mr. Dalton looked down at the swollen cheeks and forehead. He grimaced. "That goddamn car. Sorry, Lincoln, but I'm glad it's off the road for good. Too much wrong with it. I didn't want you in it, to say nothing of Isabelle." He laughed. "Twenty-five bucks, huh? Son, you got ripped off." Lincoln managed a painful nod.

Lincoln was, however, not discharged. The nurse said they had to wait until the x-rays were read by the on-call radiologist, but they hadn't been able to locate him. The four remained in the cubicle, all but Mr. Dalton dropping off to sleep. Miriam snored so loudly, a nurse came in and shook her roughly, but the moment the woman left, Miriam's head dropped and the din resumed.

At 3 A.M., the ER doctor threw the sheet back on Lincoln's compartment. He snapped, "Don't move your head. You fractured your neck."

Miriam came awake so suddenly, she fell out of her seat onto her knees. Her hands flew to the sky as she keened, "Lord have mercy." A second later, she collapsed to the linoleum and wailed so vociferously, Dalton and the doctor lifted her back into the chair.

With Isabelle's father holding her upright, the doctor went to the curtain. He shouted, "Nurse!" An old woman who had been listening to the commotion just a foot from Lincoln's cubicle straightened her back and took an unhurried step inside. The doctor barked, "Valium, five, IM, stat."

"For the boy?"

"No," he rolled his eyes, "for the lady."

When Miriam calmed, the doctor stood above Lincoln. "You fractured the dens." When he was met with blank stares, he added, "The odontoid process." Isabelle nodded. Miriam's head swooned, her eyes gazing disjointedly into the distance.

Mr. Dalton demanded, "The what?"

"It's the projection of bone at the top of the cervical vertebral column that allows the cranium to rotate." The doctor shook his head faintly at the blank stares. "You know, the bone that keeps your head from falling off."

Miriam tried to focus on the doctor. She moaned, "His head's going to fall off? Oh, my God!"

"No, he's going to be fine," the doctor droned as he rolled his eyes again. "His head is not going to fall off, madam. You're just lucky we found it in time. The neurosurgeon is coming in, and he'll..."

Miriam slipped a bit in her chair and whined nearly incoherently, "Surgeon? Will that doctor keep his head from falling off?"

A nurse stuck her head into the cubicle. "Doctor, you need to get going. You've got a heart attack in Three and an appendix in Four."

The neurosurgeon burst in at seven-fifteen. He spoke to Mr. Dalton. "Your boy has a serious fracture, but it isn't displaced, so I don't think surgery is indicated. But he will have to be in a halo for a good while."

Dalton sucked in a deep breath and fixed his eyes on the doctor. Isabelle, though, put her hand on his arm. "Let me, Daddy." He nodded and exhaled slowly, his head bobbing as if counting to ten. "Doctor, could you please tell us what a halo is?"

"Okay, but then I really need to get going. It's just an external fixation device..." Dalton drew a breath through his nose. "Well, it's like a metal ring that sits over the top quarter of the head. It's connected with rods to a brace on the shoulders to hold it in position. In the ring at the top, the halo, there are screws that come in to the skull and hold it in place."

Miriam wailed, "Oh, my God, screws in my son's head! Will they be in there forever?"

"Now, now, madam, they don't go *into* the head. The tips just touch the scalp and forehead so the head doesn't move. Keeps the two parts of the broken bone touching..."

"Broken bone?!" Miriam wailed. "You said it was just fractured."

"Same thing—fracture, break. He'll be fine if he keeps the halo on. That's going to be your job."

Dalton asked, "How long, Doctor?"

"Eight to twelve weeks—at a minimum. When the x-rays show good callus, we'll talk about taking it off. Are there any questions?"

Miriam groaned, "Calluses?"

"No, no. Callus is what we call new bone. When we see it on the radiographs, we know there is healing, and then we can determine just how much repair has taken place." He surveyed his audience quickly. They were numbly quiet, so the doctor nodded, called a nurse, and walked off.

The family was shooed from the room to the waiting area, and Lincoln was ordered to swallow a sleeper. At ten, a man wheeled a pile of chromed steel bars and variously sized silver loops through the waiting area. The din of clanking metal crescendoed as he jerked the cart to a stop at the bedside. Lincoln's eyes burst open, and he tried to wriggle off the gurney, mumbling nearly incoherently, "I need to get to the Air Force Academy. I'm late."

The man summoned a nurse and complained, "I can't work on a moving target. Do something." She injected Lincoln, he faded into a stupor, and the technician fashioned an erector set of shoulder pads sprouting adjustable rods that pointed up like so many stalks of bamboo. These were the rods that would suspend the halo. He drove the bolts in the halo forward and backward endlessly, until the last adjustments were reduced to tenth-turns and Lincoln's head sat, unmovable, plumb center inside the metal loop.

He went to the family in the waiting room and gave instructions. Lincoln was not to move a muscle for three months. He could stand and sit for a few moments but was not allowed to walk any farther than the bathroom. He was certainly not to bathe, shower, or bend over to wash himself, even with a cloth. He was transferred to a room for that day and night and would be discharged in the morning.

Lincoln woke at noon in an easy chair. He moved his eyes as far to the sides as he could, then up and down. He asked numbly, "How long?"

Mr. Dalton was going to answer but saw Miriam take a breath. She peered into her son's eyes and whispered, "Only eight weeks. It's nothing." She smiled mechanically then jerked and gasped, "Oh, my God. I forgot." She pulled the letter from her pocket and held the wrinkled envelope forward. "It's from Senator Scott's office."

Lincoln was barely able to raise his arms.

"You open it, Mom."

"Let's see. Well, they got the results of your physical, and you passed. Oh, my God. And they have confirmed your appointment, and they are sorry there was confusion, but it was because of the Department of Defense, not their office. And they wish you well, and, let's see, hope you will keep them informed on your progress."

Lincoln's eyes clouded. Bob Dalton walked to Lincoln and put his hand on the boy's shoulder. "We'll figure something out."

The next morning, Isabelle's father got a call from the District Attorney's office. Isabelle was being charged with public intoxication and interfering with a police investigation, and Lincoln with driving while impaired. He drove to the hospital, demanded copies of the blood alcohol results, then sat at City Hall, refusing to leave until he saw the mayor. The police chief and DA were summoned, and Dalton passed the lab results around. He stood. "Gentlemen, this is a new America. When someone screws up and harms another person, he gets his ass sued." He paused and locked his eyes on each official separately. "Now, it would be unseemly if the President of the City Council sued the mayor, the police chief, the DA, the City of Wilkes Barre, and an out-of-control cop for malicious prosecution." He stopped again.

The police chief grumbled. "Well, Mr. Councilmember, let me remind you that citizens can't sue the government. We are above reproach," he laughed mockingly, "especially the police."

The DA cleared his throat and held up his hand. "Calm down, Darryl. Rodman screwed up, and it isn't the first time with him. You just take care of it."

The chief answered, "If I do that, I got the union to deal with. They don't like to be told what to do."

The DA barked, "Like I said, Darryl, take care of it, or I'll bring criminal charges against Rodman for manhandling the girl, and then the good councilman, here, can bring civil charges against you and your cops." He stood, nodded to the men, and left.

Miriam wrote a letter to Senator Scott begging Lincoln be allowed time to heal and join the class a few weeks late. Four days later, two men in crisp, Dress Blue uniforms—one a captain, the other a sergeant with a sleeve crusted in stripes and overseas service bars—appeared at the hardware store. Miriam's heart leapt into her mouth, and she was unable to speak when they asked to see Lincoln. Mr. Grollier took them upstairs. They examined the boy from across the tiny living room, about-faced silently, and went back down to the counter. They explained their usual mission was to notify families their sons had been killed in action in Viet Nam, but this time they had been dispatched to inform Miriam there was no such thing as joining an Academy after the first day, and that with the severity of

Lincoln's injury, he was physically disqualified from military service forever. They were required by law to inform the local draft board of their findings.

Their parting words were, "Ma'am, I know you're disappointed, but take it from us, you don't want your son over there in the Nam. We both been there. Better say a prayer of thanks to God."

CHAPTER NINETEEN

Lincoln did not speak his first week home, and then only a few words for the next two. Isabelle brought schoolwork for him, but holding a book high enough to see without moving his head a millimeter was so enervating, he spent most of the time staring into space. At the end of the third week, Miriam received a letter from the school district informing her that, because of her son's excessive time loss, he would not be eligible to graduate with his class. Further, if he decided to continue in high school, he would have to petition to repeat his entire senior year.

Lincoln became mute again. He sat in the recliner and watched soap operas, *American Bandstand*, and the *Mickey Mouse Club*. His only excursion from the chair for those weeks was to the bathroom.

The hospital called and told him to report for a recheck. Between the weakness in his legs and Miriam badgering him to slow down, it took nearly half-an-hour to get down the steps and into the car. When the nurse came into the room, her nose and mouth were covered in gauze. Miriam asked why she was wearing a mask, and, with eyes rolling, she snipped, "You ever smell one of these halo patients?"

The next morning, just after Miriam went downstairs to work, Lincoln dragged a wooden chair into the bathtub, filled pots and cups with warm water, and scrubbed until his skin was streaked red. When Miriam came up for lunch, she walked to him and kissed his head. "That woman is nuts. You smell good, just like always. They just don't know who they're dealing with, do they?"

Isabelle began to come over after school to sit with Lincoln. She made him move his feet in cadence with the music on *American Bandstand*, and after a few days, his bottom half had learned to mimic the teens on the TV. She stood in front of him, held his hands, and danced and danced until they heard Miriam's weary footsteps on the stairs.

A few friends came to see him, and even Carl Wick, the science club teacher. Though Mr. Wick sported a broad smile, it did not hide an aura of lost hope. He had also lost weight, and was, perhaps, a bit pale. What was most alarming to Lincoln was the waning of the man's booming, navy pilot's voice. Lincoln worried his own appearance had shocked and frightened the man. He apologized, "I'm sorry to upset you, Mr. Wick. Please don't worry, sir. I'll be okay. You'll see. Maybe someday we'll go flying together."

Wick's eyes reddened. "You bet we will." He braced his hands on a chair at the dining room table and pressed his voice a bit louder. "You just don't give up, ever, ever, you hear?" Lincoln tried to nod, and Wick's eyes became murky. He patted Lincoln on the shoulder and hurried from the apartment.

At the six-week point, the neurosurgeon ordered x-rays and announced they showed some healing, He predicted another month. Lincoln beamed that he couldn't wait to get the halo off.

It would be the finest moment of his life. The surgeon glowered. "Son, when this comes off, the hard collar goes on for another six weeks, and then you wear a soft collar for six after that. So just slow down; you got a long road to hoe." Miriam's face dropped as she calculated in her mind how long it would be before Lincoln was able to work and help with the food bills.

Mr. Grollier advanced Miriam's salary a few dollars a week to help out, but she and Lincoln knew the money had to be returned someday, and Lincoln would need a job the instant he was released to work. Lincoln scoured the *Times-Leader's* help wanted section each afternoon before dance lessons but found nothing other than manual labor—an impossibility, he was advised in a call to the surgeon's office. The receptionist counseled, without speaking with the doctor, that any job requiring the use of his hands, other than to write or answer telephones, was banned for the rest of his life. He and Isabelle talked about how he would finish high school in no time, but most evenings ended with both their eyes red. When his mother climbed the stairs at six, Lincoln always pasted on a smile, but she sometimes watched from the kitchen to see his shoulders slump a few degrees deeper each day.

On the Monday two weeks before graduation, three before he should have been leaving for Colorado Springs and the Academy, Isabelle came to the apartment in tears. She pulled a chair up next to Lincoln and held his hand. "Mr. Wick died yesterday. He had prostate cancer. He never told us. He never told anyone." She pulled an envelope from her jeans. "He left a note for you."

> *Dear Lincoln,*
>
> *I don't want you to be sad. On the contrary, in many respects, you should rejoice. God blessed you with something special, and I'm not saying that to make you feel good, because that may not*

be an easy thing to live with. See, now you have to do something with that gift.

I say that you were given a lot because I look at the people in your life. You can tell a man by the company he keeps. Lincoln, think about who cares about you. Your mother was dealt a lousy hand, but she worked so hard to raise you, and look how well she did.

Then, there's Isabelle. She is a gem, Lincoln. What will be with you two only time will tell, but the very fact that a girl like that cares so much about you speaks for itself. You are a very lucky young man.

How many pilots do you know? There's Mr. Dalton. And your friend the football coach at Notre Dame (who is now the head coach!), and yours truly. Now, I'm not saying that being a pilot makes you a genius, or that it is a big deal. Not at all. If I did it, anyone can. But Lincoln, to be a good *pilot, to keep the people riding behind you safe, that takes dedication and commitment. Lives will be depending on you. The work to get there will be endless, but I know that you will travel that highway to the very end. For a man like you, it's just a matter of making the decision—nothing more.*

Okay, one more thing. I looked at your transcript. You have already passed all the core courses. You only need one gym class and one art class to graduate. Since you have a medical excuse from gym, that can be waived. That leaves art. I told Mr. Haynes, the art teacher, about your flight simulator. I'm sure it's not there anymore, but he said he'd come out to your house and you could draw pictures of the instruments and then write a paragraph about each one telling how it works, what it does, and how to use it in an emergency. If your presentation is as good as you described the simulator, he said it would qualify for an independent art project.

No matter what, Principal Dudley promised me he would convince the superintendent to let you walk the stage for graduation with your class. You see, you must never accept defeat in the important things in life. When you are sure you are in the right, and you're sure the goal is worth it, you fight back. Surely, you've heard me say that once or twice.

Now, it isn't easy to fight back. It means you have to stick your head up above the rest, and the minute you do, there will always *be someone waiting to whack it off. But you can't let that fear stop you, nor can you allow nasty tricks by small people, the bullies and the naysayers, you know who I mean, get in your way. Don't be afraid. If you do what is right, you won't lose.*

Lincoln, like I said, God gave you a lot of gifts. He expects a lot out of you in return, and I'll be standing right behind you all the way, at your six, to help you do His bidding. Never forget that.

I can't wait to watch you take on the world!

Respectfully,

Carl

Carl R. Wick

Isabelle held him so tight, it felt as if she was driving the words into his heart.

On a balmy, Thursday night in late June, Lincoln Friday walked to the stage on Isabelle's arm. When his name was called, his high school class rose to its feet cheering, "President Lincoln, President Lincoln..."

By early July, the halo was removed, and at the end of August, the neurosurgeon pronounced his fracture healed. Lincoln was discharged but handed a list of physical limitations that all but kept him ensconced in the recliner. Miriam asked the surgeon if there was anything Lincoln could do to speed his recovery.

The doctor answered, without pausing to consider the question, "Nothing."

Lincoln had become so debilitated by the months of inactivity, he could not get in or out of the car without help. He found it harder to climb stairs than during the first month after the accident, and both Miriam and Isabelle had to struggle in front of and behind him to get him to the apartment. If Lincoln tried to do a push up or walk a few stairs on his own, Miriam screeched at him to stop and give God a chance to make him better. After a few weeks, he refused to leave the apartment and made excuses when Isabelle called asking him to go out for ice cream. Eventually, he stopped taking her calls.

A week went by before she appeared at the apartment and refused to leave until he came out of his room. When he opened the door, he was unshaven and his hair was long and tangled. Still, he wouldn't talk. She burst into tears, ran down the stairs, and drove away in such a fury, he flinched with the squeal of her tires.

At the end of the week, she wrote to him. His chest tightened when Miriam handed him the letter.

Dear Lincoln,

I am sorry all this has happened to you. My father thinks you are a great guy. He told me not to bother you, to let you work things out in your head, but I miss you.

He says the mark of a man is if he can still be a man when everything around him is crumbling. He said you already know that.

If you want to go out and talk, please tell me. We can go to a show or just sit around.

Fondly,
Isabelle

CHAPTER TWENTY

Miriam increased her hours at the hardware store to pay back the advance and took a job as a waitress on the weekends. When she was mugged on her third Saturday night at the restaurant, a policeman brought her home. Lincoln was in his chair watching television, sipping a glass of ginger ale. The officer peeked past Miriam when she opened the door. His back stiffened, and he glowered at Lincoln. "Oh, it's you, huh? I thought so. Drunk again, I see?" Lincoln took a breath to answer but instead lifted himself stiffly out of the chair and went to his room. As he closed the door, the cop mumbled, "I ain't forgot about you, boy."

Lincoln couldn't sleep. The threat burned in his chest as he pondered his helplessness and vulnerability. Regardless of the truth, Officer Rodman, a bully with a gun, would hound him for as long as he lived in Wilkes Barre. Though he lay in bed struggling to find a path from his troubles, he eventually accepted there was no escape, there was no hope—he sensed only fear, and it crushed every image of the future.

Eventually, the final confrontation with Schroeder laced its way through his mind. He was so much bigger and stronger than the old farmer, but in the end, he was nothing more than a weakling who had permitted Schroeder to treat him like a farm animal. He considered how a horse, despite its power to trample a dozen men, spent its entire life in submission, obeying whoever was at the reins, even a small child. Lincoln realized he had become that creature.

He thought despondently of Honey Barre and the day she dared pull away from the groom to do something *she* desired, and how her act of defiance brought about such a painful demise. He, too, was powerless, and all he could do was roll into a tighter fetal ball and look for sleep to rescue him.

He woke at 4 A.M. and went to his dresser to pull out the letter from Carl Wick. He read it over and over then walked into the kitchen for a drink of water. Miriam was up, sitting at the tiny table nursing a cup of tea. "Mom, I never showed you this. It's from Mr. Wick. He said you were a great mom. You really are. You never quit, do you?"

Her eyes clouded. "He told me that he was going to send you a letter before he passed. I just figured you'd tell me when you were ready. I don't need to see it, though. That's between you and him."

He hugged her and listened to the story about the drunk who'd grabbed her when she left the restaurant and tore the pendant from her coat. "The SOB ran, but God made him trip, and when I caught up to him, I kicked him good, right in the head, until he dropped the broach your papa gave me. You know the one. That's when the cop happened by. He put cuffs on that bastard, and then her put 'em on *me*, pardon my French. He made us sit in the back of his car—next to each other. Sergeant at the station house made him drive me home."

Lincoln hugged her again. "Mom, that was your last night at some crap-hole diner. I'm getting a job—tomorrow. I mean today." Though she scowled quite sternly, he smiled. "Don't worry. I got it all figured out. It's going to be sitting at a desk. I'll be making enough to pay for our food." He paused for a moment. "Mom, I need to borrow the keys. Please."

"What for?" When he didn't answer, she nodded. "Okay, Lincoln. I know whatever it is, you'll do right."

He drove to the cemetery and stood over Mr. Wick's grave. After a few minutes, he choked, "Hey, Mr. Wick, I don't know what to do. You told me not to be afraid, but everywhere I look there's a trap. Every time I get close, something ruins it. I just don't know what to do." He stood waiting for a flash of lightning, a clap of thunder, but as the sky brightened, his head slumped and he returned to the car. He was not thinking when he dropped into the driver's seat, or when he turned his neck to back out of the parking lot. He spent the minutes fretting about the coming struggle to unfold himself from the car and push himself up to the apartment. As he parked, though, a vision of Isabelle appeared, and then one of Mr. Wick, and he found himself in the apartment, bent over his sleeping mother, kissing her cheek.

The next morning, he borrowed the car again and went to the YMCA. He asked to see the director. A small man in rimless spectacles emerged, eyes tightened in suspicion. Lincoln stood at near attention in his white shirt, black tie, black slacks, and spit shined shoes. He bowed slightly, returned to attention, then made his petition.

The director grumbled, "Are you good at anything?"

"I'm good at coming to work early, sir, and workin' hard. Grew up on a farm. I work 'till late." He stood a bit taller. "And I'm going to be an Air Force pilot, an officer."

"You got someone I can call for a professional reference?"

Lincoln's posture waned. He thought and thought and finally squeaked, "Chef Radicchio at the Sterling, sir."

The man nodded at Lincoln to follow into the office. The director dialed the hotel. The boy's heart pounded as fiercely as it had on his first landing with Coach Hettmans.

The man mumbled irritably, "Well, do you know where to get ahold of him?" He shook his head as he dropped the receiver into the cradle. "He moved to New York. He's cooking at the Waldorf. Your friend must be quite the chef."

"Sir," Lincoln implored, "if I give you the money, could you call him there? You can take it out of my first week's pay."

"You know, son, that's not the usual way things are done," but he drummed his fingers on the desk, picked up the phone, and dialed for a long distance operator. When they put Chef Radicchio on the line, the director asked his questions and nodded several times as a string of commentaries flowed through the earpiece so vociferously, he pulled the receiver away from his ear. Lincoln heard the waves of thunder from his side of the desk.

When the chef roared, "You send him up to here'a. I give a job to zat vun," the director allowed himself a trace of a smile, broke in, and thanked the man.

"Well, apparently, you did a heck of a job over there. He said you got a promotion about every day, and that you were a hero when the hotel burned. I remember that—something about only one employee standing his ground to fight the fire, and the same one pulled a customer to safety. That was you?"

Lincoln began in the equipment room, checking out basketballs and handballs eight hours a day. At five on his second shift, he went into the weight room and signed in as an employee. He started with feather-light weights and worked both his upper and lower body for over an hour. He was so sore the next morning, he had to roll onto the floor to get out of bed, but he repeated the process again that evening, and the next, and the one after that. The night custodian, a thickset man with a gnarled nose and cauliflower ears, glanced at him occasionally. At the end of the first week, with the room empty, aside from Lincoln, he stopped and took several steps forward. Leaning on his broom, he cautioned with a gravelly voice, "You know, kid, you shouldn't be liftin' every day." Lincoln sat up from the leg press machine to listen. "Yep, need to give them muscles a rest. You do upper body one day, legs the next." He paused and stood a bit straighter, his suddenly fiery eyes scrutinizing Lincoln's. "Son, when I was a contender, before the war…" but the door opened with a bang, and two beefy, tattooed thugs pushed their way boisterously into the room. The janitor's head dropped, and he went back to his aimless sweeping.

The next night, the custodian busied himself dusting walls, watching as Lincoln confined his workout to his upper body. When Lincoln was done, the man approached and handed him a small, tattered hardback, *The Boy's Book of Body Building*. "It's all in there, son."

Lincoln followed the workouts religiously and was soon lifting four times what he'd barely been able to take from the rack two weeks before. By the end of the month, he was running a half mile around the neighborhood each night before bed.

With his first paycheck, he stocked the fridge with Miriam's favorite foods. The scent of crackling bacon woke her the next morning. She wobbled out of her room and broke into tears as she watched Lincoln spoon butter over grits and squeeze oranges for juice. He filled the little porcelain cow with Half and Half and put out Demerara sugar for her coffee.

That night, Lincoln called Isabelle. They met at the Carvel. It was only seconds before their hands came together under the table. They were quiet for a very long time, just looking at each other; though Isabelle finally blinked, and the conversation gushed for hours. Eventually, she blurted, "Lincoln, guess what? I applied for nursing school at Penn State!"

Lincoln groaned, "And I'm handin' out towels at the Y. Not goin' to be saving lives like you, huh?"

She laughed, "You mean more like cleaning bedpans. Trade ya."

In the car, they made out for an hour, and Lincoln realized it was the first time in months he'd been aroused. As he felt himself losing control, he feared he was dragging Isabelle aboard a perilous, speeding train, one he worried neither of them would have the power to jump off. Somehow, though, they both pulled back at the same moment. When the furious cadence of their hearts slackened, they broke into giggles and gave each other a peck on the lips. Isabelle drove a few miles per hour to stretch the time before dropping him off.

Late in his second month at the YMCA, the director's assistant called in sick; Lincoln was tapped to fill in. He answered the phone, ordered a dozen tennis balls, and ran out on his bicycle to pick up lunch for the Y's monthly board meeting. As he walked into the conference room to place sandwiches and Cokes on the oval table, he looked up to see Isabelle's father sitting in a chair behind a folded cardboard sign: President of the Board of Directors. Bob looked up and laughed. "Can't keep a good man down, can they?" He stood and shook Lincoln's hand then turned to the director. "I thought he was handing out towels in the gym."

The director nodded. "Like you said, can't keep a good man down."

That afternoon, Isabelle stopped by the Y. "Hey, my dad wants to talk to you. Can you come over for dinner?"

Lincoln had met Isabelle's mom at graduation. As tall and thin as Isabelle, Kerrith was still beautiful, her blue eyes as clear as her daughter's. She wore her hair in a page boy, which made her appear even taller. Despite her regal bearing, her smile was warm, disarming, and Lincoln's back relaxed after a few minutes as he laughed freely at Bob's puerile jokes. Over veal cutlets and corn on the cob, Dalton put his knife and fork down and asked Lincoln, "You like working at the Y?"

"I like working, sir."

"I know you do. I talked to John over there. He thinks you can do better while you recuperate if you get a job that will teach you something you can use in real life. Get you ready for college, *if* that's what you want." Lincoln didn't answer. "Look, Lincoln, I know you are reliable and can puzzle out problems. I've seen you pick yourself up after what would have been the end for most of us. What I'm saying is, I want you to come work for me. My mechanics are all Airframe and Power Plant licensed. We call them A&Ps. Now, you're not going to become an A&P off the bat, that takes years at a technical school, but we need good people to do the engine teardowns before the licensed guys get to work. You'd learn more about small aircraft engines than you ever wanted to know." The color drained from Lincoln's face. "Good, I'll pick you up tomorrow morning at six, and we'll get you oriented. Don't worry, John over at the Y is on board with the plan. He told me to tell you he wishes you the best luck in the world."

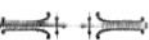

Dalton Aviation was spread over an acre of flatland at the north end of airport. Lincoln was tasked with wrenching exhaust manifolds off the four and six cylinder Lycoming engines that had to be removed, by law, from Cessnas after two thousand hours of service. He immediately snapped the heads of the rusted bolts of the first few engines he was allowed to touch, but a couple of A&Ps drifted over and showed him how gently an engine had to be treated. One of the old-timers laughed, "Son, treat 'em like a lady. No matter how rusty and cranky, gentle's the ticket. Usually get what you want." He winked. "You keep that in mind. It'll serve you well."

He used his first paycheck to buy a three-month pass to the Y's weight room, but when the director found out, he brought the money down to the gym and told Lincoln he was welcome for as long as he wanted. Lincoln increased the intensity of his workouts each week, and by Christmas, he was lifting as much as the regulars.

He also bought a Ford pickup and on the weekends made deliveries for his mom's hardware store. When the pharmacist next door heard about him, Lincoln was hired to deliver prescriptions, but on the condition he use his mother's DeSoto and wear a tie.

Most nights, he met Isabelle at the library. She was taking two pre-nursing courses at Penn State's Wilkes Barre campus. Lincoln sat across from her and read books about aviation, particularly small aircraft engines. In January, he enrolled in a physics course at the campus. Working two jobs and weekends, he was making almost enough to enter Penn State in the fall, especially if he stayed at the local campus for a term or two. He thought he might try to sneak into the R.O.T.C. program and apply for a navy scholarship, but he realized even if he earned one, someone, somewhere, would have to inform his draft board to have him removed from the conscription rolls, and eventually the record of his permanent impairment would surface. He considered moving to another city and registering with that draft board, but they would notify the Wilkes Barre board, and he would be back to square one.

He signed up for another course at the Wilkes Barre campus and, in March, registered for full time attendance. He would major in aeronautical engineering, do his first two years in Wilkes Barre, live at home, save his money, then transfer to the main campus in State College. Isabelle, though, had taken all the classes available at the Wilkes Barre site and would have to go to State College for the next round of pre-nursing courses.

Lincoln's acceptance came in the mail on a Saturday, and with it, a small scholarship. They laughed and cried and made plans to have dinner at the Sterling and then go see *Dr. Zhivago.*

Lincoln was greeted warmly by the maître d' and seated in a cozy nook in a teak-paneled section that had been added after the fire. Before the waiter brought water, a bottle of red wine found its way to their table. When they looked up in surprise, Lincoln made out Rico peering through the windows of the kitchen's swinging doors. The sparkle in the man's eyes stole his breath, and Lincoln lifted his glass and nodded in thanks. Rico opened the door slightly and raised his thumb. Lincoln waved his hand, beckoning, but Rico disappeared, and the window was soon filled with Matilda's dull stare. And then, as Lincoln and Isabelle tipped glasses, his attention was drawn to a surly face that had replaced Matilda's. Lincoln tried not to laugh. "Don't look now, but that guy, Barry, I told you about. He's shooting poison darts."

After several more glasses, their tongues became thick, and their legs rubbed more and more urgently under the table. The bottle of wine was empty far sooner than they had planned, and without having finished dinner, they found themselves in Kirby Park, veiled by a grove of trees. They touched and moved closer, and their breathing quickened as the train once again began its roll from the station. It was not long before they abandoned themselves to its energy. As the madness heightened, Lincoln opened his eyes for an instant, distantly aware only of the muted light through windows that had gone opaque from their heat.

And then there was no light or car or Wilkes Barre or work or future, just Isabelle's tummy stiffening as hard as steel, then softening, and tensing again. Finally, the locking slowed, she groaned, and went limp just as Lincoln exploded.

As his breathing slackened, a sensation of total release enveloped him, and he became aware slowly that he was sobbing. Isabelle, still trembling, clasped him in her arms and shared his tears. They lay braced together for what he was sure was the rest of time, though little by little, the world spun its way back, and they began to shiver in the cold. As Lincoln raised himself weakly, his knees slipped onto the floor. She giggled. He tried to lift himself, but one foot became entangled under the seat, and the harder he wriggled to free it, the tighter it became wedged. She laughed louder, but he soon he reached up, took her hand, and they sat again, motionless, fingers entwined, for another eternity.

When the cold began to hurt, they felt around for their clothes, and Lincoln draped his shirt over her shoulders while Isabelle slipped into her skirt. She found her bra, and Lincoln gaped at it. He desperately wanted to watch how a girl put one on, but she shoved it into her purse, snarling, "I hate that thing." It took a while to find all their clothes in the dark and turn them right side out, a process that was suspended every few seconds as they let their lips touch.

She whispered, "What, now, Lincoln Friday?"

"This, forever. I hope."

She threw her arms around him and squeezed as hard as she could, whispering, "I want to become you. To be inside you for a thousand years."

After a couple of minutes, she pulled back a bit to allow Lincoln to caress her breasts. She let her hand move slowly down to touch him, and they sat that way, in silence, until the crunch of gravel startled them. A shadow moved across the still-fogged windows, a flashlight beam diffused into the car, and there was a sharp rap on the windshield. Isabelle tried to close Lincoln's shirt over herself, but the driver's door was wrenched open. The glare of the flashlight played first on Lincoln's face, snapped to Isabelle's, and then to her breasts. Lincoln was all but blinded, able only to make out a puffy, bright red face. The odor of stale alcohol gushed into the car.

"What the hell are the two of you doing here?" Before they could answer, the voice commanded, "Get the hell out of the car and put your hands in the air." As they crawled out, the flashlight shined back on Isabelle's chest.

Lincoln hissed, "Get that light off of her. Now!"

Lincoln heard the voice grind, "Who the fuck do you think you're talking to?" just as he felt the flashlight swipe across his cheek. He fell to the ground, and the beam was back in his face then in Isabelle's. The man growled, "Shit! Turn around, girl, face away from me." He played the beam down into Lincoln's eyes. "Now, you, turn over and put your face in the dirt." The voice took several steps backward. "Okay, you, girl, on the fuckin' ground facing away from me. Stay like that. Do not look up. If you do, I'll blow the both of you fuckin' away."

Lincoln crept toward Isabelle and draped his body over hers. He stroked her softly. "It's okay, Is. We're okay." He murmured that over and over until they heard a car door slam shut and a vehicle backing up, tires squealing. They stood and held each other for a moment, but when a set of headlights played on them, they pulled apart hastily and finished dressing. They drove home in silence.

They met the next night at the Carvel. It was Rodman, the cop—they were sure—and weighed going to her father, but agreed it wasn't a great option. They went out to her car and sat for a few minutes, but when Lincoln put his hand on her arm, she shivered and pulled away. "It's not a good idea."

With finals approaching, they met in the library occasionally, though spoke very little and left separately. On Saturday night, they talked on the phone, but after five minutes, Isabelle declared, "Hey, gotta go and study. See ya."

Lincoln waited for a few seconds and murmured, "Yeah, okay."

CHAPTER TWENTY-ONE

At the end of the next week, Bob Dalton came onto the factory floor and browsed about, chatting easily with the mechanics, making his way slowly to the teardown unit. "Hey, Lincoln, haven't seen you over at the house. Everything okay? Your mom doing well?"

"Yes, sir," he barely squeaked.

"They tell me you're doing a bang up job down here. May get you off exhaust manifolds and onto heads and valves soon. Would you like that?"

"Yes, sir. Thank you, sir," Lincoln mumbled, though his eyes did not meet Dalton's.

"Well, just let me know if there's anything you need."

"Yes, sir."

After Lincoln's shift, he found a message on his windshield. It was sealed tight with scotch tape, and the paper inside tore as he ripped at the envelope. It said only, "Meet me at 7." Lincoln skipped the gym and arrived an hour early. Minutes later, Isabelle walked through the door listlessly. She wasn't wearing makeup, and Lincoln was struck at how ghostly she appeared in the restaurant's strong lights.

She dropped wordlessly into the seat directly across from him, stared at the wall for a moment, then flipped through the songs on the tabletop juke box. Lincoln asked tentatively, "I got a dime. You want to play something?"

"No." She looked up. "I missed my period." He remained silent. "I never miss my period. Never."

They sat for a long time without speaking or looking at each other. Lincoln's back straightened. "Isabelle, I heard that once, you know, you start, it throws the hormones off. It can change your monthly."

"I don't know about that, but I do know that my boobs are tender."

"Oh, Isabelle, I didn't mean to hurt you. I tried to be gentle. I'm sorry."

"That was three weeks ago, Lincoln. Don't you know what that means?"

"I guess I don't."

"Oh, Jesus, Lincoln." She stared past his shoulder for a minute. "It means I'm pregnant, Lincoln." When he sat wordlessly, she sighed wearily, "What are we going to do?"

After a few moments, he looked into her eyes. "Isabelle, we're not going to get crazy. When you got a problem, you define it, then you figure out a solution. That's what Mr. Wick always said. I wish he was here now." He stopped and thought then let the muscles in his face relax. "I know what I'm going to do. You know the coach that gave me that airplane ride?" She nodded. "I'm going to write to him. He'll figure something out. And right now, we don't tell anybody. None of your friends, no one."

"My father is going to kill me."

"No, he won't. But we just keep this to ourselves for right now. Just let me talk to coach."

"No, Lincoln. Please don't. He may feel he has to get involved to protect you and me, you know, tell our folks so that the adults can take charge and make all the decisions. I don't want that."

A week later, a letter came from Coach Hettmans.

Dear Lincoln,

I received your letter. I am sorry you are going through a tough time, but I do have some ideas. First, everyone needs to be calm. You didn't do anything to harm another person. You and your girlfriend have done nothing wrong. You need to understand that.

Okay, first, always look at the worst case scenario and get it out of the way. Let's say your lady is pregnant, which we don't even know yet, but let's just say. There are options. There are always options, Lincoln. I want you to remember that for the rest of your life.

Look, you could just get married. What's so bad about that? You can still go to college, and she can still become a nurse, like you told me. A million people go through college married with kids. A little harder, yes, I suppose, but going through college alone is not so easy either. I've been watching football players with great scholarships, with what seems like perfect lives, fall apart from loneliness. You get a job, she gets a job, and you make it work.

Then, there's always adoption. That is a beautiful thing for a couple who wants a baby but can't conceive. Happens every day.

Then there's asking your parents to help while you work, save money, and make enough to go to college. Also happens every day.

And I'm not supposed to even mention this, what with me working for Notre Dame, but I need to help you see all the options. There's an abortion. It's legal now. It's something you guys have to discuss—real hard. That means, when all is said and done, you guys will probably go your separate ways, and what will be will be.

What you and Isabelle need to do is get a pad of lined paper. Write one of the options I told you about on the top of a fresh page, draw a line down the center, then list all the positives on the left and the negatives on the right. That way, it's all in front of you. You will be surprised; suddenly, the mountain doesn't seem so tall.

Lincoln, I wish I was closer to Wilkes Barre, but if you want to talk, you call me, collect, any time when the coast is clear.

Do remember one thing. This, too, shall come to pass, and something better will take its place. Sort of like every cloud has a silver lining. The trick is in having faith that there's silver's in there and not rain, and that it's not all that hard to get to it. I promise you it's true.

Your friend,
Harlan

Lincoln met Isabelle at the Carvel that evening. He pulled a spiral notebook from his book bag while Isabelle sat without expression. His head was cast down as he etched an option on the top of each sheet, drew lines, and then began voicing the words as he scrawled them on the paper. He didn't see Isabelle's eyes redden and the tears soon bathe her cheeks.

"I don't want scientific answers," she wept so loud, several kids turned to look. "I want it all to go away. Can you understand that?"

Lincoln took her hand. "Everything's going to be okay. Look at this." He handed her the letter from Coach Hettmans.

She read a few lines and thumped it on the table. Their neighbors turned again. She whispered heatedly, "You told him?

I thought we weren't going to tell anybody. That's what you said. You promised."

"I didn't know what to do. I don't know what to do. If you have a better plan, then tell me."

She jumped from her seat and ran from the restaurant. Lincoln followed, their hot dogs untouched. At her car, she started the engine but didn't pull away. When Lincoln stepped up to her door, she stared straight ahead, leaving the window up, but after a few seconds, she lowered it halfway, though still did not turn to him.

"Isabelle, we need to talk. We can't just do nothing. Okay, I'm going to say it. I love you. And it would be cool to be together forever. And if we have a baby, then that's cool, too."

Her stare remained straight ahead, and Lincoln felt his chest tighten, sensing a helplessness as profound as when Schroeder put Honey Barre down in the barnyard. She finally turned to him. "Lincoln, get in the car before that cop comes and takes you away." He sat on the passenger's side and let his hand creep toward hers, flipping his fingers around, then thrumming them on the seat so noisily, she giggled, reached out, and squeezed his hand. But the tears suddenly gushed, and her sobs became very nearly a howl. He said nothing but held her as tight as he could. She quieted and finally whimpered, "Tighter."

They sat like that until the sun set and then drove to the park, but only to look at the spot. She sighed, "I never wanted it to stop."

"Me neither."

PART II

CHAPTER TWENTY-TWO

United States Army Primary Helicopter Training Center
Fort Wolters
Mineral Wells, Texas

Warrant Officer Candidate School was Lincoln Friday's second military assignment. His initial training had taken him from Wilkes Barre to the deep south, to Fort Benning, Georgia, for twelve weeks of basic military and infantry indoctrination. It was the first time he'd met young men up from the bayous of Louisiana, over from the mountains of Wyoming and Montana, and down from the ghettos in Detroit and Brooklyn. He lived inches away, twenty-four hours a day, from men who had never owned, or even seen, a toothbrush—teens who cleaned themselves rarely, and then only with water from the local fish pond. Many of the boys with whom he was crammed could barely read, and if they were able to write at all, it was but their names.

The other recruits in Georgia recoiled at the vociferous taunts and commands barked by privates and Spec 4s, men a year older, if that, than were they. Lincoln avoided trouble by groaning and mimicking the tortured faces of his comrades, but inside his heart, he laughed that these latest tyrants controlling his life paled when compared to Old Man Schroeder or Chef Radicchio.

He did well in Basic from the start and was quickly appointed a recruit platoon leader. A week later, the recruit company commander broke his ankle when he fell from a climbing rope, and Lincoln was pressed into service, to stand before one hundred men and bark orders. Though the drill instructors showed him even less respect than they did the rank and file, one of the sergeants took him aside and explained it was all just a scheme to test those who showed leadership potential.

On a tactical problem during AIT, Advanced Infantry Training, Lincoln's company was airlifted by helicopter into an assault. As company commander, Lincoln rode where he wished aboard the Huey and pressed his way to a squat behind the pilots. He stared in wonder at the instrument panel and the unfamiliar controls until, in a moment of turbulence, Lincoln's hand flew forward and landed on the byzantine radio console between the pilots. The co-pilot grabbed his arm and shouted through his dark visor, "Don't touch that! You outta your mind, recruit?"

Lincoln's face reddened. "No, sir, just trying to figure out the difference between fixed wing and choppers."

"That's *helicopter*, not chopper, boy, and I'll give your sorry ass a hint. To fly is human; to hover is divine." Lincoln looked up skeptically. "I'm not shittin' you, recruit. They taught a monkey to fly a fixed wing."

In the landing zone, Lincoln pushed his men out of the aircraft and buckled in for the flight back to pick up the last squad. The regular army platoon leader stuck his head in the ship and growled, "What's this, your third time back and forth? You wanna be a rotor head? Go to flight school."

"But sir, I'm company commander. I need to make sure my men get loaded okay."

The lieutenant hooted, "Get your ass in front of your men and do your job. You're a soldier, not a goddamn stewardess."

On the day after Lincoln completed AIT, he stood on line for a flight physical. It was his third time through the process, and once again, the military doctors were so fixated on meaningless physical criteria, this time the obsolete prerequisite for 20/20 vision, they failed to note the scar on his left arm, and more critically, that he could barely flex his wrist. At 6 P.M., a sergeant had them line up for the final station. Lincoln was sure it was the psychological exam, and he whooped aloud that he'd made it. The sergeant eyed him and barked, "You got a mental problem, Private?"

It was the first time anyone had referred to him as 'Private'. Lincoln raised his head a fraction and hollered, "No, Sergeant. I'm just happy."

"You're happy. They're gonna stick your ass in one of those death traps, and you're happy? You do have a mental problem. Come stand here at the head of the line. Let's let the nice lady talk to you first."

The men were ordered onto a set of outdoor bleachers. They were still in their OD skivvies as a nurse moved sideways past each man, stopping for ten seconds to ask how he'd gotten along with his mother. Lincoln responded smoothly, though his eyes, as those of his fellows, could not unlock from her colossal breasts.

An hour later, those who had passed the flight physical were handed orders for flight school and offered a two-week leave; the failures got four weeks' vacation, whether they wanted it or not, and a ticket to the First Infantry Division in Viet Nam. Lincoln was desperate to start flight school, as there were rumors the number of slots for pilots was shrinking, as they did each time Nixon addressed the nation and promised that peace with honor in Viet Nam was just weeks off. Lincoln refused the time off.

Lincoln's C-123 left for Fort Wolters, Texas, at 3 A.M. the next morning. Less than twenty minutes after it touched down in Dallas, he was aboard an olive drab school bus commanded by a grizzly man in a baggy flight suit. Chief Warrant Officer Willard Fonk ordered there be absolute silence for the eighty-mile drive to Fort Wolters. He barked that his passengers were to sit at attention and spend the opportunity perusing the geography, studying the hills and the gorges over which they would be flying for the next five months. It was little different than the speech on the bus the first day he'd arrived for Basic at Fort Benning.

At Wolters, the men were stripped to their drawers, heads shaved bare once again, and ordered into formation outside a moldy quonset hut. Chief Fonk addressed them. "You are now WOCs, Warrant Officer Candidates. In a few minutes, you will be issued gear. One of the items is exceptionally important. Can anyone tell me what it is?"

A man raised his hand. "Your flight helmet, sir!"

"Close, but no cigar. Anyone else?"

"Flight manuals, sir!"

"No. It is your hat. Your utility cap, baseball cap. You will wear it backward, at all times, until you solo. This is a rule written in stone. If you disobey it, that will be grounds for immediate dismissal. And while we're on the subject of getting your ass kicked outta here, you will run everywhere you go, never breaking stride, even into a trot, unless specifically ordered to do so by a real soldier."

Two by two, the flight cadets were jostled inside the quonset. Lincoln was near the end of the line, and he noticed that his arms and legs were reddening in the blistering, Texas sun. He dallied in the smudge of cover offered by the single tree in that acre of Texas wasteland. It cost him a dozen push-ups, and when he reminded the TAC officer that it was a court-martial offense to get sunburned in the Army, he was invited, not inaudibly, to belt out twenty-five more.

Inside, they were handed used flight suits and more olive drab boxers. “Gentlemen, and I use the term loosely, you may ask why we issue you so many sets of drawers. Many of you will need them after your first few flights.” A razor, a bar of brown soap, and an OD towel were added to the pile; at the last station, a corporal placed his fingers around Lincoln’s forehead, scrunched his face in deep thought, then pulled a tatty, globular, olive drab cloth bag from one of three bins. It looked exactly like Lincoln’s bowling ball bag at home, but when it was shoved into his hands, he was surprised at how little it weighed.

The soldier snarled, “Small, cause you’re tall, and that makes your head look big.” Lincoln fingered the orb inside and dropped his stuffed duffel to the wooden floor to yank on the zipper. The private barked, “Do not open that until you are given the order to do so. What is wrong with you, WOC?”

“Nothing, sir.”

“Good. Do not put the bag in your duffel. It is to be carried separately. Is that clear, WOC?”

“Yes, sir.”

The word, ‘sir,’ drew several lesser soldiers to Lincoln’s station. They took turns nipping at him until a man with many stripes ordered Lincoln out of the quonset. “You go wait in that field out there until I decide what to do with you. And the rest of you, get back to your duty stations.”

A few of Lincoln’s new classmates were milling about, puffing on Marlboros and Chesterfields. Lincoln zigzagged through the bulk of the class, men in their skivvies, most flat on their backs, asleep in the dirt. He settled on a tiny patch of shade behind a set of bleachers and looked about cautiously, all the time fingering the round bag. Spying not a single fully uniformed man in his neighborhood, he slid the zipper to the left. A scuffed, once-white, plastic, spherical shell peered out at him. Surreptitiously, he rotated it inside the bag and came to a jumble of frayed wires. Another turn exposed a dark visor etched with scratches as dense and deep as the furrows on the farms of Wilkes Barre. Lincoln wet his index finger with a drop of spit and rubbed at the scuffs, but there was a patina of fine dust on the plastic, and his efforts were rewarded with a swirl of new abrasions.

That scared him, and he started to pull the zipper shut, but at that instant, a sonic boom exploded over his head. He looked up, and while mostly blinded by the sun, he was able to make out the silhouette of a human form scrutinizing him from atop the bleachers. The voice thundered again, "Candidate, were you or were you not ordered to leave that bag unopened?"

"Huh? Oh, yes, sir."

"Yes, what?" Lincoln looked again, but was too distressed to answer. "And don't call me 'sir'. I work for a living. Call me by my first and middle and last name, in that order."

"I don't know your name, sir. I can't see your name tag; sun's in my eyes."

"Oh, for Christ's sake. Are you blind? The Army doesn't award wings to pilots who can't see. It's First—Sergeant—Gilly. Do you understand?"

Before Lincoln could answer, the man about-faced and ran down the bleachers at a sprint, to place himself over the sleeping mob of America's next generation of airmen. He grinned insincerely, "Welcome to Warrant Officer Candidate School. Now, off your asses and on your feet. Stand at attention."

A handful of men rose and began wandering through the red dust trying to place just where on Earth they had been dumped. After a few more screams, the rest came to their feet and meandered aimlessly in circles, one-hundred-and-twenty of the nation's elite, in their drawers, hands full with duffel bags, bowling ball bags, and burned down smokes. The private from the flight helmet station strolled out of the supply room with a World War Two movie camera, which he trained on the aimless activity.

Sergeant Gilly stood without emotion as the anarchy was recorded then spoke calmly. "Please stop in place and turn toward me. When you are in the army, you are expected to carry out orders to the letter. One would imagine you learned that in Basic and AIT. And, please, gentlemen, remember that if you are told *not* to do something, then it's best if you don't do it." He looked toward Lincoln. "What's your name, WOC?"

"Friday, sir."

"What? Oh, oh, I see. You'll tell me on Friday. Is that what you're saying? It's only Tuesday. That's a long wait."

"No, sir. My name *is* Friday."

"Friday? Jesus, I'm glad it's not Sunday. I'd have to stand here for nearly a week to get an answer out of you. Is that the day you were born on? You an Indian?"

"No, sir, my last name is Friday. No, sir, I'm a Lutheran."

"Why, I'm just tickled pink you ain't Southern Baptist like the rest of them here at Wolters. All that singin' and such. Okay. Start following orders. Do you understand?"

"Yes, sir."

"And, don't call me 'sir'. I told you, I work for a living. I am a non-commissioned officer." He glared at Lincoln. "You know what that means, Yesterday?" Lincoln shrugged. "Lesson number one in the Army, gentlemen, is that there are three tiers of officers. I thought most of you would have learned that by now. I understand that you are here to be trained to fly helicopters, and everyone knows that does not take the mental capacity of being an infantryman, or even learning to fly fixed wing, but the U.S. Army wants you to be able to retain basic information. So let me go over it once again.

"The few of you who finish flight school will become warrant officers. You are the fortunate creatures who will live in a no-man's land. That's a good thing in an army. People don't know what to make of you. You ain't fish, and you ain't fowl. That means you will be left alone. That's good. But it also means you will never get high promotions.

"For instance, there's such a thing as Command Sergeant Major of the Army and Commanding General of the Army, but no such thing as Commanding Warrant Officer of the Army, at least I never heard of such an animal. But, on the other hand, you won't be hounded for the next twenty years. Consider it is a blessing.

"Now, look here, the cream of the military in every country on God's green Earth is, and *always* has been, its non-commissioned officer corps. That's the sergeants, like me. We don't get commissions, that's why we're called," he made quote signs with his fingers, "'non-coms.' But we do all the work. See, the commissioned officers, the RLOs, Real Live Officers, the lieutenants, captains, colonels, the generals—you know who I'm talking about—spend their days at the O-Club drinking martinis and showin' off their West Point rings, making snotty comments, and giving orders for the non-coms to carry out and get the job done. Now, you are going to be, the few of you who manage to pass, warrant officers. The government will give you a warrant. That's in between a non-commission and a commission. A warrant officer ain't good enough to be an enlisted man, and he ain't smart enough to be a commissioned officer, so he warran't no officer.

"Now, this all's been going on in the world since the 1300s in England's navy. You will become the Army's technical specialists, your career devoted to just one field. Military intelligence warrant officers are Sneaky Petes for the duration. Aviation warrants fly for their whole career. You'll be the best pilots in the world—those of you who don't wash out. In the Army, commissioned officers, like lieutenants and captains, the RLOs who get their wings, they fly some, but most of their careers are spent as managers and, like I said, making high and mighty orders that I gotta figure out how to obey. Not like the Air Force and the Navy, where pilots are pilots and they fly for their whole career—or damn near—'till they can't see so good anymore.

"Now, non-coms, even the highest sergeants, salute all warrants, even the lowest ones, like some of you might be someday. But you can bet your ass they don't salute WOCs. Nobody does. And don't any of you forget, all warrants salute *all* commissioned officers. That means, even if you are a W-4, top of the pile, fifty years old, the best helicopter pilot in the history of aviation, you *will* salute a snot-nosed, twenty-one-year-old, second lieutenant.

"When you get your warrant, and you're a W-1, non-coms will refer to you as 'Sir,' commissioned officers will call you 'Mister.' When you get promoted to W-2 and three and four, you are a chief warrant officer, and they call you 'Chief,' or they can still call you 'Mister.'"

"Questions?" A few hands started to rise, but the sergeant roared, "Good, I didn't think so. Okay, each one of you take the bowling ball we issued out of your duffel bag and then fall in, including you, Saturday."

There was a bit of aimless movement. Lincoln walked toward the sergeant and spoke softly, "That's Friday, sir, I mean Sergeant, and we were told not to put it in our duffel bag."

Sergeant Gilly's head dropped and rolled left and right in disbelief. When he looked up a second later, his lips spread in a plastic smile. "Men, let us come together into ranks, like coming together lined up real nice and tidy in the pews before the Lord in church. Wednesday, do Escapillians sit in pews all straight and neat on Sunday?"

"Sergeant, I don't know. I'm Lutheran, and we do sit in pews, Sergeant."

The majority of men grasped their bags and came to relative attention, though the formation was amorphous, most of the WOCs positioning themselves to face away from the sun. It looked nothing like the ranks they'd formed twenty and thirty times a day for twelve weeks in Basic Training. The difference was that here, at Fort Wolters, no one had been preassigned to herd them into squads, rows of ten men each, which were then aligned into four neat rows, one behind the other, to form a platoon. Three platoons, back in Basic, were arranged abeam each other, dress right dress, to create a company.

Lincoln surveyed the amoeba for a moment, looked to his flanks, stepped forward, pointed to a gaggle of men, and counted off ten of them. He spoke matter-of-factly. "Gentlemen, the sooner we get this done, the sooner we eat." Some of the cadets chaffed at the man who had appointed himself commander-in-chief, but several other troops ignored the grumbling and emerged from the ranks to count out their own squads of ten WOCs.

Before Sergeant Gilly sucked in a breath to belt out new commands, he took a step back to scrutinize Lincoln and the other organizers, waiting to see how they'd respond as the griping about being manipulated by one of their own crescendoed. In fact, it wasn't thirty seconds before whispered threats about ass kickings floated about, and a few of the nascent organizers ducked back into ranks, tails between their legs. Lincoln and two others, though, remained at attention, simply pointing, then watching intensely until a reasonable formation of three platoons of forty men each coalesced.

Sergeant Gilly re-took command. "Now, all of you use your right hand to lift your flight helmet off the ground, where it should never have been put in the first place." Half the men opened their duffels and dug around to find the helmet bags.

"Why are they in your duffels? You were ordered *not* to place them in there, weren't you? Why were they in there?" He paraded about, glaring at the men who were foraging through their canvas kitbags. "Now, put your duffel on the ground and place the helmet on top with care. These are sacred objects. They are not to touch the ground ever again. Am I clear?"

"Yes, Sergeant."

Gilly strode up to a WOC in the first row, plucked the man's flight helmet bag off the duffel, then marched back to his command position. He unzipped it and reverently slid the helmet free. He held the empty bag in one hand over his head. "WOCs, think of this bag as your scrotum; it is that vital to your life. It was granted to you to protect your testicle. I say testicle, for as far as we are concerned, God gave you only one ball, and this here flight helmet is that ball. It is that vital to your life expectancy. So, those of you who got through the physical without nuts now have one. And you will need at least one ball to learn to fly." There was open laughter.

"Okay, let's be serious. Some of you may have two down there, and this makes three. That's good, 'cause you'll need all three to fly in Viet Nam. Don't be like that WOC from the last class who stuffed shit paper in his drawers and made it look like he had two. If that is the case with any of you, you're to step forward immediately." He stopped and waited. One man peered subtly to his flank. The sergeant caught the motion with his peripheral vision and added quickly, "Never mind. Just remember, you're not going to get to use your balls around here for a very long time, if ever."

He turned to face away from his audience then suddenly spun back around, his face hard. He pointed at the platoons one by one and hissed, "Let's get one thing straight. I don't give a damn about you, but I will give up my life to protect the soldiers you will be carting around in the back of your ships. *They* are the Army. This training is not a joke, gentlemen."

CHAPTER TWENTY-THREE

He walked through the ranks snarling until he came to a man in army khakis with Specialist Fourth Class emblems sewn to his sleeves and several rows of ribbons pinned above the left breast pocket. The sergeant stopped dead. "You men, you listen good. I am standing in front of a soldier. One who's been there. He may only be a Spec Four, just a hair above a private, but he's paid his dues, and now he wants to become a helicopter pilot. *This* is the man who should be here. Better pay attention. You see what he's wearing?" He pointed to a medallion above the ribbons—a silver musket on a light blue background surrounded by a silver wreath. "This is a CIB, a Combat Infantryman's Badge. This is a man who's had to face the enemy with just a rifle in his hands. You better hope you never have to fight on the ground with an M-16 like he did. What's even more important are the two ribbons right below it. There's a Purple Heart. That means this man suffered wounds in defense of his country. But most important is this red, white, and blue decoration. For those of you who don't know, that's a Distinguished Service Cross, the DSC.

That's the second highest honor a soldier can earn defending our nation. And let me tell you, for an enlisted man to get a DSC is almost like getting the Medal of Honor."

The sergeant nodded to the man. "Good to have you here, Specialist." He nodded back almost imperceptibly. "Now, the rest of you lift your duffels with your left hand and your flight helmet bags with your right." He called out, "Left face," and after a band of roving buck sergeants rotated the right-facing ten percent, they were shuffled across a draught-yellowed parade ground toward a line of two-story, Second World War barracks.

Lincoln found himself next to the man with the CIB. Halfway across the field, he gathered his courage and stole a glance at the ribbons. It was the very instant the man turned to look at Lincoln and nod. Lincoln looked to his left side to see just who the returnee had acknowledged, but there was no one there. Lincoln nodded back. The man smiled and whispered loudly, "Huber. How ya doin'?"

"I'm good. Hey, are you an instructor or something?"

"No, man. I'm just like you—nothin', lower than whale shit."

"Yeah, but you got those medals and all."

"Don't mean shit here. Each time you wanna do better, make somethin' of yourself in the Army, they knock your ass down to square one again."

Lincoln felt the back of his neck warm, and he looked behind to see several WOCs scrutinizing him. He turned and whispered to Huber. "I'm Lincoln Friday. Nice to meet you, man."

Sergeant Gilly ordered them to halt in front of a haphazard mound of their personal suitcases. As several of the men accordioned, Huber shook his head in disgust, his face more twisted than the sergeant's. He turned toward Lincoln, and his lips parted as if preparing to condemn the depths to which America's youth had fallen in the two years since he'd enlisted, but a fog of black diesel smoke blew over the company, and a dozen men began coughing theatrically. It was bare seconds before half the company was doubled over, seized with paroxysms of contrived choking. The sergeant sucked in a deep breath to regain control, but the performance ended abruptly as the trainees' attention shifted to an olive drab school bus rolling to a stop at the last billet.

When the bus doors opened, the first figure descended the steps unsteadily. Even the sergeant's jaw dropped, for there was something terribly peculiar about the creature. It was not clear if it was male or female, the jet-black hair was that long. On the other hand, it was wearing fatigues, though they were a dozen shades greener than those of the WOCs. Since the fatigues were skintight, the troops were able to determine in a micro second the lack of even a hint of breasts; they sadly accepted they were gawking at a man. His face was dark, bony, and alien. He stared back at the WOCs until the next apparition tripped down the steps and pushed him out of the way. The second man eyed the American soldiers until he was shoved aside by the subsequent passenger. Nine more of the curious figures descended. Lincoln finally recognized them as foreign soldiers, Chinese perhaps, though he was not sure, for he had never met an Asian. They lined up in a loose formation next to duffel bags nearly as long as they were tall.

Huber's eyes narrowed to slits, and he hissed, "I fuckin' knew it. It had to be my fuckin' class. Fuckin' gooks. Shit. Fuck me."

Lincoln stared at the men as they struggled to tug their belongings into the shabbiest of the row of barracks. He turned to Huber. "Who are they? Do you know?"

"Fuckin' A I know. I heard about this shit before I signed up for flight school. Fuckin' government brings over a dozen Vietnamese teenagers at a time. Teach 'em to fly so they can take over the war. It's a fuckin' joke. They can't change a fuckin' tire by themselves. Barely ride a bicycle, gooks."

Lincoln asked quietly, "Sorry, man. I don't know what that means, 'gooks'."

"It's what you call the little fuckers. Don't know where it comes from. All I know is that every one of 'em's a dick. Steal your drawers off you with your pants on. Bitches all got the clap. Oh, fuck me up my ass."

Several of the WOCs drifted a few feet closer to listen as Huber continued swearing, though as the sergeant approached, he lowered the register to an aggravated mutter. Soon, the volume of his irritation decreased, but the crimson of his complexion deepened.

A wiry, muscular little man with a two-day shadow called from the periphery. "Hey, man, if you hate 'em so much, why'd you re-up for flight school? That's three more years—with two of 'em guaranteed back in the Nam."

"What's your name?"

"Stanky, why?"

"Mind your own beeswax, Eddie Stanky. I got my reasons."

The sergeant turned back toward his recruits. "Okay, each one of you, look at the top paper in the pile we gave you. You will see an A or B or C or D. Now look at the signs on the barracks to your front. You will see an A or B or C or D painted on the wall. Now look at the man to your left. If he has the same letter as you, he is your roommate for flight school. If not, find the *first* man who has your letter. *He* is your roommate for flight school. Now, the two of you go pick your personal suitcases from the pile over there, then proceed to the billet with your letter on it. Each pair of WOCs will walk down the hall and keep going until you find an empty room. You will enter that room, place your equipment and your butt on a rack, then sit at attention, silently, and wait for further orders."

Several of the men dropped to their knees to search for the wad of documents they'd been handed at the quartermaster's.

A few dumped the contents of their duffel bags onto the dusty apron around the barracks and rummaged through mess kits, canteens, two pair of boots, web belts, OD underwear, and OD socks. A jeep screeched to a stop, and four buck sergeants exploded out of it to kick at the flotsam and jetsam and the troops, until all but ten or twelve of the neophytes had been shoved into one of the prehistoric buildings. It took another thirty minutes to redirect the stragglers, all of whom had already lost their paperwork.

In Barracks C, Huber grabbed Lincoln by the sleeve and dragged him up the stairs to a room on the second floor at the end of the hallway. Huber muttered, "Sergeants are lazy bastards. They hardly ever climb stairs. Sure as hell ain't walking to the end of the hall."

He dropped onto the bottom bed and was nearly asleep when his ears perked as the screen door downstairs slammed. He lifted from his rack, looked outside the window furtively, and when he saw the buck sergeants standing together smoking, he went to the door and nodded for Lincoln to follow. They went downstairs to the dayroom, where Huber chattered loudly, and several of the WOCs joined them. He lit a Chesterfield and offered them around, but one of the WOCs spoke softly. "Hey, man, you think it's okay to smoke?"

Huber shook his head. "No, WOC. If you smoke you, will be shot by a fuckin' firing squad at fuckin' dawn." He stared out the window for a moment then turned back. "Listen, these fuckers are going to make your life miserable for the next nine months. It's us against them. Anything you can get away with, you get away with, dig?"

He pointed the pack at Lincoln. "*You'll* take one, won't you, Friday? You ain't scared of those pussies, are you?"

Lincoln shook his head. "Ain't scared, but I promised my mother I wouldn't start. My father died of some kinda cancer.

My mother says it was from smoking during the war. Sorry, man. I promised."

When the buck sergeant swaggered back inside, Huber waited until he was sure the man was watching, then he took a final long drag and slowly crushed his smoke in a butt can. The sergeant glared at him. "I didn't hear no one give the order to light up."

Huber snickered as he let his eyes fall upon the man's fatigues, glaring at the cloth over the left breast pocket, a patch of green devoid of decoration, particularly a CIB. The man glowered then turned away from Huber and huffed orders sending the men to their rooms, where they were to empty the contents of their suitcases and duffels on their cots.

He started at the first room, picked through personal items, and chose the man's aftershave and the tassel from his high school graduation. He flung them out the window onto the dusty apron. In the next room, he took a salami from a kid named Bernstein and heaved it like a football through the screen door at the end of the hall.

Upstairs, at Lincoln's rack, the sergeant dug around until he found a photo of Miriam holding aloft a poster of an Army helicopter. She had the scribed the words, 'My Hero' across the bottom.

"What the hell is this, WOC?"

"Sir, that's my mother, sir."

"She thinks you're some kind of hero? What is she, stupid or something?"

The sergeant tossed the photo into the butt can hanging in the hallway. Huber stepped out of the room to retrieve it. He walked to Lincoln's bunk and placed it on the mattress, propping it up with a pair of socks.

The sergeant stomped up to Huber. "WOC, I don't give a shit where you been or who, or what, you think you are. I been there, too. Right now, right here, you are a piece of shit, and I'm the toilet. Do you got that straight?"

There was muffled laughter, and Huber, at rigid attention, chin sucked in, hollered, "Yes, Sergeant, I do. You are a crapper. And, Sergeant, with all due respect, that combat unit patch on your left arm, what is that?" He tapped his forehead with his index finger. "Oh, yeah, I remember now. That's the 15th-Or-Something Data Processing Brigade or Division. You were the pay guys in Nam, and I thank you for your courage, comin' to basecamp and all with our money."

The sergeant stood motionless, eyes tightening into slits as he sucked in a grand breath, but from outside the barracks, the first sergeant's voice reverberated loud enough for troops back at Fort Benning to hear his, "Fall in." The buck sergeant's face loosened, but he managed to scream, "You heard the man. Move your asses."

CHAPTER TWENTY-FOUR

On a line outside the camp mess hall, the men were ordered to drop for a dozen push-ups, then steered through a screen door onto the chow line. The first WOC placed his tray on the wooden serving ledge in front of the mess privates, a legion of sweaty, angry, grease-encased late teens who stood with ladles raised, ready to dump their soupy, grey-beige amalgam on the trays of the only creatures on Earth whose status was lower than their own. As a few drizzles dripped on the initial man's tray, First Sergeant Gilly patted the WOC on the shoulder and put his arm out to stop him. With his other arm, the sergeant made a path for the first of the twelve Asian soldiers, metal trays in hand, eyes cast down.

"These boys are our guests. And we serve guests first, don't we, men? Rest of you WOCs, outside and do a few more push-ups while our little friends here get their chow."

Lincoln watched as the dozen, pocket-sized men placed their trays, uniformly turned the wrong way, in front of the chow hall food servers, PFCs, most of whom sported Viet Nam combat patches—real ones—on their left shoulders. Several even wore CIBs, Combat Infantryman Badges. The returnees, the lot barely twenty, had been sent to Wolters to mark time and bury their lives in alcohol and drugs until ETS, expected termination of service. On that day, they would be handed a few dollars and sent home to deal with the aftermath on their own. The actual cooks, though, a group of older men standing behind the privates, wore civvies with the words "Southern Airways" embroidered on sweaty, blue work shirts.

With a dozen cockeyed, metal trays under their ladles, the servers snickered as they flipped a slice of black-burned toast purposely over the smallest compartment, cracking up as the next of their number jammed his fingers into the rigid bread, forming a crater. The third server filled it, bomb's away, with a ladleful of congealing pork grease, Crisco, shreds of yesterday's beef stew, yesterday's milk, and nuggets of undissolved white flour, splatters of which flew up to further defile their CIBs.

First Sergeant Gilly smiled thinly at the foreigners. "This is Creamed Beef on Toast, men. We call it SOS, shit on a shingle. It is very tasty, and it is good for you. Put hair on your chest."

With trays dripping gravy, several of the foreign soldiers turned toward the tables, but the sergeant pushed them back onto line for a ladleful of half-cooked, Velveeta omelet, which the cooks unloaded on top of the SOS. The lopsided trays, now mounded with a pound-and-a-half of gluey fare teetering in one small corner, tipped as the men lifted them. The sergeant shook his head disapprovingly as gunge dribbled onto the counter and then the floor. He was, though, silent while directing his guests, with hand signals and placid shoves, to seats at the rear of the mess hall.

The men sat silently, heads bowed, until one whispered and pointed surreptitiously to the bottle of ketchup at the center of the table. Another opened the lid, stuck his nose in the spout, grimaced, and turned the bottle cautiously on its side. Nothing happened. He tilted it at a greater angle—still nothing. He tipped the bottle over his eyes and peered inside. A trickle of watery, acidic, tomato sap rolled out, and the bottle dropped to the table as the man's fists flew to his eyes. The other soldiers shot back in their seats, but the victim soon quieted, and another of the foreigners stuck his index finger in the pool of ketchup that had squirted onto the table. He tasted it and shrugged his shoulders. The rest of the men resumed their head-down stillness. The first man recapped the bottle and pushed it back next to the salt and pepper.

One of the Vietnamese troops at the far end of the table picked at his mound of swill with a spoon handle, separating a shred of gummy scrambled egg from the SOS. He scraped at it until the last trace of cheese had been subtracted then used the front end of the spoon to raise it to his lips. The eyes of his compatriots swung toward him in a single stroke to gawk at the dangling morsel. As his lips parted two millimeters, the tips of several of the onlookers' tongues found their way into the open air like a nest of baby snakes. The man nibbled a corner of the egg, then another fleck, but spit it back on his plate. He wiped his mouth with his sleeve and reached for a container of milk from the hillock Master Sergeant Gilly had dumped in the center of the table. As the carton came to his lips, several of the men called out loudly and pointed to the label. The man's mouth shut with a snap, and he dropped the container.

By now, the American WOCs were seated, butts on the edge of their benches, as if cadets at West Point. Lincoln, though, did not stare forward as ordered. Instead, he watched the foreign men intently until Huber grumbled under his breath, "As usual, Army's got their head up their ass. Gooks don't eat that shit. Rice and rat and that *nuoc mam* shit, rotten fish sauce—Vietnamese ketchup. They put that crap on everything. Look, man, they don't eat our food. Simple as that. Saw it a hundred times when we tried to feed POWs. They'd rather go hungry than eat real food. Mark my words: three weeks, they'll all be dead from lack of food, and yours truly'll probably get blamed."

Stanky grinned while pretending to be looking intently at a point on the wall. "So, now, you're a fuckin' nutritionist, huh, Huber?"

"You been there, asshole? You know a single gook?"

Stanky snarled in a whisper, "Look, man, they get hungry enough, they'll eat the SOS and like it. They're not that different than us. Man's a man. My father taught me that."

"Oh, yeah? Well, I'm here to tell ya..."

Lincoln did not look up but slurred an interruption. "Huber, man, I read they eat beef in Viet Nam. That so?"

"Yeah, I guess, but it ain't cow meat. Fuckin' water buffalo from what I could see, and then it's got to be swimin' in that *nuoc mam* piss I just told you about."

"What?"

"*Nuoc mam,* rotten fish sauce. Putrid shit. Never tasted it, but I saw it in bottles when we tossed gook hootches and smashed the glass. Stank like bad pussy."

"Okay. So do they use salt and pepper?"

"How the hell would I know? Ask him." His head jogged surreptitiously toward Stanky, who had started to laugh, which brought several of the sergeants to Lincoln's table. The non-coms commenced a perfunctory session of threatening and haranguing but were drawn away by bickering at another table. Lincoln waited until they left. He tightened his jaw, lifted his tray, and strode, ramrod straight, to the Vietnamese table. Pretending to ignore the absolute silence that descended over the mess hall, he pushed two of the foreign men apart, placed his tray between theirs, and took a seat at the edge of the bench, at attention, shoulder to shoulder with the men. The diminutive soldiers stiffened, eyes trained on their laps.

Lincoln picked a few slices of chipped beef that had, on the cold trays, already become estranged from the paste of flour and congealing pork fat. He scraped away the residual grease with a butter knife, placed the slivers on a corner of dry toast, and sprinkled the jumble with salt and pepper. He turned to his left. "Friend, you speak English?"

The man whispered, "Speak English, but no good."

Lincoln went on slowly. "Well, I read all about Viet Nam in high school. You know high school?"

"High school. Yes, high school. Every man high school."

"Well, I learned that in Viet Nam people eat meat on French bread for breakfast. Is that true?"

The man turned to his compatriots and whispered a sentence in Vietnamese. The men slid together, their shoulders touching as they launched into an animated, but muted, conversation.

The man turned back to Lincoln. "Yes, Viet Nam eat bread French."

Lincoln pointed to his toast and the scraps of SOS. "It's the same thing. Try it. It's not bad, really. Hey, my name is Lincoln." With silence still blanketing the mess hall, and the cadres mysteriously standing behind First Sergeant Gilly in a corner, he relaxed and extended his hand.

The man nodded and pointed to himself. "I Nhu."

"Is Inhu your first name?"

"Yes, name Nhu."

That brought snickering from the nearby tables, and Lincoln used it as cover to add, "Well, Mr. Nhu, try it. Really. You gotta eat *somethin'*."

Nhu obscured the beef with a thicker patina of salt and pepper then wrenched at the bread with the handle of his spoon and Lincoln's butter knife. The scrap slid around on the tray; Nhu chased it but couldn't seem to load it onto the knife or spoon handle. A profound and even tenser stillness shrouded the building as Lincoln slipped the spoon out of the man's hand and turned it business end forward. Several seconds passed until Nhu opened his mouth and worked the morsel beyond his lips as if it was a cyanide capsule. His eyes closed and his jaw lifted, but all chewing motion ceased abruptly, and he just swallowed. Lincoln watched as the lump passed the stick-like man's glottis. He waited for a word, perhaps a nod, but the man's frozen expression remained undecipherable.

The eyes of both camps shifted back to Lincoln, who cut his own sandwich with the spoon handle and knife and placed a shred onto the tray of the flight cadet to his right. "And, what is your name, my friend?"

"I Dong."

"Well, Idong, why don't you give it a try?"

He wiggled his fork in front of the man's face then stabbed a piece for himself and chewed, letting his eyes smile in pleasure. Dong ground his teeth together two times and tilted his head back to help swallow but gagged violently, hurling the white and brown scrap across the table. The laughter from his countrymen was relatively veiled—it was not from the Americans.

A bellow ordered the WOCs to stand, place trays in a neat pile by the door, and fall into formation outside. Lincoln shoved what was left on his tray into his mouth and raised his palm toward his mouth, motioning with several swipes toward the foreigners, urging them to gobble their grub before it was too late, but the soldiers averted their eyes from the slop as they let it slide off the trays into garbage barrels.

The WOCs were given a few minutes before the next formation. In Building C, men from both floors gathered in the common room to talk and smoke. One asked Huber, "What the hell was that all about? Who are those foreign guys?"

"Gooks. That's who. The Department of the Army, in its infinite fuckin' wisdom, has devised a plan. They call it Vietnamization or something like that. Tryin' to teach em' to do the war by themselves. I know what I'm talkin' about. It ain't gonna work—period.

Lincoln interrupted. "Why not?"

"Because they don't give a shit about their country or about anything but their own asses. We're payin' the bills, and we're the ones dyin'. Why should they care? They don't have to. They just run away from every fuckin' battle. I seen it a hundred times. Fuckers'll leave an American advisor to die or worse—get nabbed by the VC who's gonna catch his ass, cut his off his balls, and shove 'em down his throat. I fuckin' hate 'em." He stopped short, and his face drained of color. His pupils dilated. Lincoln was struck by the faraway stare that crept across Huber's face, and he turned to look out the window to see what his new friend was scrutinizing in the Texas dusk. It was the same leaden gaze he'd seen in Mr. Wick and Isabelle's father.

Lincoln lost his train of thought, and he found himself imagining Isabelle, a thousand miles away in Wilkes Barre. The air became tense as the others saw that both Huber and Lincoln had left for other worlds. A couple of the men stood to leave but stopped short when Huber suddenly exhaled loudly. "I don't want to talk about it anymore." He turned to Lincoln. "And what the hell was that shit, you eatin' with the gooks?"

"They're our guests, guests in our country."

"Yeah, fuckin' guests. I'm here to tell ya, everything they touch turns to shit. You watch yourself. That shit rubs off. Seen it a hundred times—GIs goin' native, real saints, kissin' their asses right up until the time they trust a gook to cover their back." His eyes returned to the dayroom, and his lips tightened. "Like I said, I don't wanna talk about it."

Lincoln climbed the stairs to his room and unpacked. He followed the directives on the water-stained paper taped to a corner of the mirror that stipulated where each sock, each pair of underwear, and even a man's razor and tube of toothpaste, were to be positioned in the eight-by-eight room. He was halfway through the process when he came to the mandate for storage and care of the flight helmet. He lifted the bag and examined it under the glare of the single bulb that lit the room and began to unzip it, but he remembered the announcement at dinner that there would be an inspection of rooms at ten that night, and he was running out of time. He placed the unopened bag on the designated shelf, careful to align it precisely at the intersection of a line eight inches to the left of the socks and six-point-five inches above the right border of his dozen pair of folded, olive drab boxers.

He went to work on his olive drab tee shirts but stopped to stare again at the helmet. He lifted it reverently from the shelf and placed it on his rack then shuffled to the hallway, looked left and right, and closed the door softly. He sat on the stained mattress, his back turned to the door, and slid the zipper open. He pulled free the scuffed, white flight helmet, but there was movement in the hallway, and he jammed it back in the bag. When the footsteps faded, he tugged it free again and unwound the knotted spaghetti of wires. He followed them down two feet from the helmet to a pair of jacks, one fat, one thin. The wire from the smaller plug went to a little green microphone. He examined the grating that was meant to touch the lips. It was caked in a whitish nap, dried spit, he finally realized, the remnant of a dozen previous generations of fight cadets. The thick jack joined a worn cable which coursed up to a pair of earphones deep inside the helmet. The thin leather on the earphones was sweat-stained and nearly worn through.

He went to the shaving mirror, put his fingers in the helmet's earholes, and struggled to wrench it over his head. Though tight and uncomfortable, Lincoln was powerless to draw his jaw back from its jut or relax the pursing of his lips. He dropped the dark visor, and then slipped the second dark visor into place. He whispered, "Double dark," and wondered if they would let the WOCs use the visors the next morning, in less than twelve hours, when it was rumored each neophyte was sent on his virgin flight. After a fleeting reconnaissance of the hallway, he went back to the mirror, adjusted the chin strap, seated the helmet deeper, and smiled as it seemed to mold to his head in the warmth. With the stiffness tolerable, he lost himself in his reflection. "In twelve hours, I will be a pilot. This time, it's for real. *No* one is going to take it away." It was a very soft whisper but loud enough to mute the sound of the opening door.

Huber shot in. "What the hell you talking 'bout chump? Get that thing off your head. They'll kick your ass into the next time zone if they catch you. Not supposed to touch it for four weeks. Don't you know that?"

"No, man, I heard we get a flight in the morning. To whet the appetite."

"Well, you heard wrong. You don't get a flight for four weeks, not until pre-flight's done. Only the gooks start tomorrow. Far as I'm concerned, that's good. Maybe they finish sooner, and I don't got to look at 'em anymore. And you look stupid in that thing. Way too tight. They give you the wrong size, always extra small. They want your head to hurt so that you grab the stick too tight, and you make the chopper bounce, and that gives them the excuse to rap you on the knuckles with a screwdriver."

Lincoln tugged the helmet off, went to his rack, and began to pack the device in its bag but stopped and stared at Huber. "Man, what is it you got against these people? They seemed like nice guys. They're scared shitless, same as you and me."

"Speak for yourself. I been there. I ain't scareda shit."

"Well, my man, I gotta tell ya, I am. But I'm not takin' it out on those guys. I figure they must have something to teach me."

"Gooks, they ain't got nothin' to teach you. No different than the Negroes. Don't listen to no one in the Army unless they're white and Christian. I told ya, I been to basic, been to the Nam. Been dealin' with them Africans and Gooks for the past three years. You stick with your own kind, troop. They hate us, and we hate them. Simple. It's been that way forever, and it ain't never gonna change. I'm tellin' ya."

"I don't know, man. Had a history teacher in high school who was a Negro. Only one I ever met before Basic. He was stiff and all that, hard to understand him sometimes, but he was a great guy when you got to know him. Used to teach us about jazz after school, if we were interested."

"See, what I tell ya, jazz. Jungle bunny music."

"No, man, he was okay. Most people were afraid of him. Wouldn't give him a chance, called him a nigger behind his back, but he treated us good, the ones who acted like normal people. Every day, I learned something from him. One of the best teachers I ever had." Lincoln paused and then turned to look his new roommate in the eye. "What did those people do to you?"

Huber tossed his duffel bag on the bottom rack and lay back on it, staring at the striped underneath of the moldy mattress above him. "Nothin'. They just ain't like us."

Long before dawn, the class of Warrant Officer Candidates was screamed awake as vociferously as on the first morning of Basic Training. A stack of rubber-banded mail from home was tossed onto the floor of the dayroom, but the WOCs were not allowed to touch it. They were commanded, instead, to shave and fall in outside the barracks, in uniform, with the flight helmet bag secured under the right arm, zipper on top, tab facing forward and perfectly flat against the teeth. They were given four minutes.

Moving toward the door of the barracks, Lincoln kicked the stack of mail under a couch. When the last soul had left, he pulled it away from the wall, knelt, and fanned through the pile hurriedly and found two addressed to him. He stuffed them into his drawers, ran outside, and buried himself in a gaggle of troops at the periphery of the formation. An instant later, a squad of sergeants appeared out of the darkness. They flew through ranks like a hot wind, snatching bags from under left arms, closing zippers, and shooing the men who had forgotten flight helmets, or hats, or were wearing unmatching boots, back to their rooms.

Lincoln knew fifteen minutes would pass before the buck sergeants determined all troops were accounted for. With the sun still an hour below the horizon, he snuck the letters from his drawers. The first one had followed him from Fort Benning. It was weeks old. Miriam wrote that she had run into Isabelle, who had taken a job at the A&P bagging groceries. She and a high school friend were living together, sharing an apartment. They were both saving up for nursing school. Miriam gushed that Isabelle was even more beautiful than she'd remembered, and everybody in town prayed, when the war was over, and Lincoln came back to Wilkes Barre, they would start over again because they were the perfect couple.

The next letter from Miriam was only six days old. She wrote that there was a rumor Isabelle and a friend had moved to Florida. She didn't know where or why, but it all seemed very sudden and secretive. She asked if Lincoln knew what was going on. There was, though, no hint that Miriam had any idea Isabelle was pregnant.

Lincoln was paralyzed by the news from home. He thought back to their secret meetings in Wilkes Barre and the night she'd announced her second missed period. They sat at the Carvel and decided they would wed secretly in Philadelphia before a Justice of the Peace. Lincoln would enlist in the Army so that she would be eligible for medical benefits as a dependent. He also swore he would send his pay home, every penny of it, to help with her expenses. His chest hurt remembering that after his promises, she became tetchy and changed the subject each time he tried to make plans.

Lincoln wondered if her parents would help financially once they knew, for a private's pay was beneath meager, and he almost brought it up, but sensed that if he even broached the subject, she would make clear, in no uncertain terms, that she was not going to beg for help to solve a problem she'd created. And, he feared, it might sound as though he was testing the waters for himself. He said nothing, and they parted with just a peck on the cheek.

As the day of his enlistment neared, they met for pizza and decided, definitely, to marry. She would tell her parents, but only about the marriage, and only after he was gone. After Basic Training, before she began to show, she would move down to Georgia to be close to him and get a job until AIT was over. They would travel together to his next duty station for the birth.

The following night, though, they spoke nervously for hours about how they were too young to start a family, or even marry. In this iteration of their despondency, Isabelle would travel to Georgia shortly after Lincoln left for basic training. She would tell her parents she was going there to be near him, and that she had arranged a job as a nursing assistant. But, in fact, she would stay at the Catholic Home for Unwed Mothers in Columbus, just outside Fort Benning. They would put the baby up for adoption through Catholic Family Services.

There would be no nursing school for the moment, but Lincoln swore it would happen. He would die to make sure her dreams came true. They held each other that night and cried that it was better they not try to raise a baby as teenagers. She giggled that with her obvious fertility, there would be many future babies to carry the Friday name forward.

Two nights later, they sat over pizza and reworked the plan. They would be married the next Sunday in Philadelphia, for she simply could not accept the thought of giving her baby away. She promised to make some calls to arrange for the Justice of the Peace. They kissed gently and held hands under the table. Lincoln was sure he would spend the rest of his life with Isabelle. His heart had never before felt that joy.

On the Thursday night before their trip to Philadelphia, she phoned him at home. "Lincoln, please don't be mad at me, but I made a decision today. I need to take care of this problem on my own. I should never have let this happen, but I did, and I'm not sorry, and it's my call."

"I don't understand. Does that mean we're not getting married?"

"Yes, Lincoln, that's what it means. We just can't right now." She whispered, "I'm sorry," and ended the call.

The next night, he drove to Isabelle's house. He knocked on the door, and Mrs. Dalton opened it slowly. "Oh, Lincoln, hello. Hey, I'm sorry, but Isabelle isn't home." She stopped and waited.

"Oh, okay. I'm sorry to bother you."

"Oh, it's no bother," she answered without emotion then stood impassively until the tension became excruciating. "Well, it was so nice to see you, Lincoln." She pushed the door a quarter of an inch.

He understood and left with his head slumped. As he reached his car, he looked up and saw a light on in Isabelle's room. He was not sure if there was a silhouette behind the curtains.

When he called the next night, Isabelle answered but spoke with a sigh. "I just think we should wait. We're too young. Don't you think?" Lincoln was silent, and she added quickly. "I'll think about you a lot, but right now, it's better if we let things cool off." She suddenly gasped and blurted, "Lincoln, please, I don't want you to call me. I need some time to think things over. Please, please promise me you'll let me have some time."

He sighed and whispered, "Okay."

Her voice choked as she rasped, "Good-bye, Lincoln."

CHAPTER TWENTY-FIVE

A booming command pulled him from his trance. They were to face left. PT began that morning with a slow jog. Lincoln laughed. An order came to pick up the pace, and finally a howl, directly into his right ear, commanded them to run. A half mile down the road, one of the cadets tripped, and the company was called to a halt. As the sergeants walked threatening circles around the downed man, the other men loitered and several lit up, for clearly the morning run was over, what with a seriously wounded man. An OD school bus approached at a crawl. The men split apart to let it come to rest between them and load their wounded compatriot.

It appeared empty, and Stanky cackled, "Good, I was tired of this running shit anyway. Had enough in Basic. Don't need anymore."

But it passed without stopping, and as it did, Lincoln, the tallest of the cadets, was able to see in the windows. He made out twelve black-haired heads grouped in a rear corner. He mumbled in passing, “It’s the gooks. I think they got on flight suits. Looks like they’re going to the airfield.”

A sandy-haired man with Nordic features walked up to Lincoln. “Hey, man, don’t call ’em gooks. That’s like sayin’ wop or nigger. It’s just wrong, man. And anyway, they’re good guys.”

Huber interjected, “Uh huh.”

“No, really, they are.”

Huber snapped, “And you know because…?”

“Because I spoke to ’em last night.”

“Uh huh. You talk gook, right.”

“I told ya, man, we don’t need to be carryin’ on that way. I speak Vietnamese, yes.”

“You a returnee? Don’t see no patch on your arm.”

“I graduated from the DLI.” He turned directly to Huber. “That’s the Defense Language Institute.”

“I know what the fuck the DLI is. Then why are you in flight school?”

“I suppose I’ll be assigned to a unit training Vietnamese pilots *in* Viet Nam. But it’s the Army, so they’ll probably make me a battlefield photographer or somethin’.”

Lincoln took a step closer to the man to read his nametag. “Hey, Lockett, you can actually talk to them?”

“Some. Unbelievably difficult language. Got seven tones. Get the wrong one on a word, and you’re asking to get laid instead of passin’ the salt.”

Stanky laughed and hit Lincoln in the arm. “That’s a great language, huh?”

Lincoln asked, “You already talked to them? Really?”

“Yeah, last night. Unbelievable story, from what I could understand. They were…” but the man stopped short when a command was thundered from the head of the column. In seconds, they were back double-timing. The troop who had tripped was lagging, but there were several sergeants nipping at him, keeping his pace near that of the able-bodied.

After a couple of final loops around the barracks area, they were on line at the mess hall. Lincoln sat with Lockett and Stanky. Huber placed himself in a corner at an empty table, his gaze locked through the screen door. Stanky nodded toward him and jested, "What the hell's Audie Murphy's problem over there?"

Lincoln mumbled, "I guess the guy's still comin' down. I think that place really screwed him up."

Stanky nodded. "Probably, but what I don't get is why he would ever want to set foot back there. Once is enough for anyone."

"Not for pilots, man. You go back over and over, from what I heard." He exhaled sadly. "That's what everyone in this mess hall has to look forward to."

Stanky shook his head. "Don't think so. It'll be over soon. Already longest war in American history. I heard we're finally going to use tactical nukes. It'll last two days after that."

They were quiet for a moment until Lincoln turned to Lockett. "Hey, man, what'd they tell you, those guys from Viet Nam? You were sayin'…"

"Yeah, it was unbelievable. They were walkin' the streets of Saigon before they wound up here. I mean, they knew they had to go into the military, but each one of 'em's son of a politician or a general, so they were sure to get cushy jobs, and they were just waitin' around, sittin' in cafes drinkin' tea.

"Then one day there's fighting in Saigon. Real heavy, and a Vietnamese colonel comes to their house in a truck, shows the weeping mother a letter, tells the kid he's got ten minutes to pack, and off they go to some building. They process 'em, give 'em gear, and tell them they're going to America to become helicopter pilots. I guess they like to wear their fatigues skintight in Viet Nam, so they get issued a few pair, and there are these ladies hanging around the reception center, and they get their tailoring done on the spot.

"Next night, they put 'em in the back of a deuce-and-a-half and take 'em off to Bien Hoa. That's some military airbase right outside Saigon. Next thing they know, they're on a C-141, no windows, American food. I think they said hot dogs."

Lincoln laughed. "Imagine that was a big hit."

Lockett went on. "Actually, they said the buns were okay. Tasted like cake to them. Anyway, they landed after eight hours, for fuel I guess. On the ground for an hour, but they weren't allowed off the plane, or even to go into the cockpit and look out the windows. Next landing's at night also. They think it was California, and they're herded to another plane, a C-123, no windows, and they fly for some more hours, and around dawn, they land in Dallas/Fort Worth. Army puts 'em on a bus, and the next thing they see is us starin' at 'em yesterday.

"Not one of 'em's ever been on a plane before. What's funny is that they've flown more hours in their life than me, but they never saw what the ground looks like from a mile up. And they said the worst thing was the air conditioning. They had on like their Vietnamese clothes, and no one gave 'em blankets."

Lincoln asked, "Did they say what they thought when they saw America for the first time?"

"Yeah, they did. They couldn't believe the size of the streets and how big the cars were. One of 'em said the girls were so big, he didn't know what would happen if you get in bed with an American. Then he said he wanted to try anyway."

Stanky laughed. "Just tell 'em to tie a board across their skinny ass. Keep 'em from fallin' in."

Lincoln smiled. "At least they wanna try. Glad to hear it. Bet they'll get a chance in Mineral Wells. That's what I heard."

The Vietnamese men were not in the mess hall for breakfast. The sergeants were even more abrupt than the evening before. "Suck up your Cap'n Crunch and get your butts into formation."

With helmets tucked under left arms, they were double-timed to a brick school building, sent to classrooms, and ordered into seats. At the front of each room stood a scowling, crewcut civilian. He welcomed them humorously to the first lesson of ground school and, with chalk flying, outlined the forces that held a wing in the air.

Halfway through the lecture, those still awake saw a bus pull up to the building. The Vietnamese students trickled out, eyes wide with apprehension, several with faces a hue of blue that overpowered their dark complexions. Two of the men, with gritty, damp stains on their fatigue blouses, walked apart from the main cluster, but all were pushed together once inside the building and directed toward a classroom at the opposite end of the hall from the American cadets.

A Caucasian civilian instructor took a place in front of the Vietnamese students. He pointed to the seats. "*Jiao cac em*!" The men looked at each other, whispered for a moment, then faced forward.

The man repeated himself, and again there were puzzled expressions until Mr. Nhu mouthed in Vietnamese, "I think he said good morning!"

The men smiled and answered in English, "Good mawling."

The instructor slugged out another phrase in Vietnamese. Again, the men whispered amongst themselves then stared at Nhu. The instructor blushed and began the lesson.

The rumor was that his wife was Vietnamese, and she had trained him to speak her language. There was, however, in theory, no necessity for a Vietnamese-speaking instructor, as each of the foreign students had been thoroughly vetted and pronounced linguistically proficient to study in the United States.

But that was the same story the school had been fed about the first class of Vietnamese flight cadets many months before. They, however, had turned out to be in such need of linguistic mollycoddling, the Army had had to bus a Vietnamese woman, Hoi Chun Nguyen, a language instructor at the Defense Language Institute's Southwest Branch near Fort Bliss, Texas, to Fort Wolters. Hoi Chun admitted she had little knowledge of aviation and asked her students to educate her about the H-23 helicopters they were learning to fly. She was particularly curious about the combat tactics being drilled into them.

The daughter of a Vietnamese senator, it was assumed she was a rabid anti-communist and no particular attention was paid when she strolled around the flight line after class each afternoon and flirted with the mechanics and instructor pilots. This went on for several weeks, until she ducked into a hangar and began writing notes. Sensing she was being watched, she slipped the pad into her bra and dashed from the building.

A Spec 4, just back from Viet Nam, who had observed the woman skulking about, gave chase and tried to block her exit from the flight line, but, at the same time, was terrified of actually touching her. He ran backwards hooting, arms flapping like a sexually aroused condor, though kept at least a foot in front of her. The dance went on across the flight line parking lot just as the post commander's sedan drove by. The general saw the Spec 4 jigging about, pestering a foreign guest, and a beautiful, young one at that. He ordered his driver to stop. When the GI saw the post commander approaching at a run, he came to attention, saluted, and spoke in a soldierly tone. "Sir, I'm glad you're here, sir."

Hoi Chun, however, shrieked, "Dis pig, he lape me." She flew past the general, nearly knocking him to the pavement.

The general barked, "Driver, unholster your side arm and hold this man at gunpoint until I can get the MPs."

The Spec 4 told his side of the story without being asked. The general rolled his eyes. “You expect me to believe that, soldier?”

“Shit, yes, sir. And you need to capture her ass, quick like.”

The general nodded cantankerously for his driver to take the sedan and pick her up. As the CO’s car turned the next corner, the woman reached into her blouse, tossed the notebook into a hedge, and exploded into a mad dash for the PX. She flew past the ID checker, a huge private who looked to be asleep on his feet. When the general’s driver burst into the building, he saw the woman duck into the ladies’ room, and though the checker made a half-gesture to grab him, the driver darted in after her. There were hysterical screams from both within and outside the powder room.

When the Military Police arrived, they surrounded the room and took up tactical positions. The MP lieutenant paraded about, checking each man to insure pistols were aimed properly, M-16s were charged and on full automatic, and that the M-79 grenade launcher was loaded with a high explosive round.

There were shouts for the man to give himself up. The general’s driver opened the door a crack and tossed his wallet and ID out for evaluation. He screamed his story through the door. The MP lieutenant summoned his boss, a major, who immediately flew into a fit of pique when he discovered the M-79 grenade launcher was charged with a high explosive round instead of tear gas. Squatted and hunched forward as he blustered about the tactical perimeter, the MP commander appeared more olive drab Dungeness crab than police chief. When he was satisfied the weapons were suitably deployed, he assumed a position of authority on the sheets, pillowcases, and bedspreads aisle of the PX. Just a moment later, though, he was persuaded from his lair by a phone call at the front desk. It was the flight line with a message from the post commander that he was still waiting for an MP. The major left the lieutenant in command and raced back to the airfield to find the general pacing and the Spec 4 braced at attention on the white line in the middle of the road.

The notebook was recovered, though the only fingerprints traced through the FBI belonged to the MP who'd dug through the bushes to find it. Inside were maps of Fort Wolters' sensitive areas and page after page of Vietnamese script. The woman denied the book was hers, and no incontrovertible proof was ever found that she was the author.

The Vietnamese embassy in San Francisco was alerted. They telexed Saigon, and the woman's father threatened he and his senatorial colleagues would withdraw their support for the American war effort if Hoi Chun wasn't released straightaway. He also demanded that the original soldier, the one she had accused of rape, be prosecuted for what he termed in an angry letter to President Nixon, "...a heinous, racially motivated crimes of war." The Vietnamese senator warned he'd have lawyers in the United States sue the commanding general if his demands were not met.

In the end, the private was given an Article 15, but he was not reduced in rank, his pay was not forfeited, and he served no time on barracks arrest. When he asked if the mark would remain on his military record, his commanding officer shrugged.

The Pentagon was again without an instructor for the foreign students. The Vietnamese cadets were dispatched to barracks to wait, basically on their racks, until a solution was reached.

Three weeks later, a seasoned Viet Nam Airlines pilot, one trained in France, was flown to Texas. His English was, though, weaker than that of the cadets'. More confounding, he had become, overnight, filthy rich. His U.S.-paid salary and per diem came to, for a week's interpreting, the equivalent of a year's professional wages in Viet Nam. Granted a month's pay in advance the day he arrived, that very evening he was dragged into Mineral Wells by a throng of test pilots recently back from the war.

The aviators introduced him to the ladies of the night, local gals of black, white, yellow, and red persuasion. He vowed to spread his largess evenly before he was sent back to his star-crossed patch of earth ten thousand miles to the west. They also took him to gambling parlors, where he dropped much of his month's pay. The next night, he called a cab and returned to Mineral Wells, but by 3 A.M. he was staggering alone in a drunken miasma, searching for a lift to Wolters. A pickup stopped, and he crawled into the back. The truck pulled onto the prairie two miles from the gates of Wolters. The driver and his passenger beat him nearly to death then stole the rest of his pay and his watch. He spent a week in the post hospital.

The Vietnamese government filed another grievance with the U.S. Department of State. This time, they included the Department of Defense and the FAA, warning that if the American authorities could not provide security for visiting Vietnamese nationals, they would end the training program forthwith and sue the commanding general.

The man was flown back to Viet Nam, and a compromise was struck. New cadets would master a list of fifty essential aeronautical terms before being sent to Wolters, thus obviating the need for interpretive services. This time, the boys sent over would be scrutinized at the highest levels in Viet Nam, and funds were made available by the U.S. government to see the selection project through.

Pleased with having dodged the bullet, the post commander at Wolters thought it would be a nice touch to have at least one instructor available to the cadets who could say "hello" in that impenetrable tongue. Southern Airways found Giles Murdoch, a cook at the officers' club, who was married to a Vietnamese woman. Surely, if he had learned to live with so exotic a soul, he could be trained in the basic tenets of aviation, at least sufficiently to teach ground school.

The present class was reportedly far different than that initial, unfortunate troupe. This time, an analysis of each of the boys' communication skills had been executed by their respective, highly-placed fathers, who assured a panel of South Vietnamese generals their sons were prepared for the linguistic demands of flight training There was also a warning issued by these high ranking Vietnamese politicians that if there was any debate regarding the testing methodology the students had undergone over kitchen tables, the generals posing the impertinent questions would be relieved of command. That would mean the end of the monthly fistfuls of American hundred dollar bills, largess which arrived in nondescript wooden crates at the docks in Saigon, shipped across the Pacific to nourish the seeds of democracy in South East Asia.

CHAPTER TWENTY-SIX

Lockett was called out of class the first morning and ordered to the foreigners' classroom. He was asked to explain to the men that no Vietnamese language training manuals existed illuminating the mechanics of helicopter flight. Lockett, though, could not yet pronounce the word for helicopter and had to run to the barracks to find his English-Vietnamese dictionary. As he was sprinting back to school, he was stopped several times by cadres demanding to know what he was doing alone on post during work hours. By then, class was over and the Asian students had been bussed back to the airfield for the second of their introductory flights. The two men with stained fatigue shirts had changed into clean uniforms, but by the end of the day, they were soiled again.

Lockett was to meet with the Vietnamese that afternoon and go over the ground rules of life at Wolters. When he complained that he was missing ground school, the major told him he could make up the time at night.

For dinner that evening, the Vietnamese students were bussed into Mineral Wells to a Chinese takeout restaurant. The owner, an old man from Nanking, glared at them, for he was suspicious that, since they looked Asian, but could not speak a word of Chinese, they must be Japanese spies in Vietnamese uniforms. He refused to serve them. He screeched in Chinese that it was their fathers who had raped his people in the Thirties. He grabbed a colossal cleaver and lifted it over his head.

The students were escorted into the hamburger joint next door but were again refused service when the waiter deemed them black. By breakfast, a few of them were so hungry, they sucked down wedges of runny egg; a couple tried a few slivers of Frosted Flakes. The rest sat with arms folded as if on a hunger strike.

Lockett was dispatched to their table with orders to raise their English ability; orient the men to American food and customs; lecture in Vietnamese on the notion of calories, minerals, and vitamins; and have them start eating. All of this would be accomplished by sunset. He requested permission for Lincoln to join him, and together they sat listening to the men. The problem was not, Lincoln soon recognized, language ability. As the Vietnamese men warmed to the two Americans, their tongues loosened and their English, though heavily accented and without the slightest attention to grammar, was completely comprehensible.

As Lincoln and Lockett leaned back, Mr. Nhu looked over his shoulder surreptitiously and began to speak in a whisper. "You hear dis one? Viet Nam man, he go bank New York. He want change Viet Nam dong money for dollah, same same he do yesterday. He put ten thousands dong on table.

"Bank lady say, 'That five dollah I give you.'

"Asian man say, 'Yesterday ten dollah. Why not same same?'

"Bank lady say, 'Fluctuations.'

"Asia man, he say, 'Fluc you white guy, too.'"

Nhu nearly toppled to the floor with laughter. His friends fell about themselves. The two Americans eyed each other quickly and hooted loudly, but an instant later, the laughter terminated and the room became deathly hushed. Lockett broke the silence, his voice cracking in Vietnamese, "Gentlemen, our commanding officer wants you to be very happy here."

The men's heads canted in mystification. Nhu spoke for the group. "Maybe good America soldier talk English."

Lockett smiled, and his face relaxed. He repeated his sentence in English. The men nodded comfortably. He asked, "Is there anything we can do to help you?"

The men gathered into a tight huddle around the long couch. When they broke, Nhu spoke for them. "You see, Mr. Rocket, we not pilot. Not do good to fly. Some man seasick already."

"Well," Lockett answered, hiding a smile, "you have come here to learn to fly. Just like us Americans. We don't know how to fly, either. But do you remember how hard it was to learn to drive? It was the same problem for every American. And we all learned, didn't we?"

"Ah, you can drives car!?"

"Of course. Most of these guys are from farms. We start driving tractors when we're kids. I know you are from the city and didn't start driving until you were grown up. They're a few of us here like that, but it doesn't matter. We're all in the same boat."

Nhu's face tightened. "We not drive boat. No man here ever drive car. Only one man here ever in car. Bus, okay, car no. Most man here only bicycle. One or two scooter. Viet Nam not same same America."

Lockett turned to Lincoln. "You know, I read about this at the DLI. When the French conquered Viet Nam in the 1860s, it was just the beginning of the industrial revolution. The French wouldn't let the Vietnamese use tools. They were afraid that if the locals learned to handle even a shovel, the next thing would be muskets, and then Gatling guns, and the Europeans would lose control of the colony. You know, the Vietnamese didn't roll over at first, but they didn't have the technology to beat the French, well, not for a lotta years. The French weren't stupid. There's a ton of natural resources hidden there, but they needed cheap labor, so they limited how much land could be farmed. That freed up a work force to mine coal in the north."

Lincoln interrupted. "If they couldn't farm, how'd they eat?"

"Good question. My instructor said the French figured out just how much food was needed to keep them hungry and weak, but alive and havin' kids. That took whatever number of peasants, and all the rest got sent to the coal mines and rubber plantations.

"Had to dig out the coal with rocks and their bare hands. Down south, it's more tropical, and the French put in rubber plantations, like Michelin. French made them use sharpened rocks to tap the latex. They never worked on anything more complex than rusted, one-speed bicycles. I think it's still going on."

He winked at Lincoln. "Watch this." He turned to Mr. Nhu. "Hey, did you guys ever work on engines when you were kids?"

Nhu translated the question into Vietnamese, and all the men shook their heads. He spoke to the Americans. "Viet Nam man in room here never see engine car. First time see airplane on ground three day ago. It night, so no even see."

One of the other men laughed and said he had seen the remnants of an American helicopter that had been shot down and crashed near his house in Saigon during the Tet Offensive. The other men laughed nervously, and Lincoln's face tightened. Lockett shook his head furtively. "Calm down, man. I read that in Asia people laugh when they're embarrassed or scared."

Another man took a deep breath and spoke in English. "Father say me go America. School fly, maybe college, but no in Viet Nam for long time. So, for long time, no bomb, no bullet. Father want to save born number one son, someday he have number one son." His friends nodded. The soldier went on. "Maybe no war in long time. Maybe no more war, son fly Viet Nam Airline. Many money." He rubbed his fingers together. His friends laughed uncertainly.

Lincoln asked, "Well, you *are* here for a long time, and we want to help you. To start with, tell us what you want to eat."

Nhu took over again. "Make rice. Make chicken in pot. I show man to make. Easy. Make egg. No cheese. No Asia man eat cheese. Hollible. No can make mouth close on cheese." He laughed mirthlessly. "Not know how white people you put tooth in cheese." The men laughed.

The two American WOCs met with the commanding officer that evening. He agreed to allow the foreign guests to concoct their own bill of fare, though they would have to make do with what was on the Army's master menu for the day. Lockett also told the general that he feared the paucity of their mechanical aptitude would be a stumbling block. Lincoln added that he had worked stripping and rebuilding aircraft engines, essentially the same ones that had been adapted for the H-23. He volunteered to give evening classes to the foreigners.

The C.O. nodded. "And the classes will be open to the rest of the WOCs. You men did good work."

The next morning, Dong, a particularly tall, though stalk-thin, late teen, filled a deep-walled, thirty-inch frying pan with a thumb's length of vegetable oil, got it sputtering, and heaped in lumps of leftover rice. He stirred once, pushed the kernels into a ring around the sides, then dumped a dozen eggs into the center of the roiling pool of oil. He took a pot of leftover SOS and wrestled it to a sink, where he played the faucet over the mash then scooped out a couple of handfuls of meat and dropped them into the oil. Some of the grease sloshed from the pan, and the civilian cook from Southern Airways jerked forward and opened his mouth in protest, but the CO, who had snuck in and was standing at the periphery, reached forward and stopped him. "We'll take care of the details later, Mr. Baldwin."

The American soldiers, whose attention had been captured by the proceedings, suddenly realized the old man was in their midst, and someone shrieked them to attention. The Vietnamese, though, did not take their eyes off the food. The more the oil splattered, the more they swallowed their saliva. The colonel laughed and muttered, "As you were, gentlemen."

The foreign men stood shoulder to shoulder around the stove until Dong stirred one more time and ladled the fare onto waiting trays. The men ran to their seats, and all one could hear in the otherwise besilenced mess hall were sounds of glugging and spoons clacking on metal trays. The fried rice was gone in less than a minute. The men leaned back comfortably, undid their belts, and nodded in thanks when one of their number handed out toothpicks.

CHAPTER TWENTY-SEVEN

Though it seemed to Lincoln the ice had been broken, and the business of studying the basics of aviation could finally commence, many of his compatriots still eyed the foreign cadets suspiciously. Much of that was to be laid at the feet of Huber and his chronicles, for the WOCs remained in awe of a man who had won the Distinguished Service Cross. But several of the ordinary soldier returnees, several dozen men waiting for the day their service was over, indulged themselves at the enlisted men's club every night then went around base spinning their own war stories, the butt of which were always the perplexing little people they couldn't seem to get away from. The word "gook" peppered their tales nearly as frequently as "fuckin'", and a number of WOCs soon took up the term, some spitting it more viciously at the foreigners than did Huber, who, at least, made a feeble effort to curse the Vietnamese behind their backs. He, along with the other returnees, also warned the young WOCs to lock away their valuables when out of the barracks, babbling endless tales of GIs having been robbed and murdered in Viet Nam at the hands of the very people they had been wrenched from their lives to rescue.

By the end of the second week, though, the WOCs were exhausted by the schedule of unending PT and academic burdens. There was also constant jabbing by the TAC cadres to determine if the proto-officers could tolerate stress. It left most, but not all, of the flight cadets too tired to remember the Vietnamese were even at Wolters.

Walking after class late on a sweltering afternoon, Lincoln and Huber dragged to the front of their billets. Huber stopped short of the door, his attention drawn to a moon-faced, foreign cadet skulking past the back of their barracks, a bundle in hand. Huber shouted, "Hey, what the hell you doin' there, boy?"

The teenager bolted toward the dilapidated Vietnamese quarters at the end of the row and managed to get inside before Huber burst through the door, skidded to a stop beside the soldier's bunk, and yanked him to his feet. "What the fuck did you take from my barracks, shit bird?"

"I no take. I no take."

An Asian cadet dropped from the upper bunk and wedged himself between Huber and the man. "You no say fuck. My father Viet Nam senator. You no hit Viet Nam soldier. My father have you kill dead."

The first man shouted again over his bunkmate's shoulder, "But I no take! I no take! My father kill you, too."

Huber's face deepened into a seething burgundy as he reached around and slapped the man who was professing his innocence. The three scuffled until Lincoln came up behind and stammered, "Huber, man, don't do that. This ain't the brown boot army. Lemme get a TAC. Let those guys take care of it."

Huber shoved both men and walloped the bag off the bed with his open palm. A bottle of tea-colored liquid hit a nail protruding from the roughhewn planks of the floor. As it shattered, the hut was instantly filled with the pungent odor of rotted fish. Both Vietnamese soldiers' eyes tightened and stared forward in furious glowers, but they said nothing.

Huber looked down and froze for a moment then about-faced and strode from the shelter. The first Vietnamese soldier trembled when Lincoln whispered, "He didn't mean it, man. He just got back from Nam. I'm sorry, man. You gotta understand." Lincoln touched his shoulder but looked away when he saw the man's eyes redden.

At the barracks dayroom, there was a pile of mail, but it sat untouched as Huber gathered a circle of WOCs and talked so fast, Lincoln could see the spit flying from his mouth. "They're all thievin' fuckers, ever last one, ain't they Friday?"

"I don't know, man. I think that was some of their food, man. The way it smelled, I don't think it came from in here."

"Oh, so now you're a total gook lover, huh? I'm tellin' you, man, I had a right to slam that prick. Tell these guys I did."

Lincoln stood silently for a moment, picked through the mail, found a thick envelope from Miriam, walked up the stairs to his room, grabbed a towel, and went to the shower. Before the water ran hot, Huber was standing in front of him, his bitter, faraway eyes looking through Lincoln's. "You listen here, Private. Don't let me find you fucking me behind my back. I didn't spend no year in Nam to come home to this shit. I don't gotta deal with gooks every minute of my fuckin' life. If you fuck with me, you will lose. Do you hear me?"

Lincoln turned away and ducked under the steaming water.

Lincoln was so unsettled, he was barely able to force down his pork chop at dinner. He didn't know if he should go to the CO and tell him what had happened or keep his mouth shut. If he chose the latter, he would be considered as involved as Huber and might as well pack his things and prepare to head to jail or Viet Nam, or both. Huber, though, would get away with it because of his war record.

Lincoln climbed onto his rack and tried to sleep, but by ten, he jumped down and grabbed his fatigues to go for a walk. As he started to pull on the pants, he felt the letter from home and took it to the dayroom. There was an envelope within the one from his mom. It had no return address but was postmarked Florida and was in Isabelle's hand. He could barely breathe as he ripped it open.

> *Dear Lincoln,*
>
> *I just wanted to tell you something. I had a miscarriage when the baby was three months along. At first, it was so hard, and I wanted to write to you, but then a million people told me that life in basic training was terrible, and I thought it was better to just let things be and not bother you with my problems.*
>
> *So everything turned out OK in the end. It always does, or so I am told.*
>
> *I am feeling fine again and wish the best for you.*
>
> *Warmly,*
>
> *Isabelle*

Lincoln did not return to his room. He knew he wouldn't be able to sleep, waiting for a smash in the head from Huber or a call to headquarters to answer for his part in the incident. He eventually climbed back to the room at four and spent the next hour at his desk peering into the darkness. At breakfast, Lincoln looked surreptitiously for the Vietnamese soldier and the man's bunkmate, but neither appeared. Nor were they on the bus to the airfield, and they were missing from dinner. A day later, Huber growled, "Teach them fuckers to mess with the bull."

A week after the incident, Huber asked for a three-hour pass on Sunday morning to go to church in Mineral Wells. It was the only time WOCs were allowed off base during preflight. Though it was not possible, legally, to buy alcohol on a Sunday, he found a fifth of bourbon and, late that afternoon, began nipping at it. By 9 P.M., he could no longer stand, forced to spend the next hours on his back, glowering at the underneath of Lincoln's mattress. Lincoln rested at his desk, head lying on folded arms, in and out of sleep, drooling on his aviation manuals. He did not hear the first sniffs coming from Huber's rack, but as they became whimpers, Lincoln lifted his head and stared at his roommate. Huber was soon sobbing, and Lincoln shifted his chair to the man's side.

"Hey, man, you okay?"

Huber nodded and managed to bark, "I'm fuckin' fine," but the tears continued to pour down the sides of his face. He lifted the bottle of bourbon from under his pillow, swallowed twice, and handed it to Lincoln, who put it to his lips and threw his head back, pretending to take a healthy swig.

"What's goin' on, man? I got your six. Don't worry."

Huber wiped his eyes with a corner of his bed sheet and growled. "WOC, you don't got no idea."

"Tell me."

"Okay, but if you ever tell anyone, I'll kick your ass from here to fuckin' Saigon. You got me?"

"Sure, man." When Huber's face relaxed a trace, Lincoln spoke softly. "So, tell me, man."

Without having shifted his eyes from the underside of Lincoln's mattress two feet above his head, he monotoned, "Okay, there was this girl in Saigon. I got sent to the big city after the Distinguished Service Cross. Old man told me it was my reward for playing the game. They stuck my ass in," he made quote signs with his fingers, "Pentagon East. Huge building, all glass, air conditioned; lawns around the place, looked like fuckin' putting greens. Generals were a dime a dozen. I had to wear khakis so everyone could see my DSC ribbon and my Purple Heart." His tears stopped, and his voice hardened.

"Anyway, there was this Vietnamese girl, my general's secretary. Fuckin' gorgeous—all the ones they picked to work inside the joint were. They had to wear them *ao dai*s. You ever seen 'em? Nearly see through 'em. Makes you wanna see through 'em. Pure silk. Her hair was as long as your arm, jet black, straight, perfect. Kim Lieu—means golden willow." He stopped for a moment, and Lincoln thought he saw a new tear form.

"So fuckin' anyway, we were workin' late, and the VC hit us with eighty-twos." When Lincoln turned his head in query, Huber mumbled patiently, "Gook mortars. Eighty-two millimeter."

Lincoln mused, "Do you mean 81 millimeter mortars?"

"No. Ours are 81s. Theirs are 82s. They ain't stupid. They can use our ammo, but we can't use theirs. Anyhow, it was the first time, I think, she was ever that close to the shit. I mean, you could live in Saigon, and it was safer than Chicago. Everyone was scared, even the general. Last shit he'd seen, I suppose, was in Korea, but even there he was a REMF." Before Lincoln's face could twist in question, Huber laughed faintly. "Rear echelon mother fucker.

"I sorta took charge—and they let me. Can you believe that shit? A general lets a piss-ant private order him around. So I had us upturn the furniture and jam it against the windows. You shoulda seen the general's desk. Thing was so heavy, teak or somethin', it took the three of us to budge it.

"Whatever. One of the mortars came close, and glass got sprayed all over the place, but no one was hit. I told 'em the VC had us zeroed in, and there's gonna be a lot more where that shit came from. The general squatted his fat ass down behind his desk, and there wasn't room for Kim Lieu. I ran out to the janitor's closet, got a broom, and swept the glass up good. I told her to get flat on the floor. I didn't want to touch her. That wouldn't be right, so I, like, straddled her, and sure as shit, two rounds later, the next floor up gets a direct hit, and a hunk of the ceiling drops right where I'm on all fours over her like a fuckin' dog. Knocks me down onto Kim Lieu and cuts the shit out of my back. Woulda killed her if it had hit direct.

"So, I'm layin' on top of her, not like that was so bad, and the first thing I felt was her hair. It was so soft, like silk, and then I could feel her *ao dai* against my arms. She was cryin', and when I lifted off her, she turned over and grabbed me, hugged me so hard it hurt, but it was the best minute of my life. She wouldn't let go until the fuckin' general gets up, and he's like pullin' us apart. Doesn't even say anything 'bout my back, shirt all torn open, and me bleedin' like a stuffed fuckin' pig, whatever that means.

Lincoln was slack-jawed. "Did you get another DSC for that?"

"Hell, no. If the general had put me in for anything more than a Purple Heart, there'd have to be this whole long statement from everybody there, and his ass wouldn't have looked too hot, now, would it? So I got the Purple Heart. Better, Kim Lieu told me she had always liked me. She said I was the most handsome man there; actually, she said the prettiest man..."

Lincoln interrupted, "Well, you are very cute, after all."

"Asshole. We started seeing each other. It was like no feeling I ever knew. I couldn't think about anything but her, and I'm sure she felt the same way. But it was, like, against their ways. Her family ran away from their apartment the day she brought me home to meet them. Place was empty. Eleven people disappeared, even her niece, three months old.

"What'd you expect? The baby to be there dressed up in one of those *ao dai*s, sittin' there by herself, cold beer in hand, just a waitin' to greet ya?"

"You really are a jerk." He laughed. "You know, you're the only one I ever told this to. Between us, yes?"

"I swear, man."

"I started to do the paperwork to bring her home. We were gonna get married by a chaplain there. Good guy. Promised to keep it quiet. But she had to go and tell her sister, and her parents beat it out of the kid, and next thing you know, Kim Lieu doesn't show up for work. One day, then the next, and soon I get word she quit. Well, she didn't—her father came and told the Americans that the girl had died, committed suicide because an American had raped her and got her pregnant."

Lincoln gasped, and Huber looked at him closely and muttered, "You think I'm a piece of shit, don't you?"

"No, man. Just so happens you're not alone." Lincoln stuck his hand out for the bottle and took a full swig. "Tell me."

"Obviously, they didn't know my name, and they had never seen me, and I figured things would quiet down; but one of her uncles showed up at the gate after work one night and said if I didn't pay him, he was going to leak my name to the Americans. When I told him to go fuck himself, he spit on the ground right at my feet. I shouldn't have, but I shoved him against the building."

"Yeah, you should've."

"Next thing you know, I get a note on my rack that some gooks had come around asking about me. I couldn't go to my CO or the general, so I checked a .45 out of the armory."

"They just gave you a gun?"

"DSC, remember?" Lincoln nodded and smiled. "And the rest of the story is worse. You have no idea."

"I don't know, maybe I do."

"And maybe you do. We all have our stories. Look, I'm not feelin' too chipper. I'm..." His tongue thickened and a few seconds later, he was snoring.

Lincoln threw a blanket over him and left for the dayroom, where several of his friends were watching TV. One asked, "Where's Huber? First night I ain't seen 'im down here guzzling beer and bitchin' 'bout the channel. You know what's goin' on with that cat?"

"No, I don't. Just know he saw some shit he keeps sayin' he hopes you all don't have to."

"Why's he here?"

"I don't know. Hasn't said." Lincoln took a breath to continue but stopped. The men watched him for a moment then turned back to *Batman*.

CHAPTER TWENTY-EIGHT

After preflight classes the next morning, Lincoln hid in the men's room until the building was deathly quiet. He turned the brim of his hat forward, put his head down, and walked, not ran, between buildings to the PX. Inside, he skulked to the service counter, presented a couple of dollar bills, and asked for nickels, dimes, and quarters. He curled himself around one of the two base payphones barely hidden in a corner of the store, dialed 0, and gave the wearied voice on the other end Isabelle's number. With nearly half of his change swallowed, the operator mumbled, "Please wait."

A woman's voice came on the line, and because it had the same cadence and camber as Isabelle's, Lincoln's chest clutched forcefully. He could not take a breath to speak.

"Hello, hello, is anyone there?"

"Mrs. Dalton, I'm, I'm sorry to bother you, but..."

"Oh, my gosh, it's Lincoln, isn't it?"

He was so startled, he thrust the receiver toward the payphone, though as it began to lower onto the hook, thoughts of the last traumatic days of Advanced Infantry Training flashed across his consciousness. He was paralyzed. He could hear, and even evoke visions of, the enraged instructors cautioning that the easy days of stateside training were soon to be over, and with it would go their childhoods. The next stop was real combat in Viet Nam, and to punctuate the wretchedness of what lay ahead of them, the hardboiled sergeants imposed nearly intolerable psychological stress on their adolescent fodder. When a man broke, as most eventually did, they took him aside and, not unkindly, talked him through the process of ignoring the shock, calming himself, and moving forward as ordered, for there was no duty on Earth more sacred than a man carrying out his mission, no matter that the world was exploding around him.

Through his panic, Lincoln straightened himself. "Yes, ma'am, this is Lincoln."

"You know, Lincoln, you're not supposed to call here."

"Yes, ma'am, I know, but I need to talk to Isabelle. She's all I think about. Please tell me where she is."

Mrs. Dalton was silent for an eternity. "I can't do that, Lincoln. You know, I always liked you, Lincoln. Mr. Dalton and I still do. But we gave Isabelle our word that we would honor her wishes. She has to make her own decisions about what's best for her."

"Yes, ma'am, I understand. Could you at least call her and tell her I asked if she was okay?"

There was no answer, and Lincoln thought the line had gone dead, but Mrs. Dalton's voice broke as she barely whispered, "Let me talk it over with Mr. Dalton." She sighed, "Are you doing well in flight school, Lincoln? Bet you're at the top of your class."

"It's really tough here, Mrs. Dalton. I'm not sure I'm going to get through this. Thank you, anyway."

"You'll be fine, Lincoln. Things always work out for the best." She paused with a sigh. "Good bye, Lincoln."

He garbled a word into the mouthpiece, and the line went dead.

CHAPTER TWENTY-NINE

For the next weeks, Huber made no further mention of what had happened in Viet Nam, and Lincoln assumed what was done was done, and the man hated the Vietnamese for having kept him from Kim Lieu. Or maybe he believed her family had murdered her in their rage, an honor killing, though Lockett shook his head. He had not heard of that practice in Southeast Asia.

No matter, the WOCs were even more tired by now, and most nights, after Lincoln gave his engine lecture, they staggered back to their rooms and dropped on racks, asleep before they could undress.

Monday morning at 5 A.M., exactly four weeks to the minute from the instant they'd formed up for the first PT, a convoy of school busses carried them to the airfield for their orientation flight. Lincoln had never been that close to a parked helicopter, and here, there were hundreds upon hundreds of them, the largest collection of rotary aircraft in one place in the world, and probably in the history of humankind. Every day, fifteen hundred sorties would be flown around Wolters, and there was hardly a moment, day or night, that the sky wasn't jammed with what looked to be clouds of gnats—untold numbers of H-23s, tiny, erratic, wobbling specks in the sky. The instructors in the pre-solo phase were civilians, another of the countless contractors Southern Airways had furnished to administer most every phase of life at Fort Wolters.

Lincoln's first instructor pilot, his IP, was Tommy Donovan, a huge man, a local farmer, who had flown fighters in World War Two and then helicopters in Korea. A trace less hard-bitten and a hint more even-tempered than the active duty military instructors that would come after the first solo flight, the man was, nonetheless, humorless and severe in bearing.

As they walked around the H-23, Mr. Donovan pointed out the innumerable parts of a helicopter that distinguished it from the rest of the world's flying devices. He stopped suddenly, looked up into Lincoln's face, and muttered quite seriously, "You're too tall to fly, and I'm way too fat. I doubt if we're gonna get out of this alive. But my orders are to show you how this contraption works, and, by God, that's what I'm going to do. You got life insurance?"

"Does the Army give it to you?"

"Don't know, son, but I got some, and my agent told me just last week that I'm worth more dead than alive. So, what the hell, let's go."

Lincoln was pointed toward the right seat. Though it was where he had been placed during the two flights he'd taken in the fixed wing aircraft years before, he had always pictured himself on the left, in the command pilot's seat, when the flying began for real. He asked, "Mr. Donovan, sir, when do I get to sit on the left?"

In deadpan, he mumbled, "If we live through this flight, if you graduate from flight school, and you make it through a long time in Viet Nam, or if you make it back here as an instructor, the left seat'll be all yours. Why the hell you'd want it is beyond me." Lincoln was still thinking that through when Mr. Donovan plugged in Lincoln's flight helmet, pushed a few buttons, and asked, "How do you hear?"

"I can hear pretty good."

"No, son, that's 'loud and clear, how me?'"

Donovan shifted myriad levers, twisted controls, flipped a dozen switches, and called out, "Comin' hot." Lincoln watched as the tips of the long blades, eight feet in front of the bubble canopy, began to creep in circles. Seconds later, with the rotor turning at half speed, Lincoln searched for something to grab, to hold him in his seat as the machine shuddered harder than a washing machine spinning with a soaking rug. There was a handle, exactly like a parking brake, poking out of the floor to the left of his seat, and he grabbed at it. It pivoted up, and so did the helicopter. Donovan, though, jammed it back to the floor before the skids could break ground.

He barked, "Don't touch that. Of all the things in the world you wouldn't want to mess with, it would be the collective on a helicopter. That's like popping the clutch at a light before it turns green, and there's a car smack dab in front of you. You can drive a car, yes?"

"Yes, sir."

"Good, cause them Viets can't. And you remember what I said 'bout the collective."

"Yes, sir."

The bouncing smoothed a bit as the rotor reached operating speed, and when Donovan instructed him to push a button on the instrument panel that would illuminate the strobe light, Lincoln's hands were shaking so hard, his extended fingers poked the switch two away from the lights, and the radios went dead.

The instructor rolled his eyes, revived the radios, described each of the uncountable controls, made a call to the tower, and before Lincoln had time to ask how to turn up his earphones to hear over the din, the H-23 lifted off Lane Three, hovered a couple of feet into the air, and tipped so far forward, Lincoln was sure they were going to plow into the earth, nose first. For a moment, the machine hung in the air, but it suddenly pitched even farther, and Lincoln realized this was the certain demise Mr. Donovan had presaged. He had not, though, imagined it would happen six seconds into flight school. The man remained poker-faced, looked left and right, pulled smoothly on the verboten lever by his left hand, and the ship began to creep forward. Despite the nose that remained pointed to the ground, they began climbing.

"Sir, does that mean you point a helicopter down to go up?" Mr. Donovan didn't answer.

They flew for a half-an-hour, Lincoln given the controls only after Mr. Donovan explained how they were to say, "You've got it," "I got it," "Okay, you've got it," and, "Roger, I got it." He wanted so badly to stop the IP and tell him he already knew how to trade off control of an aircraft, but he did so poorly as he tried to fly straight and level, he decided to keep his past accomplishments to himself. The first problem Donovan noticed was that Lincoln used the pedals to turn the helicopter once they were actually flying. While the most basic maneuver in an airplane, it was just plain criminal in a helicopter.

After they landed, Mr. Donovan sat with Lincoln and read from a list of the deficiencies he'd compiled. "Friday, you have some experience in fixed wings, don't you?"

"A little, sir."

"Yeah, well, forget all of it, every single shred of that worthless information. First of all, you don't use your pedals to turn. You only use them when you're hovering. And why did you insist on pulling the nose up in the climb and point it down when you were descending? That's backward, young man. Those are bad habits you're going to break, or you're not going to make it."

"Yes, sir."

"And what is the problem you're having with twisting the throttle in your left hand? Ever drive a motorcycle?"

"When I was a kid, sir."

"As opposed to now that you're an old geezer?" He laughed at himself. "The throttle on a 23 is exactly the same. Only difference is that it isn't on the handlebars—it's on the end of the collective. Just roll your wrist around smoothly. You're a farm boy, right?"

"Yes, sir."

"Well, it's just like ringin' an old chicken's neck. Can't be that hard, can it?"

Lincoln's face turned cherry red, and Donovan looked at him curiously. "You got a problem killin' a chicken for dinner? You do, and you aren't gonna do so good in combat."

"No, sir. I'm okay killin' things."

While the orientation flight did not count, there were to be grades for every flight thereafter. It did not take much to flunk out. There was an endless supply of young men dying to get into flight school, for it was, by now, the only way to learn to fly in the military without a college education. So, Lincoln spent hours stretching his left wrist, but there seemed to be a piece of something hard inside that blocked any more than a few degrees of movement.

Then there were the differences between flying airplanes and helicopters. Despite the hours he spent hours at his desk at Wolters in the wooden chair studying the distinctions, he remained at a disadvantage. All the years he had dreamed of flying had made the operation of an airplane as rote as sauntering to the mess hall for dinner. Now, he had to forget everything and learn to walk all over again. He managed, though, to muddle along with, what he assumed were the average number of beratings per flight, until his buddy, Lockett, laughed over a beer as Lincoln complained about Donovan, "Hey, Friday, man, you lucked out. That guy's a pussy cat. He's like the most tranquil instructor in history."

After three weeks, Mr. Donovan began to teach Lincoln the art of autorotation, a skill that would allow a helicopter to land safely, even if it ran out of gas or the engine was silenced by enemy fire. Theoretically, this made a helicopter the safest form of flying. In the real world, though, the maneuver was incredibly hard to carry out. The series of lever and pedal movements was so complex, engine failure, or even a mild malfunction, usually meant death for everyone on board, even if the breakdown took place just a foot or two off the ground.

In a fixed wing airplane, engine failure, or any sudden deceleration of the aircraft to a speed too slow to keep the wings in the air, had to be followed fairly quickly by a push forward on the control wheel to lower the nose, to aim it down, so the plane would enter a mild dive and get going fast enough for the air flowing over the wings to start holding it in the air again. That was half the solution. The rest of the remedy required pushing on the power lever, the throttle, like stepping on the gas, to get the propeller turning fast enough to pull the airplane through the air. This was the maneuver Lincoln had perfected in his mind and on his simulator, and with which he had regaled Miss Kola years before.

In the helicopter, however, the opposite set of actions was called for, and they had to be carried out in a couple of tenths of a second. If the pilot failed to drop the collective, the power lever, essentially taking his foot *off* the gas, at the first whiff of trouble, there wasn't any point in trying after that, for the ship was doomed. Almost instantly, the main rotor slowed so much, there wasn't enough momentum to keep the blades flung out to the sides. They simply folded straight up like a trapped bank robber heaving his hands to the sky. That bending caused the blades to splinter into a cloud of shredded metal, converting the former exceedingly expensive aircraft into nothing more than a plunging tube of aluminum foil stuffed with condemned souls.

The next step in the algorithm of a failed autorotation was to draw a mighty breath and comfort the crew with the homily, "Prepare to die, men. It's been an honor to serve with you." If the ship had been at a decent altitude when the predicament arose, there would be, perhaps, twenty seconds to make peace with your God before the crash and the inevitable fire.

So, in the helicopter, one learned to push the power lever, the collective, that was gripped in the left hand, down, to "off", in less than a heartbeat, and at the same instant, pull back on the cyclic, the old flying stick, held in the right hand. That caused the nose to point up toward the sky. In this configuration, the rotor blades would be facing more directly into the wind and would pick up speed again, simply from the gush of air rushing through them, a pinwheel shoved out a car window.

Now, if the collective had been dropped in time, and the cyclic pulled back just right, the pilot then stole a quick look at the little gauge on the instrument panel that showed how fast the rotor was going. When it signaled a speed sufficient to hold the rotors straight out, the nose was lowered a fraction, the pilot looked out, determined which way the wind was blowing, a nearly impossible task, and turned the helicopter to head into it. Then a landing site had to be chosen, one close enough to reach with the little bit of time left in the pilot's life. With all that accomplished, it was time to begin the next set of impossible maneuvers, to set the aircraft up for a skidding landing on a smudge of ground that looked as smooth as a putting green from a mile away, but was generally filled with tree stumps, trash, and mammoth potholes.

One did not solo in a helicopter until the autorotation was mastered in its simplest form, which was over an endless expanse of flat land, where the right place to land was any place you aimed the helicopter. And that happened to be the description of the countryside surrounding the initial training areas at Wolters—prairie as far as the eye could see.

Mr. Donovan demonstrated one autorotation then warned he would chop the power any time he felt like it, to see if Lincoln could go through the drill on his own. When they climbed back into the sky after Donovan's perfect landing, he gave the controls back to Lincoln and began chitchatting. "Not bad, huh?"

"It was great, sir."

"Hey, Friday, by the way, where you from?" Before Lincoln could answer, the man queried casually, "Got any brothers or sisters?"

Lincoln spoke hesitantly but began to calm, for he had become somewhat comfortable with straight and level flight where there was no need to maneuver the throttle with his damaged wrist. His hand relaxed on the collective, and he wiped his sweaty palm on his flight suit. His mind drifted from the cockpit as he imagined the next question would be whether he had a wife or a girlfriend. As he was considering how he would answer, Donovan slipped his hand surreptitiously onto the throttle and rolled it quickly to idle. He did not, though, drop the collective to the floor. Lincoln felt the ship begin to drop at the same moment he realized the engine noise had decayed to a whisper. When the cyclic turned mushy in his right hand, he finally reacted, but it was without a speck of attention to the weeks of interminable training. Instead of dropping the collective in that golden tenth of a second, he pulled up on it—all the way—thinking he was adding power, as in an airplane. Simultaneously, he pushed the cyclic forward to lower the nose into a dive and, in his mind, force the air speed to increase and allow the helicopter to resume flying. The combination of maneuvers, though, sucked the energy out of the rotor, and Lincoln could actually see the blades slowing. The little helicopter buffeted then began to fall over on its side, on the cusp of passing into an unrecoverable tumble to Earth. Mr. Donovan grabbed both levers so hard, Lincoln's hands flew off them and into the air above his head. His knuckles rapped the top of the canopy with such force, Donovan ducked in reaction to the bang then grumbled, "Fuckin' A!" The IP pushed and pulled, though smoothly, cajoling the collective as if milking a cow. The mad dive eased off into a smolder of a descent, and he called over the intercom, "Okay, I got it. We're goin' home."

When they landed, he sat down with Lincoln in the break room and put a cold bottle of Coke in front of him. "Son, I need to be honest with you. You're having trouble with the basics. Today was just the latest example. Army needs pilots real bad, but not so bad they're gonna put you behind the cyclic of a ship full of combat troops and get them killed before they see their first fire fight. You're gonna have eight young men and a lotta mamas counting on you to deliver them into a hot LZ in one piece."

Lincoln, though his heart was quaking harder than an H-23 with a chunk shot out of its main rotor, turned his head in question. Donovan shook his head in defeat. "LZ, landing zone—where you drop off your troops and everything on Planet Earth is shooting and shoving mortar rounds down your throat. Sometimes, it's even your own guys tryin' to kill ya." Lincoln gasped. "Yeah, that's right, WOC, 'cause your helicopter puts a bulls-eye on where all the friendlies are congregating, and that helps the enemy walk mortar rounds right on top of our own guys. Look, when you get into the real thing, it's not like in the movies. I don't give a shit how brave you think you are. When you start down in a file of eight HUEYs toward an LZ, and you have to decrease airspeed to thirty knots, so slow you're not even crawling, a six-year-old gook kid could shoot you down. The AK rounds are whizzing through the Plexiglas, couple of dozen of 'em when you count the holes back at base, if you make it back to base. While all this is going down, you can't be thinking you're about to get blown away. Everything has to be by instinct, reflex. Right now, you're gonna do the absolute wrong thing and kill your crew and your load—that's ten or twelve souls. Like I said, that's a lotta Gold Star mothers." Lincoln squinted. "You don't know what that means, do you?"

"No, sir."

"Was your father in the war?"

"Yes, sir."

"Then ask him. Son, you need to get rid of the bad habits, and within the next few days. This is Week Three. Half of these guys have soloed. By the end of next week, if you haven't, you're gone, washed out, and you'll be toting an M-16 in the paddies before the rest of your pals here start Week Five. I'm not going to let you fly this afternoon. I want you to go back to main post. Eat lunch, go to your barracks, sit down, and think as intensely about what you're doing here as you ever thought about anything in your life. You need to figure out how to make the changes. It's up to you. No one's gonna do it for you. No one can. This ain't kindergarten anymore. Time's runnin' out."

CHAPTER THIRTY

Lincoln skipped lunch and returned to his room. He climbed onto his rack and began rereading the flight manual. He spoke out loud the facts he needed to drill into his head, but the harder he screamed at himself to picture the sequence of movements to transform himself into a helicopter pilot, the more he pondered the letter from Isabelle, and the sin he'd committed, and how he had marred the rest of her life.

As his mind drifted even farther from helicopters, Lincoln sensed something he had not before. It was not sadness or disappointment that things hadn't gone the way he'd dreamed. Those were emotions in whose company he'd logged countless hours, and he had begun to believe they could be risen above if he just made himself work harder. This time, his feelings were different, unfamiliar, and though not as organically painful as the fear he'd so often faced as a kid, these stabbed far deeper. It was the first time in his life he simply did not care what happened to him, or even if he lived to see himself rise above this latest failure. Though he closed the blinds and turned off the light to hide from the despondency, the darkness only deepened it. So he opened the shade halfway and climbed back onto his rack to stare hard at the ceiling, mesmerized by the water stains, culling from them fantasy images of emotionless faces—the student pilots who had gone before him. How many, he wondered, were dead, torn to pieces by ground fire because they weren't good enough pilots? But even their loss did not move him, for there was now only the impassive, enervating miasma of hopelessness.

He slept restlessly until the door opened with a boom and a gush of burning air. It was Huber. He was soaking wet, as was his hat, the bill of which was canted a few degrees short of forward. Lincoln looked up, groggy for a second, until it dawned on him that his roommate had been dunked in the pool at the officers' club, a tradition on the day of a man's first solo at Wolters.

Huber stopped dead. "What the fuck is this, WOC? What the hell are you doing in the rack? You hidin' a woman under them covers?"

It took a while for Lincoln to answer. "I'm done, Hubert. My IP told me as much today. Screwed up my first autorotation so bad, we almost died. He was TSTW."

"What the hell's that?"

"Too scared to write. You know, too petrified to make notes on his little knee pad. Didn't have to. It was burned into his brain, all my fuck ups. He listed them, each and every one. Said I only had a couple of days, and they were going to send me before the Elimination Board."

"My ass. Everybody likes you. Don't listen to 'im."

"I don't think it's about people liking you. I'm just no good at this stuff." His head dropped back onto his pillow.

"I say again, WOC, my ass. Everyone's havin' trouble, even the guys who've soloed. And, I heard Donovan's scared to let anybody go out alone the first time. Few classes ago, one of his guys rolled it up into a little ball on his first solo."

"Are you shittin' me?"

"No, man, that's what I heard. Crashes first fuckin' minute at the stick. Look, it's Friday, Friday. We got the weekend off. I been savin' another bottle of firewater for this night. Ain't sharin' it with those other dickheads. So you don't need to be sober in the morning. Anyway, I got somethin' to tell ya."

Huber slid his desk chair to the closet, pried the sheet of plywood from the ceiling, and slipped out a fresh fifth of bourbon. Lincoln's shoulders relaxed, and he laughed. "Where the hell do you get this stuff? You can't buy it at the PX, even if they let your WOC ass in there, which they don't. How do you do it?"

"Troop, listen close." His voice rose and sharpened. "I was a nearly normal kid when they sent me over there. Most of us were. But you learn to steal, and lie, and cheat, and fuckin' murder if you need to, 'cause it's the only way you're ever gonna get what you want. And that's all that counts anymore—to get what you want, the minute you want it. So now I know how to make it in the real world. I want booze, I fuckin' take it, period. What they gonna do? Send me to fuckin' Viet Nam?" He spit bitterly on the floor beside his desk. Lincoln did not move a muscle.

Huber glared through the window as he rolled open the plastic cap in a smooth twist of his fingers, flipped it into the air with his thumb, caught it in his other hand, then hurled it backhand against the wall. He handed the bottle up to Lincoln, who took a thin drag and passed it back down.

"Not that I was all that sane before I got there." Huber took a mouthful and lifted the bottle back up to Lincoln, who, this time, did not hesitate. It barely burned going down, and he took another gulp before sliding off his rack into a chair.

They were quiet for a few moments while the alcohol seeped into them. Huber got out of his soaking flight suit, put on a pair of dry skivvies, took another drink, this one a trifling compared to the first, and put his water-shriveled feet on the desk. He looked as if he was going to start talking, but his mouth closed, and he stared out the window. After another nip, he turned to Lincoln. "Like I said, I got something to tell you." Lincoln raised his eyes as the bottle stopped an inch from his face. He sipped this time.

"There's more to the story. There always is. Turns out, Kim Lieu, you remember her, she's okay. Still thinks about me, I think."

Lincoln gasped. "She called your family?"

"For Christ's sake, will you let me go on, unless, of course, you want to tell *me* the whole goddamn saga?" Lincoln belched a laugh. Huber did as well. "No, she went to live with an aunt in Bien Hoa. Your ass is gonna learn a shitload about Bien Hoa before you're done, WOC. Biggest airbase in the world, Long Binh, sittin' right next to this muddy little village. Anyway, they sent her up there so the family wouldn't be shamed."

Lincoln's chest gripped. Huber looked at him. "You okay, troop? Your face is as red as a fuel cut-off knob."

"Yeah, fine."

"Well. You don't look it. You want me to stop?"

"God, no."

"As I was sayin' before I was so rudely inter-fuckin-rupted, the family threatened her that if she contacted me, or ever told anybody about me, they'd disown her, and she wouldn't be allowed to visit her ancestors' graves. You know, those people believe in Buddhism, but also ancestor worship. A lot of what they do is supposed to bring honor on the generations that went before them. Gettin' knocked up by a hairy barbarian, that's what they call us, ain't the best way to get the ancestors to shine light and wealth on your slim ass.

"So her sister, a good kid, and fuckin' gorgeous, lemme tell ya, she writes to me from the Nam, and tells me to call her and gives me a number and a time, and I sit at home fighting with the American operator to put the call through, and she says, 'That's a war zone, don't you know? And there are regulations about allowing Americans to talk to people over there.' Then I tell her it's my wife, and she says, 'It's too dangerous.' Fuckin' moron. So I talk to the supervisor, and, eventually, she gets the sister on the line, and she tells me that Kim Lieu had the baby, it was a girl, and she was beautiful…"

"Took after her mother, apparently."

Huber laughed and stood. He put his hand on Lincoln's shoulder. "You're okay, troop."

The bottle passed back and forth a couple of times, though only sips were drawn from the half-empty fifth. "When I asked the baby's name, that's when she got real scared. Something about she couldn't tell me because the ancestors were listening. These people. So I asked how I could get money to Kim Lieu and *my daughter*, and still she wouldn't tell me, but I sent a shitload of dough over there anyway. One of my buddies from my platoon—fuckin' jerk re-upped and went back for a second helping of the shit—I had him track her down, get a picture, a hundred of them, and make sure the baby was cared for and Kim Lieu was doing okay. Turns out, she left Bien Hoa when the neighbors decided the baby looked mixed, and they were living in a tin shanty down by the fuckin' Saigon River. You know, one of those shitholes made from cut open, flattened out GI beer cans tack-welded into sheets—gook PSP, for as well as it keeps out the rain. Her family, well, the males, took all of the money and were living the life of Riley—on my fuckin' nickel!

"I didn't care so much about that, but Kim Lieu was living in a hole. And who knows about my daughter? And still, she can't call me or write to me to tell me she still thinks about what we had. What kinda shit is that?"

He sighed. "Anyway, now you know the rest of the story. I was never gonna say nothin' more, but after we got to the flight line this morning, some WOC hands me a letter that got stuck to one of his. It was from my buddy over there. He went and saw her again, gave her more money, right outta his pocket. Can you believe that? Said it was for her and the baby only, not for her shit-bird family. When he told her I had a plan to get back there and bring her here, he says she started cryin' and, like, fell to her knees calling my name. And I find out on the same day I solo. It's unfuckin' believable, troop."

He paused for a long time. Lincoln took another sip. Huber looked up and asked, "You got something eating at you, WOC. I can tell."

"Not important, man."

"My ass it isn't. Your turn. Let's hear it."

"Not very interesting, not like your story".

"Yeah, well, I'm all ears."

Huber reached up with the bottle. Lincoln waved it away. "One girlfriend in my life, had sex with her one time, and she gets pregnant. We didn't know what to do, so I joined the Army to get medical insurance. Then, she gets cold feet, decides not to get married, and tells me to leave her the hell alone. Okay, I said, whatever you want, but I'm dyin', Hubert. I loved her so much. Next thing I know, I get one letter from her couple a weeks ago, and she tells me she had a miscarriage, whatever the hell that is, and there's goin' to be no more baby, and that it all turned out for the best. And now, we should really go our separate ways. She asked me not to contact her, but I couldn't help myself, so I called her mother. All she said was that Isabelle wasn't in Wilkes Barre anymore. I sort of begged, but she wouldn't tell me where she'd gone or give me her number."

"Do you have *any* idea where she went?"

"I asked one of my high school friends, a girl, to find out. Best she could do was come up with Florida, living with a friend, Sandra Anaya. You should see that one, cocoa skin, black eyes. Anyway, they're down there somewhere waitressing."

"Does her family hate you for, you know?"

"No, man, they don't know. Apparently, she left before her stomach began to show. And even if they did know, they're great people, but they're not gonna go against what she asked. It's just the kind of folks they are. High class, like real honorable. Her old man was a P-51 jock in the war. Distinguished Flying Cross. Not a Distinguished *Service* Cross, but almost there."

"Hope I never find out how close."

Though the room was spinning nauseatingly, Lincoln did fall asleep a couple of hours later. He dreamed that he was watching Huber autorotate a HUEY into a field in the middle of Saigon, though it was really Wolters, and then try to call Kim Lieu from a payphone that Lincoln remembered from Wilkes Barre. In the dream, the operator was telling him to put a thousand Vietnamese dong in the phone, but Huber was yelling, "Gook money ain't worth shit," and he would only use American money, and it better not be any more than one dime.

Lincoln woke up and ran to the latrine to throw up.

CHAPTER THIRTY-ONE

In the morning, he dragged himself out of bed at ten. Huber was lifeless, and Lincoln considered taking his friend's hat, with its post-solo wings, and walking directly to the PX to use the phone. Though he planned to hide himself amongst the Saturday morning swarms, he knew he would be noticed, and it would be his last volitional act of flight school. So he put his own cap on, bill forward, and walked hurriedly through the gaggles of milling troops.

The clerk at the PX would not give him change unless he bought something, so Lincoln threw a pack of Jujyfruits on the counter and dropped three one-dollar bills next to it. He loaded his fatigue pockets with dimes and nickels and waited on line for the phone, and an hour later he was talking with Helen Magnuson, one of Isabelle's high school best friends. He begged her for help, to find her, and she told him to call back the next morning. He did not sleep that night.

He snuck back to the phones a day later. Helen whined, "Lincoln, I did bad in the eyes of the Lord, but you're the most wonderful man I know, and you made me laugh, and that's the only way I made it through that stupid high school. Okay, get a pencil, and if you ever tell on me, I'll make you marry me instead of Isabelle. And you wouldn't want that."

"Who says?"

"Just you write down the number and behave."

"Tell me how you did it."

"Oh, I'm going straight to hell."

"Come on."

"I went to confession yesterday and told Father Tony I was in big trouble. Usually, he comes up with a solution in a split second, 'You must say three Hail Marys, blah, blah, blah.' You know. No, you don't. You're lucky. Anyway, this time he didn't say anything for a while, and I asked to meet with him for counselling. I told him I needed to talk to Sandra, 'cause she was the only one who knew how to get ahold of the guy who, ya know, got me in a family way."

"Oh, my God. This is unbelievable."

"So, Father Tony tells me to wait in the church and pray for an hour. He finishes confession, calls Sandra's mom, gets the number, sticks his head into the church, and yells at me to go out the back door into the parking lot. He walks past like he doesn't know me. Slips me a little piece of paper, flies off to his car, and zooms outta the place like he committed a murder. I guess he had to go to confession himself, and it sure wasn't here in Wilkes Barre. So, now he's got all these problems to deal with caused by me." She stopped for a moment. "Are you okay, Lincoln?"

"Helen, I'm dyin'. They're tossing me outta here. The dream's over. I need to talk to Isabelle before I go nuts."

"You are not getting thrown out of anything. All those tough guys in high school, yeah, well, every girl thought you were the best. Handsome, polite, not some ruffian. You coulda had your pick. Bet you never knew, did you?"

"Now, you're being silly." His voice faltered. "I don't know if I'll ever be able to thank you. Someday, when I come home from Nam, I'll tell you the full story."

"That's okay. I think I know." She paused. "You be safe there. No hero stuff." Her voice cracked, but she managed to murmur, "World needs you, Lincoln." There was a click, and the line went dead.

Lincoln glanced over his shoulder at the line of angry faces on queue for the phones, so he paced around in the shadows for an hour then headed back to the PX. As he stepped off the curb to cross Van Story Street, his mind clouded with the fantasy that, in just minutes, he might hear Isabelle's voice. In his trance, his foot twisted, and he fell headfirst into a TAC officer's arms. Lincoln gathered himself and mumbled, "Excuse me, sir," saluted sloppily, and turned away to cross to the phones.

The TAC paused at the curb and called out, "Say, WOC."

Lincoln guessed, with the plethora of forward and backward hats milling about post, the officer had no idea who had soloed and who hadn't. Nonetheless, his gut clenched in dread, and the emptiness flooded into his heart. By rote he stopped in his tracks and came to semi-attention, though he did not turn toward the man.

The officer shook his head and paced around to Lincoln's front. His face came to rest just inches from Lincoln's. "You okay, WOC?"

"Yes, sir," Lincoln answered in a petulant tone.

"You don't look or sound okay. You drunk or something? Been drinking?"

"No, sir."

"Flying solo make you sick?"

That question drew Lincoln to yet another crossroads. If he answered, "Yes," he was lying to a superior, and he was done. If he answered, "No," he was lying to a superior, and he was done. "Just thinking about my girl, sir."

"Well, don't be doing that in this school."

"Yes, sir."

"You don't sound convinced. Listen to me, WOC. In no time, you'll have men in the back of your ship whose lives depend on their pilot to be thinking and making correct judgments every second of every day, not dreaming about getting laid. You got that, WOC?"

"I do, sir. You're absolutely right. It won't happen again, sir."

"See that it doesn't." He squinted at Lincoln's name tag as he barked, "Carry on." They exchanged salutes, the street emptied of men and cars, and Lincoln walked back to the phones.

CHAPTER THIRTY-TWO

Isabelle gasped, then became deathly quiet. He thought she'd hung up, but there was a whisper of breathing. He waited without a word.

"Lincoln," she moaned," you weren't supposed to call me. That was..." she gulped as if trying to catch her breath, "the deal." She spoke forcefully. "How did you get my number?"

"Isabelle, please don't yell at me."

"I'm not yelling." She stopped for a moment. "I'm dying inside. Why did you have to call?"

"I had to talk to you. I'm done here. I don't want to go home for leave before they send me to Viet Nam and go by your house and wonder if I'll ever hear your voice again. I..."

It took a while for her to answer. "I'm sorry, Lincoln. I was getting over it. I can't go through it again. Can you understand that?"

"Okay, I'll leave you alone. I'll hang up."

"Well, first, tell me, how…are you?" The cadence of her speech was uneven, her tone terse, and he realized he'd made a terrible mistake, breaking his promise.

His heart sank, but he managed to squeak, "Isabelle, are you okay?"

"Yeah, I guess. What the heck were you talking about, leaving there? Where are you?"

As he took a breath to continue, an intrusive voice blurted, "Please deposit thirty-five cents for three more minutes."

Lincoln did, and the line crackled back to life.

Isabelle went on. "Lincoln, where are you?"

"Oh, I'm still here in Texas, at Wolters."

Isabelle could feel the tremor in his voice. "Hey, Lincoln, please tell me you're having fun, that you're the best pilot they've ever had, 'cause I bet you are. Smartest and best lookin', too."

"Sweet Isabelle, I'm barely makin' it. I screwed up a flight on Friday, and they're going to kick me out."

"No, they're not."

"I'm so goddamn tired…"

"Language, please."

"Sorry, but I don't care anymore. It's so hard. This place sucks. The Army sucks. I'm worst in the class. Almost everybody's soloed except me. Never been so tired, even when I was opening the kitchen at the Sterling."

When he didn't continue, she spoke softly. "Those were good days, Lincoln. We used to meet after dark." She stopped and giggled. "Hey, do you remember that cop, Rodman?"

"What a jerk. He didn't bother you after I left, did he?"

"No way, but listen to this. My dad told me that he was found you-know-whatting in a car in Kirby Park, right next to where he bothered us, if you can believe it. He was with some girl he stopped for drinking beer. Turns out, she was a minor. He read her license wrong, and she was really a month under eighteen.

He swore he thought it was a month after her birthday. That was his excuse! 'He thought…' Jerk couldn't even count.

"You shoulda heard my father. He was screeching, laughing into the phone. First time I heard him happy in half-a-year. Anyway, Rodman made a deal saying he would quit the police department and never take another job as a cop, anywhere; if he signed the contract, he wouldn't have to go to court for statutory rape.

"My father was furious, but the DA said it was too messy to prosecute. My dad says it was really because the DA was scared that if he made a stink about a cop, he'd get a speeding ticket from Rodman's pals every time he pulled out of his driveway. Guess it's good news, anyway. First time I smiled in half-a-year, too."

They were silent for a moment. Lincoln asked, "Should I let you go?"

She exhaled as if she'd run a mile. "No, not yet, please."

"Are your parents mad at me?"

"No. They really care for you. And they have no idea about all that happened. At least, I don't think they do. They want the best for me, so they let me come down here. And I made the decision that was best for all of us. I'm sure of it, even if it doesn't feel so good." When he didn't answer, she went on. "And you don't have to worry. Everything's fine. I'm all better. I just want you to be happy. You're going to be a great pilot."

There was a demand for Lincoln to drop more change into the machine, which he did without thinking, his concentration stolen by the declaration he had dreamed of making if he ever spoke to Isabelle again. As the last nickel dropped, he waited for a moment and began. "Isabelle. You listen to me. I love you. I want you to come to Texas and marry me. We'll make our own…" There was a crackle in the earpiece and then absolute silence.

A few seconds later, the operator spoke sullenly. "Your call has been interrupted. Please wait." Lincoln feared he had touched something in his fright, but the operator mumbled there had been a malfunction in the equipment. A busy signal blurted loudly. The operator spoke over it. "I've got the line back, but your party hasn't hung up. I can't reconnect unless she does." She tried again a moment later and spoke irritably. "You'll have to call back at another time."

"Do you know when the line went dead?"

"Couple of minutes ago."

On Monday morning, Lincoln was summoned to Post Headquarters. He was told to take a seat and wait until he was called to speak to the commanding officer. He dropped onto a wooden chair, and before he had a moment to realize he was about to be expelled by the highest ranking aviator at Fort Wolters, the old man poked his head out of his office and ordered, "In here, WOC."

A black cloud engulfed Lincoln, one through which he could barely see sufficiently to maneuver through the office door. Instinct, though, seized him. He snapped to attention in front of the colonel and saluted sharply.

"At ease. Well, Private Friday, sounds like the past few days haven't been totally according to the book. Mr. Donovan likes you, but he has a job to do, and he doesn't have any leeway. None of us do. He says you really want to be a pilot, but you have a footlocker full of bad habits you're dragging around, holding you back. That, by itself, isn't the end of the world. We can teach you to fly. What is the end of the world is when your mind isn't on your flying.

"He says even when you are paying attention, you have a hard time with the collective. Cyclic's okay, and that's strange. Cyclic's the hardest. You're jerky on the collective, particularly with rolling the throttle on and off. But that's technical stuff, and it's between you and him.

"And, the next problem is your little meeting with Captain Gruese—smack dab in the middle of Van Story Street. Your mind is floating around in the clouds. That won't do. I imagine your hat on the wrong way was just part of your confusion, so I won't put you in for an Article 15 for being out of uniform on that. But I am sending you before the Elimination Board. I have no choice. Maybe you can explain it to them.

"Look, son, I'll be honest with you. This is a tough place. We're looking to weed out men who don't have leadership ability, even more than we grade flying skills—those can be learned, eventually. One of the major traits of those who can lead is concentration. When everything else is going to hell, our pilots fixate on their mission. *That's* what we bring out in our cadets. It's the difference between our military and most of the others in the world. I don't know if that can be learned from scratch. And, right now, you don't have it."

He was ordered to report the next morning to the same building. He asked around and was told there would be a tableful of officers, commissioned and warrant, and an enlisted stenographer. The scuttlebutt was that few men sent before the Board were granted a second chance. It was just another unemotional step in the winnowing process.

He put his hat on backward and took his pocketful of change to the PX. He had all afternoon, for it would be his last at Wolters.

When she answered the phone, and Lincoln paused in his usual way, Isabelle broke into sobs. "I prayed it was you. Oh, God, Lincoln, I miss you."

Barely able to make out what she was saying, he blurted, "Please, don't cry, Isabelle. I love you more than life. Come down here, and we'll get married. They let married couples live together at Fort Rucker during the second phase of flight training. I'll love you every day for the rest of my life, I swear." As he thought about what he'd said, his chest tightened, for it hit him like an artillery shell that he wasn't going to go to Rucker. He was headed straight to Viet Nam to tramp the paddies as grunt fodder for an army that considered men like him—poor farm boys and ghetto blacks—scarcely numbers, of no consequence to anyone on Earth, save, perhaps, their mothers.

There was another interruption for thirty-five cents, and as he reached into his pocket, he looked up and saw the colonel's sedan coasting down Van Story, trolling for errant soldiers. He yelled into the phone, "Gotta go, Isabelle. I love you."

Lincoln appeared at the prescribed time the next morning, the creases on his Army Tan Uniform pressed to knife blades thanks to Huber. The night before, Huber had grabbed Lincoln by the shirt and shook him. "Look, troop, I'm not letting' go of you until you make up your mind you're stayin' in this here shit-ass school."

Then Huber put on his dress uniform and pinned the actual DSC medal above his ribbons, slipped out of the barracks, and skulked to MP headquarters. He demanded to see the night duty officer, certain to be a green-tail second lieutenant. Huber virtually ordered the neophyte, who must have thought Huber had been awarded the Medal of Honor over the way he was strutting about, to issue him an iron and a can of spray starch. The lieutenant was so nervous, he began to raise his hand in salute when Huber grabbed the booty and headed for the door.

Lincoln's shoes were glistening. He had applied a coat of Crisco, also compliments of Huber, who had slipped into the mess hall at midnight. Lincoln calculated that by the time the grease had been absorbed into the leather, and the shoes had the finish of scuffed hunting boots, he would be on his way to

Viet Nam—and who cared—or reinstated, and he would declare his ruined low-quarters stolen and demand that he be issued a new pair.

At 8 A.M., he was ushered into a meeting room. Several officers in Class A greens sat at a long table. At the center was a major. Captains and warrant officers flanked him. Off to the side was an enlisted man who plunked away at a miniaturized typewriter.

The major cleared his throat. "Warrant Officer Candidate Friday, you have been brought before this Board to evaluate your fitness to remain in the United States Army Flight School at Fort Wolters, Texas. Are you aware of the workings of this board?"

"No, sir."

"Well, I will explain. Stop me immediately if you have any questions." He went on to submit the case against Lincoln, nearly word for word as the CO had presented it the day before. Lincoln was to be given a chance to speak on his own behalf, then be sent outside the room to wait, and finally called back in for the verdict.

Lincoln allowed that he understood the process and began his chronicle. He mentioned his love of flying; the years he practiced in his simulator; the loss of the appointment to the Air Force Academy; the months of physical therapy to meet the Army's overly cautious standards for rehabilitation; the eventual discovery that he had not broken his neck at all, that the doctors in Wilkes Barre had misdiagnosed a perfectly normal skeletal variation often seen in tall men; his graduation at thc top of his AIT class; and his refusal to accept an appointment to Officer Candidate School so he could apply to flight school.

The judges were silent, but their expressions softened, and after another minute, even the stenographer was at the edge of his seat. Lincoln decided to tell them about Isabelle and how that had deflected his attention.

The major asked, "Are you done?"

"Yes, sir."

"Are there any witnesses or documents you wish this Board to consider?"

"No, sir."

"Please take a seat outside, and we will call you when we are ready."

Five or six dreadful minutes passed on the wooden bench. The stenographer came out and spoke formally, "WOC, come in."

Lincoln stiffened at the thought that he was still being referred to as "candidate," and he smiled inside, but as he stood at rigid attention, the major did not order him to sit, or even stand at ease. His shoulders drooped.

"Warrant Officer Candidate Friday, this Board has made a decision on your future status at this facility. First, let me say that your journey to this school is impressive, and one I'm not sure we've ever before encountered. To put it plainly, you've got a lot of guts to have stood by your dream.

"On the other hand, this Board is not interested in your personal problems. All the good intentions in the world do not make up one iota for fact that you let matters of no military importance affect your performance to the point that you almost killed one of the best instructors this school has ever had. The helicopter is an unforgiving machine. Take your mind off of it for a split second, and you are doomed.

"Every one of us has family problems. Your private tribulations, well, to be frank, we don't give a damn about them when the lives of our troops are concerned. You may have heard that before." He stopped and looked directly into Lincoln's eyes.

"Yes, sir."

"It is the decision of this Board that you be returned to flight status as of tomorrow morning. It is our hope that you have learned a valuable lesson, and if you have, that you may someday pass on that message. You are on the strictest probation. If you make one major procedural mistake in the helicopter, or a minor one in your dealings with staff, in regard to your uniform, particularly, the direction of the bill of your utility cap; if you are found stumbling around post; or if you have not soloed by the end of next week, you will be released from this school immediately. Is that clear?"

"Yes, sir."

"Now, you've lost two days of training. You'll have to work just that much harder to make them up. You are confined to barracks—that means your room, better, your desk, until further notice. Take an hour of that time to make a decision about what you want in this world. Spend the rest of the time bent over your books, especially the chapter on autorotations..."

A warrant officer at the end of the table interjected, "Please!"

The major's lips curled up almost imperceptibly, and he spoke softly. "Son, you're a good man. You are the kind of person we want here, but it will be on our terms, and according to our rules, no matter how ridiculous or draconian they may seem to you. I trust you understand."

"Yes, sir. Thank you, sir."

They exchanged crisp salutes. Lincoln about-faced, the click of his heels nearly rattling the windows. He marched ramrod straight from the room, as if a guard at the Tomb of the Unknown Soldier. He did not see the men at the table look at each other and nod.

As he escaped the building, he exhaled and lowered his head. The shine on his low quarters had already dulled. A patina of Wolters' blood-red earth had settled into the Crisco. He laughed and made plans to bury them behind the barracks on the last day of school.

There would be no call to Isabelle. He planted himself at his desk that morning, and after writing his goals on the inside back cover of his flight manual, loosely lashed the blade of his GI entrenching tool, a short-handled shovel, to the left legs of his desk chair. He slipped the cardboard from a toilet paper roll around the end of the handle—a throttle—and smiled that he had created a reasonable collective. He fashioned a cyclic from Huber's entrenching tool and secured it to the front of his chair. For pedals, he filled his parade boots with the stripped off toilet paper, the only place he could hide evidence of what would have been a punishable waste of government property, then added socks and skivvies to the boots and laced them tightly. He arranged them under his desk, heels three inches apart, toes pointing in opposite directions, and fastened them to the floor with adhesive tape purloined from the barrack's first aid kit. He took his seat. With forefeet resting against the upper leather of the boots, he allowed himself a smile—they felt quite like real pedals.

The first simulation he carried out was the autorotation he'd flubbed. He did it so many times, his left wrist began to ache. He wrapped it in adhesive tape and did two more hours of autorotations, picturing the stage fields at Wolters. Then he imagined flying south of Wilkes Barre, each landing a feather light touchdown in the middle of the race course at Schroeder's farm. He dreamed of lifting off from the track and buzzing the main house, whooping curses at the old farmer who, in Lincoln's fantasy, ran after him, fist shaking in the air. He added landings at Fort Benning, imagining what the fields he'd drilled upon looked like from a thousand feet, from two thousand, and then from a mile above the Infantry School. When those images were crystal clear, when he could conjure terrain from above and below, he dropped his make-believe ship to five hundred feet and did a dozen autorotations from that perilous elevation. He went to his window during a break and drilled himself into picturing altitudes of fifty feet, the height at which one started pulling on control levers to cushion the fall and compose a graceful touchdown.

At 3 P.M. the next afternoon, the flight operations officer called the CO from the tower. "I don't know, sir, but the ship that Friday's in just did a bunch of damn near perfect autorotations. One looked like it was from a mile up, next from a hover, and a few from in between."

"Sure it wasn't Donovan doin' 'em?"

"Nah, sir, they were better than Donovan can do."

Donovan ordered Lincoln to land on a taxiway, and after touchdown, struggled out of the ship. He patted his student on the shoulder and smiled, "That was some nice flyin'. Take it around the pattern one time."

Lincoln's first solo hover began with a spring from the tarmac that brought him to a twelve-foot hover—he had not compensated for the lack of a passenger's weight. Lincoln's euphoria, though, blinded him to Mr. Donovan rolling eyes.

When Lincoln touched down, the colonel stepped up to the ship and opened the door. "Warrant Officer Candidate Friday, you did good, son." He turned to the gaggle of classmates who had drifted to the CO's staff car. "Time to dunk the hell outta him, men."

CHAPTER THIRTY-THREE

The instructors after the first solo were active duty pilots. All had served tours in Viet Nam—most, also, in Korea—and a handful had cut their teeth in World War II as fixed wing fighter pilots. As a caste of human beings, these were the least patient, most irritable warriors since the Huns. How a man could not squeeze a violently shaking machine into a skinny gap in a forest of old growth trees on a sloping mountain pinnacle was beyond their comprehension. "Christ almighty, WOC, get this goddamn helicopter into that clearing, *NOW*! Is there anything about that order you don't understand?"

WOC Friday drew a W-4 who'd been, rumor had it, a Marine PBY pilot in the Korean War. Lincoln was tremendously excited when that story surfaced, nearly unable to contain himself until the next morning when he'd meet the man. Lincoln was sure the new IP knew his science teacher, Mr. Wick. Hadn't Senator Scott told Lincoln how famous Mr. W. had been during the Korean War? The coincidence was eerie, but real, and Lincoln would spend the next fifty hours being trained by a man with whom he had an umbilical relationship.

"Who the hell do you think you're talking to, WOC? You think you can just make up a name, Klick, or something stupid like that, and think by kissing my ass you'll get some kind of easy time? Think again, WOC. You're already in boiling water around here, and you just turned up the heat."

Though Lincoln continued to remain in his room at night after the Elimination Board, he was not sure if the confinement had been decreed for the night of the hearing, until he soloed, or every night for the balance of the Wolters' phase. Huber's advice was, "Fuck 'em. Do what the hell you please. Who gives a shit?"

He still had interminable hours of extra work during those final months to make up for the two days he'd lost, and he kept to himself, at the books, tempted, but easily dissuaded from sneaking out to the PX for the payphones and Isabelle. He was sure she had vowed a deep love for him; he was sure she had heard him beg to marry her; he was sure he had had to hang up before she could say yes. He tried to accept that she had no way to call him, but he knew in his heart that letters would start coming through his mom.

His life had transformed. It looked as if he would go on with his class to Fort Rucker, Alabama, for the final phase of flight school, where they taught WOCs to fly the HUEY, the Cadillac of helicopters. He dreamed of both Isabelle and flying.

The CO, though, was watching him, and when Lincoln was flying solo all over Texas, the old man asked the major from the Elimination Board how it was possible to go from washing out to top of the class in less than twenty-four hours. He instructed the XO, the executive officer, to meet with Lincoln and find out exactly how he had done it. When the major reported back to the colonel and described the mock collective and boots, the old man shook his head and snarled, "I can just picture it. I give the order for a hundred-and-fifty men to sit in desk chairs wearing one pair of boots to stomp on their other pair. Word'll get out, as it always does, doesn't it, Major? The troops at Wolters are running around in scuffed footwear. And the brass at the Pentagon, you know how they are. They get a little hair up their ass, and the next thing you know, I'm relieved of command, and you aren't far behind. Major, let's be smart and keep this under our hats."

The WOCs had been so overworked after soloing, there hadn't been time to pursue their jumbled notion of international diplomacy. In fact, they rarely saw their Vietnamese colleagues, for the foreign men had been moved to a remote, rudimentary, World War I barracks shortly after the incident of the broken bottle of *nuoc mam.* The times they did see the foreign troops on the flight line, it was at a distance, and they counted only ten.

Stanky sidled up to Huber on the flight line and gave him a bump on the shoulder. "Eight, nine, ten. Gave those little assholes something to think about, didn't ya?"

Huber shoved him away and grunted, "Watch your ass, you're next."

Though the Vietnamese had begun the actual flying long before the WOCs had been given their demonstration flight, not one had soloed by the time Lincoln was tossed into the pool. Toward the end of the fourth week of flying, there were also twelve Americans who hadn't convinced their instructors they were ready. All but one, a twenty-year-old who'd had to leave for three days to attend his father's funeral, were on the bus to the airport before the sun set on the day of their Elimination Board. Now down to one hundred and four, the core class had been selected. They were called together, briefed on the next weeks of training, and then given the night off, but admonished not to range any farther than the PX.

Lincoln filled his pockets with change and steeled his heart to call Isabelle. As he walked from the barracks, a runner stopped him. "You Friday?"

"Yep."

"Follow me."

"Where we goin'?"

"XO wants to see you."

"About what?"

"Ask him."

Lincoln was led to the major's office and told to sit. Ten minutes later, the XO called him in and ordered gently, "Stand at ease, son. Friday, we got another problem child in your class. He escaped the Board today, and you will teach him to fly."

"But, sir…"

The man bristled, "But nothing, WOC. You're still on thin ice."

"Is this going to be every night, sir?"

"No, just one night, because you're going to make sure he solos tomorrow. I don't care if it takes all night. He will be flying alone within twenty-four hours. That is an order." Lincoln snapped back to attention and began to salute, but the major interrupted. "Oh, and use your own boots, not his. Yours are already scuffed. Don't need to see the destruction of any additional government property, do we?"

The man soloed the next morning. The CO was there to oversee the experiment. He quipped to the major, "I guess what that Friday guy did wasn't such a big deal. Apparently, anybody can do it. Hope to hell this kid didn't ruin *his* boots."

That night, Lincoln made plans to sneak to the phones and be back just minutes before lights out. As the men began to relax after chow, an announcement blurted from the PA that there was to be a mandatory meeting to provide details on a host of changes being initiated at Wolters. The agenda included a discussion of the sloppy dress by Viet Nam returnees and their profligate use of profanity, both critical transgressions that would no longer be tolerated at the flight school. The fort-wide assembly went on so long, most of the WOCs had long since drifted off in their seats when the CO belched, "That is all."

Those cadets still awake jumped up to salute. The major had unobtrusively moved to a position at the rear of the lecture hall, taken out a notebook, and was jotting down the names of the men who had not exploded to their feet. Lincoln, though fast asleep, was not ensnared. He was sufficiently startled by the commotion to bolt upright in his seat, but was tall enough to appear to be just a short soldier braced at attention.

The next morning, Lincoln was nearly comatose while tracking back to the airfield after an hour of flying solo over the Texas prairie. Seven miles from landing, he switched his radio over to tower frequency to announce his presence and request permission to enter the controller's airspace. He reported his position and was cleared into the pattern, but the controller broke away in the middle of a sentence to call another aircraft. At first, there may have been the trace of a smile in his voice as he addressed one of the H-23s hovering on the active runway. A few seconds later, though, his commands became so fast and brisk, Lincoln barely understood them.

The next directive from the controller was an octave higher and even faster. "Flight Cadet Nhu, you're lined up on the wrong runway, pointed in the wrong direction, and you are hovering dangerously high. For a start, get back down to three feet."

What Lincoln could discern of the pilot's reply was nasal, high-pitched, and might have been English. The controller snapped, "You are not cleared for takeoff. Fly off the runway. Now!"

The pilot declared, "Roger, this Nhu. I fly now off runway." And he did.

The controller barked, "Helicopter Green Three Six, I will not tell you again that takeoff is prohibited. You are accelerating. Slow to a hover immediately. You are lined up on the wrong runway, in the opposite direction of the flow of traffic. Everyone else is taking off *into* the wind. That is very important. Drop to three feet and hover off the designated runway and land beyond the hold line."

"Roger, this Nhu, I flying to takeoff!" The nose of Nhu's helicopter dipped, and his airspeed built.

"*Green 36, land your helicopter! That is an order!*" Or that is what Lincoln thought the man had screeched, for, even under the best of conditions, the engine and rotor clamor in a helicopter distorted nearly all communications.

"Roger, this Nhu. I fly takeoff like you say and clear to land."

The aircraft on final approach, toward which Nhu was advancing head to head, veered to the right. When Nhu lifted the nose a bit and caught sight of the oncoming helicopter, he jogged hard right, but kept his head turned to the aircraft he had just avoided, glaring at the moron landing in the wrong direction. Nhu maintained his blind climb, which placed him on a collision course with Lincoln. Lincoln looked down into Nhu's cockpit, hoping to make eye contact, but he could see only the side of the man's helmet. It struck Lincoln that the lone way to avoid a midair collision at this point was to drop below Nhu and hope the foreign cadet made no change in his rate of ascent.

Lincoln bottomed the collective, but didn't pull the nose up, knowing that he still had his engine and didn't need to use the wind to keep his rotor speed in the green arc. This wasn't an autorotation, it was an evasive maneuver, and a dangerous one. Helicopters do not like to become weightless. He dropped like a stone for three hundred feet. Though there was silence from the mortified controller, it proved to be the perfect tactic, and Nhu sailed above him by a good twenty-five feet.

The tower radioed Lincoln. The man was nearly breathless. "Blue Two Zero, that was a hell of a maneuver, impressive even for an IP. Turn left to a heading of zero-one-zero and fly the published missed approach. I'll call your inbound leg when we get things straightened out here."

Lincoln mumbled, "Wilco," and flew away from the airfield on the assigned compass heading. He slowed the H-23 to a near crawl to buy time, for he had no idea on earth what a published missed approach was or how one did it. But a few seconds later, Mr. Nguyen Van Nhu decided he was done with the day's curriculum, and he dropped in for a landing on a hover pad a quarter-of-a-mile from the runway. The controller called Lincoln, thanked him for his cooperation and astute flying, then had him turn back inbound and land.

The CO, XO, a platoon of instructors, and the man from the control tower raced out in half-a-dozen vehicles to apprehend Nhu. He was placed in the back of an MP sedan, which sped from the airfield toward Headquarters.

The CO drove over to Lincoln's helicopter. "Son, good piece of flyin'. Just don't let it go to your head."

The entire class of flight cadets was immediately confined to barracks until another lecture was hastily organized, during which a panel of senior instructor pilots and tower personnel refreshed all the aviators, and some of the ancillary personnel, about the directives air traffic controllers used before an aircraft was allowed to takeoff. The foreign students were not present.

Lockett waited a bit then snuck to the Vietnamese barracks to find out what had happened to Nhu. The man's cot was stripped, and his things were gone. The men appealed to Lockett to find where Nhu was hiding and tell him it was okay to come back; they forgave the loss of face he had visited upon them. He reassured in a mumble, "Don't worry. He'll probably be back by sunrise."

The next day, though, there were only nine foreign students on the flight line, and they spent the day on metal fold up chairs, facing into the sun, taking English lessons.

A full week passed before there was another night of lectures, this time on the importance of rolling the throttle to idle and placing the strap over the collective to hold it down when hopping out of a running helicopter. This disaster de jour had a gastronomic, not linguistic, etiology. The Vietnamese had all developed terrible stomach problems after their volunteer cook, Nguyen Van Dong, had surprised his countrymen with several dozen *nem*, a delicacy of minced raw pork dumplings normally wrapped in banana leaves, but in this case, corn husks.

The next morning, one of the men, Flight Cadet Nguyen Van Ding, was overcome with the need to evacuate his bowels. It happened while he was cruising at three thousand feet over the peaks, miles from main post. Reckoning it was a shorter trip to the top of a hill than the bottom, he managed to squeeze into a pinnacle clearing, but he sprang out of the ship and toddled, pants around his ankles, into the bushes before he had rolled the throttle to idle. He had also forgotten several other essentials the prudent pilot exercised before walking away from a live helicopter. One needed to roll the throttle all the way down, but also tighten the friction knob on the collective to hold it in the bottom, neutral, position. The ultimate safeguard was to fasten the collective to the floor with the bungee strap placed next to it for exactly that purpose. He had essentially left a car on a hill, engine running, in gear, with the emergency brake barely on. While he squatted in agony, cursing his life in America, the collective vibrated up a few inches, the throttle quivered open a few hundred more RPM, and the very light, pilotless machine lifted off. For the first second, it flew better than if a WOC had been at the controls, but a wind pushed it sideways, the rotors struck a tree limb, shattered, and the machine tumbled down the hill. Ding, his flight suit still unzipped, slid down the grade, hoping to use the radio to call for help, but the fire had already destroyed every millimeter of the aircraft, even melting the metal tubing of the hull into a crescent reminiscent of water buffalo horns. The smoke, though, was very black, and a rescue HUEY was on station before the man could crawl back up to the clearing.

Just eight souls were on the bus the next morning. Not one would sit near Dong the Cook, blaming him *not* for concocting an hors d'oeuvre made from raw pork, but for accepting the tainted ingredients with which the American military poisoned its own soldiers.

Still a letter did not come from Isabelle. Lincoln repeated their last conversation in his head a thousand times, parsing the dialogue until he could not remember what either of them had really said. Each iteration brought more doubt to his heart, and he began mistrusting that he'd heard her weep and say she had prayed he would call. Even the excuses he had invented over the weeks—that maybe she was scared to send letters through Miriam, that Miriam was secretly reading them, or that she had sent them directly to him, but the army had again misrouted them, or worse, the flight school was withholding any letter with a girl's handwriting to test his resolve—even those explanations no longer held water. He finally accepted the truth: she had said those things to avoid hurting him and to end the call as quickly as she could.

Over the next two weeks, he tried to call her, but the line was either busy or no one answered. He was so crushed, he went out with his friends to Mineral Wells, drank a dozen beers, and wound up in the back room of a tenement, in a stinking bed in a filthy room. The only thing he remembered of the night was a woman with a gooey washcloth wiping him off then running the rag between her legs. When he woke the next day at noon, he made a resolution to let Isabelle be. He would work to find himself, to straighten his path, and put as much effort into redirecting his heart as he had into learning to fly.

CHAPTER THIRTY-FOUR

Twenty weeks after arriving at Fort Wolters, Lincoln's class was dismissed with orders to report to Fort Rucker, Alabama. The final phase of flight school would commence in seven days. They would learn to use instruments to maneuver when the clouds were so thick, one could not see out of the aircraft. More importantly, the next phase included training in turbine helicopters, and Lincoln was especially relieved he'd not have to fly the H-23, the Hiller Killer, again. In the HUEY, the pilot set the throttle at the beginning of the flight and didn't have to adjust it again. In modern helicopters, the fuel was metered automatically. For Lincoln, it was to be the difference between trying to drive a standard transmission car with a frozen left foot and cruising in a hydromatic.

Huber owned a car and insisted Lincoln ride with him to Rucker. They planned to drive straight through, though the old Pontiac's transmission began to smoke in Shreveport, Louisiana. Lincoln laughed that he was the best Pontiac mechanic in the country, but Huber had not brought along a single tool, so they took a room in a fleabag motel, shared a fifth of bourbon, and vowed early in the evening not to rehash their broken love lives. Lincoln's resolve vanished at midnight, after Huber had passed out. He slipped out of the room to a payphone to try, for absolutely, positively, the last time, he swore to himself, to call Isabelle. Her line had been disconnected.

They were waiting outside the Pep Boys the next morning an hour before it opened. The clerk, just back from Viet Nam, had been a helicopter mechanic, and he called a friend in town who owned a transmission shop. The man brought the company truck and a helper, and within the hour they had opened the transmission, put in the part supplied by the Pep Boys' returnee, and replaced the burned transmission oil.

When Lincoln and Huber simultaneously pulled wallets from their back pockets, the clerk and the tranny mechanic laughed and pushed their hands away.

"You two just fly safe. Keep your heads down. No heroics, man, it ain't worth it. Trust me, I been there."

As the Pontiac rolled back onto the highway, Huber nodded to Lincoln, "Troop, I think, maybe, our fortunes have brightened."

They did not arrive at Rucker until midnight. A carburetor problem caused the big V-8 to guzzle fuel so fast, they nearly ran out on the motorway but managed to limp off and coast to a gas station at the bottom of an exit ramp. Lincoln unsealed the float chamber using a dime as a screwdriver, blew out the puddle of red Texas mud that had infiltrated what should have been the most pristine cubic inch of an engine, and they were back on the road.

At Rucker, as proto-officers, they were afforded a shabby room in a barracks that was designated a BOQ, Bachelor Officers' Quarters. It was far seedier than the motel they'd spent a couple of dollars to engage the night before, but they were so exhausted, they fell asleep on the unmade beds, using the pile of sheets and towels they'd been issued as pillows.

At breakfast, they got on line at the mess hall still so tired, they barely spoke. Lincoln slid his tray forward for a dollop of SOS but turned so abruptly when Huber screeched, "Oh, fuck me!" his elbow whacked the tray. It clanged to the floor. There was absolute silence, everyone's attention drawn to the chow line; even the seven Vietnamese troops sitting at a table in the far corner of the massive hall were on their feet to see what had happened. Huber forced his attention back to the stainless steel cauldrons of fresh eggs and home fries and bacon and sausage and SOS and buttered toast and grits swimming in butter, but sensing all eyes on him, he about-faced and marched out. After Lincoln policed the floor of his splashed shit on a shingle, he was sent back to the end of the line. When he finally filled his tray, he took it to the Vietnamese table. The men stood and shook his hand.

"Mr. Rinkin, you here now! Mr. Rocket here now?"

"Oh, Lockett, he'll be here in a couple of days. Hey, where's Mr. Dong?"

"Oh, he bad man. Okay to cook, but..."

Lincoln interrupted, "I know, but not okay to cook pork."

They laughed. "Oh, Mr. Rinkin know all about. No, Dong maybe he spy for Communit. His mother arrest in Saigon for being colonel VC. Funny thing, she work DLI then Wolter school, inter-peter, maybe long time ago. No good lady. No good son."

Lincoln smiled and asked, "Are you guys getting along all right? I mean, it looks like you're eating SOS and the rest of the stuff."

"Food okay. Get used to. Not good like Viet Nam food, but pretty good."

When they finished and stood to leave, Lincoln noticed one of the foreign cadets slip something into a paper bag and bootleg it like a quarterback. When the man passed Lincoln, he smiled to himself at the scent of rotting fish sauce.

Huber was still growling when Lincoln found him in the dayroom watching soap operas. He looked up at Lincoln and hissed, "Don't start with me, troop."

"I know, I know, but these guys are okay. They're on our side." He related the story of Dong's dismissal.

Huber laughed, "So, now, we're rid of Ding and Dong. Rest of 'em'll be gone soon. 'Nother one of your Army's great plans gone astray."

At mail call the next week, on the first day of classes, the company clerk shouted Lincoln's name, and his heart shot into a wildly rapid beat. He could tell from across the room that the letter was in his mother's hand, but it wasn't until he reached for it did he realize it was quite thin. Miriam had seen Isabelle in a car, but hadn't been able to tell who was driving. At least, she thought it was Isabelle, but when she asked around, no one seemed to know. She reported that Mr. Schroeder had suffered a stroke and was being pushed around town in a wheelchair by his wife, who had to stop every two or three paces to wipe the drool from his chin. "See, Lincoln, there is a God."

The married WOCs were permitted to live with their wives in the Rucker phase. There were billets for these families, but with the massive buildup of troops for Viet Nam, housing on many bases was at a premium, and couples were given additional pay to find apartments off base. Stanky was one of the few married WOCs, and his wife joined him in a trailer between the city of Enterprise and Fort Rucker. On the Friday before classes began, Stanky and his new bride sat with Lincoln and Lockett at a pizza parlor near the PX. As the sun began to set, they went their separate ways.

A woman in a sweatshirt and a hat walked thirty yards behind the Stankys and waited until they got into their station wagon. She jumped into a beater car and followed them to their trailer. She waited a minute, took off her hat, fixed her hair, and knocked on the sheet metal door. Both Stankys came to see who it was. When she told them why she there, they opened the door wide and dragged her inside.

The three sat and drank beer. "The problem is, I don't know if Lincoln hates my guts or still wants to get married. Could you ask him if he wants to come to the Rawls Hotel tomorrow? I mean, just so we can talk?"

Stanky laughed. "You mean can I ask him in about twenty minutes? He'd be nuts to pass on you." He turned to his wife, "Sorry, Sweetie," then back to Isabelle. "He's got a good head on his shoulders. He's no fool. Hardest working guy I ever saw."

"So, he's doing okay? He told me he was flunking out."

"Well, he finished third in the class, and that was after he had to make up some days when he flipped out about somethin' or another."

Isabelle lost the color in her face then sat up straight and protested that Stanky didn't need to go back to Rucker that night; the next day would be fine. "It's been eight months; another day is okay."

"No, it ain't."

He grabbed a few bottles, and Isabelle asked gently, "Mr. Stanky, three more beers?"

"Yeah, two for your man, and one for the taxi driver. Shoot, Lincoln'll tell y'all, alcohol only counts in helicopters. This is Alabama, Doll. You're in the Deep South now. Around here, y'all get pulled over if y'all *don't* have a beer in your hand, and 'specially if y'all ain't got one for the cop."

After the tires squealed and gravel sprayed against the trailer's foil sides, the two women sat quietly until six empties sat on the coffee table. Isabelle's eyes reddened as she mumbled, "I wouldn't be surprised if Lincoln refused to get in the car, and he told your husband that he never wanted to see or hear from me again. I deserve it. I treated him so badly, and the whole time, I thought I was protecting him. I screwed up, and now I'm dragging you guys into it."

"Don't you give it another thought, Honey. You're our first friend here, and my husband, oh, I love saying that, he talked about Lincoln a lot. How his mind was somewhere else for a while, and he had all that trouble..." She stopped herself and stared into the eight square feet that served as the kitchen. "Look, I'm going to make a couple of pork chop sandwiches. Got some deep-fried okra, too. Want that on the sandwich, or on the side."

Isabelle relaxed and laughed. "I don't think I've ever had okra. What is it?"

"Girl, you really are a Yankee, aren't you?"

"Pennsylvania. Is that bad?"

"Oh, my gosh, no, I just never met anyone from a mile farther north than Dahlonega. That's in Georgia. Smoky Mountains. More beautiful than you can imagine."

"Maybe someday. Maybe, if Lincoln sends me away, I'll drive through there on my way to wherever."

"'Fraid not, Honey. Only time y'all be leavin' here'll be with your man. I know 'bout these things."

Isabelle's eyes clouded, and her new friend slid over on the couch, put her arm around Isabelle's shoulder, and held her tight.

When Stanky got back to Rucker, there was a fire on main post, and he had to park a mile from the BOQ. He went on foot to the mess hall and found Lincoln sitting with Huber, who was groaning, "The gooks already got their familiarization flight in the HUEY, and we gotta go through a bunch of recips still. Did you know that? You gotta learn instruments in the same old shit we flew at Rucker. Fuckin' Army."

Lincoln laughed, "Hey, sooner they get checked out in the HUEY, the sooner they go home. That should give you a hard on just thinkin' about it."

Huber shook his head. "I guess I'm going to have to beat the wiseass outta ya yet, huh?"

They looked up surprised as Stanky trotted to the table. Lincoln laughed, "What's up, man? She ditch you already?"

Huber hit the table with his palm. "See, a wisenheimer. What'd I tell ya?"

Stanky was very serious. "No, look, Friday, I need your help at the trailer. You're a farmer, right?"

"No, I'm a fuckin' nuclear engineer. Tell 'em, Hubert."

"Come on, man. You know plumbing, right?"

"Some. How can I help ya?"

"My place is flooding. I don't even know where to turn off the water main. Could you come out and take a look?"

Lincoln thought for a second and nodded. "Okay, no problem. Let's get it taken care of before Monday."

Huber put his fork down and grunted, "I'll go along with you guys. Give Friday here some pointers."

Stanky's eyes opened so wide, Huber laughed, "You look like a some kinda flyin' bat. You sure you don't want me along, hold your hand?"

"Nah, that's okay, man. My car's only got room for two—still full of our furniture. You're a big guy, Huber, broad shoulders. You won't fit. You just stay here and relax. You were in the Nam and all that…" Stanky turned and dashed for the door.

Lincoln shrugged and chuckled, "Army really knows what they're doing when they pick a WOC, huh?"

At the car, Lincoln shook his head at the empty station wagon. Stanky mumbled, "Just trust me, man." He handed Lincoln a beer, and they sped south toward Enterprise. Neither spoke for a few moments, but Stanky finally sucked in a breath and, looking straight ahead, asked with a quaver, "So, Friday, you got a girlfriend, married?"

"No, man. Married to the helicopter."

Stanky laughed too hard. "I mean, you ever have a girl?"

"Yeah, long time ago. Didn't work out. Great gal, but she figured she could do a lot better than me."

"What was she like? I mean, do you ever think about her?"

"Tryin' not to."

"Well, I mean, what if she just showed up? I mean, havin' a girl here. That make you happy?"

"Stanky, what the hell are you talking about?"

"Just wonderin', man"

"What's goin' on?"

"I don't know. Just met this lady. Me and my wife. Said she wanted to get to know a pilot. Just thinkin', you might be game. She's cute, man. Just wanted to make sure you ain't spoken for."

Lincoln glared at Stanky. He was about to demand Stanky tell him what he had planned, maybe a foursome, or worse, a threesome with Stanky's new wife, but they pulled into the trailer park, and Stanky jammed the car to a stop thirty yards from his single-wide. Lincoln was still glaring when Stanky flew out and jogged to the trailer. His wife looked out the window and called over her shoulder, "You wait here, Honey."

She met Stanky just outside the door. "Well, what'd he say?"

"I don't know. He didn't."

"But that's him in the car, right?"

"Yep."

"Well, why did he come if he didn't want to see her?"

"I didn't tell him she was here."

She threw her arms into the air with frustration and shouted, "You didn't?"

"Well, sort of, I did, but not really."

Lincoln sprang from the car, his face tight with irritation. He started toward the two of them. Isabelle, who had not been able to see into the car with the setting sun in her eyes, burst through the door and ran toward Lincoln. He stopped short, stared, and felt his knees wobble. She threw out her arms to steady him, but he gathered himself, stood erect, and reached out to brush the tears from her cheek with the back of his hand. They did not touch or kiss, seconds flowing as they stared at each other.

Lincoln mumbled, "I'm dreaming."

"No, I am. I am. Is this real?"

Lincoln bent forward and kissed her lips so gently, she wasn't sure he had. She opened her eyes, screamed, and jumped into his arms. As he spun her 'round, the Stankys embraced. The two couples came together slowly. Isabelle and Lincoln were tugged into the trailer and pushed onto the couch. There wasn't much conversation until Stanky's wife sat up straight in her tattered recliner. "Well, why don't we take a walk and let these folks talk about things."

Stanky giggled, "Nah, let's have another beer."

She stood and grabbed him by the ear.

Isabelle and Lincoln spoke softly for a few moments and agreed to go to her hotel, but they swore to each other they would do nothing but talk. They swore it.

Isabelle drove them to the Rawls in Enterprise, the finest lodging in the county. She told him she'd chosen it for the most important moment of her life. He laughed, "Mine, too."

There was a bottle of red wine in the room, but they stood face to face and swore solemnly a third time they would do nothing but talk. They vowed it for a fourth as she poured the first glass. When the bottle was drained, Lincoln shot off the couch. "You wait here, Isabelle."

He grabbed his wallet and yelled over his shoulder as he flew through the door, "Don't leave town."

At the little store in the lobby, he perused the shelf of cigars, chose the fattest, and ran back to the room. Isabelle giggled as she took another bottle of wine from her suitcase. Lincoln grinned, but then groaned, "Oh, my God!" watching her pull the cork free.

As she turned to the sideboard to fill the glasses, Lincoln pulled the cigar from his pocket, opened the metal container, slipped the band off very carefully, and tried it on his pinky. When she faced back, the wine sloshing a bit, he took the glasses from her, put them on the coffee table, and dropped to a knee.

"Isabelle, I love you. I missed you more than you will ever know. I don't want to miss you again. Will you marry me?" He took her left hand and slipped the cigar band onto her ring finger.

She dropped to her knees and was barely able to form the words, "Will *you* marry *me*?"

They both cried as he carried her to the bed. Their clothes were off well before their bodies touched the crisp sheets. They made love on their backs, on their sides, standing, kneeling, and in every other position between the ceiling and the thickly carpeted floor.

When they were done, they hauled themselves back onto the bed and twisted their sweating bodies into a perfect sphere. Before falling off to sleep, Lincoln spoke broodingly. "Sweet Isabelle, we screwed up. Bet we're back to square one."

"Don't fret. That's not going to happen again. I'm on the pill."

"Why? How did you know you were going to find me? And maybe I would be too scared to, you know."

"Uh huh."

They slept nude, wrapped together, unmoving, until after ten the next morning, when they made love again. It took them an hour to dress and leave for breakfast. The afternoon was spent searching for a rooming house Isabelle could rent until they married, and then they went back to Rucker to talk to a chaplain. She claimed to be Lutheran, like Lincoln, to avoid the humiliation of begging a priest to marry them and have the service performed at the back of the church. The man agreed to do it two Saturdays hence.

Stanky gave away the bride; his wife was the bridesmaid. Huber showed up in his Dress Blues and stood with Lincoln as best man. Lockett sat with the Vietnamese soldiers and translated. When the ceremony was over, everyone shook hands, even Huber with the foreigners.

For a wedding gift, the guests bought the newlyweds tickets to the theater in Enterprise, where Elvis Presley was performing that night in honor of the soldiers at Rucker. Huber called ahead and got word to the producers that Lincoln, a pilot on his way to Viet Nam, and his brand new wife would be in the audience. When they arrived at the ticket kiosk, the agent took them into the theater through a back door and down a dark hallway. A moment later Elvis, in full regalia, exploded from his dressing room, shook both their hands, and invited them in.

"Sure proud of ya flyin' those whirly birds. I was in the Army, ya know. Germany. Got a lotta respect for you guys." There was a soft knock on the door, and Elvis smiled. "Hey, looks like it's time to go to work. Someone's gotta pay the heat and light. God bless, and you keep your head down. See y'all when you get back." He patted Lincoln's shoulder and bowed slightly to Isabelle.

They were directed to front row center seats, and after "Love Me Tender," Elvis asked Isabelle and Lincoln stand. He introduced them then led the applause.

Over the next weeks, they moved into housing on post and bought a German Shepherd, Zeke. Lincoln spent every second he wasn't in the helicopter with Isabelle. He reveled in the flying, and Isabelle reveled in seeing him so happy. It did not matter that he got home late most nights, for they would make love then loll in bed as Lincoln told her of the HUEY's super-sensitive controls and how, more than once, he had been forced by the IP to weave a pencil between his fingers. "Hurts like hell if you grab the cyclic too hard. You know what I mean?"

"Oh, yeah, hate it when that happens."

At the end of nine months of flight and military training, Miriam stood to pin on Lincoln's warrant officer bars. The next day, Isabelle pinned on his wings. There wasn't a hint that Isabelle's parents disapproved of the marriage, and Isabelle and Lincoln promised they'd have a full wedding back in Wilkes Barre within the next few months.

A few days later, back in Pennsylvania on leave, Lincoln received a telegram from the Department of the Army. His assignment to a newly formed regiment in Maryland had been rescinded. He was, instead, ordered to join the 36th Assault Helicopter Company in Viet Nam. He was to report in three weeks. Isabelle and Zeke moved in with her parents.

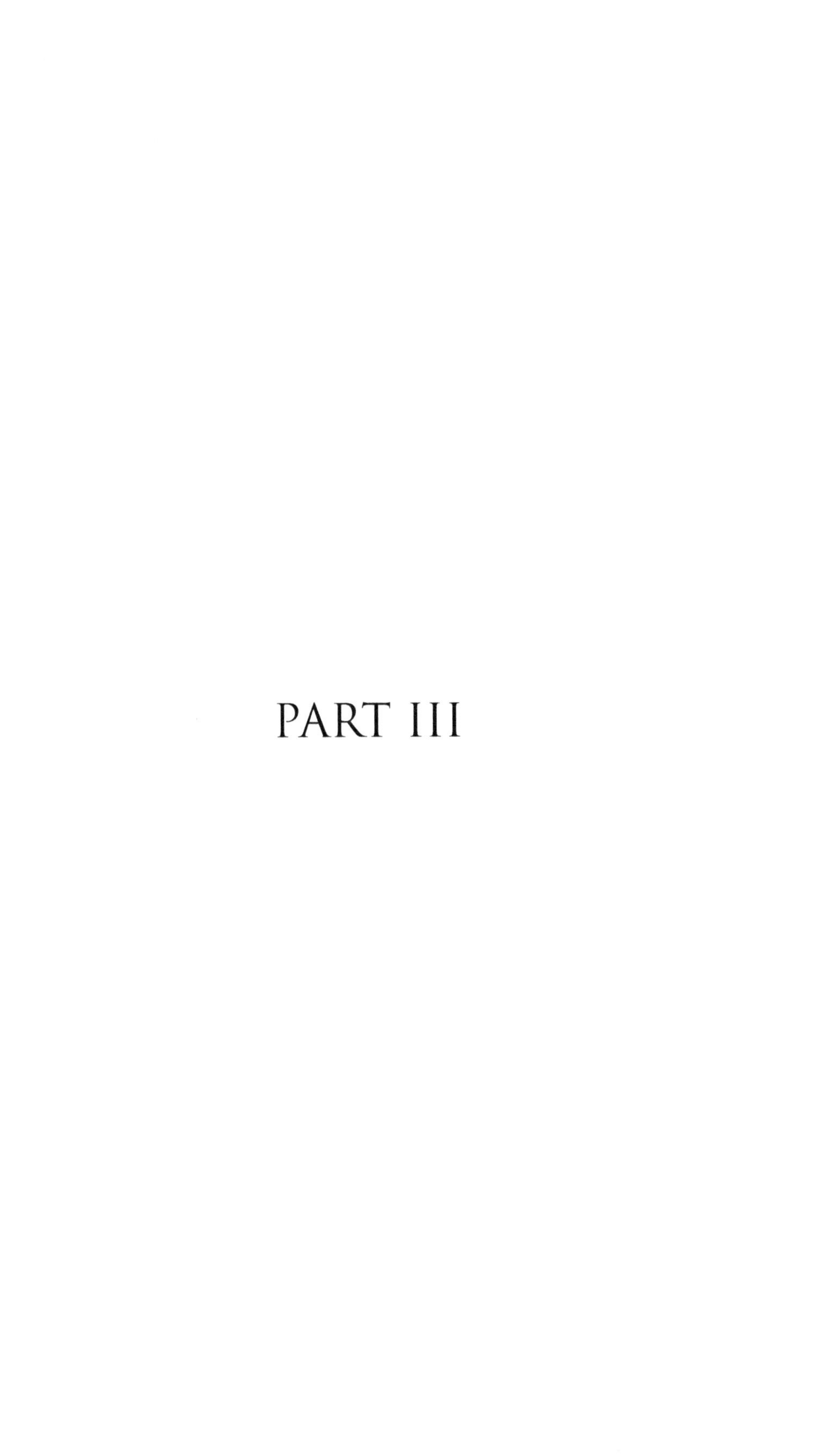

PART III

CHAPTER THIRTY-FIVE

36th Assault Helicopter Company
Mekong Delta
Republic of Viet Nam

The 36th's digs were in one corner of a neat, square mile of red earth cut from the Michelin Rubber Plantation in the Mekong Delta. The nearest town was My Tho. Though they were forty miles south of Saigon, the unit operated nearly the length of the country. Lincoln's helicopter company was commanded by a senior major, who, though a pilot, spent most of his time on the ground putting out the fires stoked by his fifty or so pilots, and as many enlisted crew members. With ancillary, non-flying personnel, cooks, armorers, and supply sergeants, there were often two hundred names on the unit's DD-1, the Morning Report.

Lincoln arrived with six other pilots, the largest number of aviators to report in one day in the history of the unit. Lincoln was the least experienced, but because they had been lined up by height, and because Lincoln stood a head above the rest of them, he was the first called into an office for an interview with the XO.

The captain looked up from an open file on his desk. "Says here, you did okay in flight school. Finished near the top of your class."

"I think Number Three, sir."

"So you figure you're a pretty good pilot, huh?"

"No, sir."

"Who was the best of your class, in your humble opinion, and why?"

"Troop named Huber, sir."

"Why do you refer to him as a 'troop', Friday?" He had used fingers to make quote marks.

"Well, sir, he was prior enlisted. Got the DSC here in Nam and then won the Soldier's Medal back at Rucker, sir."

The second part of the sentence piqued the XO's interest. "Sit down, son, and tell me about it."

"Well, sir, he was in a 55 when one of the B Models lost its engine on a practice autorotation, which turned into a real autorotation, and the IP must have had a heart attack…"

"Not surprised to hear that. Was he one of the old guys?"

"Yes, sir, almost forty, from what I heard."

"Ancient. Go ahead."

"The student pilot was one of the Vietnamese kids they sent over to go through the school."

"No wonder the guy almost died."

"Did die, sir."

"Jesus. Okay, continue."

"My friend, Huber, he was the first to see the smoke, so he dropped in next to the ship; and no matter the fire, he ran into the aircraft and saw the student struggling against his seat belts that he forgot to unbuckle. From what I heard, the flames were just about to engulf him. He could see that the IP was already dead. He knows about these things, sir, and he pulled the student free and went back to extract the IP. It just wasn't right to leave him there.

"Huber got his face burned a little. Some of the upperclassmen said it was an improvement."

"Assholes."

"Yes, sir. One wrist was pretty bad, but it was his left, his collective hand. When I graduated, he was just getting out of the hospital, and he was going to repeat the Rucker phase to see if he could handle it."

"Hope he does. We need men like him."

"Oh, he will, sir."

"Okay, Friday, back to the business of war. We need to get all new pilots trained up in the right seat first. Let me warn you, it may take months before we get a spot for you as aircraft commander, but the good news is that the more experience you get on the right, the better chance of making it through the year. At first you'll be itchy to find the little commie bastards and rain hot lead down on their malevolent asses, but it won't be long before that phase passes, and you'll be happy when we send you out to deliver beer and mail.

"We want full concentration every second you're flying, no hot dogging, no heroics; you just spend your time trying to do it one better than the last time. You do that, you'll be surprised. Instead of doing insertions way up at four feet, and patting yourself on the back, you'll be cursing yourself if you're an inch over a foot. Be able to use the distance between your skids and the ground to strike the official one-foot stick that's at the Naval Observatory, or wherever the hell they keep it.

"I'm gonna put you in with Bob Roetchsoender. W-4. Best pilot I've ever seen. You think he's in his rack asleep in the barracks, and maybe he is. You make your approach into here three knots too fast, and somehow he knows; and he's out of the barracks, and his arm's around your shoulder, and he's sayin', 'Friday, good to see ya. Hey, on those approaches, we'd like to see thirty knots. Makes it a lot easier for the guys in the tower to sequence arrivals and departures.'"

As an FNG, a Fuckin' New Guy, or peter pilot, as fresh aviators were known, Lincoln was assigned a corner room at the end of a rickety, single-story BOQ. It was less than thirty square feet. Each tenant was issued a five gallon Gerry can to fill with water from a five-hundred-gallon tank on wheels that sat outside Lincoln's window. He was pleased that he didn't have to walk far for water, but the tank was also a gathering spot for the pilots, who assembled there to brush their teeth and bullshit. The din went on from long before dawn to long after midnight.

The toilet was a four-holer outhouse just feet from his other window. He believed that, too, would make his life easier, but it was a hope shattered when, overwhelmed by the heat, he opened both unscreened windows. That launched a wraparound scourge: added to the yacking of his associates was the odor of their GI excrement, which wound up being less toxic than the daylight swarm of flies that took the shortcut through his room from the crapper to the stagnant puddles under the water trailer, and the clouds of anopheles mosquitos born and raised in those puddles, who waited until dusk to take flight. Louder even than the insect drone and whine, and the human bullshitting, were the taunts of compatriots congregated at the water tank, who demanded Lincoln close his windows to stifle the noxious cross draught.

The water in Lincoln's Gerry can was freezing in the morning. Shaving in it was more painful than shaving dry, so Lincoln hung the can upside down from the ceiling and slid his tiny field desk two feet under it. He liberated a four-foot length of copper fuel line from the maintenance shack, ran it down from the Gerry can, rolled the lower half of the tubing into a flat coil, and left the last foot of copper straight. He laid the coiled segment against a hot plate and closed off the tip with a piece of neoprene tubing pinched shut with a paper clip. Just minutes after plugging in the hot plate, he had a washbasin full of running hot water.

His pleasant mornings lasted for several days, until he returned late one afternoon to find the entire contraption gone, Gerry can and all. When he complained, a lieutenant, the unit fire marshal, told him it had been confiscated as an ignition hazard in the paper-thin, wooden barracks.

A week later, Lincoln was walking through the commissioned officers' BOQ and passed an open door. He glanced in to find out how the upper crust lived and saw his thermodynamic apparatus, including paper clip, erected by the window. He asked around and found the room belonged to the fire marshal. When Lincoln challenged him, the lieutenant explained arrogantly that *his* room was equipped with a fire extinguisher. "And what were you doing snooping around my stuff, anyway?"

Each room had a wired, crank field telephone that rang at night when a pilot was needed. The problem was, most of the phones were on the same line, and the system rang constantly. If a peter pilot had been asleep and too groggy to make out the name being ordered to the flight line, he had to get up, ask around, and hope someone else had heard correctly. More than once, Lincoln was in his flight suit, boots barely laced, in the right seat, getting ready to start the turbine engine when the aircraft commander hopped in with another pilot and asked Lincoln what the hell he was doing there.

Meals were served in a clean, airy, screened mess hall. The cooks were all US soldiers, but the vegetable peelers and dish washers were locals, mostly young women, who the GIs behind the counter chased around as if dogs in heat. The lower ranking officers often had to stand on line and wait until the servers were done propositioning the women, who sat in the back over tubs of potatoes and carrots. The senior officers had their own little room off the main hall and were served from a menu by a contingent of draftees too delicate to be sent to the front lines.

Lincoln's first flights were milk runs down to Saigon to pick up treats for the senior officers: cognac, Cuban cigars, and white linen tablecloths. Chief Roetchsoender was happy for the light duty, and he was the only one the CO could trust to fly into Saigon and not disappear for hours into the brothels. Lincoln's helicopter company was attached to an infantry brigade, and, occasionally, their commanding officer, a full colonel, sent a helicopter to the harbor in Saigon to land on the fantail of a ship, pick up a secret package or two, and fly back to headquarters.

On one of those sorties, the chief schooled Lincoln in the radio procedure critical to weave through Saigon's complex, treacherous airspace. He guided his student through the ridiculously steep approach to the boat, and when Lincoln finally spotted the tiny space the chief was pointing to on the fantail, he had slowed to the point that the helicopter was essentially at hover speed, the tail section of the aircraft swinging left and right, doing the HUEY shuffle, as he over-controlled the pedals in his fright.

The chief laughed when Lincoln called over the intercom, "That boat's bouncing up and down. What do you recommend?"

"I recommend you put it down on that big 'H'. You know, the one everybody else lands on."

Lincoln tried to work the collective up and down to match the pitch and heave of the landing pad, but he got out of sync for just an instant, there was a bang, and the chief stole the controls and jammed the collective to the floor. That ended the flight. He said nothing to Lincoln but put his fingers melodramatically into his mouth to count teeth.

Lincoln's head dipped in contrition. The man looked over and smiled. "No problem, Mr. Friday. They don't teach you how to land on moving targets in flight school. Just one of about ten thousand vital moves you're gonna have to learn on the fly. No pun intended. Just hang in there and add each experience to your playbook." Lincoln nodded sheepishly. "I'm serious. Go back tonight and write down the approach and try to remember how you were working the collective when that little blip in your flying nearly knocked me unconscious."

There was laughter over the intercom from the door gunners, and the chief snapped, "Quiet down, or I'll have him do it again. Or, maybe, MacClenny, you wanna scoot up here and give it a try?"

"Hey, Chief, you serious?"

"You see, Mr. Friday, what I've had to deal with?"

On the trip back to basecamp, Chief Roetchsoender called over the intercom, "Mr. Friday, let's do an autorotation, just for practice."

Lincoln lifted his head to nod, but the throttle had been rolled to idle before his chin could drop. His left hand flew to bottom the collective; his right drew the cyclic back until it was nearly buried in his gut. All of it was done before the chief's next heartbeat. Lincoln guided the ship toward the massive, open field directly to their front. At five hundred feet, he called out the algorithm in minute detail, and within seconds, the chief rolled the throttle back on and turned to Lincoln. "Okay, you've got me convinced. Nearly broke my damn wrist, you dropped the collective so fast, and the cyclic? Jesus, whacked me in my stomach. Got a hernia or somethin'. Gotta go on sick call along with MacClenny back there, who needs to see a psychiatrist. You better hope this doesn't wind up in surgery, Mister Friday. Now fly me home."

Lincoln was turned loose the next morning to fly as co-pilot for a W-2 who had been in-country for eight months. Though there were regulatory limits on how much time a pilot was allowed at the controls, the man had already logged over one thousand hours. He had also survived far longer than the average pilot, who, it was estimated, would be at the stick for only four or five months before he was killed or wounded.

The first day they flew together, the XO granted the venerable W-2 a vacation by letting him fly replacements, mail, and beer, "ass and trash," out to grunts in the Mekong Delta. After they dumped their cargo, he ordered Lincoln to fly east toward the South China Sea and land on a secluded beach. The crew skinny dipped for ten minutes until one of the door gunners swam into a school of jelly fish, and his face puffed to twice its usual size. The aircraft commander ordered them aboard and was airborne in seconds. Ten minutes into the flight, he looked back at the gunner and changed course from Normandy Basecamp and its sickbay to the evacuation facility in Vung Tao, twenty miles up the coast. There would be fewer questions at a hospital.

He was wrong. An administrator at the 93rd Evacuation Hospital, a first lieutenant, stood the chief up against the wall. "Food allergy, my ass. This is jelly fish envenomation. I know about you pilots and your afternoons on the beach. We don't have the time or the staff to be treating not-line-of-duty problems here. You're the man's superior officer; he's your responsibility, and his treatment's going to come out of your pocket."

The chief, at semi-attention, spoke past the lieutenant's shoulder. "Hey, sir, let me tell you, sir, I am way past me warning you rear echelon mother fuckers that if you fuck with the bull you get the horn. That phase of my stay here ended after week fuckin' one." He glanced up at Lincoln, who had drifted a few feet back and stood behind the non-inflated door gunner. The pilot jerked his eyes, to draw Lincoln to his side, then took a step toward to the lieutenant. He managed to switch places with the officer then herded the man along the wall, around the corner, and into an empty hallway.

"You look here, asshole, mother fuckin', un-rated REMF, when I bring you a casualty of this here war, you drop to your pussy, faggot knees, give me a blow job, and then cure the mother fucker." He grabbed his crotch and rubbed it up and down. He shot Lincoln another look, and his new co-pilot clutched his own groin. The healthy door gunner pushed between the two pilots and began rubbing away. A moment later, the sick crewman wobbled to the periphery, and the four closed the semicircle around the lieutenant. As the last millimeter of a perimeter was established, and the four combatants were hammering away at their crotches, the lieutenant jammed his back against the wall and let go a fart that rumbled the corridor.

The aviators began howling; even Jelly Fish nearly dropped to his knees. The aircraft commander swung his chin over his shoulder toward Lincoln and boomed, "Tonto, our work here is done."

They trotted to the ship, checked to make sure Jelly was breathing, opened the first aid kit, and fed him six of the twelve aspirins and all six of the antihistamines tablets. Halfway through the flight, the aircraft commander glanced back and laughed. "You look like a fuckin' puffer fish. You ever seen one of them things? They eat that shit in Japan. I know, man. I was stationed there. Colonel's pilot, until some un-rated RLO screwed with me when I took my girlfriend, Yumi, up and gave her a couple of minutes at the stick.

"I hate them unrated asshole officers. Never been to flight school. In a word, fuckin' worthless."

From the back of the helicopter, the well door gunner grunted, "That's two words, Chief."

"Whatever you say, professor. Now, Jelly," he turned to look at the casualty, "when we get in, you take off your harness and pretend to fall out of the ship right onto your face. That'll explain the whole thing. Shit, who knows, might buy you a day off, maybe even a Purple Heart."

There was no answer from Jelly because he was no longer conscious, a victim, not of the disease, but of the cure. In fact, his face had returned to normal, but his brain was pickled in Benadryl. The pilot called for the medics to meet them at the flight line, and after the man was carted off, the aircraft commander owned up to the XO about the antihistamine, but claimed it was administered after the door gunner was overwhelmed by a swarm of local insects when they were taking off after delivering their trash to the grunts. Lincoln stood in the background and nodded during the interrogation. The XO looked up at him one last time, and Lincoln smiled, "That's the way it happened, sir."

When Jelly came to, he pissed and moaned about a headache for a day, and then for a week about constipation.

Lincoln was shuttled to different aircraft commanders over the next couple of months, each watching and evaluating him. He was beginning to fly insertions, and the command pilots gave him more and more time at the stick. On his fifth mission into a hot landing zone, the VC were close enough to track him inbound with light arms fire. It was the first time he saw bits of Plexiglas fly off the canopy, and he wondered how the enemy could be such poor shots, or how the Lord had placed him in just the right locus of space to spare his life.

When he got back to basecamp and was checking the damage, the mechanic called Lincoln over and showed him the accumulation of spent AK-47 lead under the seat. He had been protected by the thick piece of steel boiler plate that sat under his butt. He wrote a very loving letter home to Isabelle that night but did not mention he was no longer doing the beer runs.

CHAPTER THIRTY-SIX

Isabelle had taken a job as a nursing assistant at Wilkes Barre Hospital. They put her on the general surgery floor, and within weeks, she was an acting circulating nurse in the operating room. With it had come a pay raise, and she increased, despite their protests, the amount she gave her parents for rent. But it was as far as she could go without a nursing degree, and she began to take courses at Penn State's local campus again.

She enrolled in physiology. Her lab instructor was a diminutive man, John Rosemary, a graduate student on loan from Penn State's main campus. Though Isabelle wore the thin wedding band Lincoln had bought at the PX at Rucker, Rosemary stood just an inch behind her during the first session, and in little more than a whisper asked if she was married, or if she was wearing the ring to keep guys away.

She turned and smiled broadly but warily, "Oh, very married, and to a great guy."

There was a humph, and a second later, she thought she felt something touch her behind, though ignored it and went on setting up the day's experiment.

In the middle of the next session, he wandered back. "So, where's this husband of yours? No one's ever seen him. He around?"

She turned quickly this time to face him and caught his hips moving toward her as if to grind at her rear end. She gasped but quieted and spoke down, an inch from his face. "My husband, if you must know, is in Viet Nam. He's a helicopter pilot. Any more questions?"

Rosemary stood stunned for a moment but quickly sneered, "Yeah, well, how many babies has he killed? He eat any of 'em?"

She tried to remain poker-faced, but her façade broke. The months of fear, of loss, her husband doing the most dangerous job in the war, maybe on Earth, all of it surfaced, and she was shocked at how fast her fury rose, how the pressure in her head went from a controllable fester to nuclear proportions. While Rosemary was, as a graduate student teaching Bio 201, exempt from the draft, she had no idea what Lincoln's life had become. Was he ever out of harm's way for an hour or two, maybe on the weekends? Was there even such a thing as a weekend in war? It was daytime at home and dark in Asia. Was he in the middle of a night resupply or dustoff mission? Walter Cronkite often shook his head and reported those missions as the most demanding of the ridiculously treacherous maneuvers pilots were called upon to do a dozen times a week.

With the vulnerability of not knowing whether her worst fears had materialized, that the news would be there to greet her when she got home, a bolt of rage tore through her. Rosemary saw the venom in her eyes and took a step back in retreat, but Isabelle's palms rose, and she shoved him in the chest. He stood motionless for several seconds, then stepped back and became entangled in a stool, arms sweeping wildly as he fell onto his back. As he hit the floor, several full beakers crashed, soaking him with foul-smelling chemicals.

He rose unsteadily and howled, "Get out of my classroom! I just failed you in this course. You will *never* become a nurse."

She sprang for the door at the back of the lab and was in the hall before his words reached her. She ran into the road crying. At first, she turned left and headed at an unsteady jog for the administration building, but was gripped with fear at the thought of what she had done, and so reversed course and stumbled in the other direction toward her car. She drove home and sat in the driveway, the engine running, until her mother came out. Kerrith Dalton's face hardened at just the first few words of the tale, and she drew Isabelle from the car into the house and urged her onto the couch.

She poured two glasses of wine and in a few minutes, with the whole story on the table, Isabelle sighed, "I hope I broke his neck."

Kerrith laughed, "If you didn't, your dad will. This little bastard will cease to exist within the next few hours." She called her husband at the plant, and he was in the driveway and out of the Olds 98, it seemed, before the phone was in the cradle.

He called the Wilkes Barre campus, but the dean would not talk to him on the grounds that an investigation of an assault was in progress. He phoned the main campus at University Park but was fed the same excuse, so he rushed out of the house and drove to the local dean's office. He walked past the receptionist. The dean yelled at her to call security, and as Bob Dalton was led away, the dean hissed, "I can see where your daughter gets her violent ways."

Late that afternoon, a police car rolled into their driveway. A pimply-faced, young man said he wanted to come in and speak to Isabelle. They said nothing when he walked past them and looked around the living room. He asked where she was, and they reported, with great solemnity, that she had left, and they weren't sure when, or if, she'd ever be back.

The boy looked at them skeptically. "If you lie to a *police officer*, you will be arrested and charged. You want to think about your answer again?"

"How old are you, young man—nineteen?"

"That is none of your business. And it just so happens, I'm twenty-two."

"Get your watch commander over here. Now!"

"You don't give the orders around here, I do."

Dalton called the police station, and the supervisor was there in a few minutes. "Look, I'll be honest with you, pal. Your name ain't the best down at the station. You got Rodman fired, and we haven't forgotten that. You wanna be smart? Cooperate with us and tell us where your daughter is, and we'll go easy on you."

"You got a warrant to be in this house?"

The young cop interjected, "Don't need one," but the sergeant waved at him to be quiet.

"We don't have a warrant, but like I said…"

Kerrith Dalton took a step toward the sergeant and raised her index finger to make a point. The young cop, seeing her approach his commander, body blocked her. She fell to the ground and gasped for breath. Dalton cocked his fist, but instead of hitting the man, dropped to his knees to tend to his wife. She screamed around him, "Get out of my home!"

Still on the ground, she winked at her husband, and let her head fall to the rug. "Oh, my God, you killed her! Oh, my God." He stood, went to the phone, and cried aloud that he was calling the District Attorney's Office.

The two cops tore out of the house. Kerrith opened her eyes and whispered, "Are they gone? I didn't hear the door close."

"It didn't. They were too scared. And you were so good. You should get an Oscar."

Isabelle rushed down the stairs and yelled that she had seen the whole thing from the landing. "I'm not putting you through this. I'm turning myself in."

"The hell you are. You've got enough on your plate. Anyway, this is a tempest in a teacup. But I'm going to follow up with Israel Sirota, see just how we go about suing the lot. We'll include the two deans, Penn State, and at the top of the pile'll be your pal the lab instructor. They'll settle, and it'll cover your room, board, tuition, and books, just like a football scholarship. All expenses paid nursing degree—not bad for an afternoon's work, huh? And I hope you knocked a few teeth loose."

Isabelle wrote to Lincoln that night.

> *Dear Love of My Life,*
>
> *Well, school's going okay. Had to straighten out one of my instructors. Think he got the message like a Cassius Clay punch in the chest.*
>
> *You know, I was thinking today. This world is a rough place. I love my parents a lot, and they have my back like a steel plate, but when it comes down to it, it's really just you and me from now on. Nothing else matters. I vow to care for you, no matter what comes our way, and it looks like no matter how hard you try to avoid the crazies, they have this radar that finds you. So, we will battle the bastards together. Oops—language, please.*
>
> *Time is passing too slowly, but every day is one less than the day before. I don't want to wish our lives away, but I will until we can hold each other and sleep for ten days, touching, never stirring.*
>
> *I'll love and cherish you.*
>
> *Soon and then forever,*
>
> *Is*

CHAPTER THIRTY-SEVEN

Lincoln had received good marks from the pilots with whom he'd flown. He was coming up on five months, the time a peter pilot became eligible to assume command of an aircraft. Though he was excited about the possibility, it was also terrifying to think he'd soon not have a seasoned pilot next to him to pull his ass out of the fires, which erupted more fiercely each day. As the political situation at home worsened, soldiers were permitted to do less and less to protect themselves. As he'd improved, he went along on an increasing number of hot insertions and extractions. Over the past ten nights, he'd been called out at two and three in the morning several times to drop into a firefight in the middle of the jungle and extract ten fully-equipped infantrymen, despite the D Model Huey's weight limit of about eight.

"Which two do you want to leave behind, Mr. Friday?" asked the aircraft commander when Lincoln balked at knowingly overstressing the ship. "Lemme me show you how to do it. Book's all wrong."

The pilot slid the HUEY back and forth like a car stuck in snow, until there was a jerk, followed by a sensation of spinal compression, as if in an elevator at the Sterling Hotel. Moonlit shadows suddenly moved vertically as the ship lifted into the canopy. The main rotor struck the tops of the banana trees that surrounded the landing zone, and a path was cut for the rest of the helicopter to enter the climb. Once they were in the air and the pilot eased up to eighty knots, Lincoln turned back to look into the heap of exhausted infantrymen. He expected a grateful thumbs up from the troops for whom his crew had so exposed themselves, but there was no movement, for all the men were asleep. He glanced further into the back of the ship to see the door gunners slumbering. The aircraft commander turned the controls over to Lincoln, and a moment later, the AC was snoring.

Lincoln wasn't scheduled for a flight the next morning, and he planned to skip breakfast and sleep in until nine, though as he rolled over on his cot, he smelled bacon and coffee. It was overwhelming, and he trundled to his feet, shaved in seconds, and was in the mess hall. Barely able to keep his eyes open, he groped for a seat in the corner, at the far end of an empty table, hoping to be left alone to fill his belly and drop back into the sack. He nodded as he passed two men but did not look at them, nor they at him.

Halfway through his eggs, he had a sense of déjà vu but ignored it until he couldn't. He looked up. It was the same second Huber did. They screamed and nearly tumbled out of their chairs to jump toward each other.

Huber spoke first. "Fuckin' troop, what the hell are you doing here?"

"Winnin' the war so you don't need to be here. Holy shit! You made it!" His chest clutched as he allowed his eyes to scan Huber's face and the burn scars. At first glance, they looked far less hideous than Lincoln remembered, but there they were, and there they would endure, as a reminder, for the rest of his life. After a few minutes, though, Lincoln smiled to himself that the stains seemed to fade, and then disappear, as the conversation warmed.

Huber had spent weeks in the hospital, had undergone several skin grafts, and had was returned to duty. He graduated two classes later and wasn't at all unhappy that he'd logged a lot of extra time in the HUEY stateside.

Lincoln looked him square in the eyes and smiled. "Serious for a minute, Hubert. You look great."

"Thanks, man. At first, they told me, with my face problems, I'd be removed from active duty. Too disruptive, they claimed. I was pissed. I save a fuckin' pilot, but I'm too ugly to sit next to him? My old man, Jap POW in the war..."

Lincoln interrupted, "So that's how you come by who you are."

"He's okay. Never told you 'bout him. He was out of the loop for a while, but it's all patched up now. Hope I turn out like him someday."

"You already have, my man."

"Anyway, my old man went berserk about the face thing. Senators and all that. Next thing you know, they pack me up, roll me onto an Air Force hospital plane, and I'm in LA at a clinic; some private plastic surgeon's hangin' over my bed, and then I'm asleep, and then I wake up lookin' like a fuckin' mummy. Just like in the movies. I gotta wait a week, and everybody gathers around, and they peel off the bandages, and what you sees is what you get." He became very quiet. "Taught me a lot, the whole thing did, troop. Even more than being here last time." He was silent again for a moment then laughed. "Musta made me handsome or somethin'."

"You always were."

"Thanks, man, but suddenly, I got more ladies than you can shake a stick at." He stopped talking, and Lincoln was about to ask about Kim Lieu when Huber snorted, "Didn't connect with them. Still hung up on you-know-who. Man, what the hell's gonna happen next?"

The XO stuck his head in the mess hall and called, "Mr. Huber, let's get you oriented. And, Friday, glad to see you're up and well fed. We got a new assignment from brigade. Old man wants you and Chief Marconi to go down to Saigon. Chemical Corps over there wants to talk to us about an experimental program. You two go find out what they want. The orders said it would take couplea days. Enjoy yourself in the mean city. And don't volunteer or show too much interest. We already got all the work we can handle killin' gooks."

Huber's eyes opened wide, and he stared at the XO for a second then grinned at Lincoln. "We'll catch up at the O Club."

CHAPTER THIRTY-EIGHT

Two mornings after the incident in physiology lab, Isabelle was still in her pajamas at eleven. She refused to go to school and sat at home watching television, far more quiet than usual. Zeke would not leave her side, and when she broke into tears in the middle of the soaps, he lifted onto his back legs and embraced her with his front paws.

Bob Dalton met with Israel Sirota, his attorney, the day after the incident. Israel had managed to squeak out of Berlin in '38, at the age of thirty, just after he'd graduated from law school. During the war years, he was nearly paralyzed with worry about his family in Germany, and it wasn't until '47 that he went back to his books and passed the bar exam in Pennsylvania. Now in his 60s, very thin, bald, and unkempt, he had semi-retired but still held an abhorrence for governmental abuse of power that shocked even Bob Dalton at times.

"Israel, you're going to work yourself into the grave with bitterness."

"Good. As long as I take a thousand of the *momzers* with me. You know what is a *momzer*?"

"Of course. A bastard."

"But a *mean* bastard of the worst kind. Anyway, so what's the problem? Ah, first, how's your son-in-law?"

"Sounds like he's been given safe duty. Fine with us. No need for a hero in the family. Just a need for a family."

His chest felt a bit uncomfortable with his careless mention of what still burned deep in Israel's heart, but the man leaned forward, gave Dalton a tap on the side of the arm, and nodded. "And you take care of them with your life. Thank God you have the chance."

Dalton went over the entire story, from the night Rodman covered Lincoln's accident to the night in the park, the officer's termination, and the nightmare that afternoon. Sirota commented quietly, "*Oy vey*, Robert. Where do we start?" He pulled a yellow legal pad from his desk, held up two pens, laughed, "We're going to need more ink than is in one," and started logging the tale. He asked questions as he wrote and had soon filled several pages.

When the tale was finished, Israel sat quietly, chin in palm. "Robert, please do not be mad at me, but you may be simply pounding sand going after these bastards, particularly the police.

"Look, you and your family are law-abiding people. You've never had to deal with these *momzers* before, and I mean the whole legal system. It is an abomination. Corrupt to the core. Think about the innocent people that get caught up in the storm. Tens of thousands of them every year, beaten senseless by the police, and then beaten penniless by the courts, all the time begging someone to listen to the truth. No one in the system ever does. It is as if they are deaf to reason, deaf to anything but their own interests.

"But the cops, the lawyers, and the judges, all of them, I am sorry to say, rely on these cases to keep the gears turning and the money flowing in. Arresting and trying petty crooks is rubbish. Your kind of people, on the other hand, you have the money to pay bribes and big fines. You can be milked for huge sums to stay out of jail. The worse they make it for you, the faster you pay. Shake down a prostitute or heroin addict. That makes great sense, doesn't it? You get ten dollars out of them. *Bubkis.*" He glanced at Bob.

"I know, Israel. It means 'nothing,' and I'm beginning to get the picture."

"Robert, excuse me, with all due respect, you have no inkling of what's going on, and it's only getting worse. You know, I'm getting near the end of my race, and to be truthful, it's not so awful a thought when you consider where this society is headed."

He looked away, deep in thought. When he turned back to his client, he shrugged. "So, in the end, my friend, if you want to go ahead with a wide-ranging suit, I'll do it, but I want you to know what you're up against."

"So, they can bust into my house and assault my wife with impunity?"

"Now, Robert, let's think about what happened yesterday. Strip it of the emotions. First, you let the cops into the house. You didn't have to."

"Of course, I did. The kid wanted to come in on police business."

"Excuse me, Robert, ignorance of the law is no excuse. You know that."

"What do you mean?"

"Well, you were under no legal obligation to let that officer into your house. He did not have a warrant, did he?"

"I don't know. I didn't know."

"It was your right *and responsibility* as an informed citizen in a democracy to ask to see it." Dalton's face hardened. Israel smiled weakly. "Please, not to kill the messenger. Okay, we move on. He told you the police were investigating an assault committed by your beautiful daughter, who did, in fact, commit said battery. Is that true?"

"Self-defense."

"But it's not the cop's job to make that determination, is it? That's the court's job. And the little prick was retreating when she let him have it. Right?"

"He assaulted her. She was protecting herself."

"Better check the laws. As I said, he was retreating. She should have called the police. And your wife took a step toward a police sergeant in the middle of an angry confrontation. Yes or no?"

"Come on, Israel. She's an older woman."

"Robert, are you listening to yourself? I said we must look at the bare facts, not the emotions, yes?"

"Go ahead."

"The young officer had to make a split-second decision, and he didn't draw his service weapon or punch her. No, he used the appropriate amount of force to protect a fellow police officer, and, again, in fact, Mrs. Dalton was not harmed physically, was she?

"Oh, and you can't lie to a police officer who is investigating a possible felony. Even if the little putz at school caused the whole thing. And you both lied, didn't you? So, sir, you can see why my best legal advice is to cease and desist."

Dalton dropped his head, thought for a moment, then stood and shook Israel's hand. "As always, sir, you are the consummate legal scholar and level-headed friend."

"I don't know about that, just been at it for centuries. Let me know if you hear a single word from any of the parties, though I think you won't. And Isabelle is to attend her classes and ask around if anyone saw that instructor touch her. There may be grounds for a civil action. But I have a feeling the young man will not be working there very much longer. Let me know."

CHAPTER THIRTY-NINE

Lincoln and Marconi were given bunks in the Chemical Corps' enlisted barracks in Saigon. Marconi protested, so they were pointed to a GP Medium tent and issued air mattresses and a couple of old sheets. The next morning, they were directed to a classroom set with twenty-four places along sweaty, OD tables. In front of each seat was a perfectly aligned, soggy pad of paper and a pointed, number two pencil. A bird colonel, without wings embroidered over his left breast pocket, bristled into the room and ordered, "Seats!" The two dozen rated pilots dropped indifferently into rusting, metal folding chairs. Several scratched the inside of their ears with the pencils; others fanned themselves with the pads, though all bitched about the heat, the shitty accommodations, and the distance they had had to crawl the night before to find a bar.

A white-bearded, bald civilian in grey overalls took a place at the podium. He pulled a handkerchief from his pocket and cleaned his rimless glasses. "Gentlemen, I am Doctor Pavel Kratok. My degree is in biochemistry, and I have been engaged by both Monsanto Corporation and Dow Chemical to adapt Agent Orange to the struggle in which we are engaged in South East Asia. I will now present an introductory course in the use of this defoliant…"

A captain in the front row smirked, "My wife uses defoliants."

"That's exfoliators, and if you don't mind, Captain, this is not a joking matter. The more you learn about this chemical, the more successful you will be in delivering it appropriately, and the sooner all of us can go home. In that regard, it is a lifesaving biological.

He turned to his blackboard and wrote so feverishly, the chalk crumbled and his fingernails scraped the slate. One of the majors hissed, "Jesus, cut that shit out!" The colonel at the rear of the room cleared his throat.

Soon, strings of carbon hexagons bound to free Cs, Ns, Hs, Ss, Cls, and OHs stretched across and down the board. He turned smartly to face his benumbed audience. "Chemically, Agent Orange is an approximately one to one mixture of two phenoxyl herbicides, 2,4-dichlorophenoxyacetic acid and 2,4,5-trichlorophenoxyacetic acid in iso-octyl ester form. As you can readily see, these are exceedingly complex molecules that have been in development since World War Two.

"They have been created to remove foliage, that is, denude the countryside and deny the enemy their jungle sanctuaries and food. We are here to train you in the niceties of its delivery via U.S. Army aircraft. Basically, choppers."

The captain with the vain wife harrumphed, "We refer to them as helicopters, not kitchen tools."

After the undercurrent of derisive laughter faded, the professor went on. "Very well. The Air Force has its own program. They spray it from low-flying C-123s. We've specified they fly no higher than two thousand feet to make sure the air is fully saturated with the agent. That is crucial."

A major raised his hand. “Excuse me, but last time I looked into the range of an AK-47, it seemed to me, not that I’m an expert, but it wouldn’t be too hard to hit a slow-flyin’ whale that close to the ground.”

“Major, I’m afraid I’m not the man to talk to about the Air Force program. I can give you a name when we’re done, and you can follow up if you’re that concerned.”

“What I’m concerned about, Professor, is you telling me to send my men in their,” he made quote marks with his fingers, “‘choppers’ out to fly low and slow over jungle that harbors tens of thousands of little bastards with guns powerful enough to macerate every helicopter in South East Asia. You get my point?”

“The parameters of the altitude and air speed profiles we’ve developed are designed to maximize the eradication of most, if not all, of the flora with which the chemical comes into contact. A tremendous amount of work has gone into developing an agent that is deadly to the canopy that hides the communists but does not harm, first and foremost, humans. This is a remarkable compound, gentlemen.”

The major, a shade of red more intense than pickled beets, drew a deep breath, but the colonel interrupted from the rear of the room. “Gentlemen, the Department of the Army is not going to send you up to be sitting ducks. It’s not the way we conduct business. You will fly with escorts. And that’s the last word on the subject. Doctor, please carry on.”

Lincoln was soothed by the reassurances this intellectual, elderly man had proffered, but he noted some of the more senior officers in the audience rolling their eyes. A chubby old man, a lieutenant colonel, stood, and before the instructor recognized him, grunted, “Excuse me, Doctor, but that’s the same line they gave us when we were at Los Alamos, and they made us sit in a trench a couple of miles from the frickin’ atom bomb. Half those guys are dead from cancer.”

"Well, I doubt it was a couple of miles, as you say, nor is it half, but I had nothing to do with the Manhattan Project. What I do know is that Operation Ranch Hand, the code name for our project, has been going on in Viet Nam since 1961, and I have never heard of a single side effect of Agent Orange on humans or animals.

"Now, as you may know, Agent Orange is not orange at all. It is a colorless, oily liquid and smells like insect spray. Well, you ask, if it isn't orange, why do we call it Agent Orange? It's simply because the fifty-five gallon barrels it comes in are painted with broad orange bands to distinguish them from fuel products." He laughed emotionlessly, "Great stuff, but you wouldn't want to fill your gas tank with it.

"If used properly, we will be able to strip about half of South Viet Nam's land of its foliage." He saw the eyes of several of his students harden. "Not to worry, gentlemen, that leaves sufficient, arable land to maintain the present population of the South. Granted, Viet Nam will not be the rice bowl of Asia it has been for centuries, but the peasants might have thought about that before inviting the Commies in for dinner.

"And, granted, there are going to be villages up in the mountains that will not be able to sustain themselves. It'll force the populace down into the cities. On the other hand, that will hurt the enemy soldiers who get food from those people. Our communist friends will have to leave those regions, as well, and concentrate in the lowlands. Makes them an easier target. That's the whole point, isn't it? Again, those villagers have buttered their own bread by supporting so heartless an enemy."

The lieutenant colonel broke in. "Look, they don't have a choice. They don't supply the right number of bags of rice, their families, especially the kids, are dragged into the middle of the village at night, forced to kneel in the dirt, and executed with a bullet in the back of the head. VC persuasion. Very subtle. So, let's not get too comfortable with what we're being ordered to do."

The full colonel at the back of the room spoke harshly. "Colonel, at ease. We're not here as humanitarians. Not another word from anyone in this room about the nature of Agent Orange or how you are going to deliver it. *Not one more word!*"

The next lecture concerned the specifics of spraying from HUEYs. They learned that a crew would come out from Saigon in 18-wheelers to convert two gunships of each unit into sprayers. The two-hundred-gallon tank would fill the entire back compartment, but there would still be a little room for the door gunners, who were to be trained to operate the sprayers in flight and refill the tanks on the ground.

Dr. Kratok turned back to the blackboard. "Okay, let's get down to specifics. You might want to take notes." He spoke as he scratched away with a new piece of chalk. "You will fly at seventy to eighty knots, and with that weight and all the equipment hanging outside causing parasite drag, that's about all you'll be able to do. If you stay relatively fast, you will stay ahead of the spray."

A major was on his feet. "What about turns?"

"What about them?"

"When we turn, we'll fly right back into the cloud, won't we?"

The full colonel screeched, "Goddamnit, Major, I told you no more comments. Report to me after class."

The last session was a Chemical Corps-produced, black-and-white movie, purportedly of a D Model Huey actually spraying over the countryside. It was out of focus and filmed from such a distance, the men could barely make out a cloud-enveloped dot in the sky. Most of them were asleep when the lights came on, including the colonel.

Lincoln and Marconi radioed their headquarters in the Delta, and a ship flew in two days later to carry them home. When

Lincoln looked for Huber, he found his friend had been sent, with a detachment of helicopters, up-country to support the Marines at the DMZ. Lincoln asked why the Marines couldn't fly their own helicopters, and the XO scoffed, "Because they're Marines. You ever watch them operate? Like take a hill?"

"Can't say as I've had the pleasure, sir."

"Well, it's something to behold. You know how we saturate a hill with artillery and air support before we send soldiers up it? Well, they take the hill first and then call for air support. Crazy mother fuckers. Hated to send your friend up there to cut his teeth, but we're not doing so good in the casualty department of late, down here, anyway. Hope he'll be okay."

"Shit, sir, Huber? He'll be back with the Medal of Honor before the week's out."

Three weeks later, Huber was still not back, but the truck with the sprayer equipment rolled into basecamp. Lincoln was rousted from his bunk an hour after he'd put his head down at 7 A.M. He had been out all the past night flying American corpses and near corpses to hospitals and graves registration depots. One victim, a Vietnamese village chief who had harvested the ire of local Viet Cong guerillas and suffered the vaporization of his hut with mortars, was in such desperate shape when Lincoln's dustoff ship skidded in, the crew intercommed the pilots that they couldn't tell if the man was dead or alive. When Lincoln looked to his left, the aircraft commander was asleep, so Lincoln mumbled, "Well, one should live by the adage, always err on the side of caution."

"Huh, sir?"

Approaching Saigon, Lincoln shook the aircraft commander's shoulder and spoke over the intercom. "Donny, let's drop this local off at that Vietnamese hospital down by the river. Let them make the decision. That's why they get paid the big dongs."

When they arrived over the Saigon River, Lincoln looked down and realized there was no way to weave a HUEY through the jumble of electrical and telephone cables, to say nothing of the miles of drying laundry, so he shook the pilot awake again and asked what to do. The man took control, yawed and pitched and rolled—left and right, up and down, forward and backward—until few pieces of the local's clothing survived the rotor wash. The ship dipped through a hole in the wires the size of a Volkswagen and settled onto the ground.

Three ancient, Vietnamese orderlies in dirty hospital whites arrived with a primitive stretcher to claim the body. As the helicopter was about to lift off, a diminutive young woman in a crispy, white nurse's uniform emerged from the front doors of the hospital and asked a gunner, "What his name?"

The man called the pilot. "What should I tell her, sir?"

The aircraft commander grumbled, "Shit, I don't know. Tell 'em Nguyen Van Thieu."

"That's the president of Viet Nam's name, ain't it, sir?"

"You got a better idea?"

"Now, she wants to know where we picked him up."

"Oh, for Christ's sake. Fuckin' Hanoi." Up came the collective, and they were gone.

A couple of hours later, Lincoln had to get up and supervise the installation of the spraying equipment. He had assumed command of the spraying project, for it had taken so long to get the equipment to basecamp, Marconi had rotated back to the States.

The crew from Saigon allowed this was their first field installation. The original installers were dead or in the hospital after their truck had hit a mine on the last outing.

Since the forklift they needed to remove the tank from the truck and slip it aboard the HUEY had been reduced to Christmas tree tinsel in the explosion, a dozen enlisted men were co-opted to maneuver the massive vat. It had, though, been designed without handles or surfaces that could be grasped. When ropes and two-by-fours failed, Lincoln's CO ordered the maintenance section to weld handles onto the sides of the tank, but no one there knew how to Heliarc aluminum. They sent a HUEY to Long Binh to fetch a trained welding crew and their equipment, but those technicians were already up north working on a secret project to protect aluminum-hulled M-113 Armored Personnel Carriers from rocket propelled grenades. The scuttlebutt was that an armor lieutenant with a degree in engineering had convinced his commanding officer to Heliarc-weld pivoting, four-by-eight sheets of aluminum to the sides of the personnel carriers as standoff. When the vehicles were on the roads in convoy, and at their most vulnerable, the sheets would be extended four feet to the flanks, and the North Vietnamese rocket propelled grenades would explode early and not pierce the side of the vehicle. The concept was sound, but when the welders finished the prototype, and several commanders gathered to test the idea with a captured B-40 rocket launcher, the round exploded as the colonel pulled the trigger. Four men died—two of them, welders.

So it was a week before another Heliarc specialist could be flown in from Japan. When it was done, the tank installed and the sprayer wands poking from the sides of the ship nearly as far as the tips of the main rotor blades, the crew chief tried to slide the back door shut to get to the fuel nozzle and gas the ship for a trial run. The handles, though, were in the way. The welder had gotten as far as Saigon before they got word to him to return, and it was past midnight when he arrived, so he left his kit at the airstrip overnight. By morning, his tank of helium, the gas needed to weld aluminum, was empty, drained by a platoon of infantrymen just in from the field who believed sniffing noble gasses while smoking joints intensified the high.

The welder, twitchy at being back in the boonies, chose not to wait a week for another tank of inert gas and removed the handles with an acetylene torch. He melted a hole in the Agent Orange tank. The harder he tried to patch the imperfection, the larger it grew. The man became so enraged, he smacked the torch against the side of the tank. That shot a blob of steaming metal onto his arm, and his fatigue jacket ignited. He dropped the flaming torch, and a wiring harness under the floor directly below the flames melted. The XO relieved the man of his duties, gave him an Article 15, and ordered another welder flown in. Patching the hole was easy. Replacing the wires, though, took ten days; and another two were vaporized test flying the ship.

The night the helicopter was signed off, Lincoln was ordered to the XO's office. He told Lincoln to accompany him to the O Club, where they were greeted by a dozen, beer-chugging pilots who shook Lincoln's hand while the XO announced Warrant Officer Friday was now an aircraft commander.

His first flight in the left seat was a spray mission to shower a wooded area just outside his basecamp that had provided cover for enemy snipers. One assassin had hit a private who was sitting in camp in a metal folding chair getting a haircut from a local Vietnamese barber. When the blood exploded out of the man's head, several GIs waiting their turn tackled the barber and nearly beat him to death, assuming he had cut the soldier's neck with his straight razor.

Lincoln inspected the helicopter and the spraying equipment before takeoff. His door gunners had filled the tank with Agent Orange, and though there were supposed to have been chemical suits for the full crew, they, too, had been lost in the mine explosion months before. By the time the crew had dipped buckets into the orange-banded, fifty-five gallon drums and topped off the onboard tank, they were saturated with the herbicide. The crew chief bitched, "Sir, this shit stinks. Makin' me itch."

"Young Crew Chief, I'm all trained up on this stuff. Perfectly harmless. It's been proven in scientific studies."

Lincoln called out the starting sequence, his new peter pilot called the tower, and two Cobra gunships hovered up and took positions to the flank of Lincoln's ship. Finally, a command and control HUEY with the XO aboard cranked up.

Lincoln grunted, "When the Air Farce goes out on a spraying mission, they do it with five to seven C-123s, each of them armed with Vulcan cannons, and two fighter jets fly circles around them. Everybody goes along for security. We get two Cobras and the old man, who, you can be sure, won't be dropping below five thousand feet, even if they lose an engine or run outta gas. Don't worry, they'll figure a way to stay away from this shit."

Lincoln was the last to lift off. The other aircraft climbed out as fast as they could sprint, though the spray ship struggled to gain just a minimum of air speed and altitude. They weren't a mile away from basecamp before the crew chief cackled over the intercom that he was going crazy itching. Lincoln turned and looked at the man. His face was swollen. His lips were half watermelons. Lincoln called back, "Crew chief, you need to get those lips under control. Get the First Aid kit out and take two, *and only two,* Benadryls."

"Sir, they told me to ditch the First Aid kit to save weight."

"Save weight? What's that, a whole extra pint of that shit we're haulin'?"

"Why are you yelling at me, sir? And I ain't feelin' so good."

"Okay. We're goin' back." Lincoln radioed his intentions, and they made a half circle in the sky and dashed toward the airfield. As they were on final approach, the crew chief began to lose consciousness. His last act before passing out was to put a death grip on the sprayer trigger. A thick cloud of Agent Orange puffed from the aircraft, but the pilots didn't see it until the other door gunner called up front. Lincoln told the man to go over to the stricken crew chief and stop the release, but there was no way to get past the tank to the other side of the ship.

They had no choice but to land, get the sprayer turned off from the outside, and send Lincoln's first casualty as an aircraft commander off to the hospital. As they hovered in carefully, believing the tank was still mostly full and the ship, thus, very heavy, the rotor blast sent clouds of defoliant out to the sides, saturating the far corners of the basecamp. Most heavily soaked, aside from the crew, were the neat lawns of St. Augustine grass, seed for which had been sent to the CO by his retired parents in Cape Coral, Florida. The man cultivated a green belt of fifty meters around his headquarters to control the blowing, red earth churned up around the clock by the helicopters.

It was three days before the crew chief could be replaced. As the new man came out to the ship for training, he did not realize the spray wand was as delicate as a paper straw, and he put his boot on it to climb aboard. It bent, and when he yanked to straighten it, the metal cracked. The wand plinked to the ground.

The CO was not devastated that no further spraying sorties could be mounted from Normandy Basecamp. The entire position had been rendered a Mars-scape, every blade of grass, every bush and banana tree in camp, and for a quarter of a mile beyond, had shriveled to weightless, brown threads. The only area not denuded was the patch of upwind jungle from which the Viet Cong took potshots at the now totally exposed Americans. The detritus of dead flora worked its way into the water supply, the fuel tanks, and the chow. When the helicopters flew, the CO's quonset was consumed by untold cubic yards of fine, red dust, some of the drifts as high as his windows. By the time the new wand arrived, the CO had demonstrated to the high command that Agent Orange was being carried by the winds to Saigon and sucked into the central air conditioning at Pentagon East. Spray missions, thereafter, flew out only from specialized installations hundreds of miles to the north. Lincoln was sent up there. It was the same night Huber got back down south.

CHAPTER FORTY

Isabelle returned to class two days after her dad had talked to Mr. Sirota. Rosemary was still the teaching assistant but remained crudely aloof, making frequent snide comments about the capacity of women to meet the challenge of pronouncing the various organs of the body. He pointed at one of the female students and jeered, "How do you pronounce, 't-e-s-t-i-c-u-l-a-r'?"

A couple of the co-eds approached Isabelle after her first class back and suggested they meet for coffee at the Student Union Building. They had witnessed the shoving incident but hadn't heard what led up to it. When they met, both women reddened, and their faces tightened.

Jennifer nodded. "Ladies, I have a plan. Let's get a couple other girls involved. Strength in numbers."

The cabal grew to five. They gathered again the next day after lab and finalized plans. The mission would take place during the double lab session on Friday. Jennifer volunteered to do the very dirty work portion of the proposal. She flirted with Rosemary several times on Thursday, and by Friday morning, when the bell rang at ten, starting the twenty-minute break, he was already hovering. When Jennifer was sure everyone was out of the room, she took a big step away from the lab table, as if to leave. She pretended to be surprised and embarrassed when she bounced into him, grabbing his arm to steady herself. She ran one hand down his side, along the front of his thigh, and let her fingers brush the material near his crotch.

"Do you remember when you said the word 'penis' the other day?" He was too breathless to answer. She looked around the room surreptitiously. "There's got to be somewhere we can go so you can," she raised her finger to make quote marks on either side of his zipper, "instruct me."

Rosemary's hue deepened into a sweaty magenta, but he managed to grunt with a deep tremor in his voice, "There's a prep room on the next floor." He turned and walked toward the door without looking back. She followed to a rear staircase where Rosemary, head down as if pondering a great question, took the first steps reticently. He suddenly jerked straight and bounded past the landing. He stopped in front of a locked door, pulled a full key ring from his pocket, fumbled trying to find the right one, and hissed loudly, "Shit, come on, goddamnit," until the handle finally turned. He went in without holding the door open for her. She shook her head, rolled her eyes, looked back to the staircase, smiled at the shadows, and waited until several giggling faces appeared. She ducked into the room.

Rosemary had taken only a few steps inside. He stared at Jennifer's blouse, his eyes as wide as the bottoms of the glass beakers on the work table. She, by reflex, began to bring her arms up to cover herself but smiled sickly, let her arms drop, and pooched out her breasts. His eyes swelled.

She drew in a deep breath, took a stride to stand directly in front of him, and whispered, "I don't have much experience. You're going to have to tell me what to do." When his hands trembled as if he'd been cursed with early onset Parkinson's, she whispered throatily, "You know, show me and touch yourself the way you like it. You know, to make yourself hard. I want to see a man hard. I never have." She ran her fingers over her breasts ever so lightly.

Down came the zipper. Jennifer's palm came to her mouth to stifle a laugh, but Rosemary spoke quaveringly, "Yeah, I know. But I think it can get *even bigger* if *you* touch it."

She howled, "Oh, my God!" There was a brief pause then a crash as the door flew open and four women sprang in, the front two with cameras. One was a Polaroid.

Wearing a look of studied disgust, Jennifer turned toward Rosemary, waited for the girls to get into position with cameras aimed, and put both hands out as if repulsing him. After a few shutter clicks, she twisted her face into an expression of melodramatic terror, refining it as the two women moved about the room working their cameras. A deer caught in the headlights, Rosemary managed, after a dozen shots had been snapped, to fold himself mostly into place; but as he tugged on the zipper, he caught the tip of his substantial foreskin in the teeth. His screamed "SHIT!" was louder than the laughter of the five women.

The Polaroids were blurry, almost to the point of worthlessness, and the girls were devastated. They would have to wait to see the Kodaks, which a friend promised to develop, for if they had them processed at Woolworths, the prints would be confiscated as pornographic. They blew up several of the better shots, and the women took them to the associate dean. After he caught his breath, and his color cooled to a deep red, he dismissed the women, telling them he had to discuss the matter with the University's administration.

A week later, after the pictures had been mailed to the main campus and reviewed, the women were recalled to the associate dean's office. "Girls, we have a situation here. You have created and distributed pornographic material, and you did so on Pennsylvania State University property. That is grounds for immediate dismissal. This is a venerable institution, one which any scholar would be proud to claim as his alma mater.

"Now, if for some reason, you were granted forgiveness and allowed to graduate from Penn State, you would not want your university sullied with the type of scandal that would certainly grow from *your* actions. Am I correct?" The women just stared, slack-jawed. "So, the dean has reviewed your academic and disciplinary records, and as first-time offenders, he has generously agreed to suspend the matter if you agree to sign contracts not to divulge the nature of this incident for a minimum of four years." He opened his desk drawer and pulled free a stack of papers.

The women signed, the dean's secretary witnessed, and the meeting adjourned. They walked silently to the Student Union Building, but once inside, disintegrated into uncontrollable laughter. Jennifer finally squeaked, "I think I wet my pants."

CHAPTER FORTY-ONE

By the time Lincoln's chemical warfare activities were placed in the hands of a less senior pilot and crew, he had been to Hawaii on R&R and spent nearly every minute of it at the Hilton Hotel on Waikiki with his arms draped around Isabelle. She levelled with him about the incident with Rosemary, and Lincoln vowed to find him when he got back and pull off his nuts. Straight-faced, she remarked, "Better get good at micro surgery."

She was thrilled to hear that Huber was well and hoped the two would get to fly together before June when Lincoln was expected to DEROS, Date Expected to Return Over Seas. But they still hadn't been in basecamp together for more than a few hours.

Lincoln bought Isabelle a diamond necklace and gave it to her on their last evening together. She cried all night and couldn't get on the bus to go with him to the airport the next morning.

When Lincoln arrived back at Normandy a few days later, he had to go through a check ride to make sure his skills hadn't withered in the two weeks he'd been gone. His check pilot was

Marconi, who'd been home for a couple of months but had already shipped back. The man was promised a slot as a check ride and test pilot if he agreed to an immediate return to Viet Nam, to be held there for only six months, then guaranteed two years stateside before being sent back again. Everyone knew the war would be over by then, so he accepted the offer.

Before they took off on the check ride, Marconi sat with Lincoln on one of the nylon, folding beach chairs the crews had begun to carry in the back of the ship. Marconi told him of the research that had been made public at home, but not to the troops, about the toxic effects of Agent Orange, and how there had been a sudden upsurge of birth defects in the children born in villages that had been sprayed. "Shit's even travelin' on the wind down to the cities."

Lincoln thought for a minute then laughed humorlessly, "You remember that jerk, what was it, Crock or something? The one who gave us the class on Agent Orange? Said it was completely safe."

Marconi spit. "He was a crock all right. There's a bunch of studies show a big uptick in the number of leukemia cases in our guys coming back from the Nam."

Though Lincoln seldom visited the Officers' Club, he went that evening with Marconi for a beer. While they talked, the screen door flew open and several pilots pushed in noisily, Huber in the lead. When they saw each other, Lincoln and Huber rushed together, nearly toppling to the floor. As they pulled apart, Lincoln's heart smiled, for Huber's scars were nearly gone—and it had been less than a year. He was thin, his face chiseled, and he looked more like an actor than a soldier.

Introductions were made all around, the drinking became serious, and soon Lincoln and Huber found themselves alone in the back of the quonset, talking so fast the table rumbled. Huber had been in-country for several months but had not been able to sneak away to Saigon. He complained that they watched pilots closer in the war than they had even at Wolters. He guessed his only chance to find Kim Lieu would be during an in-country R&R, if he lived long enough to get one.

Just a week later, Lincoln's helicopter company was detached to a different infantry brigade at Brandywine Basecamp, north of Saigon. This was to be the first of a series of maneuvers in which the American and Vietnamese infantry troops would work side by side—Operation Scrambled Egg. The ground portion of the venture was old hat to the planners at Pentagon East. Huber had gone on these missions years before. New was the use of Vietnamese-piloted HUEYs flying alongside American aircraft to carry out troop insertions. The Vietnamese would transport only their countrymen, the Americans only theirs, and there would be no comingling. A file of American slicks, HUEY troop carriers, would enter the landing zone and drop their men. When they were clear, the Vietnamese ships would come in. Once landed, the two ground commanders would meet and make a final assessment before penetrating the jungle to engage the enemy.

Legions of interpreters were brought in, both American and Vietnamese, some familiar with flight operations and others with infantry maneuvers. They had been culled from a dozen units throughout the South. The helicopters were flown in one by one or in small gaggles, spaced many hours apart over several days, to preserve the element of surprise. When Lincoln's company was assembled at Brandywine, the brigade commander from Normandy flew out and met with them the afternoon before the first day of the operation. The pilots were squashed into a GP Medium tent with just ten chairs, all taken by non-pilot, senior officers. Most of the airmen sat on the dirt floor. Others milled around bitching loudly about the heat, the rain, the mosquitos, the dust, the mud, the poor excuse for food that was the fare of the infantry in Viet Nam, the lack of shelter while eating—which allowed the crappy paper plates upon which the so-called chow was served to fill with rainwater and dissolve in the diner's hand—the drinking water that had become contaminated with aviation fuel, the aviation fuel that had become contaminated with drinking water, the lousy selection of Kool Aid available to mask the taste of the fuel-tainted water, the latrines that were nothing more than very narrow ditches dug from the muddy earth over which the user straddled—one foot on each bank—the lousy selection of comic books available while one did his business, and, finally, the kids who congregated at the perimeter wire and sold phony Coke—orange-dyed sugar water—and diluted 33 Beer, all for exorbitant prices.

The colonel's assistant stepped briskly into the tent and called the mob to attention. The Old Man shot in on his aide's heels. "I am very glad to see my flock integrating so well into our new environment." He paused, looked in the eyes of his soldiers, and began on a positive note. "Men, this is quite an opportunity. You have been carefully selected..."

Huber interjected, "Sir, you mean carefully condemned..."

"Mr. Huber, I know where you're coming from, and I respect your opinion; but ours is a special unit, and I will tolerate no negativity. If you want to get yourself confined to your BOQ for the evening, keep jabbering."

"Roger, sir. The Vietnamese suck. Now, could you make that for the next week?"

The undercurrent of laughter grew to such a rumble, the colonel's lips tightened, but the pilots pointedly averted his glare, and he forced a few snorts of bogus amusement, then became deadly serious. "Gentlemen, every man in this room is an officer. You know very well I don't make the rules, but I do carry them out. And you will as well. Then we can all go home and raise our families and hope like hell our kids don't get sent to another shithole like this to do it all over again. I will get you home if you act like the professional aviators you are, both in the cockpit and during the planning stage of your missions. I saw it in the islands during the war. Over and over. Meticulous planning, attention to detail, can-do attitude. You wanna go home in one piece, you listen to me. This ain't my first rodeo."

A powerful silence cloaked the room as assignments were handed out. The colonel had gone so far as to have photos taken of the countryside around the various LZs. He had flown out days before in his command and control ship and ordered his pilot to simulate the final approaches into the chosen landing zones and a dozen other decoys. He used his own eight-millimeter movie camera to detail the real flight paths. The men studied the photos and made sketches; the films were looped over and over. Aircraft commanders used their watches to time various segments of the flight, calculating where their ships would be on the approach when the aircraft ahead was dumping its troops.

The flight leader called on the men to name various trees, freaks of nature, that had grown taller than the rest and could be used as checkpoints. When the christening degenerated into a Rorschach test of erotica, the colonel slapped a palm on his desk, and the checkpoints became Green One, Green Two… He nodded and left the tent. The men squeezed together around tables and calculated air speeds and altitudes at those markers, and how they would react if this ship or that one went down, who would break off for the rescue, and who would fly cover.

That night, the two dozen American pilots who had been assigned the first mission, that was to commence at dawn, were slouched in a corner of the O-Club bitching about the inevitability of failure any time the two sides came together. They were doing so in whispers, for the CO was sitting at the bar with his Vietnamese counterpart, both men nursing martinis, the Vietnamese colonel's first ever cocktail. Occasionally, the American officer turned surreptitiously to eye his men and stare pointedly at the building number of empties until the pilots nodded. The old man nodded in return then went back to his futile attempt to communicate with the Vietnamese colonel.

As the evening wound down, the screen door opened and everyone looked up curiously to eye the late arrivals. Lincoln and Huber nearly flew out of their seats as Lockett stepped inside and removed his hat. They didn't notice the diminutive soul on his heels. Nearly in tears, the three classmates dropped at an empty table, and Huber yelled to the bartender for a reload. The colonel cleared his throat deafeningly, and Lincoln laughed, raised his index finger, and declared, "Just one, barkeep."

Lockett called out, "And one for my friend here."

Lincoln and Huber looked up to see Mr. Nhu standing near the table waiting for an invitation. Lincoln rose and took his hand. Huber nodded slightly.

Lincoln put his arm around Nhu's shoulder and guided him onto a chair. "Mr. Nhu, I am so happy to see you, but I thought, last time I heard, you had, you know, gone home..."

"Mr. Rinkin, I so happy to see you. No, I no go home. You not believe story. He took a breath as if to begin the saga, but stopped as Lockett put two sweating beers on the table. While the American pilots guzzled, Nhu watched furtively out of the corner of his eye, waiting until the men looked up before taking his first swig. When Huber smiled thinly, Nhu sat a bit straighter and tipped the bottle up for a deep swallow. The men became silent and turned to him. He tried to restart his story, but his tongue had already thickened. He looked at Lockett. "Mr. Rocket, you tell. You better than Nhu for story."

Nhu had appeared before the Elimination Board, so mortified, so overwhelmed with shame, he had not been able to squeak a single word of English in his defense. All he did was hold up his helmet, wiggle it in front of the board chairman's face, and point inside. The major had shrugged, thrown up his hands in frustration, and dismissed the foreigner.

For two weeks after the decision to eliminate Nhu, he made fervent pleas to be heard, but every time he began to explain, his tongue froze, and his evaluators shook their heads at the time and resources already squandered on so hopeless a cause.

As Nhu's special visa was running out, he buried his pride and telexed his father, who telexed the Pentagon, who telexed the commanding officer at Fort Wolters, who flew up to Washington to meet with his CO and the Deputy Secretary of Defense. An interpreter from the Vietnamese Embassy was brought to the Pentagon by limousine. Nhu's argument was that the quality of the equipment inside his helmet was so poor, even an American student would have been confused by the calls from the tower on the day he essentially shut down United States Army aviation.

The principals examined the helmet. Nhu pointed to the size placard on the inside—Extra Large. The Deputy Secretary glanced at Nhu's head. He grunted, "Very funny."

Nhu grasped the nuance, recognized the theatrical potential, and popped the device on. It barely touched his head. He spun it several revolutions, as if a malfunctioning droid. A high-pitched lament accompanied the painstaking removal of the headgear, and that was followed by animated pointing at the inside components. The tattered earphones had likely seen service during World War Two; they were that thrashed. The Deputy Secretary pulled the helmet out of Nhu's hands and stuck his finger inside to jiggle the piece of broken copper wire that poked through the center of the left earphone. "How did your G-4 let junk like this find its way aboard a million-dollar aircraft?"

"It was an H-23, sir, and they aren't all that expensive."

The Deputy Secretary flushed, but he spoke quietly. "General, you will reinstate Mr. Nhu. You will provide him and his countrymen with serviceable equipment, and the man who issued him the extra-large is to receive an Article 15. This shit is going to stop." He stood and left the room.

Nhu accompanied the general back to Texas aboard a mammoth C-141 military transport. They were the only passengers. It was a very quiet three hours.

When Lockett was done, Nhu smiled at Lincoln and Huber. "I recircle at Wolter. Work hard on fly. Work hard on English. Do okay, not great."

Lincoln shook his head. "I think you mean *recycle.* And you sound terrific." He turned to Lockett and Huber. "Can you imagine being sent over to China to learn to fly? You don't know shit from shinola about aviation or even driving a car. The language is friggin' impossible, and the asshole supply clerk fits you with an extra-small helmet, I mean extra-small by Chinese standards, and he laughs at your ass when you put it on. And then the jerk in the control tower is screaming at you so fast, even the Chinese students don't know what the hell he's talking about. And all this on your second solo." Even Huber nodded.

The pilots and gunners were on the flight line at 4 A.M. The complaints about not enough sleep, headaches, and the cold were louder than the engines coming hot. The infantry boarded and slings were traded between the crew and the soldiers about smoking on the helicopters; a near fistfight erupted over the man who pulled a Ballantine beer from his pack and wouldn't share with his buddies.

The first stick of American aircraft lifted off at ten, three hours late. They rendezvoused at the designated point in the sky and made their insertions. The LZ was cold, and it was a routine milk run from point A to B. No one was squealing about taking fire; in fact, it was so quiet on the radio, Lincoln let his peter pilot do the whole flight while he sat back and took pictures of the magnificent countryside.

The Vietnamese flew sixteen ships from their own base in the Delta to make the insertion alongside the Americans. It remained cold when they arrived. In the command and control helicopter, the colonel sat with his operations officer, the infantry brigade commander, the Vietnamese air boss, Lockett, and Nhu. The two interpreters spoke to each other but dared not utter a word to the brass.

The infantry commander, Colonel Bierline, sighed in relief as he spoke on the intercom. "That's good. We got enough troops on the ground now, the bad guys would be fools to engage. Let's get some boots into the peripheral LZs and start pinching in on the bastards."

There was discussion aboard the command and control ship, just to make sure, about which of the various outlying LZs had been assigned to the Americans and which to the Vietnamese. There were nods all around when it was certain everyone was on the same page, and radio calls were made to sub-commanders. In the C&C ship, the soldiers marveled as the lines of helicopters far below reversed course and headed away from the original insertion point.

A moment later, though, Lockett tapped Nhu on the shoulder and pointed at two sticks of helicopters, one Vietnamese and one American, coming from different directions but closing on the same outlying LZ. The lead aircraft had not yet spotted each other. Radio calls were made, and both sticks slowed but continued the approach. Then another two sets of helicopters appeared, both headed toward a single LZ. Maps were checked, code books scrutinized, frantic calls made, and the gaff finally discovered. The names of the outlying LZs on the American maps bore no relation to those on the Vietnamese charts.

Colonel Bierline, the overall commander, understood the potential for this becoming a military calamity of Waterlooesque proportions, one to be discussed and studied for centuries to come. He thought for a minute and decided to err on the side of caution, withdraw the troops already on the ground from the safe, still-cold LZ, end the operation for the day, go home, regroup, and live to fight another day.

He forced himself to remain calm, to the point that he was able to key the intercom and, with a smile in his voice, sigh, "Well, the best laid plans of mice..."

He was interrupted by a roar on the radio from the American ground commander that his troops had suddenly become the target of enemy rockets, mortars, and automatic weapons fire. With the Vietnamese ground commanding officer one of the first killed, his men were in complete disarray, and most had retreated at a mad sprint back toward the original LZ. They were begging to be extracted, but the American ground commander warned that any attempt to send the helicopters to the LZ, or the airspace within two miles of it, was suicide.

A moment later, he called to relate a devastating increase in ground fire and the retreat of his infantrymen to a defensive position near the LZ. "Shit, everybody is shooting at everybody." Those were his last words. A mortar round detonated in the trees over his head, and the entire command group was disabled.

Bierline called the next lower tier of commanders, company grade officers, and was able to restructure what was left of the battalion. The Vietnamese, though, were in even greater disorder. Their air commander aboard the C&C ship was shaking so hard, he could not speak, so Nhu lunged forward and took control of the radios. When his words quieted one of the indigenous captains, Nhu advised him to regroup, form a defensive perimeter with the Americans, and hold that position, no matter the cost. He turned to Lockett to ask if the Americans could pop smoke and identify themselves. It would allow the two company commanders an opportunity to meet and establish a coordinated response. Lockett talked it over with his colonel, who discussed it with the infantry brigade commander, and it was done.

What was left of the two friendly units consolidated near the LZ, leaving behind antipersonnel mines to detonate as the enemy advanced. The C&C ship was running low on fuel, but before going off station to refuel, Colonel Bierline ordered his pilot to drop in and put Lockett and Nhu on the ground to coordinate the helicopter portion of the extraction.

Both men were handed PRC-25 radios and M-16s from a gun rack in the back of the ship, and as the aircraft touched down, Lockett gulped, closed his eyes, and jumped free. Nhu followed, and in the rotor wash was pushed on top of his counterpart. The two laughed so hard, it was a chore to stand up and run for cover.

The two pilots made contact with the American boots, and Nhu set out to find his countrymen. Only a few shots rang out in his direction from the Vietnamese troops before he low-crawled and cursed his way into their defensive halo. He arranged a meeting with the Americans, and a few more rounds whizzed by as the two companies began a small, but aggressive, forward movement toward the enemy, a tactic to drop more mines and afford them a greater physical margin when the extraction came.

A Vietnamese platoon leader had been killed, and Nhu took command of that unit until the helicopters arrived. He went to each man and told him to be brave and that he would make sure they got out, but they would only survive if they fought as if protecting their mothers. "Because you are."

The C&C ship was back on station. A report came that the friendlies had pushed the VC a mile deeper into the jungle, and the colonel called in an air strike. The jungle glowed orange with napalm. The heat, even two hundred yards away, was oppressive, and many of the men sat smoking cigarettes during a lull in the air attack, shaking their heads at the wholesale obliteration of kids their own age.

When the air cooled, several small teams of infantry moved forward to probe the enemy line, assess the battle damage, and drag back their own dead. Nhu and Lockett went along to determine the extent of the buffer zone. They found enemy soldiers burned beyond recognition but still alive. Lockett radioed for American medics. They could also see rustling in the hills another half mile from the LZ, the remnants of their enemy. One casualty, a VC, feigned death until he opened an eye and recognized Lockett as an American. He very slowly drew his AK-47 toward him, and as his finger closed on the trigger, Nhu caught the movement out of the corner of his eye and sprang toward the man but tripped and fell on top of him. Though the AK fired, the round landed in the dirt. Several of the Vietnamese soldiers wanted to execute the man right there, but Lockett prevailed, convincing them he was of intelligence value. Several Vietnamese soldiers were ordered to make a litter and haul the man to the LZ, but he died less than a minute after they left, and they dumped his remains on a pile of the other burned casualties.

Lockett thanked Nhu. The two men sat and smoked a cigarette. Lockett mumbled, "You know, Lieutenant, the instant I radio the VC position to my CO, that's another couple hundred dead cousins of yours. Do you think I should do it?"

Nhu nodded. "My friend, it is not our decision."

Within five minutes of Lockett's radio call to the C&C ship, the hill erupted in greasy, carroty tracks of flame.

The extraction took place, and the two friendly units returned to their respective bases to lick wounds. Platoons were reconstituted, helicopters patched, pilots and crew members replaced, the dead sent to graves registration, the wounded flown to hospitals, and at eight that night, debriefings were held. Where the snafu at the outlying landing zones came from was not revealed, nor was much effort put into an investigation. It was done and would not happen again. New plans were put forward for the morning, and the aviation colonel limited his men to one beer apiece. No one griped.

Nhu was called before the Vietnamese air boss and disciplined for usurpation of command. He was also called into Colonel Bierline's office, though secretly, and told he was being put in for an American Bronze Star with "V" Device for Valor, to acknowledge his work that day. Lockett was, as well.

Huber was furious at the turn of events and growled about the loss of American lives due to the Vietnamese screw up, but his pals were too tired to argue with him. When Nhu was invited to their table, Huber got up, left his half-finished beer on the table, and went to his tent.

CHAPTER FORTY-TWO

The same operation, but into a different set of LZs, commenced at dawn the next morning. Huber was the co-pilot two ships behind Lincoln. As the day before, the first insertions were into cold patches of scrub near the hill where Lockett had reported the enemy movement the day before. Given the easy-to-calculate rate at which the enemy moved—they had no vehicles and could not come into the open to use roads, or even cross patches of exposed land—the perimeter of what was left of their unit should have been evident.

But probes by the American scouts found no sign of the enemy, other than the skeletal remains of soldiers who had been killed and then eaten by animals from rats to tigers. The latter were sufficiently Pavlovian to recognize that, where there were explosions, fresh meat was often available. The Command and Control ship radioed all units to push outward toward various, lesser LZs for extraction. That way, the colonel could report to his superiors that he had at least one patch of land in Viet Nam that was free of the communists, if for just an hour. The ships back at basecamp were refueled and given new missions. Nhu and Lockett were issued up-to-the-minute maps, their code books were checked and rechecked, and they were dropped off at basecamp to board the lead ship of their respective country's helicopters. They were to sit in the back and keep an eye on the geography.

The extractions began with columns of HUEYs making precision approaches, but the infantrymen were very slow in boarding, as they were masters in the art of vaporizing time, thus limiting their exposure to yet another opportunity to be slaughtered. The pilots, though, were not happy with the slow pace, for they were sitting in the open, at low altitude, barely crawling along, while the ships on the ground loitered.

The first stick was so slow, the next was already on station, circling before half of the initial helicopters were off. It was a hopeless traffic jam in less than a minute, and when all the ships were appropriately situated as hovering ducks, the automatic weapons fire burst from the jungle. Some of it was directed at the pilots, some at the tail rotors. Both tactics worked, and several ships fell from the sky, so many oak seeds.

Lincoln had a full load, and as he went into the climb, Plexiglas was flying about like glass from a shattering window. One round managed to squeeze through a tiny gap between the boiler plate under the seat and the vertical armor that protected the co-pilot's back and neck. The co-pilot pitched forward onto the cyclic. The door gunner sprang forward and pulled the man off the control stick by yanking on the deceased's helmet. Lincoln managed to pull the ship out of its dive, and he joined the other aircraft heading back, though was told to break formation and proceed as fast as he could soar to a hospital. He looked again to make sure and radioed it was too late.

The Vietnamese helicopters took similar fire, and three of their ships crash landed. Nhu told his pilot to go back, drop the infantrymen to make room for the casualties, and let him out to see who was alive. Nhu led the wounded to the ship, but it was too heavy, so he kept the less badly hurt on the ground with him. There were a dozen frantic radio calls, and another Vietnamese HUEY dropped in to pick him up. Several soldiers on that helicopter were forced off at gun point to allow the injured aboard. Nhu stayed on the ground with them. As that ship lifted off slowly, due to the overload, a tiny man, perhaps just a boy, popped out of the brush and pointed a shoulder-mounted tube at the helicopter. Nhu saw the child's eyes shut tightly right before the roar, the whoosh, and the disappearance of the ship in a flash of blue and red. As little pieces of smoking OD debris floated to the ground, the startled boy turned to run, the rocket launcher still on his shoulder. Nhu and his compatriots hesitated, but one of the men howled in rage and fired. He missed, though the others opened up to cut the child to shreds.

Another ship came in to rescue Nhu and his soldiers, and this time the Vietnamese infantrymen laid a cloud of lead over the entire perimeter, shooting blindly, but effectively, for there was no return fire. Since Nhu's helicopter was the only Vietnamese ship left, he joined the American formation. He smiled ironically when he heard Huber over the radio and congratulated himself on his improving English. He had come so far, he was able to recognize a particular voice in such a foreign tongue. He wondered what it was about the Vietnamese people that the man so despised, though he doubted he would ever find out. He shrugged, leaned back, closed his eyes, and tried to nap.

Just seconds later, there was a bang, and Nhu shot upright in his seat. A bright flash was just fading from the helicopter to his front, the last aircraft in the American column. The pilot appeared unable to control the ship, and it was soon sliding left and right, pitching up and down. The other American ships did not realize their trailing aircraft had been hit, and when Nhu tried to radio the Americans, he realized his radio had taken a bullet.

The American helicopter finally entered a rapid descent, one far beyond the skill of any aviator to arrest. Nhu told his pilot to follow it down. The man balked for a moment; Nhu pulled his .38.

The damaged helicopter plunged into a stand of trees and hung, rocking slowly, nose down, JP-4 pouring from bullet holes in the fuel tanks. The rotor wash from Nhu's ship whipped the oily liquid into a froth that engulfed the still-steaming engine.

Nhu hooked the rescue rope around his waist and ordered the door gunner to lower him. The hull of the downed helicopter was so slick from leaking fuel, he was unable to hold himself against it, so he swung out and back several times until he sailed through the back doors. The gunners were both dead, their heads hanging limply, and Nhu understood their necks had been broken in the crash. He lowered himself to the pilots' seats. The aircraft commander was gone; there was no doubt. The co-pilot, though, was breathing, but only in tiny, feeble, gasps. Blood was dripping from his mouth onto the instrument panel.

Nhu unbuckled the man and tried to pull him out of the seat, but the American outweighed him by seventy-five pounds. Slowly, though, he worked a leg free, then the other, and the man's torso fell forward. Nhu untied the rope from his waist and placed it around the soldier's chest, leaned out the pilot's door, and motioned for the gunner to lift. The crewman did not realize the rope was no longer anchored to Nhu, but to a man inside who required the gentlest traction to maneuver him through the door. The gunner motioned for the pilot to hover up quickly to get Nhu out of there before the ship exploded, but the American's helmet caught in the door. The entire downed aircraft jolted as the wounded co-pilot's body jerked to a stop. Nhu screamed up to the gunner, but the man could not hear or see him, so Nhu ripped the wounded co-pilot's helmet strap open, and the limp body burst free to dangle at the end of a rope over the jungle.

The moment the wounded man's weight was out of the ship, the center of gravity of the downed helicopter changed incrementally but enough to send it tumbling down several more feet. The dripping fuel was now directed into the hot section of the turbine engine, and the ship began a slow burn that was confined to the outer skin. Nhu could not hang on outside long enough to hail the rescue ship, and as the fire spread, he jumped free into the lush, second layer of canopy then climbed down on vines until he could drop into the scrub. He ran from under the burning ship just as it exploded. Fire rained to his back and sides, and he slid to the jungle floor, where a bit of unburned air hovered.

The rescue helicopter drifted off a hundred meters, until the flames died down, but when it went back, though the door gunners searched desperately with their eyes, there was no sign of Nhu. It shot back into the sky and dropped the wounded man at the American basecamp. The medics did what they could to stem the bleeding they could see, but it was clear the wounded man was losing blood internally, and all they could do was run IV fluids as fast as the solution could be pumped. As the helicopter lifted off to evacuate him to the hospital, the medic turned to the CO and shook his head almost imperceptibly.

The old man called Lincoln to the headquarters quonset. "Friday, the ship we lost was Huber's."

"I know, sir."

"Well, he's alive, but they told me it doesn't look like he's gonna make it. I'm sorry. I know you two go back a ways. Why don't you go ahead and gather his personal belongings. Bring 'em up here, and we'll write a letter to his family together."

When Lincoln got word of Nhu's death, he sat on his cot and held a towel against his eyes to stifle the tears. He took a cigarette from a pack lying on a buddy's bed and sat numbly, facing the wall. He reread one of Isabelle's old letters; she had told him he was the best man in the world and that everyone who knew him was sure, no matter what he faced, Lincoln Friday would always do the right thing.

He jumped from his rack, grabbed his helmet, and jogged to the flight line. He had been checked out in what the pilots called a LOH, a "loach," a light observation helicopter, and begged the CO to let him go out with an observer to gather his Vietnamese friend's remains.

The old man looked Lincoln in the eyes. "That little shit is the bravest man I ever met in this place, bar none. Now, Chief, what happens in these situations is always the same. You lose more men and equipment in the rescue attempt, attempts, than got lost in the original disaster. That is a law of war. On the other hand, remember what I was saying about going home, and doing it with pride, and all that other crap?"

"I do, sir, but it didn't sound like crap."

"Well, Chief, I'm retiring in a couple of months. Don't you dare tell a soul. I know who you are, and I trust you. You're probably my best officer, including the whole bag of commissioned. This was the worst day of my career, and there isn't any point in staying on active duty. There will be no star for yours truly, and to be honest, even if there was, I'm not so sure this line of work is all that good for the health of a fifty-year-old. So, Lincoln, you take a loach and try to bring back that man's essence, something to give his parents, to whom, by the way, I plan to deliver his decorations personally."

"Thank you, sir, but I have to remind you, I'm still a just a W-1. You said 'Chief.'"

"Friday, I may be a colonel, but I'm not as stupid as most. You are a W-2 because I just promoted you ahead of your contemporaries. Go find something of Mr. Nhu for his family."

Lincoln rousted Lockett, and the two tracked down the pilots of the Vietnamese ship that had rescued Huber. One insisted he go along in the back to show the way. When they found the ship's melted skeleton, Lincoln tossed a smoke grenade to mark the location for the helicopters behind them to drop in and gather the lost American crew's remains.

They hovered over the site, but with the rotor wash, there was nothing to see, aside from the wildly undulating jungle vegetation, a thousand hands waving at them to go away. There was, though, a sudden, tiny flash that caught the Vietnamese pilot's attention. He tapped Lockett on the shoulder and pointed down. When the American fixed on the ground, he realized they were being engaged with small arms fire. They could actually see the eyes of the man shooting at them, and Lockett pulled his .38, aimed as well as he could in the shuddering aircraft, and pulled the trigger. There was no way to tell what the round struck, but it wasn't his enemy, for the soldier was still upright. Lockett stared through his sites even more intensely, and was about to take his next shot, when he realized the man was dressed in an OD flight suit and was waving a signal mirror. Lockett screamed, and Lincoln hovered the small helicopter at a mile per hour, if that, toward a tiny clearing. Nhu followed at a run, and when they dropped in, he collapsed as they pulled him aboard. The flight back was silent, for each time one of the men tried to come up with something to say, it faded before it came from his mouth.

Nhu was airlifted by an American HUEY to the same facility at which Huber was being operated on in a last ditch effort to stem his internal bleeding. The next morning, the old man let Lincoln and Lockett fly to the hospital to check on them. Huber had survived the surgery but was unconscious. A doctor came in and told them Huber had torn his liver, ruptured his spleen, and had lost so much blood, it was unlikely he would wake up.

They went to see Nhu. He was in a chair, staring blankly out a filthy window. The areas of his head, back, and arms that had been burned were bandaged. He looked worse than Huber. They sat with him for a while, listened to the story, and returned to tell Huber just who had saved what there was of his life. There was no way to know if he heard them.

Two days later, the CO sent a private to fetch Lincoln. His chest gripped with the inevitability of the news to come. "Your friend Huber asked to see you. You and Lockett go there and tell him if he wants a job, we'll find a place."

Huber was on his back, eyes vacant. Lincoln asked if he had heard what he and Lockett had told him days before. He shook his head. They related the story of the rescue, and that it had been Nhu who'd come very close to sacrificing himself. Huber turned away and closed his eyes. The tears, though, pressed through.

He asked to go see Nhu, but the doctor wouldn't allow him to sit up, so Lincoln and Lockett put Nhu in a wheelchair and trundled him from the Vietnamese side of the hospital to Huber's room. The American tried to speak, but words would not come, and, instead, he began to cry again. Nhu lifted himself out of the wheelchair and lowered himself onto the foot of Huber's bed.

CHAPTER FORTY-THREE

When Isabelle received the letter describing Nhu and Huber connecting in the hospital, she sat with Zeke on the couch, his head in her lap, and tried to imagine what the war had fostered in the hearts of such innocent men. She laughed at her own problems, the full load of courses, exams that came nearly every other day, and the worst, trying to get into nursing school, given her reputation.

She sat with her father that night in the living room. “Poppy, I really want this. But what’s going to happen when they find out about that thing with Rosemary?”

“Not a damn thing’s gonna happen, Sweetheart. You want to go to nursing school, you’ll go. You’ve got your interview in six days, right?”

“What if they bring up the whole mess?”

“Then you deal with it. Let’s get an answer ready, and if it comes up, knock ’em dead. In life, doll, you define the problem, you come up with a plan, you stick to it when all looks grim, and you fight until you get it done. Learned that in the war when all seemed lost, and the walls were crumbling around us. In the long run, like looking back now, it's easier than being afraid and doing nothing."

The day before the interview, the five friends drove together to Hershey, to Penn State's new medical education complex. They were each handed a packet of forms and instructions. Isabelle was the only one scheduled to be interviewed by the dean of the nursing school. She couldn't sleep that night and sat up writing a long letter to Lincoln, embarrassed by her petty life and lack of strength. In the morning, she tore the pages into shreds and took a cold shower, imagining that was what Lincoln was doing at the same moment half a world away.

The dean of the nursing school was sitting at her desk in an austere office. She came to her feet formally and shook Isabelle's hand so firmly, it almost hurt. Her close-cropped, salt and pepper hair and military bearing gave her the demeanor of a sergeant major. Her clothing, though, was frumpy and unpressed, her shoes clunky.

"Have a seat, Mrs. Friday." Isabelle nearly gasped at the greeting, one of the first times since her wedding day that she realized who she was. "Well, thank you for coming here to evaluate us. As you know, we only recently opened our doors. We're being watched very carefully. Right up the road is the University of Pennsylvania, oldest medical school in the new world, and here in Chocolate Town, we are the youngest. We have to be especially careful who we choose to represent us. And *you* have to be careful to choose a school that fits your needs and your personality." Isabelle's chest clutched, and her face reddened. "Tell me about yourself and why you want to come here, to Hershey."

"Well, ma'am, I'm married to the finest man on this Earth. He's a helicopter pilot in Viet Nam. And he's having a rough time, not like us at home." Her eyes dropped. "And I'm going to be a nurse, and I'm going to do it here, at Penn State, because this is where I live, and this is where I can do my part to make this world a better place."

The dean stood and came around her desk. She bent forward and put an arm around Isabelle's shoulders. "I know you will. Hershey would be lucky to have you."

The room became unnervingly quiet. Isabelle tried to speak, but nothing came. The dean retook her seat. She smiled at Isabelle and commented, "You look like you just got word you won the Irish Sweepstakes."

Isabelle grinned, "I did."

"No, you earned it. Okay, let's get some housekeeping out of the way. The reason that you are sitting here at my desk, not talking with another interviewer, is because I wanted to meet the woman who stood up for herself when a snake tried to humiliate her. I'll be direct. Those two deans involved are from the olden days, relics. The world is changing, or at least America is. You are not to assume, from the way you and your girlfriends were treated, that Penn State tolerates women being considered sexual objects or dull liars who imagine things happening to them that really did not. You have as much right to an education with dignity as any man. On the other hand, you have an obligation to work for your grades and not rely on a pretty face and a seductive smile to get you through, not in my school, at least. But you already know that.

"I have reviewed your credentials and spoken with your professors. Every grade you earned was an A, and in a very competitive pre-nursing curriculum. Everyone respects you, but please remember, they are mostly from the nursing profession. When you become a nurse, you will deal on an hourly basis with doctors. That will be the greatest challenge of your professional life. Caring for patients will come naturally to you. No question.

"I'm sorry to tell you this, but the arrogance you are going to face is extraordinary. Some of the doctors you will encounter are superb; many are not. The latter are usually the ones who have been groomed from grade school to go to the best colleges, tour Europe the summer after graduation, and then start medical school. Don't get me wrong. They work hard, very hard, but so many believe viscerally that they are superior in every way to both their patients and nurses.

"All of this breeds contempt on both sides, but it is hidden under a veneer of collaboration and teamwork that lasts only until the doctor has a fight with his wife or gets a ticket coming to work, and then off come the gloves, well the doctor's gloves. Hell to pay for anyone who doesn't lick his shoes for the next twelve hours. And then there's the cooling off, and a few less eggshells to walk on, and then a few days where they realize they've been jerks, so everything is peachy keen for a bit; and then it happens all over again—and then again. Every once in a while, you get a medical director who has leadership ability and won't tolerate the infantile behavior, but they are few and very far between.

"I'm telling you this to let you know you will be facing innumerable humiliations as your career proceeds, and that you're going to need to find subtle ways to fight back. That brings up another trap—medical students and residents. These are two classes of human beings on the bottom of the pile. It's easy to take out your frustrations on them because they can't fight back. You will be co-opted into joining factions to pick on certain ones. Kinda fun, but it just fosters deeper resentment in the end, and it makes the vicious cycle only more vicious, because they will grow up to become real doctors someday. I hope you will rise above it.

"Okay, I've talked long enough. You will be getting a wagon-load of acceptances. I hope you will consider Hershey when you make your decision. And if you do, I will not bother you, but I hope you will bother me. You are going to hear all sorts of stories about the witch they appointed the first Dean of the Nursing School—Mrs. Hitler they call me, and I'm not even married." She laughed heartily, and Isabelle's eyes glowed.

That evening, she sat with her parents on the porch and faced west, watching as the last filaments of sun faded. She smiled to herself that Lincoln was seeing the first traces of that very same light, a world away in Viet Nam. She drank two martinis. She told them of the letter that had arrived that day from Lincoln. Huber had been banged up but was doing fine, and he now loved the Vietnamese.

Her letter to Lincoln blazed with the positive strokes she had received, and in it, she wrote in big numbers the months, weeks, days, hours, and seconds until it would all to be over: two months and change, "5,443,200 seconds, oops, I mean, 5,443,197, oops, now I mean, 5,443,192!" The next morning, Zeke could sense her exhilaration and pranced alongside her to the mailbox, leash held loosely in his mouth.

CHAPTER FORTY-FOUR

On a day off, Lincoln hitched a ride to the hospital in Saigon. Huber was slouched on a beaten recliner in the lounge. A bit of color had returned, but he had lost more weight. Lincoln greeted him by laughing, "Hubert, you need to start eating. You're beginning to look like Nhu."

Huber shook his head. "I can't. Not hungry."

"Is it because of the surgery?"

"No, man. All I can think about is finding Kim Lieu. All these months, I've been trying to get some time off to come to Saigon and start looking. And when I finally wind up smack in the middle of town, I can't fuckin' walk."

"Hubert, let me ask you. So, when you got to Saigon, how were you going to go about finding her? I mean, it isn't as though you availed yourself of the Basics of Vietnamese Language night course they offered back at Normandy. Yeah, you made a commitment-and-a-half to get back here, but you ain't got a plan."

"To be honest, troop, or do I have to call you Chief?"

"Yes, you must call me Chief, and it is customary for an underling to come to attention and salute when I, your superior officer, enter a room."

"Okay, asshole, in answer to your question, I just thought it would happen. She would suddenly appear at the door. I did good here last time. I did good in flight school. I just thought God was finally on my side, and that He would take care of the rest."

Lincoln thought for a minute. "You may be right, but God helps those who blah, blah, blah. You need to make a plan, boy."

"Yeah, maybe when I can get out of a chair without two nurses—fuckin' male nurses, thank you—pulling me to my feet, I'll hit the streets."

"My ass. The second you can hold yourself up in a chair for three minutes, your slim butt'll be back in a slick doing it all over again. Like I said, you need a plan, and as fast as you're getting better, you better come up with one quick-like."

Lincoln's assault helicopter company remained attached to the 33rd Mech. They continued to do joint operations with the Vietnamese and, occasionally with Australian helicopter companies. When Nhu was discharged from the hospital, he was given two weeks off, an "in-country R&R," but much of his time was spent attending award ceremonies in front of his countrymen, and then in front of the American brass. Colonel Bierline recommended Nhu for the Distinguished Service Cross, the very medal Huber had earned for exceptional heroism on his first tour, but that was quashed by the brass at Pentagon East, for a Silver Star was the highest award available to a foreign combatant working with an American unit.

Bierline and the aviation battalion commander were so irritated, they flew to Saigon, ready to pound tables. A deal, though, was struck awarding Nhu a Silver Star for rescuing Huber. His

Bronze Star was upgraded—for taking charge of so desperate a situation and saving Lockett's life—to another Silver Star. That would mean a Silver Star with an oak leaf cluster to designate the second award—nearly unheard of, even in American military annals, but surely a first for a foreign soldier.

Nhu invited Lincoln and Lockett to his parents' home in Saigon. He led them down a dilapidated, steaming alley that opened into a seemingly separate city walled off by a thousand shops crammed one next to the other. The eight-foot wide, twelve-foot deep stores were segregated by the nature of their wares: fifteen denture makers in a row; then a sudden switch to wicker chairs, just chairs, that went on for eight or nine iterations; and then the inventory switched to rice bowls, and nothing but rice bowls of every shape and color for the next six shops.

Nhu ducked into a skinny gap between the wig retailers and a row of writing paper vendors. Outside each of the latter, seated at a table just inches off the ground, was a wispy-bearded man in traditional, but moth-eaten, Chinese garb. With nib pen in hand, the man arrogantly looked away from a potential customer until the fawning, illiterate citizen bowed and handed over a sheet of just-purchased paper. The old scribe brusquely queried the client as to what was to be said to a government official or far-off relative, and without another word, dipped his pen painstakingly into a tiny bottle of India ink and scratched out the document in Vietnamese letters or exotic Chinese characters. When the peasant paid his bill, the penman pulled a worn, leather pouch from his underclothing and carefully inserted the few, clammy, penny notes.

The three soldiers wandered through yet another alley into a residential area, stopping at a crumbling stucco building. Nhu directed them up an exceedingly dark, narrow, worn-out stairwell, one so low, Lincoln had to stoop and use his hands to steady himself. At the tiny landing on the third floor, they came to two doors facing each other, both protected by an outer lattice of steel mesh worthy of a federal penitentiary.

Nhu turned to one and smiled broadly. He opened several locks with ungainly, rusted skeleton keys and called out to announce himself. He needn't have bothered. His mother and father were sitting in wicker chairs just inside the first of three microscopic rooms. A single, low-watt light bulb in a small, crystal fixture lit the room unevenly, giving it the look of a secret society assembly. Nhu's parents jumped to their feet, bowed slightly, and took their guests' hands, holding them for many seconds. Tea was poured, cigarettes offered, and a bowl heaped with withered, unshelled peanuts was placed before them.

Nhu watched his guests' eyes closely as they surveyed the room. He spoke quickly. "My mother Chinese, father Vietnamese. Mixed marriage. Only certain place they can live in peace." He waited several seconds while Lincoln and Lockett screwed up their faces. "I do not want to say, but America, you not see white and black together. For us it is the same—hide always."

Lockett asked, "But Lieutenant, your father is a government official. If he's, I don't want to say, you know, not accepted, how did he get elected?"

"I do not want to say such a thing, not accepted, but my father, he so smart." Nhu's arm swept out toward the crammed bookshelves. He pulled Lockett into the next room. Its walls, too, were lined with books, the shelves encroaching on the negligible living space. In the tiny bedroom, just a bit of real estate was left for the mahogany planks that served as his parents' bed. The rest of the sixty square feet was choked with mountains of books, a desk piled with his father's papers, and a 1920's typewriter.

Lincoln looked questioningly at Nhu. "Did you grow up here, I mean, in this apartment?"

"Yes. Where you are stand." He pulled aside a cloth that covered a three-square-foot closet. He extracted a tatami mat, unrolled it on the floor, and laughed, "Home, sweet home."

Nhu's mother served platters of traditional Vietnamese food, *cha gio*—egg rolls—*pho*, Hue crab, and fried vegetables; his father lugged a bathtub-sized pot of streamed rice to the table. The elder Mr. Nhu pulled several Tiger Beers from a washbowl filled with ice, and they ate for an hour. Nhu drizzled a few drops of *nuoc mam* onto Lincoln's rice. A moment later Lincoln took the bottle and poured on some more.

Lockett watched Lincoln for a few minutes. "Hey, this your first Vietnamese meal?"

"Yeah. Wish I'd known six months ago."

Lockett laughed. "We used to go out with our instructors at the DLI. Took us to little places in Frisco. We practiced our Vietnamese. I was so excited when it actually worked. I ordered a bowl of rice. Waiter came with three because I had said it three times to make sure I got it right. Tell ya, Linc, I feel as close to these people, the Vietnamese, as I do anyone at home."

"Makes you wonder what the hell we're doing here. Blowing up the place building by building. Wish I understood."

Nhu's father eyed Lincoln's empty bowl. The man scooped two paddles of rice into it and handed him the *nuoc mam*. Lincoln nodded and turned to Nhu. "Would you please tell your parents how happy we are to be here? Tell them that we think you are a great guy, and a great pilot, and most of all, a great hero."

Nhu blushed and said nothing, though his parents' eyes glowed. When Lockett translated officially, they laughed.

The three went to see Huber in the morning. He had developed an infection in his surgical wound and was back in bed. He had also lost more weight. The doctor waited until he drifted off to sleep then called the three soldiers out of the room. "You need to get him turned around, fellas. His immune system isn't working right because he's starving. Can't synthesize protein to make antibodies to fight the infection."

Lincoln asked, "Isn't he getting antibiotics?"

"Of course. The best we have, but they can't handle the problem on their own. His immune system has to do its part. Gents, this is serious."

When Huber woke, Lincoln peered directly into his friend's eyes. "Hubert, the gig's up. We're gonna get things turned around. You are going to tell my pals here what this is all about, and then we are going to come up with the plan you obviously haven't made. Get started, young man."

Huber growled a few strings of profanity and finished with an, "Okay, what the fuck." His audience's eyes were glued to the face that seemed to have become more skeletal than before he had napped. His saga went on for half-an-hour, much of it centered around the idiocy of the officers at Pentagon East. Every order, he declared, was based, first, on what would keep the officer out of dutch with his next higher level of command and then, when it was judged sufficiently benign, its value in engendering brownie points for promotion. An occasional notion about what was needed to win the war came third in the list of priorities, and finally, in last place, was the merit that directive might have in bringing soldiers in the field home alive and sane.

When it was all done, though Lincoln and Lockett were silent, Nhu leaned back and laughed. "It all so simple. We go find you Kim Lieu. She make own decision. This new Viet Nam for woman. You see."

The three men returned to Normandy and flew a dozen more missions with the combined force. After a few days, the planning and the assaults became routine, and they felt ready to counter the tactical maneuvers the VC had drawn upon during the first few missions. By the end of the month, the VC and the North Vietnamese regulars were nowhere to be found during the day, when aerial assaults could be mounted, but they remained everywhere at night. Mortar attacks became so commonplace, a bunker was excavated behind the Officers' Club and a fridge dug into a wall so the patrons could retire to the underground tavern and continue drinking until the enemy ran out of shells for the night.

Lincoln was sent back to the spraying detail for a couple of weeks, a plum of an assignment, for it was out of harm's way. Or so it was touted, until a spray HUEY was shot down by a kid with an AK-47; and the men were pickled in Agent Orange when the tank ruptured, despite a soft autorotation. Lincoln swooped in to salvage the crew. One of the downed door gunners vomited a jet of Agent Orange in the back of the ship. Lincoln yelled to the man not to worry, "That shit's harmless. Just bug spray."

Lincoln, Lockett, and Nhu asked for a three-day, in-country R&R. They would spend the time in Saigon searching for Kim Lieu. They visited Huber, who had begun to eat and was out of bed. He gave Nhu all the information he could to start the search, and the three took a cab into the heart of Saigon, near the grand Binh Thanh Market. Nhu donned his dress uniform and went to Kim Lieu's parents' home. He made up a tale about the government seeking children of American soldiers, products of Operation Mixed Egg. The U.S. government had promised, he explained, monthly sums to families tainted with barbarian blood. Their faces brightened with interest.

Nhu told them he had to see the mother and child and take them, *without* the grandparents, to a central registration point. That's where the struggle began. The Vietnamese knew their government well enough to fear their daughter would be kidnapped and sold into sexual slavery, for it was clear that, to have slept with an American savage, the woman had essentially declared her promiscuity to the entire world.

Nhu fought and fought, but they wouldn't give in. Nhu smiled and said he would give them time to think about it and would be back in the morning with the first installation of cash, just in case they changed their minds.

The three stayed in a crumbling guest house nearby and were at the edge of the alley that led to the parents' cardboard and tin shanty by 5 A.M. At sunrise, the father popped out of the hut and moved surreptitiously, though like a dart, into the dawn shadows, past refugee villages, through alleys that led off alleys, until he ducked into a sturdy-looking, cinderblock shelter. When they got closer, they realized the blocks had been piled on top of each other without cement. The three hid behind a corner and waited for fifteen minutes. The man exited, trailed by two young women, one carrying a parcel wrapped in moth-eaten blankets.

When they got back to the man's home, Nhu waited a few minutes and went to the door; Lincoln and Lockett took positions towering just behind him. Nhu held up a five-dollar military payment certificate three inches from the father's eyes. It was a good two-week's food money, and Nhu pledged it was just the first of monthly payments that would come for the next five years.

Without taking his eyes off the cash, the father yelled over his shoulder. A curtain of dirty cloth hanging from the ceiling was pulled aside. Two women holding babies stepped forward to stand, eyes cast down, behind the old man. Both children appeared to be of mixed blood, and Nhu asked who was who. When the women looked down in silence, Nhu jammed the money behind him into Lincoln's fist, about-faced, and nudged the two soldiers outside.

"No, no," the old man spluttered in Vietnamese. "Maybe they can tell you a little, but not too much."

Nhu handed the money to the man, who took a step to the side of the girls, turned his back to them, and shoved the bill into his drawers.

Lockett snipped, "I won't be taking *that* fiver back."

Nhu asked the girls, in English, if one had had a boyfriend at an office in Pentagon East, a man who had saved her life. The more striking of the two stood motionless as the color drained from her face. Though the father did not understand a word, his face wrinkled in distrust, and he slid back in front of Kim Lieu.

Nhu spoke over the man's shoulder. "We need to talk you. So important."

She froze for a minute then managed to smile uneasily and answer disinterestedly in English, "One hour, at the big market, but I don't want to say name of it. But you know B T. Where they sell fish."

Lincoln laughed under his breath. "How romantic!"

Kim Lieu blushed. "Okay, maybe vegetables."

Lincoln winked. "Oh, much more enchanting."

She hid a smile as the old man turned to glare at her.

They met at the Binh Thanh. The three pilots made sure she wasn't being followed as they drifted toward "Vegetables," a section of the massive market that, by itself, was as large as the entire Safeway in Wilkes Barre. "Rice and Beans" was even grander.

Lincoln laughed, "It'd take ya two weeks to do the daily shopping."

Nhu corrected him. "No, only few minute. You only go to relative stand. Or maybe same stand you go for twenty year. Very easy. Same as you know to go for buy rice bowl or false tooth. Only family or friend to buy from. Otherwise, no can trust. Not family, he give you bad fish for much money. System work."

They saw Kim Lieu, for she was much taller and far more regal than the other women. She was holding the baby in blankets, but was so tremulous, the child was bouncing and began to cry. They nodded for her to follow to a section of the market with dozens and dozens of tiny, steamy, grubby food stands. Nhu sat across from Kim Lieu and ordered *pho* for the four of them.

He laughed, but not happily, "Maybe only food here in market not kill American. Maybe be boiling whole day, maybe two." He turned to Kim Lieu and spoke in Vietnamese, then to his Western friends. "From now we talk English. No secret. This too important. Who to start?"

Lincoln raised his hand vaguely. Kim Lieu's eyes locked his. "Miss, I am not going to play any more games. You know a man. His name is Huber." Her eyes reddened, and Lincoln paused to puff a trill of air from his lips. "Well, he is our great friend, and he is here in Viet Nam, actually in Saigon, and he wants to see you."

She took a diaper from a bag and covered her eyes. They waited. The baby cried harder, and Kim Lieu put her down and told her to stand on her own. The toddler did, but when she got a full view of the Americans, she grasped her mother's leg desperately. Kim Lieu covered her face again and mumbled barely audibly, "Where is he?"

Lincoln spoke calmly. "In the hospital, but he's fine."

"How did he get here?"

The three men looked at each other. Lincoln went on. "He became a pilot so he could come back to Viet Nam and find you and the baby. Got a little banged up, wounded, but Lieutenant Nhu, here, saved his life, so he's okay now. Just that he won't eat because he's so sad not to see you. Doctor said that if he doesn't start eating, he may not be okay."

When she uncovered her face this time, her eyes had hardened. "I cannot see him. My families forbid it."

Nhu's face heated. "Who forbid? You father? No, he want money. Mr. Huber, he really love you, want you, not money."

Nhu went back to slurping his soup, ignoring her, though both Lincoln and Lockett sat motionless, butts puckered, as tense as they had been on their first flights at Wolters. She turned toward them. "No, I cannot go to see him. If I do, I never leave him."

The two Americans gasped. Lincoln managed to squeak, "You mean you really love him? Still?"

"Hieu is kindest man there is. He is gentle as baby. He help everybody. When he has only little money, he give it to buy food for a man on the street. And he is so beautiful. All my girlfriend say he is most beautiful man in Viet Nam."

Lockett turned to Lincoln. "Huber!?"

Lincoln laughed, "I know. It's the water. Somethin' funny in it—evil weed drainin' from the GI bases, or LSD, maybe. I don't know. Somethin' though."

Kim Lieu spoke to Nhu in Vietnamese. He turned to his friends. "She say you no understand Mr. Huber. He no so simple. Miss Kim Lieu, she watch him long time before even say 'Good morning.' Miss Kim Lieu already go to college. She not peasant. She say he made from steel but need to be…" He stared up at the ceiling in deep thought.

Kim Lieu whispered behind her hand. Nhu nodded and laughed, "Yes, he need temper steel. But she also say she cannot give up to see family and go ancestor grave. If father take away, she become like Mr. Huber, not eat and die."

Kim Lieu then spoke in Vietnamese, rapidly and with concern. Nhu waited patiently then answered in English. "No, no, he okay now that we help him find Miss Kim Lieu."

She answered again in Vietnamese and stood. Nhu translated. "She angry I try to shame her to see Mr. Huber. But I understand she have great problem. Maybe we go back talk to Mr. Huber and come to answer."

Kim Lieu lifted the baby and held her tightly as she started toward the door. Lincoln ran to her side and took the liberty of touching her elbow as lightly as he could. "Let him see his baby. Come to the hospital. You stand outside the room. We'll show him from the door. I promise I will be gentle if you let me hold her."

She nodded. Lincoln was struck silent, for he had never seen a creature bearing such wounds upon whose face nothing was revealed. As they rushed out, Lockett threw three dollars on the rickety table, and the proprietor's eyes opened as wide as the *pho* bowls he had served fourteen hours a day, seven days a week, every day of the year, for the past thirty years. Stupefied, he watched them weave through the stalls until he lost sight of them as they emerged into the blistering daylight.

At the hospital, there was a bit of disturbance when they first walked into the American ward, but the lies bounded from the three soldiers' mouths like a swarm of H-23s, and they were soon standing outside Huber's room. Lincoln checked with a nurse on their friend's condition, and he said the man had improved and was eating again. Lincoln put out his arms to take the baby, and Kim Lieu lifted her but paused and froze. She pulled the baby back into a tight embrace and stepped up to the doorway.

Huber was staring at the ceiling, forming images only he could have conjured from the burgeoning mold. He must have sensed motion at the door, for his face turned in that direction, but he perceived nothing and looked away without expression.

Kim Lieu tightened and took a rigid a step into the doorway. She whispered, "Hieu. It is Kim Lieu."

His head craned toward the sound, but it was just the recurring phantasm, and he turned away. His friends stepped into the room and urged Kim Lieu forward. Huber looked up again. There was an instant of tranquility before the air was sucked from the room as Huber exploded in a thunderous howl. It quieted, though, as his tears erupted.

Kim Lieu gasped. The baby wailed. Lincoln and Lockett became lightheaded and paced about the room aimlessly. A bevy of staff collected at the door, one of whom, an ancient Vietnamese woman from Housekeeping, toddled in, looked at Kim Lieu, then at Huber, listened to Nhu's quavering narrative, and scooped the baby into her arms. The woman cooed and rocked the baby until it quieted, then she went into the hall, quickly surrounded by her co-workers.

Kim Lieu's face was wet with tears as she shuffled toward the bed and sat on a far corner. Huber reached out to take her hand. She hesitated, but he drew her toward him with the gentlest stroke of his fingers. She slid closer, and then closer, until she rolled onto her side and embraced him. He placed the pillow under her head and they stared at each other, faces barely an inch apart. When the pillow became damp, he slipped the dry side under her head tenderly.

Huber whispered, "The baby," and Lincoln ran into the hall to retrieve the child, but it took some time to find the housekeeper, who was circled by her minions, shoveling rice into the child's mouth with chopsticks. When Lincoln brought the baby back to the room, she scrutinized Huber, and he looked away, trying not to scare her, but she reached out and tugged on his nose. He kissed the top of her head.

The nursing supervisor had heard the rumor and strode indignantly to the post-surgical floor. He stood silently at the door but gathered himself and addressed the couple tangled in an army hospital bed. "The regulations state that a man and a, you know..." Kim Lieu looked up and smiled alluringly. The man stammered, "Everything okay in here?"

"Could not be better, sir. Thank you for taking such care of my husband."

Lincoln, Lockett, and Nhu gaped. Lincoln took the nurse by the elbow and drew him into the hall. "We'll be back in an hour, I promise. We'll take his wife home. Could you turn your head for a while?"

Kim Lieu and Huber were in the day room when they got back. Huber had showered and shaved and was holding the baby, who had fallen to sleep in his lap.

The three pilots spoke softly that they had to get back to Normandy, and Huber looked up and tried to thank them, but nothing came. Lincoln wagged his finger at his friend. "You deserve it."

CHAPTER FORTY-FIVE

Isabelle shared the letter about the reunion in Saigon with her parents. Her father smiled. "You have a hell of a husband, and we have a hell of a son-in-law—the best."

She gave them the countdown—five weeks and a day. Lincoln had received his new assignment, the 3rd Armored Cavalry at Fort Lewis, in Washington State.

"I know, Poppy, it's very far, but it's not forever."

"No, it isn't, Doll. I was stationed there after the war. McCord Air Force Base, right next to Lewis, Camp Lewis, then. Most beautiful spot in the country, once you get used to the rain."

She laughed. "Maybe, if it rains all the time, Lincoln won't have to fly so much, and he can stay home and help me study."

Isabelle had written to Pacific Lutheran University in Tacoma, not far from Lincoln's new duty station, to ask for permission to take nursing classes that could be transferred to Penn State when Lincoln was done with his service. She had long since been accepted into the School of Nursing at Hershey, and the dean had written to the administration in Tacoma to help sort out the nuts and bolts. The only roadblock came from an administrator at Penn State's main campus, who had the final word on the application of credits earned at other institutions. He was a well-known, rabid, anti-war activist and had opposed allowing Isabelle to matriculate at Penn State in the first place. He stood before the admissions committee and sought to censure her as an army wife. "She has a responsibility to either divorce her husband, or, at the very least, convince him to desert and join the anti-war movement. If she is not willing to do that, I question her commitment to the healing arts."

There was an hour of bitter discord, but a final compromise was reached requiring Isabelle to appear before the board and assure them of her devotion to non-violence. The dean of the nursing school stood and asked politely for a fifteen-minute recess to gather her thoughts. What she gathered, though, was the senior and mid-level staff of the College of Nursing, twenty-three white-uniformed women who flowed into the meeting hall and formed a crescent behind the dean.

She stood rigidly. "I resign," she announced and turned her head toward the nursing staff.

Each woman spoke softly. "I resign."

Isabelle had already bought the textbooks and was putting in twelve and fourteen hour days cramming anatomy, biochemistry, and the basics of gastroenterology into her head when the dean called to confirm that the transfer had been approved. She and her folks celebrated that night, and when her mom went to bed, her father spoke softly to Isabelle. "Hey, Nurse Friday, I need a consultation, if you don't mind." He sat on the couch and complained that his stomach hurt.

"What do you mean by stomach?"

"Well, down here." He pointed to the lower right side of his abdomen. "Not been able to go to the bathroom, either."

"For how long?"

"I don't know. A day or so."

She looked in his eyes and screwed up her face. "How long, Poppy? Tell your nurse the truth."

"Okay, maybe a week."

"And you're just getting around to mentioning it?"

"Well, you know how I feel about things. If it ain't broke, don't fix it."

"Oh, my gosh, but it *is* broke, and we're going to go to see Dr. Heldman at sunrise. No ifs, ands, or buts."

"Heldman's been dead for years."

"Not that Dr. Heldman. His son took over the practice. Everybody loves him."

An x-ray of Bob Dalton's abdomen revealed loops of distended bowel, some filled with fluid, some just air, some with both. Dr. Heldman ordered a barium enema to see exactly where the blockage was, and if it was simply a twist in the bowel, or, though he didn't mention it at that juncture, a tumor.

It took three days to schedule the test, then four more to be given the results. It was a tumor, almost certainly cancer of the large intestine, and while they would operate, the chances of survival were, Isabelle knew after she went to see her dean, very small.

He was sapped of energy after the barium enema, and spent the day in bed, asleep by nine. Isabelle sat with her mother that night and explained what was likely to happen. The tumor, along with a segment of bowel both before and after the growth, would have to be removed to make sure all the diseased tissue had been taken out of the body. Had the growth been in the middle of the large intestine, there might have been a chance to cut it out and reconnect the two halves, but the x-rays showed the cancer toward the end of the bowel, near the rectum. When the surgeon was done removing a wide margin of cancer-free intestine, nothing would be left to connect at the far end. Isabelle sighed. The surgeon would have no choice but to fashion a colostomy, what was left of the bowel sewn to an opening in the front of her father's abdomen. The waste would dribble into a plastic bag, one he would wear until the traces of cancer the surgeon could not have seen and removed consumed his mind and body.

Kerrith poured two glasses of wine. "We need to sit down with your father and lay it out, the whole truth, just like you did for me. He would not want it any other way."

When they had their family meeting the next night, Bob drank three quick martinis and laughed sadly. "I know. Now, what we're going to do is come up with the best solution, given the facts we know at this point. We're not pulling any punches. We don't know what the result of the surgery is going to be, but one thing is for sure, I won't be able to work for a couple of months, probably more. So here's what I see. Every several days, some guy comes to me asking to buy the business. I politely, believe it or not, tell them to shove it where the sun don't shine. I must have thirty business cards of fat corporations who want to get their paws on the place. I will choose four or five and get them to murder each other over a price. The money goes into bonds. We live on the interest, and very nicely, I might add, and we wait and see what happens. That way, the business does not control us—we remain in command."

He leaned back, smiled, and downed another cocktail. "Anyway, the place has become a pain in the rear since, out of the clear blue, yours truly is legally responsible for one of my rebuilt engines that runs out of gas because the pilot was drunk when he took off and forgot his new engine was fifty horsepower hotter than the old one, for which he paid more than his mortgage, just so he could be a big shot and brag about it, and it sucks gas twice as fast as the old one, like I drink Martinis tonight, which was only ten miles an hour slower, the plane that is, than the new one. Are you following me?"

"Robert," his wife spoke seriously, "we won't be making any major decisions after the four martinis you've managed to inhale in the last ten minutes."

"Yes, Kerrith, dear."

CHAPTER FORTY-SIX

Isabelle did not write to Lincoln about her father, but her letters had clearly lost their tenor, and he brooded quietly. That was not his only care. His battalion was being scattered to the two corners of Viet Nam. He was being sent further south. Huber, who had suddenly gained fifteen pounds and was as chipper as Lincoln had ever seen him, had been returned to flight status. He was sneaking down to Saigon nearly every other day while his buddies covered for him.

Huber and Lockett were called to the CO's office. Both were promoted to Chief Warrant Officer Two. The colonel apologized to Lockett for the delay, but explained that because he had been assigned additional duties as an interpreter, it had eaten into his flying time, and his promotion had taken a hit. When Lockett raised his index finger to speak, the CO grumbled, "Don't ask me, Lockett, I just work here."

They grinned broadly until the old man told them they were being sent up-country for the rest of their tour. When their time came to return to the States, they would fly home out of

Da Nang, five hundred miles to the north. He would not see them again and shook their hands warmly. They were dismissed to pack everything they owned and report to the flight line for a waiting Air Force C-123. As they walked to their rooms, Huber understood he would not set foot in Saigon again for the rest of his tour.

Halfway to the barracks, Huber stopped short, cursed, and broke into a sprint to his room. Minutes later, when a HUEY started its engine for a routine run to Saigon, he loped up to it, threw his duffel in, and climbed aboard. Lockett watched as the ship lifted off to the east.

The next morning, Lincoln and his crew were sleeping beside their HUEY, waiting for written orders to fly to Saigon, land on a boat, pick up three celebrities, and transport them around South Viet Nam to lift morale. A jeep pulled up next to the helicopter. A captain was driving, and two Vietnamese were riding along, a striking woman in her thirties in the front and an ancient lady in the back.

The captain shook the pilot awake and asked impatiently, "Hey, Chief, sorry to bother you, but where'd you take that Vietnamese guy the other night? I can't find him anywhere."

"What guy? Excuse me, sir, but who are you again?"

"Oh, yeah, I'm J.W. Weathersby, S-5 for the 33rd Mech—civil affairs officer. You're the dust-off that flew into My Co two nights ago, yes?"

"What's My Co, Captain? I'm sorry, sir, I don't know what you're talking about."

"Two nights ago—the village of My Co. I called and asked you to medevac my counterpart—tall Vietnamese guy who was wounded at the north end of the vill. Hey, I'm not trying to bust your balls, Chief. Thank you for coming in, but I need to find him. You said you took him to the Sai Gon Hospital."

"Oh, yeah, I remember now. Yeah, we took 'im down there. He was fucked up. Crew chief said he didn't have a chance."

"Yeah, but I went down there yesterday, and they never heard of him."

Lincoln called up to his crew chief, who was sunning himself on the roof of the helicopter. "Hey, Tommy, where'd we drop that local two nights ago?"

A small man with a bristling Mohawk hairdo, red bandana, and a heavy Bronx accent piped up, "The usual, sir, wasn't it? Yeah, yeah, that's it. I remember, for sure. The Mayo Clinic. You know, down by the big market."

Lincoln smiled acerbically. "See, I told you, Captain. I promise, we didn't keep 'im. Take a look in the back of the ship if you don't believe me."

J.W. snapped, "Chief, listen to me. I searched every ward of that shithole hospital, every goddamn bed, stared into every face. The lady at the front said there was no helicopter that night."

"I'm sorry, sir, I got no reason to bullshit you. That's where we dropped 'im. I don't know what to tell you."

J.W. stared out at the red mud of the helicopter base and finally sighed, "Okay, Chief, I believe you."

"Why, thank you, sir," Lincoln added sarcastically.

"I'm sorry, Chief. I didn't come here to piss you off. Look, the guy was my best friend here. At the least, I need to find his body." He started to walk off, then turned back and added with a smile, "Hey, I gotta ask you one question, Mr. Friday. How the hell did you get into that place, and at night? There's wires everywhere."

"I didn't, sir. Old chief, been flying an hour or two since he got home from the Korean War, dropped it in. I see you're rated, got wings. That guy's like magic. Hope they don't send you or me back enough times to learn to fly like that. And, I'm sorry you lost that local, sir."

The captain walked up to Lincoln and shook his hand, adding, "Hey, man, I'm sorry. Thanks. You guys were great the other night. I'm sorry. You're a good man, but this whole fuckin' place sucks. I'm never fuckin' comin' back. Watch me now."

Lincoln's eyes reddened. "A fuckin' men, sir."

The captain got back in the jeep, spoke to his passengers, though mostly with hand signals, threw his arms up as if in capitulation, and drove off.

Lincoln leaned back to resume his nap when a runner stopped in front of him. "Sir, old man wants to see you, ASAP."

"What about?"

"Sir, if I knew that, would I be a Spec. Four?"

"Was he mad?"

"He's always mad."

Lincoln walked slowly, watching the dust whorls settle on his boots. The colonel sat him down. "Relax, Chief. Now, Lincoln, we have a situation. Several situations. I know you're supposed to be picking up, who is it?"

"I think Willy Shumaker, Willy Hartak, and that big guy, yeah, I mean yes, sir, Mr. Belvedere, Sabastian Cabot."

"It can wait. Here's what's going on. First, your pal Huber missed the flight for Da Nang. As of tomorrow's Morning Report, he is AWOL. Maybe I'll list him as a deserter. He had some money in the bank around here, what with his DSC, the Soldier's Medal, and his wounds, but he's cashed his last check. Heroric sonofabitch or not, if he ain't back by tomorrow's Morning Report, I'm going to fry his ass—court martial—life imprisonment. Now, you and I both know where he is."

"You know, sir?"

"Chief, I am aware of everything. I am the all-knowing eye in the sky, and don't you forget it. So, you are going down to Saigon, find him, and get his slim butt back here. Everybody knows he owes you big time. I just hope he hasn't forgotten. That should give you some leverage to pull his fool ass out of a fire that's stoking up by the second. Somebody else can take the big wigs around.

"Okay, and the next item, I'm sorry to tell you this, but I heard from the Red Cross today. You have been granted a Compassionate Leave. Your father-in-law is very ill, apparently, and they want you home. I've arranged a seat on the Freedom Bird for you tomorrow at noon.

"So get Huber back here, and God speed. I'm about to lose my two best pilots. His pecker got him where he is, but, through you, he has a faint chance to get it back in his pants."

"Begging your pardon, sir. This wasn't about sex. He really loves her, and they have a beautiful baby together."

"May be, but *I* got a beautiful daughter, and I miss her more than you can dream. And I will miss you, too, Friday. You're the best junior officer I ever had. I hope you will consider staying in, get the morons in Washington to send you to college, get a regular commission, and knock 'em dead." He stood, shook Lincoln's hand, reached into his pocket, pulled out four five-dollar military payment certificates, and handed them to Lincoln. "For your cab into Saigon and Huber's back to the helicopter."

Lincoln stiffened and put his hands behind his back. "Can't take that, sir." The colonel gave him a bump in the shoulder, and before he turned away, he nodded. "Didn't think you would. But get it done, son."

The XO met him outside the door. "Gonna miss you, Chief." He stopped and looked into Lincoln's eyes. "Got nothin' more to say. Pack your stuff. There's a LOACH waitin' to give you a hop to Saigon. It's gonna hang there until seventeen hundred hours. Get that joker aboard. That's an order."

Lincoln was dropped at Tan Son Nhut Airport. He took a cab to the Binh Thanh Market in Saigon and traced what he could remember of the path to Kim Lieu's. Playing charades, and with his warmest smile, he coerced a cute schoolgirl to take him down the final alley to the cinderblock hut. He knocked on the tin door and slid it aside an inch.

Only Kim Lieu's sister was there. She couldn't understand Lincoln, so he went out into the alley and found a boy who knew a few words of English, gave him a dollar, and they went back to talk to the sister. Six times, seven times, eight times he explained to her that if he didn't find Huber, the man would be sent to jail for the rest of his life. He demonstrated by pulling a calendar from the wall and mimicking year after year. He drew a stick figure behind bars, scratched the word "Huber", and drew an arrow to the shape. Then he wrote the years, 1968, 1969..., but quit at the year 2000, when her face twisted in confusion.

She cried, grabbed Lincoln by the shirt, and pulled him through a set of alleys, deep into the privation of Viet Nam's civil war. He looked away when the cachectic, hunkering denizens of that slum lifted empty rice bowls, begging with their eyes for Lincoln to put something in them. When he came to a little girl with a half-filled bowl, he glanced at it and saw ants crawling between the grains, probably the child's major source of protein and vitamins. As he passed an old lady gutting a rat next to a pot of dirty boiling water, he became lightheaded and leaned against a hut to steady himself.

The sister jumped into a shelter even more wretched than the cinderblock shanty and pulled Kim Lieu out, who blocked the way when Lincoln took a step toward the door. Back and forth, back and forth, until Kim Lieu finally ducked inside and came out to whisper to her sister. Kim Lieu's shoulders slumped, and she drew Lincoln by the arm to the doorway.

At first, Lincoln could barely see into the gloomy hovel, but after a few seconds, his eyes grew accustomed to the darkness. Huber was sitting in a padded chair, a dozen empty cans of 33 Beer piled by his side on a tiny, shredded wicker table.

Huber slurred, "Fuckin' troop. Now I got you involved. Fuck me."

"Listen, Hubert, I don't got much time. My father-in-law's really sick, I guess. I gotta leave in a few hours. Look, old man's gonna forgive you your trespasses, but you need to get your still-slim ass back there before Morning Report."

"And never see *my family* again?"

"As it is, they know where you are. If you play your cards right, you can go home in a few months and take Kim Lieu and the baby with you, or at the worst, send for her when you get established back there. Or, knucklehead, you can spend the next ten to fifteen in Leavenworth."

"What the fuck am I gonna do, troop?"

Lincoln pushed his way in, took Huber's duffel bag from the corner, stuffed it with what he could see of the man's belongings, turned to him, grabbed him by the tee shirt, and yanked him to his feet. "Kiss her good bye." As they moved through the door, Lincoln turned back to Kim Lieu. "You two will be together again. I promise."

Lincoln's Freedom Bird lifted off into clouds so thick, the ground disappeared before the wheels were up. He was happy not to have to watch that tortured land disappear.

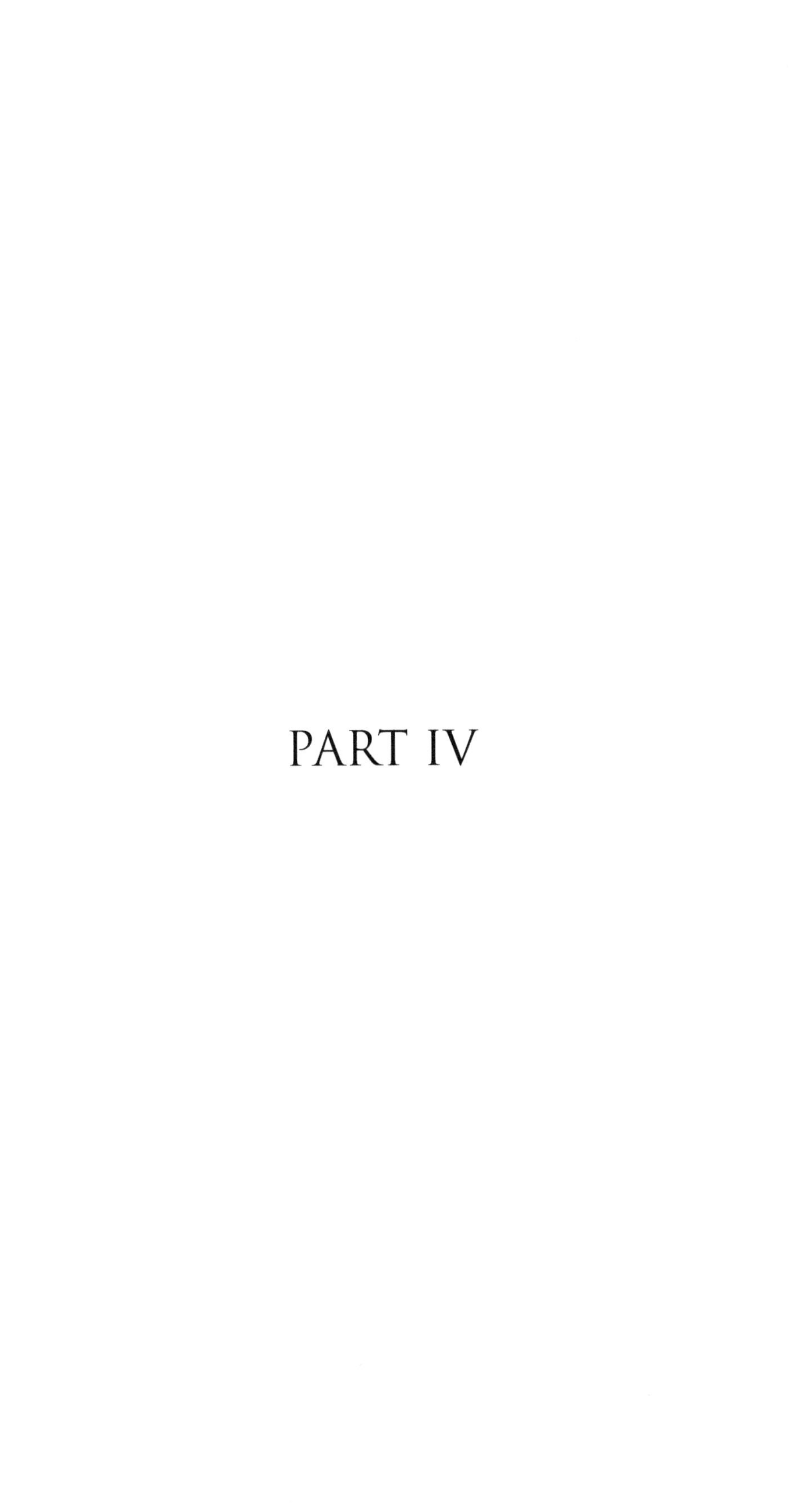

PART IV

CHAPTER FORTY-SEVEN

Bob Dalton's surgery did not go well. The tumor had wrapped itself around the bowel and then snaked south toward the rectum. It had invaded so far, there was nothing useful left of the last quarter of his colon. The surgeon cut a hole in the inside wall of his patient's abdomen, pushed what he could salvage of the bowel tube through it, then sewed the perimeter edges of the tube to the outside. It was a stoma, an opening for the waste to drool out, around the clock, into a bag that would never fit very well. The day after surgery, a blood clot formed in his leg, though no one noticed, and the next day a piece of it broke off and showered his lungs with tiny particles of clotted blood. He could barely breathe, even lying flat on his back.

By the time Lincoln arrived in Wilkes Barre, nearly seventy-two sleepless hours after leaving Viet Nam, Dalton was in a rented hospital bed in the living room. His face was skeletal. Lincoln gasped, Huber's appearance suddenly crossing his mind.

"Lincoln, thank God you're here." He struggled for breath. "Come, sit down." He coughed a couple of times while trying to catch his breath after lifting his hand to take Lincoln's. "Need to tell you a couple of things. First, I am so proud of you. You didn't run away. You did your part, and now you can lean back and be proud of yourself. I want you to know that I think of you as a son. I was going to turn the business over to you, but you still have those years you need to give back for going to flight school. It's unavoidable." He stopped to catch his breath. "But, there's gonna be enough money that none of you will ever have to worry.

"Okay, Lincoln, business discussions are out of the way. Hey, tell me about the rescue, the one with your friends Nhu and Huber. Been waiting a long time to hear that one."

Lincoln laughed. "Dad, it's unbelievable." He was so happy to have something to say to pass the time. He began the story, recounting a plethora of Huber's antics in flight school. He lost himself in the portion of the tale about Nhu nearly flying into him at Wolters, and was soon talking to the wall. He glanced to the left, saw Bob's face relax with the slightest smile, and was relieved the tale he was spinning brought distraction to a dying man. When he got to the part about Nhu dragging them through the alleys of Saigon, he stole another peek at Bob. The smile had not faded, and Lincoln was going to continue, but he noticed what looked like dust on his father-in-law's unblinking eyes.

Lincoln stood and tried to pull the man's eyelids down but couldn't. He held Bob's forearm with both his hands and, through his tears, wished him a good journey. Lincoln's last words to him were, "Dad, if you can, get me word what it's like on the other side."

At the funeral, hundreds upon hundreds of mourners from Wilkes Barre and beyond covered the cemetery. The police refused to attend, so Lincoln organized the aircraft mechanics into a platoon of traffic directors. After the priest's words, a retired general from the VFW stood at attention in front of Kerrith. Though it was not customary for the wife of the deceased to rise, she did, and accepted the impeccably folded American flag with a subtle bow. She remained at attention during Taps. Her expression was, though, serene, and when she took her seat, both Isabelle and Lincoln glanced at her sideways. Her tranquility soothed them.

Isabelle and Lincoln settled into life at Fort Lewis in Washington State. The magnificence of the scenery muted their sadness. They kept the windows of their bedroom open wide to allow in the pristine mountain air. After several weeks, Lincoln began to sleep again. The majesty of Mt. Rainier, where they spent a weekend loving each other at Paradise Inn, high on the mountain, further softened their loss.

Kerrith called every other day. When Isabelle cautioned that the phone bill was going to be more than the house was worth, Kerrith laughed. "Sweet child, don't you worry about money. One day, you know, my voice may not be on the other end." After that, Isabelle called *her* every day.

Lincoln found himself back in a tiny, under-powered, rickety H-23, the regimental commander's personal pilot. But the duty was wearisome, for the only time the old man came near the air field was during annual maneuvers. The colonel had become terrified of flying after his C&C helicopter crashed in Viet Nam. He spent three months in the hospital at Ft. Lewis and was then assigned to lead Lincoln's cavalry unit. The colonel and his driver went out to Gray Army Airfield one afternoon, just to look at the helicopter. The old man picked away at the peeling paint with a fingernail, rolled a bit of it up in his fingers, and asked to see the logbook. The ship had been retired from the flight line at Fort

Wolters because it had too many hours on its airframe. He had walked away and not been back to Gray Field since.

The colonel ordered Lincoln to make sure the helicopter was airworthy once a year, when the generals came out from the Pentagon to watch the armored cavalry demonstrate its combat readiness. The rest of the time, he and the aircraft were to be available for the squadron commanders, but, in truth, they had no time for flying. The lieutenant colonels' lives were dominated by the need to put out an infinite number of fires on the ground, for those were the days the Army was crumbling under the virus with which the war in Viet Nam had infected it. Racial tensions, drugs, anti-war sentiment within the ranks, bitterness over the way in which combat returnees were humiliated, and the obvious hunger of the upper ranks to protect their careers rather than lead men—all of it created strains in everyday life that were worse than those of the war itself.

Lincoln felt the poison and steered clear of every soul dressed in army green. When the regiment was sent to Yakima, east of the Cascade Mountains, for M-60 tank gun training, he would often set out at dawn in the H-23. Deep into the desert, he dropped into remote craters that had probably never before been explored by modern humans, or any humans. He'd land and use his entrenching tool, the same tiny shovel he'd converted into a collective the day before he soloed, and unearth prehistoric artifacts which he and Isabelle took up to the University of Washington for donation to the Burke Museum. A little bronze plaque with the Friday name was attached to the glassed-in case that held a skull which looked like it came from a massive, bovine creature, but flashed three-inch canines that had remained needle sharp over the millennia.

They shopped at the commissary and PX, buying nice things for their new home. Lincoln fell in love with knockwurst, which was sold all over post from hotdog carts, just as it was in Germany, where so many soldiers had learned to relish it while on tank duty in the aftermath of the war in Europe. Then he developed a taste for Arby's roast beef sandwiches, coffee, and chocolate chip ice cream. While showering one morning before heading to the flight line, he noticed he had developed a bit of a gut, and he weighed himself at work—he had gained twelve pounds in twelve weeks. He told Isabelle, and though she said he was more handsome than ever before, Lincoln began jogging that evening and limited his knockwursts to two a week.

Four months into their stay at Ft. Lewis, a telex came to their quarters while Isabelle was at school and Lincoln was grinding through paperwork for another promotion ahead of his contemporaries. It was from The Department of the Army, Aviation Branch. Lincoln's bowels clenched as he tore at the envelope. It was as he feared, orders sending him back to Viet Nam for a second tour. He would be granted a leave, to start in two weeks, and was then to report to the transfer station at Oakland, California, for the flight back to Asia.

He went to see his CO. The old man growled, snatched the phone, and ordered the post operator to connect him with Aviation Branch. "This is a damn priority!"

A colonel on the other end explained that because Lincoln had been released early from Viet Nam, he had not officially completed his commitment, and would have had to go back after six months anyway. The CO covered the phone as Lincoln argued he had come home only a couple of weeks early. The personnel officer in Washington suggested the colonel quickly file papers recommending Lincoln be sent to college and granted a regular army commission upon graduation.

After the call, the colonel warned, "I'll do it, Chief—today, if you like, but you realize that if this goes through, you'll owe two more years for each of the four years of schooling the Army's going to pay for. And you still have a couple to work off for flight school, so that's ten more. Adds up to a career commitment. Are you ready for that? Is that what you want?"

True to his word, the papers were filed before the close of business that afternoon, but the request was quickly denied by the very career officer with whom the colonel had spoken. The personnel officer's recommendation was that the papers be resubmitted when Lincoln returned from the coming tour.

The colonel shrugged. "Sorry, Chief. You're not the first, or the last, to take it in the butt from the career mavens in D.C. My recommendation is for you to go back and do your time with a smile. The war's winding down. I doubt you'll serve a full tour, and you definitely won't have to do it a third time, like so many of your pals, including me, have. Then, you'll be free to stay for a career, and you'll have a great record to bolster you. Or, you can tell 'em to shove it. I wouldn't blame you if you chose the latter, my friend. Their loss."

Lincoln had not told Isabelle about the orders until the night that the final word came from the Department of the Army. They sat together for the cocktail hour. She wept. Lincoln was too numb to cry.

She muttered, "It would have been nice if they told us before we moved out here, before I went through all that to get my credits approved, before they made us leave mom."

"They're not nice. You and I are just parts in a machine. One breaks, throw it away. That's why most of us hate the Army. FTA we said every morning when we got up. Fuck the Army."

They drank for another hour and stumbled to bed, where they made love over and over between their tears.

Lincoln managed to avoid showing up for duty with the 3rd Cav during those last two weeks, often finding himself first on line at sick call complaining of a rash that covered the lower half of his body. The doctors could not decide on a diagnosis, so they restricted him to quarters to prevent its spread to the other aviators. He spent the time, though, with Isabelle, often accompanying her to class, where they sat, shoulders touching, the envy of a hundred cooing nursing students. That was until he wore his uniform to a lecture. Several of Isabelle's friends gasped at the sight then turned their backs. She stopped going to class, but it did not matter. She would not be there to finish her courses—the work and tuition for naught.

They drove cross country to Wilkes Barre, the car stuffed with the sum of their worldly belongings, a full-grown Zeke squeezed between pots and pans in the rear seat. They moved back in with Isabelle's mom, and she took the house off the market. It seemed only days before Lincoln hefted his duffel bag aboard the Greyhound for Philadelphia, then the flight to California, and finally the leg back to Asia.

CHAPTER FORTY-EIGHT

The major at the assignment desk in Bien Hoa looked up from Lincoln's file and quipped, "That was quick. Let's get you back into the Delta, your old unit. Less to learn that way. Three days there, and you'll forget you were ever home."

Lincoln sat alone in the corner of the O Club that night. He was nursing his first beer, not because he was curbing his drinking in anticipation of flying again in twenty-four hours, but because he was too lethargic and depressed to get up for another. He picked at the peeling plastic of the tabletop, nearly comatose in the wicked evening heat and mugginess he'd hoped never again to suffer. The scream that shocked him out of his reverie came from directly over his head. His eyes shot up to see Stanky shaking in excitement.

Lincoln exploded off his stool and into an embrace with his old friend. "What the hell are you doing here? Don't tell me they screwed you, too."

Stanky dragged a stool over. “Goin’ home. How ’bout you, Linc?”

“No, man, back for a second helping. Where you comin’ from?”

Stanky explained that he had been offered an extension of ninety days, with a guarantee of eighteen months at home if took the deal. He had just come from flying with Huber, and Lincoln begged him to tell him what was cooking in his old unit.

“Linc, the story is unbelievable, what happened to Huber when he got back the afternoon you went to see him in Saigon. Don’t worry, I know the whole story. You did good—saved a man’s life, in a way.

Stanky chugged his beer, put his hand up for Lincoln to wait, ran to the bar, then dropped back at the table with four more beers. “Anyway, Huber was told to have his ass out at the flight line at zero six hundred the next morning. They were sending him up to the new unit near Da Nang. When his plane landed that afternoon, his new CO up there, some West Pointer, he went there to stare at Huber, but wouldn’t talk to him. XO marches up to Huber and assigns him as the sanitation officer. Told him he wasn’t gonna fly anymore.

“The guy he was replacing was an RLO, real live officer, a first lieutenant, if you can believe it. Got malaria, supposedly from sleeping in town with whores without a mosquito net. I mean, the asshole was down there every night, and *he* was the one in charge of making sure every swinging dick in basecamp was using a mosquito net, and *he* gets malaria. He also misses the Sunday morning malaria pills, shacked up the night before, and he couldn’t get back ’cause a mine went off on the road, and the engineers closed it for a couple of days. So our pal the lieutenant wasn’t there to hand out the pills, another one of Huber’s new duties, and the old man went nuts.

Lincoln snorted, "I can just picture it. Huber handing out pills and sayin', 'Now, First Sergeant, I want you to take this little green one right here in front of me, and then, in ten minutes, I'll trust you to swallow this big one.'"

Stanky rolled his eyes and went on. "So this guy, the sick lieutenant, he wasn't rated, but as far as the new old man was concerned, neither was Huber anymore, so Huber got the duty. Now's when it begins to get complicated. Stick with me. See, there's this other lieutenant, FNG, fuckin' new guy, West Pointer, of course, who'd actually been to flight school. Well, he arrives with a hair up his ass, this one. Thinks he's fuckin' commander-in-chief or somethin'. Makes the senior warrant officers call him sir, even when they're flying, and he tells them what to do in the helicopter. Just made first lieutenant, got, what, three hundred hours under his belt; and he's tellin' a W-4 with three thousand, and twenty years older than him, he's teaching 'em how to fly. Ready for this? He made 'em practice autorotations, and when they're back on the ground, he goes over their performance, like back in Wolters. Gave 'em a grade!

"So one of the crew chiefs snuck into the jerk's BOQ room and put a dead rat in his helmet. Guy was off on a three-day, in-country R&R. That was enough time, in this heat, for the thing to melt. I mean the rat. All that juice got into the earphones, everywhere, and then the air in the BOQ. When the guy got back, someone had already busted the door down to his room and threw the helmet a hundred yards into the brush. Lieutenant had a stroke, man. Yelled at everybody, but no one would tell him anything.

"The supply sergeant said he'd requisition a new helmet, but in the meantime, the CO ordered him to go and find the thing, soak it in vinegar overnight, then pour in baking soda in the morning. Asshole did it, and of all places, in the latrine. That shit got all over the place, on the toilet seats, burned the old short hairs every time you did your business.

"Now, everybody was pissed, and they went to the XO to complain. So the old man sends him to Saigon to work at one of those buildings down there. To me, it's a sad waste of a pilot, even a Pointer, but who would want to be up same time as him?

"So, the old man has no choice. Huber sits right seat for a while, then a couple of ships go down, and, presto, Huber's an aircraft commander again. One of the best sticks I ever saw, and just like his track record, manages to pull people's asses out of the fire, man, like on an hourly basis.

"So that's his story. We were getting' shipped all over the place, so I wouldn't be surprised if you get sent up there with him. Sure you want to hear the rest? You look tired."

"I am tired, but don't stop. I love this shit."

"Okay. Most screwed up unit I ever been in. CO, yet another fuckin' West Pointer, only like thirty-eight or somethin'. Young for a full colonel. Supposedly got promoted ahead of his contemporaries a bunch of times. Got them stars in his eyes already. You know how they get, them colonels, when they think they got a chance to make general. Can't live with 'em.

"It's a nut house. Every morning before the sun, Linc, every troop is out by the mess hall, even the cooks and supply sergeants, out in that humidity doing PT, and for seven days a week. He's a madman. When he shows up on the flight line, your crew, they gotta stand at attention. Aircraft commander steps forward, salutes, reports—you know, name, rank, tail number of the helicopter—as if the old man didn't already know. Then he looks you up and down, says, 'Carry on, Mr. Stanky,' and back we go fixin' the damn ship. Just wasted a whole lotta time, as far as I could see.

"And he don't trust no one with one of," he made quote signs, "'*his* aircraft.' Always crawlin' up on a ship, loves to inspect the Jesus Nut. Look, even a monkey knows, the Jesus nut comes loose, the main rotor spins right off the mast. You ever seen a J nut come loose?"

"Can't say as I have."

"No, and it never happened in the history of HUEYs. Kinda funny, though, if it did, you wouldn't have anything to autorotate with, would you?"

"You would not."

"Exactly. All you would have was a few seconds to pray to Jesus. But anyway, it never happened, but there he is, checkin', makin' sure. When he didn't find a single deficiency at the top of any rotor in the company, or in Viet Nam, for that matter, he got a hair up his ass about all sorts of other nuts and bolts. Took to carryin' a torque wrench in his back pocket. When he found a nut too tight or too loose, he'd unscrew the thing and fling the son of a bitch as far as he could. Mechanics never knew which ones he was going to choose when he went on the war path. Spent their days forgetting about important things, I mean like fluid levels. Pissed away their time trying to guess which worthless screw the old man was going to attack."

Lincoln and Stanky spent the next hours laughing, becoming very quiet when Stanky told Lincoln who had not made it. They walked back to the barracks together silently, shook hands, and planned to meet in the morning, but Stanky was woken before dawn and told a seat had opened on the Freedom Bird leaving in an hour. He was gone before Lincoln arose.

When Lincoln reported to the airport later that morning, he was handed orders that superseded those of the afternoon before. He was to fly up north to Da Nang and join the very unit from which Stanky had just escaped.

At the new basecamp, the CO looked him up and down, asked him a few aviation questions, then growled that all new aviators, regardless of how many combat hours they had flown, would undergo several check rides before being allowed to sit at the controls, even as co-pilot. "All you men are peter pilots until I'm good and ready to say otherwise."

The colonel assigned Lincoln to fly with Huber for the first test flight. They took off and flew to Da Nang, sent the crew to the PX, and settled into an American restaurant on the base for what, they swore, they would limit to only two hours of catching up.

It was during the third hour that Huber told Lincoln about contacting an Army chaplain and asking the man to perform a quick ceremony joining him with Kim Lieu. The minister shook his head as he described the difficulty of marrying an indigenous woman in a combat zone. The paperwork to bring her home, especially with a child, was daunting, but the most imposing obstacle was the regulation that a soldier's commanding officer had to officially approve the union. The old man back down south, still Huber's official CO, had refused to see Huber the afternoon Lincoln had convinced him to return to duty. The only word he got from the colonel was an order, delivered by a private, to report at zero six hundred the next morning for a flight as a passenger on an Air Force C-130 to the unit near Da Nang.

Later that day, the West Pointer who commanded the detachment in the north was present when Huber's plane landed. The colonel had been ordered to make visual contact with his new, valiant, but troubled, warrant officer, though, he, too, declined to speak to him. Just as Stanky had recounted, Huber had been assigned duties of uncommon degradation, including, but not limited to, supervision of the local Vietnamese who had been hired for pennies a day to incinerate the GIs' feces. There was also a nightly patrol to confirm the troops were using their mosquito nets, and then there was the weekly corralling of the whores who had been permitted into camp. Huber was to have them queued at seventeen hundred hours every Tuesday, at afternoon sick call, to be inspected by the camp doctor. If the physician deemed a girl pure, he handed her a 3x5 piece of green construction paper, which she handed to Huber, who stamped it, the seal of venereal approval.

Actually, a fair percentage of the ladies of the night—and morning, and afternoon—employed by the basecamp were carrying strains of sexually transmitted microorganisms no bacteriologist on Earth had yet encountered or imagined existed. Those girls, mindful of their copious, polychromatic vaginal discharge, sent grandmothers, mothers, sisters, and best friends to stand in for them at sick call. Since most of the women of that province were named Nguyen Thi Hoa, and they all looked exactly alike to the American eye, there was no way for Huber to know who he was certifying, and he used his stamp liberally, nodding politely, pretending he was sitting before Kim Lieu's family members.

Then there was the incident with the lieutenant and the reeking flight helmet, and Huber was finally allowed to fly, though he was warned to venture no farther than the officers' club once he finished the day's airborne missions. The CO also disallowed his fraternization with the locals and warned that if he discovered Huber within a quarter mile of the massage parlor, of which Huber was to remain the inspecting officer, he would be sent back to the feces-burning detail, not as a supervisor, but as the man who stirred tainted helicopter fuel into the latrine barrels so that the waste could be cremated.

After Huber reported to the old man that Lincoln was the best pilot he'd ever flown with, Lincoln was given the right seat of a beaten HUEY. The aircraft commander, a warrant who had been in-country for five months, asked Lincoln respectfully if he wanted to do most of the flying, but Lincoln shook his head and sat with his eyes fixed, flight after flight, on the panorama of that beautiful, but deadly, star-crossed land.

A month passed, some pilots died, some rotated home, and Lincoln found himself in command of the newest ship in the fleet. His bearing changed during the first flight, and several sorties later, the crew spread word that Lincoln was the coolest head they'd ever flown with. Though the door gunner was tapped to become a crew chief on a different aircraft and receive a promotion to sergeant, the man refused to leave Lincoln.

The CO came out to the flight line to see just what all the fuss was about and strapped himself in the back of Lincoln's ship, making the excuse that he wanted to take notes as they dropped into LZs and design procedures to make insertions more efficient and safer. After a few flights, he called Lincoln into his office for a debriefing and to throw ideas around.

The colonel asked, "Chief, have you ever heard the expression, 'Ship of the line?'"

"No, sir."

"Learned about it in the Command and General Staff College at Leavenworth."

"That's also where the army prison is, sir, isn't it?"

"That's true, and let me tell you, the course was like being in prison. Backbiting, anything to get an edge on the next colonel. Dog eat dog. Only thing kept me going was staying in shape. That's why we do PT. It's like medicine for the soul.

"Anyway, 'ship of the line' is the way the British used to engage in naval battles. Those old wooden ships would line up bow to stern, broadside exposed, and go at it with the enemy. If a single ship panicked and broke ranks, that was an offense punishable by death for the captain. It was a stupid way to fight, devised by stupid, arrogant commanders who closed their eyes to the possibility of innovation. And, that about sums up the way we are going about it here.

"I want to try different ways of inserting troops. I'm tired of our 'ship of the line' tactics, sending my men to fly in a crawl, in line, broad sides exposed. I want to come up with something new. But we need to make sure we figure out every possible way it can go wrong. I'm not experimenting with the lives of my men.

"So I want you to talk with your pilots about coming into LZs from random directions and at random times. If we can get the enemy to fire in all sorts of directions, maybe we can triangulate and pinpoint them. Go to the O Club and have a beer or two, but not three. I'm buyin'."

Though Lincoln had hoped to spend the balance of his tour carting ass and trash, he walked back to his tent, head drooping, imagining ways to avoid the colonel's directive. He made an excuse not to go to the club that evening, but ten minutes later, he pulled himself from his rack and made his way to the bar. The ideas flew as fast as the beer, and he recorded them in a notebook. He dragged Huber along when he went back to the old man. The colonel took seven helicopters off line duty for a day to let them practice at safe LZs near headquarters. When they were ready, he joined Lincoln for the first test.

Though aircraft were converging from seven directions, each pilot knew exactly who was approaching from his left and right, and just how many degrees he had to turn to remain clear of the traffic. They continued to practice on the ground and in the air so often, it became a reflex. And while there was sporadic small arms fire when they put the plan into action, the VC couldn't get a bead on a helicopter approaching from the north before another was thundering overhead from the south, firing away at the jungle from which the enemy was shooting. After the first mission, the old man inspected the ships and discovered just three bullet holes in one aircraft, but the crew chief swore they had been there for months because maintenance had refused to patch them, as they were in non-vital areas.

The colonel chose several landing zones, but only those that lent themselves to the new plan. He'd first land men in peripheral LZs then march them toward the central LZ to sweep the area before the main insertion. He would catch the VC coming and going, a set of pincer movements that cleared the enemy from large loops of countryside. The enemy body count was rising, the friendly casualties were decreasing dramatically, and the pioneering tactics drew the attention of the brass in Saigon, and then Washington. Several senators flew to Viet Nam for a briefing, and the brass at Pentagon East urged them to fly up to Da Nang to see for themselves. They were scheduled to arrive in the morning and fly in the C&C ship at eight or nine thousand feet to scrutinize an insertion. Jet lag was bandied about as the reason the dignitaries didn't arrive at basecamp until past four.

Nonetheless, Lincoln's colonel smiled ecstatically when the sixteen-helicopter delegation spewed out the four senators. The generals lined up by rank behind the politicians like so many ducklings. When the colonel formally invited them to fly along in the command ship as planned, there were no takers. He smiled, "We fly real high, way above the action. Gentlemen, I can assure you I am not suicidal."

One agreed to go along, a man who had served in Korea as a clerk for a legal affairs general in Seoul. The colonel had him ride in the adjoining seat aboard the C&C helicopter. Before the ship lifted off, two of the generals, who were staying behind to provide security for the dignitaries, called the colonel aside and warned, "You fly high and no hard turns. No hotdogging. Don't you embarrass us."

Lincoln led the mission. He was the first to drop in and insert his men. Huber, flying head to head with him, peeled off to the right as planned, and Lincoln flew away from the path Huber had used inbound. Soon, there were ships cluttering the sky, clouds of locusts—olive drab bugs flitting east, west, northeast—dropping into a rice paddy here, one there. Neatly coming together over the chosen check point, stacking themselves at different altitudes, they gently descended into a perfect file to fly back to base to pick up the next load of boots.

"It's a ballet," commented the senator in the command ship, and the entire crew flushed with pride.

On the next sortie, Lincoln flew third, allowing one of the more junior pilots to have the experience of dropping into an LZ with no one flying ahead of him to set the approach parameters. Huber remained second, and Lincoln called him on a separate frequency to warn him to be careful, for a newer aircraft commander was at the controls in front of him.

The colonel's helicopter, not privy to the nitty gritty details of the operation, continued to circle at five thousand feet. The senator called over the intercom, "Gettin' a nose bleed up here. Colonel, I want to get closer and take a look at it from another angle."

The pilot turned to look at the CO, who pointed generally in the direction he wanted to fly, rather than calling coordinates over the intercom, which would have forced the pilot to bring his eyes into the aircraft and search the map. The old man also pointed down with his index finger then held up three fingers.

The pilot acknowledged the order to descend to three thousand feet by nodding and mimicking the CO's hand signals. The aircraft commander turned to the co-pilot and called over the intercom, "Your ship."

There was a delay, as the co-pilot was adjusting his helmet, and the aircraft commander repeated the command with a bite. "You got it, Lieutenant."

"Oh, okay, I've got it."

"You got it."

The colonel called from the back on a private intercom line. "We need to stay above the ships forming up, but I want the senator to be able to look into the LZ and see how the troops are reacting on the ground. We need to show him there's no confusion, despite guys being inserted from so many directions."

The man in the right seat was a peter pilot, in-country for a just over a month. He was flying in the CO's ship that day, nominally, because the colonel liked to give his junior officers a chance to prove themselves, but really, because the young man's father was a lieutenant general, the rank every colonel on Earth longed for. A word from the very junior officer that his commanding officer had let him fly a senator around on a combat mission could not hurt.

Unbeknownst to the aircraft commander, though, the directive to descend had been issued while the co-pilot was fussing with his helmet. The young officer was ignorant of the plan. Nonetheless, when control was transferred, the aircraft dropped steadily for several hundred feet, but only because the lieutenant was so nervous, he was unable to steady his left hand on the collective and maintain altitude. The CO and the aircraft commander assumed they were in the planned descent, and though the forceful maneuver drained the color from the senator's face, the ship was on the way down, and they went back to their maps. When no one chewed the co-pilot's ass for having lost so much altitude, he very slowly tugged on the collective and tried to return to five thousand feet before anyone discovered his gaff.

The number one troop ship was light, having off-loaded its infantry, and was ascending rapidly, nose down, during the climb. The pilot was anxious to rise above the incoming ships quickly and arrive at the check point to impress Lincoln that he didn't need a babysitter.

At the same time, the pilot of the command ship looked up and snapped, "You're supposed to be descending to three thousand." Before the aircraft commander could take back control of the helicopter, the co-pilot dropped the collective as if entering an autorotation. The ship began to sink rapidly, and the pilot grabbed the collective to ease the rate of descent that had everyone essentially weightless, barely held in place by seat belts.

There was sufficient chaos aboard with papers, maps, and grease pencils floating past faces, that no one was looking outside to see the nose-down troop ship approaching from below.

The first anyone knew of the imminent mid-air collision was the instant before the impact, when the aircraft commander of the troop ship looked up and saw the undersurface of the C&C aircraft fifty feet above him. He smashed the collective down, and though the rate of climb waned, it did not stop, and his main rotor struck the skids of the command helicopter, lopping them off. It also shattered the blades of the troop ship into a cloud of black shards. The helicopter sank from the sky, tumbling, though so slowly, it gave the impression of a gentle descent. The optical illusion did nothing, though, to repeal the laws of physics, and what was left of the helicopter drilled a hole in the jungle earth so deep, the explosion and fire that followed was mostly underground. The smoke that eventually escaped was as black as a beaten eighteen-wheeler's, and it caught Lincoln's attention a mile away. By reflex, he began a turn toward the smoke to reconnoiter, but he saw Huber enter the LZ and drop his infantry, and realized he must not abandon the plan.

Lincoln called the first ship. There was nothing but static. He called the C&C helicopter. No reply. He radioed Huber and told him he was unable to contact either aircraft and directed him investigate the smoke.

Huber answered that he saw a helicopter in the distance limping along and then, with a high-pitched tremor in his voice, called, "Goddamnit, the skids are gone."

As Lincoln off loaded his infantry, he called Huber and told him to follow the wounded aircraft. He would investigate the smoke. Lincoln raced to the plume of black, but by the time he was hovering over it, all that remained of the helicopter were dying licks of sooty, orange fire. He looked out and saw Huber chasing the C&C ship, which was losing altitude, barely able to fly, but headed toward a clearing.

Huber followed and dropped into a high hover over a good-sized rice paddy, one right outside a village. He waited to see what was going to happen before he put himself on the ground and couldn't move aside if the CO's helicopter lost all control.

The damaged ship tried to slow to a hover, but a piece of the hull, a sheet of OD skin that had been hanging by a single rivet, broke free. It was swept down in the rotor wash, expelled sideways into the air outside the rotor disc, blown back up by air bouncing off the ground, and, finally, sucked down into the blades. The helicopter plummeted to the ground and, without skids, rolled over several times. Huber landed behind it, but not so close that the coming explosion would consume his aircraft as well.

Lincoln dropped in next to Huber. The co-pilots of both helicopters were ordered to remain on board and secure the aircraft, keeping them ready for an instantaneous departure, while the two aircraft commanders ran toward the wounded ship. The four door gunners pulled their M-60 machine guns free and followed, automatically dropping at the corners of the compass to form a defensive perimeter.

The C&C ship was on its starboard side, the occupants hanging from their locked seat belts, most unconscious. The senator, however, had unsnapped his seatbelt as the helicopter hovered, crawled to the door, and jumped free. He started to run for a ten-foot berm that surrounded the primitive farming hamlet, but as the hull struck the ground, it rolled wildly and crushed the man. Lincoln crawled in from the side door, which was now the facing the sky. He looked straight down and saw the civilian pinned on the ground under the other door. It was clear he was gone.

Lincoln tried to free the passengers but found it impossible to open the seat belts with all the weight hanging against them.

Worse was the lack of range of motion of his left wrist. He had Huber squat below each man, come up, and lift the wounded slightly with his shoulders so Lincoln could open the buckles. They lowered the victims slowly out of the aircraft. The last man to be freed was the aircraft commander, who was semi-conscious and tried to tell Lincoln what had happened.

When the six men were placed on the ground, necks protected and bleeding stemmed, Lincoln went to his crew chief, who was lying prone, facing the village, M-60 charged, finger stroking the trigger. Lincoln kneeled and explained the plan. They would place three of the men in each helicopter, place packs and ammo cans around their heads to prevent neck movement, then everyone would jump aboard, and they would fly directly to the evacuation hospital in Da Nang. The gunners were to board the helicopters, man their machine guns, and provide cover as they took off. Once in flight, they would stand guard over the casualties to ensure no one woke up and began thrashing about.

Lincoln stood to go back to his helicopter and brief the copilot, but he saw a flash from the village and then peasants running into huts. There were more flashes, and he soon realized the little cracking sounds around his head were not insects but supersonic AK-47 rounds, just millimeters away.

The helicopter machine gunners all crawled into position facing the village and began firing indiscriminately. Lincoln shouted for them to wait until they were absolutely sure no civilians were in the line of fire. After the next couple of bursts, the machine gunners emptied belts of ammunition toward the muzzle flashes, and as they stopped to reload, it appeared the enemy guns had been silenced. There was, though, an unnerving stillness in the village that was more distressing than the firing. For two minutes, nothing happened, and the pilots came to their knees warily then took a few steps toward the wounded. Gradually, the silence was broken by the wail of female voices coming from the mud and grass huts, a howl that gained in measure until the paddies vibrated. It was like nothing Lincoln had ever heard, a lament so final and hopeless, it chilled his heart.

Huber called out, "Fuckin' A, musta just dusted a few of the cocksuckers!"

The lull in the firing from the village continued, and the two aircraft commanders slithered close to the ground, pulling the wounded toward the waiting helicopters. Huber yanked feet; Lincoln supported necks and heads.

As the air cleared of dust and smoke, the gunners began sliding along the ground toward the two serviceable ships. The protracted silence reassured them, and the men rose. They lifted the casualties aboard slowly, deliberately, taking time to situate the bodies and insure necks were stabilized. As they raised the colonel, however, a booming crack a hundred meters behind them lifted mud and water into a cone. A second later, another explosion erupted farther out. There was a period of stillness, and the Americans worked faster, but two more explosions followed, the gush of mud and water now but sixty meters across the paddy.

Huber screamed at the gunners, "Scum bags are walkin' rounds into us. Level the fuckin' village." Lincoln's crew turned to look at their aircraft commander, but this time, Lincoln said nothing.

The closest mud and straw huts quickly vaporized, and a moment later, the thunder of only one explosion at a time rolled across the paddies. With several more bandoliers of M-60 machine gun fire, all the guns were silenced.

The casualties were loaded, crews boarded, and the pilots wiggled into their seats. As Lincoln slipped on his helmet, two new explosions lifted earth and water eighty meters away. This time, the mortar tubes were in the forest, opposite the village. As the door gunners swung their M-60s toward the wood line, a shower of Plexiglas fragments blasted through the aircraft as enemy machine gun fire spewed from their flank.

The co-pilots had long since radioed for support, and two Cobra gunships called that they were minutes out. Lincoln wondered if he should lift off, and become an even larger target, or wait for cover from the Cobras. He decided to remain there until the gunships arrived, and when he radioed the plan to the other helicopter, Huber switched to the gunships' frequency and implored, "Get your asses on station."

One of the pilots radioed back, "I'm peddling as fast as I can."

Lincoln stared at his map, studying the coordinates he would relay to the Cobras to help them locate the enemy, but as he began to jot down the numbers, a mortar round landed thirty feet to the rear of his side of the helicopter. He looked back by reflex and saw the door gunner's left arm shredded by the shrapnel, blood spurting out the door and puddling on the stubble of last year's rice. Lincoln jumped from the aircraft, and ran to the man. He cut a length of seatbelt with his knife, wrapped it about the wounded man's arm, then gritted his teeth and tightened until the hemorrhage became a trickle. He pushed the gunner gently onto his back next to the other casualties. As Lincoln climbed into the cockpit, a new cone of Plexiglas fragments shot into his left arm. He looked down to see his wrist covered in blood. He pushed up the sleeve of his flight suit. Half-a-dozen flaps of torn flesh surrounded the old scar.

His mind numbed as the pain reached him. In seconds, he was left with only the image of Honey Barre in the moments before old man Schroeder put her down. His chest relaxed, softening as he thought of her, and how they were sharing so mystifying an experience. Then even that vision began to dissolve, first at the fringes, then wisps of color and form fading. His head slumped.

He was not aware of the vibrations that built in the paddies, not even when they ripened into a thumping roll. The two Cobras had arrived on station. The din as they bore down on the village was doubtless the loudest sounds the tenants of that condemned patch of earth had ever heard, or ever would. The violence of the air the gunships had set in motion rocked Lincoln's body so hard, it forced his head to shudder, and with that slap came meager threads of consciousness. The blinding light from the gunships' rockets added another lance of stimulation, and the fire that consumed the jungle woke him sufficiently to feel, deep in his chest, the disquiet of knowing he was supposed to be doing something. Though Lincoln remained dazed, he thought he heard voices crackling in his earphones. He was not sure if he was dreaming when he heard his co-pilot speaking to Huber. "Sir, Chief Friday's hurt. He can't talk. I don't think he can fly."

Huber ordered both ships to take off, and he called the gunships to advise them of the new plans. Lincoln's co-pilot gulped, straightened his posture, and began to pull up on the collective. As the skids became light, the ship drifted a bit left, then right, some forward, and a little backward, before it settled into a stable hover. It was a sensation as familiar to Lincoln as sitting in a chair, as much a part of his world as breathing. Hovering stirred the deep interstices of his mind, and by reflex, he, too, straightened and forced himself to concentrate.

At three feet, the co-pilot lowered the nose and was about to take off, but a screaming whine filled the helicopter, a violent banging shook the last cobwebs from Lincoln's consciousness, and the engine ground to a halt. The heavy main rotor, though, continued turning, grudgingly surrendering its momentum. As it bled energy, it allowed the skids to touch back down as lightly as any time in the co-pilot's fledgling career.

Nonetheless, whatever had brought the aircraft down had also ruptured the fuel tank, and the rotor wash sent JP-4 spewing inside the helicopter. With the oily liquid scudding into a tornado within the ship, some of it seeped into Lincoln's mouth. That was the final stimulus. He became sufficiently alert to stammer that they needed to abandon the aircraft. When the other door gunner heard the order, he asked the co-pilot to help him move the casualties to Huber's ship.

Lincoln's eyes opened fully, and he worked himself free of his seat. He cut his own seatbelt and wrapped it up and down his arm, stemming the bleeding. It was also a splint sufficient to allow him to help transport the casualties—six wounded from the C&C ship and his door gunner. The rest of Lincoln's crew jumped aboard Huber's bullet-ridden helicopter, praying it had enough left to lug them out of what was fast becoming the worst afternoon for American aviation since the Korean War.

Huber counted heads. "We got ten thousand bodies to medivac outta here. Boiling, fuckin' muggy afternoon. Too hot to get off the ground. Fuckin' Charlie's got a bead on us. It ain't gonna happen." Huber jumped free of his seat and asked his two gunners if they wanted to stay behind. Both unstrapped, secured their M-60s, threw out cans of ammo, and crawled backward to a copse of trees that grew out of a rocky finger protruding into the paddies. Lincoln's gunner jumped free and sprinted back to his downed ship for the remaining M-60.

Lincoln snatched an M-16 rifle from the back of the helicopter, ordered his co-pilot to sit left seat on Huber's aircraft, and told the two co-pilots to make a running start and then head out at treetop level, where it would be harder for enemy troops to see exactly from which direction they were coming.

The co-pilots radioed to brief the Cobras, and the two gunships dove in to spray a ferocious curtain of lead and rockets into the tree line. An instant later, the HUEY raced across the paddies, dodging and weaving so violently, the tip of the main rotor nearly struck one of the dikes. The co-pilot in the right seat aimed for the edge of the jungle at full throttle, waited until he was just meters from the trees, and pulled the cyclic into his belly. The G forces crushed them in their seats, but he pushed the cyclic forward an instant later, and they began to float. He skimmed trees until they were a mile from the village, then jumped into the climb, and disappeared in the clouds as they raced for the evacuation hospital at Da Nang.

The Cobras made another pass, this one for reconnaissance, and the trailing gunship suddenly pulled up over the paddies and came to a near stop. The pilot radioed that he had seen movement in the tree line to the right flank of the five Americans on the ground. The VC were stealing around to ambush them. One of the door gunners turned that way and began firing.

Under the cover of the M-60 machine gun din and radiance, a black-clad man fulfilled his resolution to die, if that was what it took, to rid the land of his ancestors of the latest foreign invasion. He stepped out of the jungle, lifted a rocket launcher—one longer than he was tall—pointed it in the vicinity of the Cobra, closed his eyes, and pulled the trigger. The missile smoked out of its simple tube and just nicked the tip of the tail rotor of the slower gunship. It was enough, though, to send the helicopter into a spin, as if a maple seed. The aircraft was still throbbing, splinters of main rotor showering them, as Lincoln and Huber arrived at the wreck.

Huber moaned, "Shit, it's covered in JP-4. Don't fuck around. Get 'em out, *now*!"

The two dazed men aboard popped the canopy but sat unmoving, still belted in as Lincoln and Huber climbed onto the hull. Huber grabbed the edge of the canopy in his hand and howled like an Olympic weightlifter as he ripped the Plexiglas free.

Lincoln saw a stream of fuel working its way into the back of the engine. He called to Huber, "Gonna have a fire in about three seconds. Haul ass."

They lifted the gunner out of the front seat onto the ground, then wedged the pilot out of his barely shoulder-wide cockpit. Huber reached in, pulled free the onboard first aid kit, and threw it to Lincoln just as small orange flames, no brighter than fire starter on a charcoal grill, dribbled from the engine. They soon seeped onto kerosene that had pooled on the ground. Huber and Lincoln pulled the men away into the paddy and hid with them behind a flimsy, dike wall. The flames burgeoned, and they were not surprised with the explosion that followed as fuel, rockets, and machine gun ammunition cooked off, shaking the province.

It was the first time Lincoln realized the sun was setting. All that was left of the last day of his life were darkening rays of magenta bathing a blotch of land that had, an hour before, been nothing more than a primitive, ageless rice field. Lincoln thought of the aboriginal peasants who tended the land following the same agricultural tenets as had man since he'd started his crawl across the Earth. And now, sixty minutes later, it was littered with the detritus of the most modern of mans' conceptions.

Huber looked at Lincoln. "Let's see the arm."

"I'm fine, man."

Huber reached forward and unwrapped the nylon strap. He quaked for a moment but tightened his jaw, pulled bandages from the first aid kit, and covered the wound. He crawled off to scrounge about in the patch of trees until he found a branch the thickness of an index finger, which he folded several times and bandaged to Lincoln's arm as a proper splint.

Lincoln added snidely. "So, now, you're an orthopedic surgeon."

Huber looked at him sideways. "A what?"

The three door gunners squirmed backwards in the mud to join the others. The two men from the Cobra were conscious, though one was weeping. The pain from his neck was so severe, he wanted to die. The other man babbled about horses then lay back and smiled.

The other Cobra radioed for a dustoff, but it was now a night mission, the tropical sun having evaporated just that quickly. With the darkness, the VC would sneak into position long before the rescue helicopter located the downed Americans. The enemy was wise. There would not be a single shot until the dustoff came to a hover. In the confusion and din, and the certainty that all of the Americans' hands were off their weapons loading the wounded, the rockets and machine gun fire would come from the flanks and cut them down. When the ship disintegrated, the VC would use the light from the flames to pick off any remaining flicker of life.

The other Cobra skidded in. The gunner sprang out of the front position and helped stuff one of the wounded crew into his tiny seat. The ship lifted off straight up, a rocket ship, and dashed to a nearby clearing, where the pilot lugged the man out and went back for another of the injured. Huber told Lincoln to go aboard, but he refused. "Load my crew chief. *I* signed up for this bullshit. Fuckers in D.C. *made* his ass come here."

When the Cobra returned, two RPGs flashed from the wood line, but it was too dark to see the smoke trail and fix from which thicket the rockets had been fired. When no explosion shuddered the paddies, Lincoln shook his head, trying to imagine how the VC could have missed from so close.

He shouted, "I'm about tired of this shit, Hubert. Slide to your left and get ready to put some fire on the wood line, but wait 'till I tell ya. I'm gonna swing 'round the other way and get behind these assholes."

"Don't do it, troop. Stay together!"

"Fuck no, we're sitting ducks. I'm goin' into the tree line. When you hear my M-16, stop your shootin'."

"Don't do it!"

"Fuck you. I don't feel like dyin' tonight." And Lincoln slipped off along a ditch toward the woods. When he came to the edge of the forest, he put a hand in front of his mouth and screamed to Huber, "*Now*!" The VC may have heard him, but when Huber discharged his M-16, the enemy turned their guns toward him, firing magazine after magazine. In the cover of the noise and smoke, Lincoln sprang to his feet and ran deep into the woods until he came directly behind the VC. In their arrogance or ignorance, they had not put out rear security, and he dropped into a crawl to slip along the deadfall until he could see the silhouettes of heads against the flicker of moonlight. He considered what he was about to do, shook his head, and growled, "Fuck it." He came to his knees and sprayed the formation to his front until two of his three magazines were spent. When Huber heard the distinctive sound of the M-16, he ceased fire and drew back to provide security for the wounded.

After a few seconds, the VC still able to fight turned to fire blindly at Lincoln. He used the chaos to slide to his left and low-crawl around the formation of enemy until he was peering straight down a trench full of the remaining Viet Cong. He waited until the Cobra began its thunderous approach before crawling toward the closest man. He walloped him over the head with his pistol, and the man fell silently into the mud. Lincoln saw three VC arming a rocket launcher, came to his knees, and fired point blank into them. They fell. Lincoln expected that was to be his last volley, and the last act of his life, for he was now completely exposed in the trench. The soldiers, however, remained fixated on the helicopter, and Lincoln rolled up and out of the trench, crawled behind and parallel to it, then took a stable, prone, firing position as he'd been taught in basic training. The remaining VC fell one by one. He muttered a painful, final prayer after each shot, not because he was about to die, but because his death would so hurt Isabelle.

He went on firing single shots, waiting for one of the enemy soldiers to drop into cover, assess the situation, and return meaningful fire. Those men, though, did not have that fundamental training. They were young, peasant boys whose experience of decision making had hovered around whether to first feed the water buffalo or the pigs. So he lay on his belly and calmly finished his work. When nothing moved, he screamed to Huber that he was coming back. His heart was at once weightless with the knowledge he had survived. They were out of danger, and he was going home; but in the next second, a dark cloud shrouded him as the image of little men falling at his will burned deeply inside of him. It so blurred his consciousness, he came to his feet and walked slowly, perfectly upright, from the wood line.

Huber shouted, "Get your butt down, troop!"

Lincoln snarled, "Don't need to. We kicked 'em in the ass."

Lincoln was barely done with his quavering bravado when green, AK-47 tracers erupted from the village, the enemy gunners zeroing on his silhouette. To the Americans watching, it appeared as though Lincoln was surrounded in a shimmering, jade cape, a surreal testament to the man who had saved them. Lincoln sneered haughtily, but an instant later collapsed, clutching at his foot. Huber slithered forward and pulled Lincoln behind a mud wall. At that moment, the Cobra reappeared over the treetops, entering a gun run. AK-47 tracers arched up, away from Lincoln and Huber, lighting the sky with emerald flashes.

Huber radioed to alert the pilot his helicopter was the target of ground fire and told him to hide until the Americans could suppress the last of the small arms. The ship skidded sideways, looped up and over the hill that jutted into the paddies, then settled to the ground. The pilot waited, the engine at full power plus a few percent, his trembling hand pulsing on the collective, staying light on the skids, eyes locked on the temperature gauges.

The Americans on the ground began to take fire again. The lead dustoff ship arrived and radioed, but Huber had sent them off to hold out of range of the small arms and rockets. As the moments passed, fire from the village intensified, now with the report of several machine guns. By that point, word had gone out from the propaganda cells in each primitive settlement along the dirt highway that the final helicopter battle of the war was underway. Insurgents from across the countryside left their families, carrying with them World War One, bolt action rifles, knives, and shovels—any piece of steel upon which they could lay their hands—to join the victory struggle. In between long bursts of automatic weapons fire, the frail popping of squirrel guns maintained the background static while the big guns reloaded.

Then rockets began to fly overhead toward the spot in the sky the Cobra had occupied thirty seconds before. Huber laughed, "Fuckin' idiots. Okay, troop, let's take a look." He yanked up on the piece of hanger wire pilots used to hold bootlaces in place. In case a foot became entrapped in wreckage, a man could pull the loop at the top of the wire, slide it up, let the laces threaded around it pop through the eyelets, and pull his foot free that quickly.

Lincoln's ankle had been hit. Huber brushed aside a small spicule of bone that had been cut from the tibia by a bullet. There was, though, surprisingly little bleeding, and Huber dressed the gash, slid the boot back on, and wrapped it tightly in the laces.

"Troop, it looks like none of us is gettin' outta here. Even these duds'll bring down the gunship if it tries to pick us up. I think I'm going out for a little stroll." He called to one of his door gunners, "Hey, Billywankle J. Moose, lemme hold some M-16 rounds. I'm near out."

Spec. 4 William Wankle scrounged about and put together a single full magazine. Huber gave him a pat on the shoulder, and they both laughed. He turned to Lincoln and grinned. "Fuck me and the horse I rode in on. See ya."

As Huber low-crawled out to the flank, mimicking Lincoln's tactics, silhouettes of men crossing the berm from the village toward the Americans popped out of the night. He came to his knees to improve his field of fire and very slowly took aim at the VC. He carefully discharged single rounds, a tactic that was more confusing to the approaching infantry than if he had put out bursts. He shot one man at either end of the line of soldiers—aimed back to the right then to the left—on and on, until the terror of not knowing who was next sent the few remaining scrambling back over the berm.

Huber was there to greet the remnants. He fired careful, single shots, and the last of the enemy went down. While the infantry charge had been neutralized, there were still machine guns, rocket launchers, and mortars deployed in the village. Despite being out of rifle ammunition, he moved forward, pistol in hand. He charged it very quietly then crawled furtively through the dead and wounded toward the profiles of the heavier weapons. One by one, the VC gunners were taken down by the punch of Huber's .45.

With the cessation of the explosions, it became deathly quiet in the village, but as the men's hearing accustomed to the calm, they could discern dying soldiers crying, wretched tremors that came from both the wood line and the village. Lincoln called the dustoff leader, but they had stayed as long as they could and flown off station to refuel. They promised that two other rescue ships would arrive in minutes.

The Cobra heard the conversation and dropped in seconds later. It made a few runs carrying the wounded, one by one, to the safe clearing. Soon, only Lincoln and Huber were left.

With the next approach of the gunship, Huber yelled for his friend to get in, but Lincoln spit, "I'm not leaving you here alone. Might fall in love with one of the VC ladies and decide to stay."

"Who said I was staying? Get in. I'll ride steerage."

Lincoln hissed, "What the hell you talkin' about?"

"Just get in and watch. Teach ya somethin'."

Huber told the pilot to come up into a low hover, and he monkey wrapped his legs and arms around one of the skids. The off balance gunship shot over the paddies, the pilot pursuing supersonic speed, though he was cautious not to make sharp changes in attitude. He dropped into the next clearing, hovering at two feet to let Huber untangle himself. The pilot threw a flare to signal the rescue ships. The original gunner dove into his forward seat, the canopy slammed shut, and they were gone. Neither Lincoln nor Huber ever saw them again.

As the dustoff ship lifted from the clearing, Lincoln looked down at the village, at the fire feeding on what was left of the straw tinder in which these people, and untold generations of their ancestors, had passed fragile lives. He muttered, "Who gives a shit."

BOOK II

CHAPTER FORTY-NINE

Wilkes Barre, Pennsylvania
40 Years Later

As the van pulled into the driveway, Lincoln Friday lifted out of his recliner and limped onto the front porch. He smiled as the side door slid open automatically, and more broadly when the steel ramp slid out like a black tongue. An electric wheelchair rolled onto it. The woman in the chair looked up and beamed at Lincoln then raised her hand shakily in a fragile wave. After she pushed a series of buttons, the ramp lowered to the paved driveway, and she wheeled off toward a wooden ramp that led up to the porch. The chair bounced as it hit the uneven edge on the wooden incline.

Lincoln bent forward, as if to take a step toward the wheelchair, though caught himself and regained his full height. He laughed aloud, "Speed Queen, welcome home." She braked to a stop in front of him, and he bent forward to kiss the top of her auburn hair.

Slowly, she extended her neck to look up at him. Her smile stole his breath, and he was wordless until a stocky, broad-shouldered man in his thirties emerged from the driver's seat, packages gathered in both arms. He dashed up the ramp, placed the boxes on the woman's lap, and threw his arms around Lincoln.

The woman maneuvered her wheelchair with a tiny joystick to lead the parade into the house. Isabelle, in an apron, dashed into the living room. She touched the woman's face, hesitated, then looked up and threw her arms around the man.

"Sit, sit. The usual, Mike?"

"Of course."

"And, Sabrina, you still on that 'alcohol is the tool of the devil' kick?"

"Mom, what are you talking about? Red, if you don't mind."

Isabelle rolled her eyes. "Oh, I forgot. That was Mike, wasn't it?"

Mike turned to Lincoln. "Dad, looks like, once again, Mom's gotten into your stash of the evil weed."

There was easy laughter as Isabelle disappeared into the kitchen. Lincoln asked, "So, how was the trip? You drove like halfway around the world."

Sabrina nodded. "Not that bad. The new van is amazing. It's more comfortable than being home, as long as Chuck Yeager here stays clear of the authorities."

"Heyyyyy, cop let me go in Wyoming, didn't he? And so did the one in Cedar Rapids..."

"And the one in Ohio."

"Wasn't quite up to the level of a class three felony."

"You think your pardon might have had something to do with me sitting brokenhearted in the backseat, eyes red, a lost waif? And the handicapped plates and the disabled sticker you happened to flash while you were handing over your 'license, registration, and proof of insurance, please.'"

Isabelle placed a beer on the coffee table in front of Mike and turned back toward the kitchen. He called out after her, "Hey, Mom, you were a felon once, weren't you? Like you assaulted the police or something?"

She came back in with a glass of red wine and placed it on the fold out tray of Isabelle's chair. "Nah, that was Nana. I only beat the tar out of a professor."

Mike cringed. "I'm lucky I'm only a high school teacher."

Isabelle mused for a moment. "That's so long ago. Seemed like the end of the world at the time. And, as usual, it passed, just like everything else. Why does it take so long to learn that?" She stood quietly for a moment then bent over to cap the glass of wine with a plastic lid that held a straw. She touched her daughter's cheek tenderly. "You're more beautiful each time we see you. I mean it. Hey, wanna sit in your recliner, Sweetheart?"

"Nah, I'm fine. What with the new car, new chair, I'm livin' large." She drew her torso forward with difficulty to take the straw into her mouth, pulled a long draw of the wine, let herself fall back, and smiled peacefully.

Isabelle brought Lincoln a beer then settled into the third recliner with a glass of white wine. It was soon quiet but comfortable. Mike waited a moment and broke the silence. "So, Dad, what's the latest on the HUEYs? You sign the contract?"

"As Isabelle's dad's old lawyer, Israel Sirota, always said, '*Oy vey*!' I wish he was still around to help us, and in about a thousand things. Supposedly, the helicopters are sitting on the ground in Pakistan, where they've apparently been for a very long time. How they got there is beyond me, and the sellers won't say. Must have been the week we were pissed at India, and Reagan, or whoever, and sent the Pakistanis military equipment. I called the State Department and tried to find someone at our embassy in Islamabad to go look at the parts, but they said they couldn't get involved in private, commercial deals. Sellers sent pictures, but who knows if they're real?"

Mike laughed. "I can't imagine the possibilities."

"On the other hand, if it's real, it'll be the buy of the century. Fifty wooden crates, all different sizes, as small as a shoe box to twice as big and long as your van. Three as big as the couch—the engines, they said. I figure just those are worth three or four times the twenty thousand they want."

"Does that include shipping?"

"That's another eighteen thousand. I figure we could probably slap together two serviceable helicopters with the three they're offering. Just had to retire one of our ships. Two HUEYs would double our present lifting capacity. They'd pay for themselves in a few weeks. Your father-in-law is a brilliant businessman, Michael." He was interrupted by the ladies' groans. "Enough about my toys. Catch us up on the court case."

Mike nodded to Sabrina. "Your turn, Sweetheart."

Lincoln held up his hand. "Excuse me for a moment. Nature beckons, yet again." Isabelle went to the kitchen to bring refills, crackers, and cheese.

When Lincoln limped back in, Sabrina forced her shoulders out of their sag and began. "Okay, here goes. Like I told mom on the phone, it's still making its way through the process. Trial date still hasn't been set. It's maddening. Doctors at Friends of Beneficence remain adamant they followed accepted procedure, and every motion they submit harps on my medical history, that the Agent Orange paralyzed my left arm since birth. The fact that I'm ten times worse after I went to their ER, and all of a sudden, now my legs are paralyzed, too, well, that's just the 'natural progression' of the disease, or so they claim. I mean all of the progression happened in a half hour?

"But whether the doctors are guilty or not doesn't seem to make a bit of difference. During the depositions, the hospital administration lied so many times, I wanted to run 'em down with my chair—the old one."

Lincoln grunted, "And that was a hunk."

Isabelle laughed, "Vehicular homicide. Serve 'em right."

Mike snorted, "Jees this is a violent family—Grandma on down. Must run in the genes."

There was a softening of the air. Everyone sipped from their drinks and sat back. Sabrina shook her head with a wry smile. "Really, you should have seen it. Stuff we knew wasn't true, and they're swearing under oath it is, but we couldn't say anything. Like when Mike saw with his own eyes that ER doc throwing instruments when he was supposed to be putting the central line into me. And all his cursing at the nurses. They swore it never happened that way, but the motions judge ruled that Mike couldn't testify because he was just one person, and it was his word against theirs, and he wasn't a health professional, anyway. They actually made the argument before the judge that if it had been both of us to testify to that guy's behavior, there may have been an argument, but I was unconscious, and it was exactly because he was cursing and throwing things that I was. Then they threw in that that behavior is tolerated in the 'heat of battle,' especially when they were working so hard to save my life.

"They'd do or say anything to make excuses for what that doctor did. They probably hate him, our lawyer said, but with all that money on the line, the facts are irrelevant. Mr. Jennings told us they couldn't fire or even discipline that guy, not even mention the incident on a piece of paper and put it in his personnel file, because if they did, it would make it obvious they knew the truth all along and let him continue practicing in their ER. But Mr. Jennings couldn't say that up front, so he used, like subterfuge; he'd look up at the ceiling in the middle of questioning that guy and pretend to be talking to himself. 'Do I want this guy touching my children?'

"The other side, they'd be on their feet screaming, 'prejudicial, inflammatory,' and they threaten to go to the motions judge and have Mr. Jennings sanctioned. There was one time he pulled a dime from his pocket and slid it across the table toward their attorney. 'Go ahead, give him a call.' Lot of harrumphing after that, but Mr. Jennings just looked out the window.

"With each expert they hired, they got him to say all my problems were from the Agent Orange. I guess they were trying to get us to settle, said that if the case went before a jury, they would be able to link the trouble moving my left arm before I got sick with the problem I'm having now. The fact that I can't walk after that night in the ER is just part of the Agent Orange syndrome. They had their experts each say the same thing: 'When you see a single congenital defect, look for some more defects, 'cause they always come around eventually. Sadly, in this case, the stroke was the eventually.' So they're blaming everything on the Agent Orange."

Isabelle snapped angrily, "The two problems don't have a damn thing to do with one another—the effects of the Agent Orange and what that charlatan did to you in the ER. One was a neural tube defect; no matter what the VA doctors claimed then, we know it really was now. And the other was a stroke, no matter what the hospital swears. The first problem's below the neck, the other's above."

"But mom, you have to admit, to a jury, they look the same. And in order to convict the hospital of malpractice, the standard is not beyond a reasonable doubt, that's for criminal trials. Here, it's the preponderance of the evidence. That means one more expert on their side than on ours. They have dozens lined up. Got money to fly them out from God knows where, pay all their expenses, and then hourly fees of like a thousand dollars. We can't come near competing with that. System's rigged."

Lincoln added distantly, "Funny, the lawyers used just the opposite argument when you were born with the neural tube defect. We knew it was from Agent Orange. VA did, too. Everyone knew. It was happening here—children of returnees—*and* in Viet Nam. All of a sudden, huge numbers of kids with holes in their spinal cords being born to parents who'd been exposed. And the government wouldn't accept a single thread of responsibility. Fought every single case to the death, no matter what it cost in legal fees. Spray and betray. Shoot, they wouldn't even concede that I'd ever come in contact with the stuff. Do you know that story, Mike?"

"Not sure I do."

Isabelle groaned, "You know it very well. Stop being polite."

"Well, maybe heard it once..."

Mike laughed. "Go ahead, Dad, I need to hear it again. Learn something new each time."

"Well, it wasn't in my records that I had been exposed. I mean, it wasn't something the Army kept track of. How could they? That stuff was sprayed from a half-mile in the air in the middle of the day. Hot as hell out, blew everywhere, what with the unstable atmosphere..."

Isabelle groaned. "Dearest husband, this isn't the Weather Channel. Let's get on with the story." She laughed and stood to refill the drinks.

Lincoln waited until she returned. "Okay, okay. Anyway, when I finally tracked down my old crew chief, who, by the way, had lymphoma from Agent Orange, to prove that we had sprayed that crap all over the countryside, VA said it didn't matter what he said. They claimed your defect, I'm sorry Sweetheart, I mean the chromosomal abnormality..."

"Bullshit, Poppy, it is what it is."

Lincoln's eyes hardened. "Anyway, they said it wasn't on the list of Agent Orange-caused problems. But *every single disease* that's on that list now had been denied at one time or another. We couldn't even prove it was a neural tube defect. Didn't have MRIs in those days. Looked like one to all the doctors we asked to testify, but that wasn't good enough for the VA, and since the VA was the defendant, the burden of proof was on us. Benefit of the doubt went to the accused. They always came up with one more doctor to say there was no so-called scientific proof that your condition, if it was a neural tube defect in the first place, was associated with the Dioxin in Agent Orange. Over and over, they claimed it was fate, or maybe even a stroke caused by a non-attentive obstetrician who let your head come out of the birth canal too fast. Then they'd drop their heads sadly and mutter, 'A tragedy, but not the government's fault. Maybe you should seek redress from the hospital that delivered the baby.'

"And when we scratched and dug up one more doctor for our side, they found and paid two more to say it wasn't the Agent Orange, that you were just the victim of the percentages, or maybe physician malpractice, that any baby could be born that way. By the time we were done, their lawyers were so irritated with us, they stopped shaking their heads in sympathy. You should heard 'em yammer at the administrative judge, 'Your honor, these people are bound and determined to squeeze the government for what may have been a product of their life style. Why, Mrs. Friday freely admits that the night their baby was conceived, they each had a glass of wine, or maybe it was two. She doesn't seem able to recollect just how much alcohol she consumed."

Lincoln glared at the wall. "They had all the money in the world, every penny of it from our tax dollars, to stay one expert ahead of us, to swear to the court that it was just luck of the draw."

"And maybe it was, Poppy, but I'm doin' just fine. I wouldn't trade my life for anyone I ever met."

"Sweetheart," Mike interjected heatedly, "and I wouldn't trade you for any soul on this Earth, but what that goddamn doctor did to you in the hospital that night was *not* fate. I don't know about Agent Orange, but what I saw with my own eyes was malpractice. The sucker was busy cursing at the nurses and throwing things to cover up that he couldn't stop his hands from shaking and start the damn IV, and give you back the blood you lost from the ectopic pregnancy, that he didn't believe you had in the first place, and let you sit out in the waiting room and bleed, just because he was pissed off at the doctor who sent you down there in the middle of the night and made him work." Mike was screeching, "He was guilty of malpractice and worse, period. The hospital knows it, and yet they do nothing. If they win, I just don't know what I'll do. I may just make sure that doctor doesn't ever set foot back in the ER, except maybe as a patient."

Sabrina's face tightened, "You'll do nothing of the sort. We'll win, and if we don't, we will go on loving each other, and we'll have a great life. Don't worry, we don't need to do a darn thing. It will be taken care of. Always is." She drew a swallow of wine through her straw. "So, when do we see Nana Kerrith and Grandma Miriam?"

Lincoln stood. "And on that happy thought, I think I'll just sprint to the ladies' room, if you'll excuse me."

Isabelle laughed. "The Queen doesn't announce."

"Yeah, well, I gotta go, so your highness, pardon me."

As Lincoln limped to the bathroom, Sabrina asked, "Mom, is dad going more now? I read there's a lot doctors can do for that."

"It's getting worse, but your father says every guy he knows has the same problem, and when they go to the doctor over at the VA, they get kicked around worse than on sick call, and the pills cause impotence and loss of, you know, the drive."

Sabrina laughed. "God forbid."

Lincoln came back and dropped into his chair. His left elbow brushed the arm rest and pushed his sweater up a few inches. Mike glanced over and saw how withered his father-in-law's forearm had become. The hand was atrophied, skin loose and hanging, except for an area of gross swelling on the back of the wrist. He asked, "Hey, dad, when those helicopters get here, are you going to be doing the work on them yourself?"

"Unless you wanna do it."

Mike smiled glumly. "You don't have any elves you can round up from the woods to do it for you? I mean, what with your wrist and your ankle."

"I know. We'll see."

CHAPTER FIFTY

Lincoln stared through their bay window as the sun began to set beyond Wilkes Barre's western farmlands. The silhouette of a tiny Cessna floated above the fields, scurrying home before dark. He pictured the minimal cockpit, laughing to himself at how complex and weighty it had all seemed a lifetime before. He spent a moment trying to fathom how the seemingly endless years had so swiftly evaporated, then shook his head, sighed quietly, and looked up at Isabelle.

She spoke softly. "Flying, Sweetheart?"

"Yep." She queried him subtly with her eyes. He nodded back and turned to Sabrina. "Sweetheart, we have a surprise."

Mike shouted, "You guys are pregnant!"

When the groaning faded, Lincoln went on. "We have special guests for dinner."

Sabrina sighed. "Wait. I thought we were going to go see the grannies."

"Yep, we will. Tomorrow night. Don't worry, they've been in Wilkes Barre for a hundred years; they'll still be around in twenty-four hours." Isabelle glared at him. "Okay, ninety years. Sabrina, I don't know if you remember, but there was a man, he was from Viet Nam. You called him 'Uncle No.'"

Sabrina gulped. "Oh-my-God. I was just telling Mike about him two nights ago. I do remember him. I think it was the first time I was ever near someone who didn't look like me. I was so scared. I think it made him uncomfortable. That's kind of bothered me a little all these years."

Lincoln shook his head. "Nah, you were perfect. You were so beautiful, such an important milestone, in all of our lives—even his. So he leaned forward to touch your hand, but then he got scared that it might not be the right thing to do in America."

"Poppy, I remember the whole thing. He came close and made sounds, and he smiled at me, but then he jumped away. I guess he was scared he'd frightened me."

"Not scared, Sweetheart. Probably just overwhelmed that he was finally safe, and you couldn't realize at the time that you were his glimpse of the future, that men like him, and me, had a chance to live in peace. He didn't know what to do. He had been through so much, and there you were—his good fortune staring him in the eye. He thought *he* was lucky, but without him, truth is, none of us would be sitting here today. Anyway, he told me that seeing you was the first moment he realized the nightmare was over."

At six o'clock on the nose, the doorbell rang. A swarthy, diminutive Asian man stood at the threshold. He held himself rigidly erect, his eyes telling of profound anxiety. He bowed, as if standing before the emperor of Viet Nam, then slowly brought himself back to attention. Without a word, he turned stiffly and placed his hand gently on a pretty woman's forearm. She took a step to his side and bowed modestly.

The man spoke with a thick, Asian accent. “Mr. Rincoln, this Nhu wife. She is Quynh. It mean ‘bird.’”

Lincoln gasped, “Oh, Mr. Nhu, this is such an honor.” He shook her hand first, though so gently, it was hard to know if he had touched her.

Nhu turned again and waved impatiently at two early teens, their lips puffed over braces. His hand was palm down as he beckoned them. The girls stepped forward and, after delicate bows, stood ramrod straight, eyes lowered. Nhu spoke facing Lincoln. “This Tu.” He turned quickly, pointed at the older of the girls, then snapped forward. “That mean ‘star.’” He nodded at the younger one. “This Xuan, that mean ‘spring.’”

The two men looked into each other’s faces, then came together in an embrace that brought a hue of red to Isabelle’s and Quynh’s eyes. Mike bent forward and held Sabrina. The girls, though, remained rigidly inexpressive. When Lincoln spoke, his voice cracked. “Please come into our humble home. It is our honor.”

Isabelle asked what she could bring to drink, and Lincoln offered Nhu, “Beer, wine, maybe something stronger?”

“No, Mr. Rincoln, Nhu drive back to hotel tonight. Never drink drive.”

Lincoln nodded. “Of course. I know who you are.”

Mike laughed and turned to the girls, who were sitting as severely as they had stood. “Young ladies, how ’bout a glass of wine, maybe liquor and a cigarette?”

Mrs. Nhu smiled, but the girls’ eyes widened. Nhu giggled. “Mr. Rincoln, you son-law, he just like you. Make to feel welcome. Make to laugh. Make easy to be guest.”

Sabrina nodded. “Yes, Mr. Nhu, he’s very funny.” She turned her wheelchair toward her husband. “You’re hilarious,” she chuckled dryly, “aren’t you, *Dear*?”

Mrs. Nhu’s lips curled up.

Lincoln spoke. "Sabrina, Mike, you don't know just who's sitting here, but Mr. Nhu is an amazing man. We'll eat dinner, and then, after, Mr. Nhu, would you tell my family the whole story? I've waited years to hear it all at once."

"Mr. Rincoln, my greatest friend, my story nothing. I embarrass to tell when so many Vietnamee people go through so much, and also you go through so much for to help Viet Nam."

After dinner, they settled in the living room. Mike helped Sabrina into an easy chair and covered her legs with a blanket. She pulled him forward and kissed his lips gently. The girls gasped. Nhu laughed. "You see, this how good man treat good wife. You be lucky grow up marry man such like Mr. Rincoln and Mr. Mike."

Lincoln made Mrs. Nhu take his easy chair. At first, she demurred, but he led her by the arm across the room. She smiled as she lowered herself, then waited a moment, turned to her husband, and spoke firmly in Vietnamese.

Lincoln asked, "Is everything okay?"

Nhu laughed. "Oh, wife fine. Say Nhu must drink wine. She drive. Truth? She better driver than Nhu."

Lincoln laughed, "Yeah, but can she fly a HUEY?"

"That also better than Nhu."

Quynh laughed and spoke for the first time that evening in full sentences. "Not really. He's better on the collective, but I'm pretty handy with the cyclic. That's why we get along so well."

Lincoln's family sat, jaws slack, until Isabelle laughed. "Quynh, were you born here? Your English is amazing. Better than mine."

She laughed. "No, I was born in Saigon, but I have to admit I came here when I was only seven, so it was learn English or perish. Bao Chien, he's the amazing one. And that means 'protective warrior' in Vietnamese."

Lincoln nodded. "And so he is. Well, Mr. Nhu, it's time, my friend. Please tell us the story. You have to. We're going to make it into a movie."

Nhu took a swallow of wine. "Guess time for Nhu to speak. Fun to tell, now, but not fun to live. Well, year 1975, Nhu still flying HUEY for Vietnamee Army. I now become major. Make good money—maybe twenty dollar for one month." There was quiet laughter. "Then the war go very bad. Communit, they come from North, NVA, North Viet Nam Army. I in Xuan Loc, fly from old base of 11 Cav. That American unit, tanks. They leave and give us basecamp, I think Seventy-Two.

"Then one day, end April '75, Xuan Loc gone. NVA take overnight. All my friend prepare to die, but okay because they soon to see ancestor, thank ancestor for good life. I say, that stupid. We see ancestor another day. Now, you come with me. NVA never take Saigon. I tell them take rifle, two magazine, nothing more. I carry fifteen friend in HUEY H model. We land Saigon. It chaos. Many helicopter take off for American ship at sea. All pilot take family. I want to go, but never leave without mother, father, grandmother, grandfather. So I leave helicopter in airport. Go to gather family. They too scared to leave house. Mr. Rincoln, I forget, you know house!"

"Yes, we were there with your parents. They were so good to us. They had so little, but they shared. I never forgot. Please, though, go on. But wait a minute, I'll be right back."

When Lincoln dropped back into the plastic chair he'd dragged in from the patio, Nhu was whispering to his girls to sit up straight. He smiled, and Isabelle leaned forward. "Yes, Mr. Nhu, please go on. I haven't heard even half of this story. Lincoln, did you know all of this?"

"Less than half."

Nhu nodded politely. "Okay, but you tell when Nhu talk too much." There was laughter and, with another quaff of wine, the tension in his jaws and shoulders slackened. "So, Nhu helicopter still in airport, and family sit in house with arm across chest, say we safe here, not in machine that go up then fall from sky so easy."

Lincoln laughed cynically. "They weren't that far off. I'm sorry. Go on."

"Communit, next day, they drive tank into Saigon. War over. Every soldier throw away uniform and gun, but Nhu bury M-16 under brick of house. Put magazine in big tin can.

"At first couple year, Communit, they not do bad. It look like thing settle down. Then all of sudden, '79, they come to house and take away all who work for American. My father, he politician. He go. Brother, he professor English. He go. But Communit, they know from neighbor Nhu can fly. They talk to Nhu, tell Nhu they leave alone if fly helicopter for Communit army. Say to officer, first must let father, brother go. He slap face. *I* spit on officer face. Go to concentration camp next day.

"For five year, sit in small room with fifty men. Almost no food. Maybe little rice, green leaf, I think from local tree. Maybe fat of pig, one small bite, one time in week. Then '85, they open door. We go home. Must walk. Take many week. Countryside very poor. Farmer people hand some small food, but they have nothing for self.

"When get home, slowly, all family come together."

Lincoln stood. "Mr. Nhu, just give me a minute."

With Lincoln back, Nhu took a breath to continue. The room was utterly silent. Even the girls were transfixed. Nhu saw their expressions and spoke quietly. "I never tell children story. They too young to understand. Now, maybe okay.

"Eighty-Nine, I so skinny. Family skinny. Everybody, maybe nothing to eat for years. I get out pencil. I write down mother, father, everybody, how much kilograms. I add up. It like six American. Can take every one of family in H-model HUEY. That fifteen people. My job on street to fix shoe. That all Communit government allow Nhu to do. No one watch me. So, go for little afternoon walk to Tan San Nhut Airport. Look for full day. Communit still have American helicopter capture at end of war. But Nhu don't know if have fuel.

"Nhu go to friend. She lady who can sew. She make Nhu North Viet Nam flight suit. I captain again. Lose one rank." He laughed—the others did not.

"I just like Mr. Huber. Not care." Nhu's very dark complexion suddenly flushed. He stopped talking, his head dropped, and he stared at his feet.

The quiet thickened, and the air became so charged, Lincoln quickly stammered, "Yeah, our old friend, Huber. Yeah, but that's for another time." He paused. "Well, Mr. Nhu, please go on with the story. It's really unbelievable."

Nhu drew a deep breath. "So, Nhu walk onto flight line. Some soldier salute. Nhu almost laugh. Growl at them to get to work. Nhu go to HUEY. Turn on master switch, look at fuel gauge. Tank empty. Next one, empty. Next one, full. But Mr. Rincoln, you remember. HUEY cost all money in world, but they put in cheap fuel gauge. Maybe five dollah. Crap."

Quynh's eyes flew open. "Bao Chien!" she nipped in Vietnamese, and his eyes dropped shamefully. She shook her head and muttered, "Less than one glass of wine."

Nhu waited a few seconds, took another swallow, and resumed. "So I check fuel tank itself. Fuel full. Nhu go home, tell everybody eat all food in house, take gold that left, all money that left, and family take bus to middle Saigon. Nhu leave them at hospital with big helipad. Back to Tan San Nhut. No helmet in ship. What to do?"

Lincoln laughed. Nhu thought for a moment and chuckled as well, but the rest of the room was silent. Lincoln spoke this time with a smile in his voice. "Mr. Nhu and his helmet! But that's also another story, for another time. Please Mr. Nhu."

"Nhu jump in ship, forget to untie rotor. Start to push button. I say, 'Oh,' then the s-word." He shot Quynh a glance. She rolled her eyes. "Nhu jump out. Some police, they look at me. I untie, very slow, like just part of mission. Then start for real. Come hot, but have no way talk to tower. But who care? I jump off into climb for so light. First time ever fly only man on board HUEY. Approach hospital. Grandfather and mother on mother side, they too afraid. Refuse get on. Finally, Nhu get out, forget to tie down collective, I so scared and angry, and pick up grandparent and throw on. Then everybody get on."

Lincoln cried, "Oh, my God. Don't tell me!"

"But collective behave, and off we go."

Lincoln put up his hand to stop Nhu. "I can't stand it. You just started flying with fifteen souls aboard and nowhere to go?"

"No, no. Nhu have plan. Thailand. If we fly to Cambodia-Thailand border straight line, maybe fuel okay. Range of Hotel-model HUEY maybe three-fifty mile. Saigon to border Thailand maybe three-twenty-five. Maybe land inside Cambodia. No matter. Many Vietnamee walk from Saigon, all across Cambodia to refugee camp. They call these people walk full trip, 'platform Vietnamee.' Who know why."

Lincoln pulled himself to his feet. "Mr. Nhu, hang on for just a minute."

When Lincoln returned, he saw that Tu's and Xuan's heads were hanging, eyes nearly closed. He nodded to Isabelle subtly, and she turned to her guests. "Mr. Nhu, you've travelled so far today. All the way across the country by plane, then all the way by car from that awful airport in Philadelphia. Why don't we continue tomorrow morning at breakfast? How about we meet you at your hotel? The restaurant's great. Did you know Lincoln worked there when he was a kid? Tried to burn the place down."

Sabrina laughed. "Not *that* story again."

Lincoln lifted his head and grinned. “And a heck of a fire it was. Then they fired me, not for causing it, but for trying to put it out. Makes sense. After all, this *is* Wilkes Barre.”

Isabelle turned to Quynh. “How ’bout ten? That’ll be seven your time. Is that too early?”

The girls’ eyes rolled. Quynh shot them a look. There were hugs—an especially long one between Lincoln and Nhu.

CHAPTER FIFTY-ONE

They rode together to the hotel in Sabrina's van. Isabelle and Lincoln sat in the third row of seats, just behind Sabrina. As they passed Kirby Park, they turned to look at the spot, now totally hidden in a copse of trees. They squeezed hands, and then again as Mike drove very carefully into the parking lot of the Sterling Hotel.

Lincoln brought his lips to Isabelle's ear and whispered, "Haven't been here in years. This is the very spot I bought that stupid old Pontiac. Who knows how life would have turned out but for that twenty-five bucks?"

Isabelle put her head on his shoulder. "It's all for the best. Thank God for that car. For everything. For you." She kissed him gently on the lips. When they looked up, Lincoln saw Mike's soft eyes in the rearview mirror.

The Nhus were sitting in the lobby and vaulted to their feet as the Americans entered the hotel. The hugs were even warmer than the night before, and it was some minutes before Nhu rushed to the restaurant door to open it for Sabrina's chair. Mike sidled up to Xuan and Tu as they entered the dining area. "Hey, you guys, last time I ate here, they were serving deep fried alligator. We ordered some for you."

In one voice, the girls moaned, "Maaaaaaam! Is that true?"

Quynh laughed, "You bet it is. This is the East Coast. That's what people eat here. You're gonna love it." The girls took each other's arms and stopped short. Quynh shook her head. "Come on, you two. Can't you take a joke?" They shuffled, an inch at a time, past tables, ogling plates, until Quynh walked back to them and hissed, "Act like young ladies, or I'll send you back to the room." Their eyes rolled once more.

Sabrina spun her chair toward Mike. "Good work, Mr. Ambassador."

After brunch, they sat back, and Lincoln prodded Nhu to go on with his story.

He began, "I think I tell you we take off from hospital. Whole family lay on floor in back. We get a thousand feet, that when all screaming and crying begin. 'We gonna die, we gonna die, never again see ancestor grave.'

"I get so sick tired of all screaming, I turn around and yell at them to shut up, or I come back there and push out loudest, then next loudest, until all gone. Suddenly quiet except for cry, everybody cry. Get sick tired of cry, and Nhu turn around again. 'You stop cry now, or I come back there.'

"Nhu friction down collective and put on cyclic trim to hold still. Then I turn around and pretend get up from seat. They see Nhu two hand off controls and more screaming. Not so smart for Nhu. Finally, talk quiet to them, just enough over engine noise. Tell them ancestor tell Nhu save family one way or other, not matter. Ancestor say helicopter bring them close to heaven. That what Vietnamee believe is God. We have no God, just heaven. They believe Nhu smartest in family for fly, and they believe that Nhu speak to ancestor because Nhu always come so close in helicopter.

"We fly southwest. Low, slow, not burn too much fuel. We go for three hour, then hear twenty-minute fuel warning scream like evil spirit. Fly on, looking to see if Camboda-Thailand border. No way to tell. Then five-minute fuel warning. 'Whoop, whoop, whoop,' so loud, all start cry again—maybe Nhu cry also.

"Nhu pull out circuit breaker to stop sound, because not want that to be last thing family hear before all die. See clearing ahead and land like put baby in cradle. Everybody look up. Happy, smile. Then engine stop all by self, out of gas. Nhu not have to do shutdown sequence. No post-flight inspection." He and Lincoln laughed. The others stared.

"We get out. It graveyard. Everybody scream and cry again, so Nhu order them like recruit to move rear end, get ass walking." Quynh raised her eyebrows. Nhu lowered his head, but as he tasted the bitterness of the memory, his face tightened, and he lifted his head, looking away from his wife.

"Think we still in Cambodia, so take compass and family walk west. Thick jungle. Mosquito big enough to pick up dog and carry him into air like H-23."

Lincoln turned to the audience. "That was our training helicopter in Texas. That's the other story I was telling you about." He pushed himself to his feet. "Hang on there, Mr. Nhu. I'll be right back."

Lincoln was gone longer this time, and when he returned, Nhu stared at him. "Mr. Rincoln okay?"

"Fine, fine. Just ah, you know, gettin' old. Please go on with the story. It's amazing."

Nhu looked at him for another minute before continuing. "Okay, so family walk and come to village. Never see house like this in Viet Nam. Swamp, so some house build on four pole high in air. People have nothing, but give us little rice. We ask if we in

Cambodia or Thailand. They not know where they live. They say live, then say name of village. That all they know. Some not know even what is Cambodia or Thailand.

"They send us on trail, and we come to next town. Bigger. Now, we know still in Cambodia, and we in trouble. They take some gold not to call Khmer Rouge. That Cambodia Communit. We leave middle of night, for tomorrow they take more. We know how Communit in Viet Nam say they come to save life and spirit of little man, then strangle family to steal gold, steal future. Pol Pot, he kill twenty-five percent Cambodia people. All in name of Communit. He will kill Vietnamee people, like Nhu family, just same as slap mosquito. So, we go again.

"Next town in Thailand. We give some gold, or they tell police, who come and take all gold. So we march, so hungry, so tired, to refugee camp for Vietnamee people. It not much better than jungle, but there have food and American doctor. One man, he was soldier in Viet Nam; now he doctor and come to camp to help. He speak Vietnamee, but not so good. My family laugh at him. Nhu yell, want to smack family. Say to them, 'This man leave family American, help you for free. You laugh? What wrong with you?' Sometime, they so stupid.

"So, we settle in. Sometime, Thailand soldier come and sneak into lady hut and rape. They laugh. They look for gold, but we hide most. Hide pretty good. Leave little to let soldier steal. We finally complain to Red Cross. Mosquito, snake, thief everywhere. We get three liter water every day for drink, cook, wash clothes, bath. Everything for sale: water, salt, sugar, cigarette. Guard beat you if you complain, then let Thailand young man into camp at night for girl. These one they steal medicine, food, and sell back in morning. You no buy, they take you out in jungle and shoot. Then they charge family for price of bullet.

"Doctor who like to speak Vietnamee, he very kind. I want to write letter to Mr. Rincoln, but doctor not know where Mr.

Rincoln live. No idea. I ask doctor if he know Mr. Rincoln. He laugh, but he say when he back to States, he look for my friend. He call to Army in D.C. when he get home. He say Mr. Rincoln pilot. Army contact him to Fort Rucker. They not want to give information, but doctor from New York, and he good at tell tall tale. He send Mr. Rincoln letter, and Mr. Rincoln do unbelievable. He sponsor Nhu family to come to U.S. Unbelievable."

Lincoln smiled. "No, your courage is unbelievable. Your family, they deserved a break."

"But so much money for you to bring, now thirteen, to U.S. Three grandparent die in camp. Early. Maybe better. When we get here, government very good to Nhu family, but send to North Dakota. Not same as Viet Nam, so I save money to take family to San Francisco. So many Vietnamee there. Why not go Californa? Have nothing better to do with life.

Isabelle interrupted. "But Mr. Nhu, you have done so well. Excuse me, would you please tell us how you got started in business? From the little I know of it, that's another mind-boggling story."

The waiters and busboys were hovering, a step closer every few minutes, so Lincoln finally went to the maître d' and asked if they should go. The man told him they were getting ready for a wedding reception that night. Lincoln laughed. "Well, sir, that's really crazy. I was a busboy here, what, forty-five years ago or so. It was my first night on the job. It was a real fancy wedding. One of the guests was this beautiful young gal. And, guess what? I married her."

The man looked at Lincoln. "Wait a minute. Are you the one who won that medal in Viet Nam?"

"Well, I won *a* medal. Don't know if I was *the* one."

"Friday, isn't it?"

"Yes, sir, it is. How do you know that?"

"Mr. Friday, please let me show you something." He pulled Lincoln through the swinging doors into the chef's office. Other than grimier walls and small holes in the linoleum that had grown into gaping hollows in the floor, it had not changed in half-a-century. The man pointed at a sepia newspaper clipping in a cheap frame. As Lincoln focused on it, a blanket of numbness settled over him. It was a picture of him standing with President Nixon, receiving the Medal of Honor. Under it was a handwritten caption. "Lincoln Friday worked in this kitchen as a pot washer, dish washer, sandwich man, and short order cook. He helped put out the fire that nearly destroyed the old hotel."

When Lincoln went back to the table, everyone looked up questioningly. His face was wan, and he sat dazed, until Isabelle put her hand on his arm. "Oh, yeah. Sorry." He told the story, but ever so briefly, then explained they had to leave the dining room so the staff could set up for the wedding that night.

Isabelle stood and came up behind his chair, leaned forward, and kissed his cheek. She laughed, "It's all just one great big circle, isn't it?"

Lincoln placed a credit card with the bill, and the waiter took it hurriedly to the desk. He was back sooner than there had been time to run it. Lincoln asked, "Is there something wrong with the card?"

"Oh, no, sir. Mr. Ambriano wants you to know this one's on the house."

Mike piped up. "The tip, too?"

Sabrina turned her chair to the waiter, whose face was paler than Lincoln's. "I'm really sorry for his behavior. That's another one of his feeble attempts at humor. I live with this twenty-four, seven. I'm the one who deserves a tip."

As the party rose to leave, Mrs. Nhu tried to explain to her daughters in Vietnamese, then in English, why everyone was crying with laughter. The girls stood, though, without expression.

CHAPTER FIFTY-TWO

They drove to a small, but attractive English Tudor in a quiet, affluent neighborhood. Kerrith Dalton walked off the porch a bit unsteadily. Her hair was white, though perfectly coiffed. She had remained slim, her face regal. Nhu thought it even more stately than decades before. The Nhus were cautious, though, when she extended her bony, gnarled hand. They touched her so softly, she harrumphed, but quickly smiled warmly and put her arm around Mr. Nhu's shoulder. She squeezed hard and laughed, "I'm not going to break, you know."

She had not seen Nhu since the late Eighties and had had only pictures of the girls. As she took an erect step backwards to look at them, her demeanor relaxed and her eyes reddened. Lincoln went to her side and put an arm around her waist. She straightened. "Well, everyone, inside. Let's greet Miriam."

Lincoln's mother was in a wheelchair. Her complexion was ashen and her eyes yellow. Though her tummy and legs were covered with a blanket, it was not hard to see the outline of her belly. It was if she was eight-months pregnant. She lifted a skeletal hand toward Nhu.

"Oh, Mr. Nhu, I didn't think I would ever see you again. God is so good to us. And this is your lovely bride. My, my, you did well for yourself."

Mrs. Nhu bent forward to take Miriam's hand, but Miriam pulled her forward into a hug. Quynh froze the instant she sensed the skeletal frame but recovered quickly and added with emotion, "If it wasn't for your Lincoln, we would not be alive. So, thanks to you, we are all here."

Miriam spoke with effort. "The children, they're so beautiful, like you. Come closer girls. I want to see you."

Tu and Xuan stiffened. They shot a harrowed glance at their mother, who took Xuan by the hand and led her to Miriam's side. Tu followed obediently but stood, shielded, behind her sister. Miriam lifted her hand slowly and reached for Xuan, who pulled back reflexively and bumped into Tu. Then Mrs. Nhu pushed her forward. When their fingers touched, Xuan became stock-still. Miriam looked up and laughed weakly. "You're as pale as I am. Sweetheart, don't be afraid. I am Uncle Lincoln's mama. He's nice, isn't he?" The child nodded fleetingly, and Miriam laughed again. "He and your papa are the nicest men you will ever meet, and Michael, too."

Kerrith cleared her throat, asked what her guests wanted to drink, then started pushing people toward the chairs she had dragged in from the four corners of the neighborhood. The girls shot to the two farthest from Miriam.

There was small talk about the Nhus' first trip to the East Coast as a family and their plans to drive to D.C to visit the Capitol and the White House. Miriam asked the girls what they thought about flying, but they looked to their mom, begging silently for her to answer.

With a lull in the conversation, Lincoln sat up straight. "Well, when we were at breakfast, Mr. Nhu was recounting how his family got here, but we had to stop just when he started to tell us about going into business down in California. Mr. Nhu, Mom and Mrs. Dalton know about your trip from Thailand, but they don't know about how you became so successful. Actually, Isabelle and I don't know the full story. No one's going to chase us away from here, so take your time."

Nhu looked at his wife, who nodded faintly. "Okay, but very boring." He sat silently for a moment, staring out the window, then drew a deep breath. "Okay, Nhu come to San Francisco, not yet have child or have wife, but have to make money to feed family. Many too old to work, not speak one word English.

"So, Nhu take job. In States, Vietnamee woman do fingernail, maybe cut hair. Man work drive cab, maybe gardener. Nhu can no learn name of street in San Francisco. Too many name of Spanish. So, find refugee man from Saigon who hire Nhu do garden work. He terrible man. Like usual boss Viet Nam. He treat countryman like dog because he boss. He say, if not work for little money, he call government, make trouble. It lousy job, like peasant, but pay bill a little. So, they send Nhu up and down I-280—go to rich man house and cut grass, rake, trim. One day, Nhu in front yard nice house San Bruno, next to San Francisco Airport. Nhu spend too much time look up at airplane land, take off. I think how ground look from in air. But I never fly again. This America. Pilot only American. But working, family safe, so life okay."

Nhu stopped and looked back out the window into the lush gardens. All eyes remained wide, waiting for his heart to return to them. He began again slowly, his voice tinged with a whisper of bitterness. "So, Nhu trim walkway of house. Front door open. A man—tall, handsome—he dress in dark blue suit with four gold stripe on sleeve. Hat have gold band. Look like navy officer. Then, see he have gold wing on chest. Nhu turn off trim machine as man walk by. He almost not nod, head so high in air.

Nhu realize he not navy. He airline pilot. I want tell man Nhu have many hour as pilot. I want talk him about flying, but he in big black car and gone. Never look back one second.

"So, Nhu maybe angry at rude man, but then think, why that man have so much? It must be will of heaven. That how Vietnamee think. Heaven, maybe you call God, Heaven tell what you fortune in life. No other choice. Not complain. If complain, Heaven strike man down.

"But then Nhu think. He spend time in U.S., be around good man like Mr. Rincoln, Mr. Rocket, Mr. Huber. So, maybe by now, different mind than Vietnamee man. Nhu say to self, 'Why not fly again? This *is* America. When we take citizenship class, they teach you: work hard—do good life.

"So, if Nhu decide to fly, Nhu fly. I tell boss 'go to hell.'" His wife's shoulders dropped again. Nhu's face became as tight as Lincoln had ever seen it. "Nhu no care. I tell him go to *hell.* He slave driver. Own countryman worse of all. So Nhu go to San Francisco Airport. They have helicopter school. They laugh when come in, tell Nhu graduate American Army Flight School. Want to convert military license to civilian. They laugh harder. But Nhu pay for three lesson. Very much expensive. Nhu not care.

"First lesson, instructor, he not let me touch. He do all flying. Maybe he need time for logbook, but Nhu angry." He stopped. This time, the faces turned away as tears welled in his eyes. When he began again, he straightened himself in his chair and forced the quaver of anger from of his voice. "Second lesson, I say I want fly whole hour. He look at me like I crazy. Minute I get into helicopter, I tell him again. He let me touch pedal for a second. I tell him I now take collective. Mr. Rincoln, I so embarrass. Look like mosquito fly around—up, down, sideway—same first day Wolter. He take control. He laugh. Then I say, angry, 'I pay; I fly.' Man scare Nhu hit him. Back to pedal. Two minute, no problem. Then collective three minute, no problem. Cyclic, five minute.

Come back like ride bicycle. Then, I tell man I hover for five minute, then tell him, 'Now I fly by self!'

"I tell him I call tower to hover taxi to active. I call. Clearance they give. I taxi for takeoff, and off we go. Easy, like walk again. Instructor, he red in face and sweat. I tell him I make approach. This too much, and he say. 'No, man, too dangerous.' I not fight in cockpit, so he land, and Nhu march in to see owner. She American, but mean like Chinee dragon lady. I tell her, if not get new instructor, go to other helicopter school. She hiss like cat, say, 'No threaten America woman.' She say, 'This not China.'

"So, I go to El Granada, near Half Moon Bay. Take lesson from old man. He Army pilot in Korea War. He now logger pilot. He good man, and soon, Nhu get ticket—then have to get commercial. Borrow money from family. They not want to give, only take from Nhu. But Nhu work hard, get commercial, then old man give job pulling log from forest. Loggers rough men, but good person. They like Nhu; Nhu like loggers.

"Nhu work seven day week. Make good money, and one day, boss, he say, 'Enough, enough.' He getting scared of fly in helicopter. Nhu laugh. He not laugh. He say he done. He sell me business if Nhu can pay. What to do? Too much money, but he let Nhu pay slow at first years, then after five year, pay off.

"Maybe three year after buy, need new engine. Nhu always look in helicopter magazine for cheap engine. Then, Nhu angry again. Why Nhu always go to buy cheap? This America. Not think so small all the time. So, see new technology in magazine. Can convert piston engine helicopter to turbine jet engine helicopter. Cost too much, but carry much more log every day. I tell old boss. He say good business idea, so he add me two more year to pay off.

"Then get government contract to clear deadwood near coast. It called Loma Mar. At end of day, Nhu land, tell ground crew go drive home. Nhu take helicopter to airport for overnight security. Before Nhu take off, car pull up to field. Man come over. He say he pilot in Viet Nam, now doctor. He speak some Vietnamee. I so excited, wonder if he same doctor in Thailand refugee camp." Nhu paused to let his audience's jaws drop. "He not." Nhu laughed and went on. "But he tell Nhu fly HUEY in Viet Nam, Eleven Cav. He go to flight school before us. Come home, become doctor. He say Nhu come to his office for flight physical. No charge.

"Next day, somebody put big tent up in field near where Nhu ground crew set up fuel truck. End of day, Nhu land, and doctor there again. I so happy to see. Ask doctor what is tent. He tell me is revival meeting tent. Nhu not understand, and he try explain Nhu what is revival. Still not really understand, so doctor, he say me stay until night and see.

"Doctor and Nhu drink beer, wait. Sun go down, a hundred car park and go into tent. Man on stage very big, black suit, black tie. He quiet, head down until everyone sit. Then he start slow, cannot hear, but loud and loud, and soon he scream that every man do sin. Only Lord save, stop do sin. Doctor, he laugh, but very hard to see. When over, man on stage, he sweat like horse. White foam come from mouth. Doctor laugh again.

"So Nhu go to doctor office. His nurse look at me and smile, ask if I Chinee or Japanee. I say Vietnamee. She all happy, say friend upstairs business office Vietnamee. She ask Nhu if marry. When I say no and shake head sadly, she all happy again, say she introduce. And I meet wife.

"Now, three helicopter. Five pilot. Eighteen employee. Pain in ass." Quynh threw her hands up in defeat. "Own hanger in Half Moon Bay. Send helicopter all way to Oregon, Washington. Charge little, but do much work, and company okay. So that is story."

Lincoln excused himself. Isabelle smiled. “That is the longest, well, in the last five years, I’ve seen Lincoln sit in one place without getting up.”

When Lincoln retook his seat, he shook his head. “Mr. Nhu, you add up all these stories, and you’ll have a book.”

“Nhu not speak English to write letter to friend.”

“Nah, you do it with a ghostwriter. What the heck, your daughters can be the ghosts!”

There was a gasp from the corner, and the girls’ eyes widened. Xuan tugged on her mom’s blouse. Mrs. Nhu turned and patted her on the shoulder, “Not that kind of ghost, Sweetheart.”

CHAPTER FIFTY-THREE

The next morning, Lincoln and Nhu drove to a café near the hotel for breakfast. Nhu asked why they just didn't eat at the hotel, but Lincoln shook his head. "Nah, they'll just give it to us for free. That's not right. You pay your way, Mr. Nhu, and so do I. We both learned that in the service. Better way to live."

Nhu asked, "So, Mr. Rincoln, it is the time you tell me about our friend Mr. Huber. I not want to hear in letter. I want to talk you face face. That respect I have for him.

"Well, this is going to be hard, my friend. He was the kind of man that tried so hard, and nothing *ever* worked out for him. Nothing. He did a lot of good in this world, but he never realized it. Makes me so sad."

"Me, too. You know, in China if save life of man, then you responsible, take care of that man forever. So, Nhu responsible for Mr. Huber, but fail."

"No, you didn't. He was just one of a million. No one cared. You know what they say: 'Viet Nam vet, crazy fucker; they all are. Angry, mean drunks.' At least that's what you hear at a party when the draft dodgers've had a drink or two. They all ask me how come I stayed sane. I never answer, but then I don't say anything for the rest of the evening. That's when they get scared. Keep their eyes on me like I'm no different from the rest of the vets, just a wild animal looking for a place to go postal. Especially, they watch my hands. If I twitch, they get all flustered, like I'm reaching for a gun or a Bowie knife."

Nhu laughed uncomfortably. "I hope you joking."

"Of course. Partly, at least. Still angry, though. Aren't you?"

"Maybe. But you know Vietnamee man; he know life very short and unhappy. But it from Heaven so cannot change. He must accept and wait for good fortune to come next day. He only hope for good fortune, but not can make happen, that for sure."

"But look what you did."

"Like Nhu say, his idea come from America friend. Other world out there, learn from U.S. Army. Viet Nam no one teach that, even in college. Still, you see how scare Nhu children. We try explain them not listen to relative. Not be so afraid of everything in life, but maybe Quynh and Nhu not even realize, when we teach right and wrong, there be some our own fear; it still come through."

"No, your kids are beautiful. Well behaved. They are what they should be." He stopped for a moment and thought. "Mr. Nhu, what do they want for the future?"

"Xuan say she want to be doctor, and Quynh say no problem if work hard, but then Xuan say she not real American, not good enough."

"What do you believe, Mr. Nhu?"

"Nhu honest with best friend." Lincoln looked up, surprised. "Yes, you only friend who know what we do in my country. Mr. Rincoln's heart and mind always know what right thing to do, still if no one tell him.

"Remember first night eat at Wolter. Mr. Rincoln come to table and cut up food to give Vietnamee soldier, like he care we eat. For Vietnamee, not so much food in our country, even for okay money family. So food very, very much important. You come to help us. Other soldier hate us. We talk at night, hope you not wash out flight school. Every Vietnamee pilot like Mr. Rincoln. We try to like other GI, but they hate us."

"I don't think they hated you, Mr. Nhu. You were different, and people don't do well with things that aren't familiar. Human nature. And think, most of the WOCs were kids, children, just off the farm. They listened to guys with just a little more experience than them. Again, just human nature. And there was a lot of anger from the returnees. They should never have been sent to Viet Nam in the first place, and when they got back, some of them got caught up in the anti-war movement. Lotta drugs, *lotta* drugs, and they reacted just like you figure kids would—like little jerks. They were all mighty pissed off, for good reason, and some of them were too stupid to understand you guys were in the same boat they were.

"Don't forget, a lot of the soldiers at Wolters and Rucker—not the pilots or WOCs—but the support troops, they hadn't even graduated from high school. They were just drafted off the streets. Some were sent by judges who said, 'The Army or jail; take your pick.' Those were the ones who wound up in combat units. Lot of their buddies died. And now they were back, and the Army made them wait six or eight months to get discharged. It was just to have a pool of cheap labor to sit around and play nursemaid to a bunch of flight cadets. All they did was complain, tell everybody just how pissed off they were. Army couldn't do a damn thing to 'em. See, they would say to an officer giving 'em shit, 'Whata you gonna do to me, sir? Send me to Viet Nam?' Then they laughed in guy's face. You fellas didn't see that. You couldn't see that their anger wasn't at you but at the Army, for taking even more time from their lives, and for what?

"Even in the mess hall, Mr. Nhu, there were days I was afraid to go in. Thought there was going to be a prison riot. Hey, there were mass mutinies at some posts. Bet you never heard that. Pentagon is the best at switching stories around until no one knows what the hell's the truth. I'm sorry you guys got caught up in our problems."

"No, Mr. Rincoln, some of WOC and soldier leave Vietnamee alone. Some terrible. But you help us, and we never forget. Still write letter to few alive and always say Mr. Rincoln reason we make it. Mr. Rincoln best friend of life."

Lincoln took his hand and squeezed it between both of his. "That's about the nicest thing anyone has ever said to me."

Nhu nodded and spoke softly. "But time to tell about Mr. Huber."

Lincoln laughed bitterly. "Well, you know that he almost got court martialed for living with Kim Lieu."

"Yes, Kim Lieu tell me."

"Of course. I forgot. Well, he and I wound up in the same place, the 249th Evacuation Hospital at Camp Drake, near Tokyo. He was worse than me, and I didn't get to see him for the first couple of weeks. Then I insisted, and they said okay, for a few minutes, but they ordered me not to talk about what happened that last night when we got wounded. I asked why, and they said it was classified.

"Classified my ass. I figured it out after I left Huber. That mess out there had to be one of the worst fuck ups of the war. Dead United States Senator. Dead top level colonel. Good man. Dead helicopters all over the countryside. Bunch of United States senators all part of the whole mess, maybe the reason it happened. And those toads ran back down to Saigon the instant they heard the first reports of a downed aircraft with one of their pals aboard. Assigned like a dozen Cobras to fly shotgun for 'em. You know what I mean by shotgun?"

"Fuckin' A!"

Lincoln leaned forward and hugged Nhu. "So blessed you came to see us. Anyway, they took *our* cover with them back to the rear. I mean, the Cobras that should have been out with us that night spent the evening in Saigon at the club in the U.S. Embassy.

"Brass lied through their teeth, saying the senator got killed when one of the door gunners got hit, and the senator took over his gun. Of course, he didn't have any bullet holes in him, according to the autopsy that his wife insisted a private doctor do back in Virginia.

"Turns out, the asshole was so scared, he undid his seatbelt and tried to jump free of the ship as it was hovering. He didn't give a shit that everyone else was sitting tight. That's when something hit the main rotor; the ship went in, rolled, and crushed the asshole. Deserved it, yellow bastard.

"Then, when Huber and I were put in for the Medal of Honor, the brass lost *my* paperwork, and they accused Huber of being out of uniform. They said he had a .45 in his holster instead of the issue .38 that pilots were supposed to carry. Huber always carried a .45. It was usually the opposite. The ground officers wanted the .38, because the .45 doesn't have any accuracy. So, there was a lot of bartering on the part of the grunt platoon leaders to get rid of their .45s. But Huber wanted a sidearm with some punch, so he traded his .38 for a .45 plus a bottle of bourbon. Or maybe it was two bottles.

"But don't worry, the government found a way to keep the whole thing quiet. That was until my Isabelle got involved. She and my mother-in-law went apeshit when I told them the whole story. It was years of letter writing and trips to D.C. before William Proxmire—he was a senator, good guy—took an interest. So, finally, I go to D.C. and get the award, but Huber's was still working its way through when it happened.

"Lemme back up. When Saigon fell, Huber was flying at Rucker. They made him a test pilot. When a helicopter was repaired, he was the one who flew it first to make sure it was airworthy. They started him out as an instructor, but that didn't go so well. He told me he'd get so pissed at the students, he'd give 'em a shove in the cockpit."

Nhu shook his head. "Maybe they put him in jail. Even in Viet Nam Army, you no touch lower man."

"I know, but now he had a DSC, DFC—Distinguished Flying Cross—a Soldier's Medal, two Purple Hearts, couple of Bronze Stars, and a dozen Air Medals. And he was up for the big one, Medal of Honor. So, if he screwed up, they had to find a way to hide it. No matter what he did, his mistakes, he was one brave son of a bitch

"Anyway, when Saigon fell to the commies, Huber was cut off from Kim Lieu. He spent all this money trying to send telexes to her through the Red Cross and the Embassy. Nothing. Never heard a word. He was a madman. Left the Army, took a job on a ship to Laos—assistant fuckin' cook. I'm sure that worked out real well, if any of them didn't die of food poisoning.

"Anyway, Pathet Lao was taking control of the country, but it was like a gentle revolution. In the morning, until noon, the old government was in control. At noon, there was a siesta, and then at about 2 P.M., the communist government took over. So, you start your nap with the royal government in charge, and when you get up a couple hours later, the post office has stopped selling stamps with the king's face and started peddling ones engraved with the hammer and sickle. Next morning, the whole mess starts all over again.

"So, Huber gets there with a wad of cash. He hires some goons to take him into Viet Nam, get him to Saigon. He goes down the Mekong River in like a canoe. Gets as far as the Cambodian Border. The Khmer Rouge capture his ass. He buys his way out and then turns around and asks *them* to help him to get to Saigon. But the Cambodians fuckin' despise the Vietnamese, I mean, really hate them. So they say if Huber gets to Saigon, it will make a Vietnamese woman happy, and they can't allow that. He backtracks to Vientiane and steals a Russian helicopter."

Nhu laughed. "This man I like."

"Yeah, well, no way he's going to get anywhere near Saigon. That's eight hundred miles. Gas mileage on a Russian pig isn't much higher than in one of their tanks. He drops into a big, open field on the Cambodian-Vietnamese border and walks into Viet Nam. Gets captured, *again.* They take pity on him and bring him to Hue. He sits there for like two weeks while the commies in Saigon make a decision. I mean, they would be happy to get rid of Kim Lieu and her kid. They're outcasts, mixed blood. But they also know she's gonna want to take a couple of dozen family members, and that's gonna to open a can of worms." Lincoln stopped and queried Nhu with his eyes.

Nhu nodded once again. "I know what means worms."

"So, they send him back to Vientiane. I guess there was air traffic between the two countries for a while after Viet Nam fell. They tell him before he goes that Viet Nam will be opening up in no time, and they will allow him back with open arms. Huber believes them.

"He comes home, but his head is so screwed, he can't hold a job. Starts with grass, then it's cocaine, and at the end, heroin. He was living on the streets in San Diego, then he got a job working at LAX servicing aircraft, but he fell off the wagon..." Lincoln looked at Nhu, who nodded. "Got fired and was homeless again in a couple of weeks.

"I went out there. Isabelle was so scared. We had a new baby with problems, and she made me promise not to bring him back. I knew she was right. Fuckin' A, she was right. Always is, but it hurt. I gave him a roll of hundred-dollar bills that woulda choked a horse. I guess he went through the wad in a week. He called me crying. Said he was a disgrace to our friendship, to the military of the country that had paid for his flight training, to this and that.

"I told him, I said, 'Hubert, as usual, you are full of shit, my man.' He laughed, so I told him, 'You don't owe anybody a damn thing. They owe you. Think of how many lives you pulled out of the fire. How many kids probably have your name, been named after you? My own daughter, Sabrina Huber Friday, for Christ's sake."

Huber was quiet for a while, and he said, 'You really think so, troop?'"

"I said, 'I fuckin' know so.' Then he gets real quiet, and like in five minutes, finally says, 'So what do I do?'

"I told 'im, 'Go down to the VA in San Diego. They're treating depression now, finally. All free. Can you hold on for two weeks? That's what it takes for the pills to start working. Give it a try, will ya?'

"I called ahead and told 'em who Huber was—and who I was—big deal, so they listened and promised to give him preferential treatment. Took three weeks to get an appointment. They told him he wasn't suffering from PTSD." Lincoln looked up at Nhu, who nodded again, and Lincoln went on. "They said it was a readjustment disorder or something like that. No, it was an adjustment disorder, different than real depression or PTSD, because Huber's was due to a specific situation, but real depression just happens because of genetics." Nhu bobbed his head. "They said he wasn't able to deal with a particular problem, I guess, like he couldn't get back to Kim Lieu and the baby. They told him there was evidence that the Vietnamese government was beginning to relax a little, and he'd be able to get there soon. They told him the best he could do was save his money so he could bring the family to the U.S. And they said when they were reunited, all his problems would disappear. They sent him to a chaplain. Good guy. Promised to get the paperwork done.

"Sounded a little strange to me, Mr. Nhu, but just a few days ago, I was listening to Public Radio, you know, NPR. I heard with my own ears the head of the VA say the same thing, that all these guys coming home from Iraq with mental problems, that it wasn't PTSD, but this adjustment thing. I mean, I could sort of see that in the guys coming back from the Middle East, because it was fresh in their minds, but then I looked into it, and they were still patting the First Gulf War guys on the shoulder and telling them to give time a chance. But they'd been crazy for damn near ten years, and the VA was turning 'em down for PTSD allowances because this general, the head of the VA, he said right on the air that it was getting too expensive to pay all the soldiers who had put in for benefits.

"Anyway, they told Huber to take pills, and he actually went to the VA pharmacy to get them, but they were twenty-four bucks, and he didn't have any money left over. I guess Huber got a little nasty, if you can believe it, and one of the pharmacy techs told him to use some of the money he was pissing away on drugs. Huber walked out and gave them a group finger. Security came and escorted him out of the building and told him he couldn't come back until he saw a psychiatrist who could say he wasn't going to be violent.

"He called and told me the whole story. I offered to give the VA my credit card number, but he didn't want to do that. He told me he was so pissed at the VA, he was feeling better. Gave him something to think about. And, you know, he sounded better than I'd heard him in a long time. I told him, if he wanted, I'd come back down. No way, he was much better, and I thought maybe that VA guy, the Secretary of Veteran Affairs, was right. I mean, a big shot general and all, he must a known what he was talking about, right?

"It was the last time I talked to him. From what I gathered, he'd gotten his hands some money and bought drugs for the house. 'This round's on me.' I can just hear him. Then he drifted away from the crack house and went down to the tracks and ate a train."

Nhu's head plummeted, and his eyes closed. The two men were quiet for a long time. Nhu finally turned to Lincoln. "I wonder people walk by on street, do they know what story have Huber? Maybe they not so happy with smile if they hear."

"You know, Mr. Nhu, they all have their own problems. We need to be happy that Huber did what he did. Like I said, a lotta families are around because he lived for as long as he did." Lincoln paused and went on slowly. "Do you ever have dreams about the war?"

Nhu nodded. "Mostly dream about Communit. They come to take away father, brother, me. That worse than war."

"I'm sorry to ask, but did you ever think about suicide?"

"Nhu Vietnamee. We different from America. Like Nhu say yesterday, if fate say this happen, then this happen. Also, have too many family take care. But truth, sometime like sea wave come over head and so sad. Why brother kill brother? For Communit government? It stink—but old government stink. Million dead for nothing get better.

"Oh, Mr. Rincoln, not worry one minute. Nhu never hurt self. I am so lucky man. Heaven good to me. Family is so good, and Mr. Rincoln, I never forget."

Lincoln sighed. "Well, it's back to the real world. Let's go see what the ladies are up to."

When the Nhus drove away the next morning, Isabelle and Lincoln stood with their arms around each other in the driveway, waving. Isabelle turned to Lincoln. "Did you see the girls? They were crying when Quynh said it was time to go. Wow. What a blessing you've been in their lives, Lincoln Friday, in so many lives. You are a good man." She nuzzled him, and they walked back into the house arm in arm. She made coffee, and they sat in the living room quietly for a half an hour.

Several months later, Lincoln and several other Medal of Honor recipients were invited to Washington, D.C. to sit with their states' congressional delegations during the president's State of the Union Address. Isabelle was shown to a seat in the balcony. When the speech was over, she joined Lincoln on the floor of the House.

A man in a suit marched up to them and muttered, "Both of you, come with me, please."

The president looked up as Isabelle and Lincoln approached and drew himself into an erect posture. They were introduced. He asked if Lincoln's limp was related to his service, and Lincoln allowed that it was. The president looked him in the eye. "Sir, have you been cared for with dignity and respect by the Veterans' Administration?"

"Mr. President, to be honest, sir, most of us with jobs try not to rely on the VA."

The president looked at him a bit harshly and asked, "Because?"

"Frankly, sir, a Viet Nam vet trying to get an appointment, well, sir, it takes forever. Or so my friends say. Iraq and Afghanistan take precedent, and they should."

The president peered at Lincoln's name tag. "Mr. Friday, I'm sorry and embarrassed to hear that. I will look into it." He gazed into the air, as if making a mental note of the conversation, then extended his hand. As they shook warmly, the president placed his other hand over Lincoln's. He turned to Isabelle. Something about her eyes stopped him, and he spoke quietly. "Thank you and your husband for your service. It's wonderful citizens like you who make this job worth it." He bowed ever so slightly, though his entourage of sentries had tired of the small talk, and he was bustled off before he could say goodbye.

When they got back to Wilkes Barre, Isabelle and Lincoln sat in their rose garden over a glass of wine. She hummed, "You know, Sweet Lincoln, it ain't too shabby when the President of the United States stops to chat and tells you that you made a difference."

He put his arm around her shoulder. "Don't much care for his politics, but you gotta admit he sounded genuine. Makes me think maybe he actually cares. But who knows?"

Lincoln stood and excused himself for a moment. When he sat back down, Isabelle spoke softly. "Sweetheart, do you think we ought to get you into the doctor. It's getting really bad. What is it, three times a night, now?"

"Nah, it's no problem. Every guy I know..."

"Every guy you know isn't my beautiful husband."

CHAPTER FIFTY-FOUR

Isabelle had medical insurance through her work, and over the years, though Lincoln was not included on her policy, the helicopter company had been doing sufficiently well that he had seen and paid a local doctor out of pocket, the rare times he had a problem. He had contacted the government about being treated at the VA and had been promised that with his Purple Heart, he was entitled to priority care. He could sign up any time and be seen immediately, the representative assured, so there had never been any urgency.

Slowly, as that year slipped by, Lincoln began limping to the bathroom five and six times a night. While that had happened a few times over the years when he drank too much coffee late in the day, it had now become standard fare. But he told Isabelle all that meant was that now he was at the level his friends complained of when they were in their late fifties. He still felt well, and he was so busy with the company, he did not have time to take off two, and maybe three, days to drive to Philadelphia and see a doctor. While the VA hospitals in New York were closer, the reputation in Philly was not as dreadful.

And there was still the deal to buy the three disassembled HUEYs sitting in crates in Pakistan. With the downturn in the economy, despite the Fridays' pristine credit rating, his bank had balked at a loan, as there was no way to evaluate the quality of the merchandise. He would have to locate a licensed aircraft and power plant mechanic in South Asia to inspect the parts. He set out to find ex-pats working in Pakistan—first, just a civilian he might hire to locate an American or British A&P mechanic. The next step would be to gather the technician's credentials, submit them to the bank, and if satisfactory, hire him to open the crates and inventory, grade, and photograph the components. Then the bank would hire a local A&P to review the results, and a loan for eighty percent of the price would be approved. The cost to Lincoln for the inspection process would be in the range of ten thousand dollars, which the bank refused to include in the loan.

Lincoln thought he might fly to Islamabad and do the inspection himself, but he discovered getting a visa for a commercial enterprise there would take many months and thousands of dollars for physical examinations. Graft for the host of business licenses would top the price of the merchandise. He called Bell Helicopter in Texas, and they put him in contact with their representative in Islamabad, an American warrant officer who had flown helicopters in Iraq. He took all the information from Lincoln, as well as Lincoln's background, and promised to get back to him.

Two days later, the man called from Pakistan. "Hey, sir, are you the Lincoln Friday who won the Medal of Honor in Nam?"

"I am. How the heck did you find that out?"

"Are you sitting down, sir? You remember a pilot from flight school by the name of Lockett?"

"Oh, my God."

"Yes, sir. He's my supervisor back in Fort Worth. He's going to be giving you a call, if you don't mind, just to say hello. Spoke pretty highly of ya. Told me to get my butt down to Dacca on the next flight and get the job done, no charge. Says the country owes ya."

The photographs showed enough parts for two serviceable aircraft, two D-Models, not the extra powerful H-Models that had been advertised, but more than enough to make good business sense. After he and Lockett spent several hours catching up, Lockett contacted Lincoln's bank and made arrangements for a report under the auspices of Bell Helicopter. There was no charge. The loan was approved, and the man in Pakistan supervised the transport of the crated helicopters parts to the docks in Karachi.

Lincoln received an e-mail that the ship had sailed but had several ports of call before reaching the East Coast. The estimate for delivery was a month-and-a-half.

For several weeks, Lincoln was at his hanger making preparations for the arrival of the freight. He contacted old friends in the Philadelphia area, retired A&Ps, and offered them union wages to help reconstruct the aircraft. One, working as a greeter at Wal-Mart, offered to pay Lincoln to be part of the project. He laughed, "They stuck me at the door. Told 'em I'm an angry old man. Hate people. Said they ought to put me in the back unloading vegetables—somethin'. Told 'em I'm in good shape, promised I wouldn't take no sick days. Working behind the scenes, I figure I wouldn't be pissin' off the customers. Think these geniuses listen to reason? Right to the front door with me. Do I sound like a happy man to you, Linc?"

A week before the container ship was to arrive, Lincoln had taken to sleeping at the hangar several days a week. He came home on Friday and was up every hour during the night hobbling to the bathroom. Nearing dawn, relieving himself began to burn. By seven, he was running every ten minutes, though he was able to squeeze out only a few drops, each one so agonizing, he had to force back tears. By ten o'clock, he began to sweat, then his back began to throb on the left, just above his hip.

Isabelle had been vacuuming but stopped and declared, "That's it. We're going to the doctor."

"Nah, just worn out from all the work. Almost done. I'll take the weekend off, be like brand new by Monday." But as he jumped up to rush to the bathroom, he became dizzy and dropped to his knees. Isabelle gasped and raised her voice, a response so unusual, Lincoln followed her to the car.

At a walk-in clinic, they were seen by a nurse practitioner, who ordered a specimen then examined him by very lightly taking her fist and thumping his lower back out to the sides. The left flank was so sensitive, even the light percussion nearly lifted him off the table. Lincoln argued that he had probably pulled his back with all the lifting he'd been doing at the hangar, but the woman shook her head. "Well, Mr. Friday, your urinalysis shows a bladder infection. That's not a big deal, but I'm worried the bacteria have begun to creep up out of the top of the bladder, goin' north toward the kidneys."

She explained it was not terribly unusual for an older man to get a bladder infection, usually, because the prostate grows so large, it begins pinching on the urethra, the tube that carries urine from the bladder to the outside. "See, when that happens, the urinary stream's not strong enough, anymore, to wash out the occasional bacteria that crawl in through the tip of the penis. And they start dividing and multiplying and swimming up the urethra to that nice, warm home in the bladder."

The nurse practitioner showed them the urinalysis report. There were masses of bacteria and white blood cells. She discussed with them the danger of not treating the infection aggressively, for Lincoln was already showing signs that the bacteria had indeed crept up past the bladder and were beginning to take root in the kidneys themselves—pyelonephritis, a potentially deadly infection. That was the source of the back pain, the sweats, and the unsteadiness. She warned that it was not unheard of for the kidneys to suffer permanent, life-threatening damage if the infection was allowed to grow for too long, "For instance, Mr. Friday, until tomorrow."

She recommended Lincoln be admitted to the hospital and treated with intravenous antibiotics. She explained that taking the drug by mouth, at this late stage, was unlikely to drive the concentration of the medicine high enough in the blood to kill the bacteria already consuming the kidney.

Lincoln asked, "What if I take a double dose by mouth? Will that raise the concentration?"

"Yes, it will. Problem is, you take that much, you'll be vomiting your guts out before the medication has been absorbed. Nearly all of it'll wind up in the toilet bowl. In the end, you get an even lower concentration in the blood. That make sense?"

Lincoln smiled and spoke politely. "Yes, it does." He then went on to explain that he had no private insurance. The nurse suggested he be seen at the VA in Philadelphia, that day, for admission. She left the room to consult with her supervisor who accompanied her back to the room. After fifteen minutes of discussion, the doctor agreed, with a grunt, to start Lincoln with an antibiotic injection and directed him to take antibiotic pills over that day. He stipulated that if Lincoln wasn't able to get an immediate appointment at the VA, he would, no matter what, without fail, return to the clinic before it closed that evening.

When the doctor left the room, the nurse also prescribed a pill that would numb the urethra, to blunt the burning pain, but warned it would turn his pee bright orange. "I'm telling you this so that you won't flip out at three in the morning and call me!"

Isabelle laughed, "Don't worry. I'm a past master at UTIs. I just didn't think men got them."

"They usually don't unless, like I said, something is blocking the flow of urine. Let's get you feeling better first, and when things calm down, we'll have a urologist take a look."

Isabelle called the VA and asked for an immediate appointment. They looked up his name, but there was no record of Lincoln having sought, or having been approved for, medical care. Isabelle asked if they could do it over the phone, but the woman explained it was a process, one that could take weeks, especially if there was anything unusual about the veteran.

Isabelle asked, "Does having won the Medal of Honor make any difference? We were told he would get priority care."

"That's what I meant by unusual. Sometimes special cases take a lot longer. You know, he's free to come to the emergency room and sit until all the registered vets have been seen."

Lincoln, though, was feeling dramatically better by late afternoon and sat down for a meal. Isabelle called the clinic and gave them an update. The nurse called back after she had spoken with the doctor, and they agreed, given the circumstances, to wait overnight, as long as the Fridays promised to return in the morning. By sunrise, Lincoln was feeling so much better, he told Isabelle he was going to duck into the hangar to do one little job, and that he'd meet her at the clinic at nine.

When the debris and smoke cleared, he ate breakfast, and they were at the clinic as the doors swung open at eight. The doctor examined him. Lincoln's back was much less tender, and his fever was gone. He pronounced Lincoln improved, but far from cured, and allowed him to continue with the oral medication. He made him promise, though, to return again the next morning, when they would discuss increasing the time between visits to two days. He also, essentially, ordered Lincoln to see a local urologist by the end of the week.

Isabelle called the VA. The same set of conditions for an appointment were proffered. The clerk told Isabelle to apply on line and wait until the application was reviewed. She estimated it would be three weeks before treatment was authorized. Isabelle tried to schedule an appointment to save time once the paperwork was accepted, but the woman became huffy and warned, "Clearly, Madame, you are unfamiliar with the VA system. When, and if, your husband is approved, *then* you will be able to access the system. Please don't ask me to violate regulations."

By the end of the week, Lincoln was back to normal, but kept his word, and presented himself to the clinic. He appealed to the doctor for permission to wait a few weeks before seeing a specialist. Lincoln's urine was crystal clear, and under the microscope there were no red or white blood cells. He was also getting up only once or twice a night, far better than the past couple of years. The doctor opined Lincoln had been suffering from a low grade urinary tract infection for a long time, and now that it was under control, the situation was less dire. He made Lincoln agree to see a local urologist within ten days if he couldn't get into the VA. Isabelle and Lincoln talked it over and decided to chance that his application would be approved before then. They felt, with his priority status, he would be seen quickly, and so, with handshakes and pats on the back, the Fridays left the clinic relieved.

CHAPTER FIFTY-FIVE

Three days later, Lincoln received a call from a dockside warehouse. The ship had arrived ahead of time, and he was being charged by the half-day for storage. He drove to the Port of Philadelphia and walked his fifty-some crates through customs, a process that took two days and the transfer of thousands of dollars from his bank to the federal coffers. The trucks he had hired to haul the goods to Wilkes Barre did not appear. The drivers had gone on strike the day before, and Lincoln was stuck with more storage fees, so he drove back to Wilkes Barre, rented trucks, hired a dozen men from the VFW, and led the parade back to the docks in Philly. The striking drivers threw rocks, so Lincoln's men aimed their vehicles at them and gunned the engines. After a picket fence of jabbed middle fingers raised by both sides, the trucks rolled north to Wilkes Barre.

It took another two days to offload the freight and stack the crates in the hangar, most of the time frittered away on negotiations with the acting airport security director, who refused to let the trucks onto the sleepy facility. The rent-a-cop wagged his finger in Lincoln's face, admonishing he had not been pre-advised of the potential threat to national security posed by cargo from an enemy nation. Lincoln presented the letter he'd presented to county officials and pointed to the stamped and signed authorization on the bottom, but the man refused to open the gate because *he* had not been alerted. The airport director and the guard's boss were out of town at a security meeting in Washington, so Lincoln cajoled the county commissioner to drive over. The security guard did not know who or what a county commissioner was, so he pocketed the keys and locked himself in his office. Three sheriff's deputies threatened to knock the door down and arrest the man if he didn't open the gate.

When the parts were stacked in three-quarters of the hangar, Isabelle met Lincoln at the airport restaurant. They clinked glasses and laughed that they had done the impossible, and for only triple the original price.

At 8t A.M. the following Monday, his two A&P friends arrived, and the larger crates were pried open. They hoisted the engines free, and Lincoln was delighted that two came with paperwork from a Honeywell technician establishing that they both had over twelve hundred hours remaining before TBO, time before mandatory overhaul. The third was due in three hundred hours, and they put that engine aside as a backup. It was already toward the end of the week before the engines had been inspected and the list of needed parts finalized—a dozen inexpensive seals and a few bolts.

It was to be one of the happiest weekends of his life. Each engine, had it had only half its life left, would be worth three times the entire investment he'd made, if not four. And there were three of them. When the ships were reassembled, his company, Friday Lift, would move up to the next level in value.

CHAPTER FIFTY-SIX

That Saturday, they received a letter from the VA stating that Lincoln had been approved for care. He was not to be given priority until he submitted proof from the Department of the Army that he had earned a Purple Heart. There was a rumor that a congressman from the Midwest was working on a bill to include Medal of Honor winners in a special priority group, but it was far from reaching the Floor.

In the meantime, Lincoln was free to avail himself of the VA's medical services, but warned he would be afforded only standard precedence. Isabelle called Monday morning. The VA Hospital of Philadelphia had not yet caught up with the care-approval arm of the agency. They had no record of a Lincoln Friday. The clerk advised Isabelle to call back in a week. She did—and was told the first appointment with a urologist was four months off. The explanation was that the veterans of Lincoln's age, millions of men from the Viet Nam era, had aged to the point that nearly every one of them suffered from an enlarged prostate gland. It was the biggest problem in their lives—and also in the lives of those who worked at the VA. Isabelle took a deep breath to calm herself and made the appointment.

Lincoln was out at the hangar at six in the morning, making coffee and putting out Spudnuts. The men arrived at eight. They sat together talking for a few minutes, then drifted, donuts and coffee in hand, to one of the engines that was resting on a mount. They touched it as lovingly and warmly as if it was a brand new grandchild. One of the men followed the maze of thin aluminum tubes with his fingers, his mind refreshing itself as to where each molecule of fuel and oil was destined.

The phone rang. Lincoln walked back to his cluttered desk. It was Isabelle. "Sweetheart, I just got a call from the home. They think your mother may have had a stroke. They were trying to get her out of a chair, and she tumbled. They think her hip is broken, so they sent her to the hospital."

Isabelle and Lincoln waited in the hallway as an orthopedic surgeon examined Miriam. When he came out of the room, they stood to talk to him, but the man excused himself and walked down the hall to meet with the neurologist. The two physicians stood cogitating, chins resting in palms, until the orthopedist heeled around and dashed to the elevator. The neurologist walked past them into Miriam's room. Isabelle shook her head in disbelief and strode in behind him. Lincoln trailed.

They watched as the neurologist tapped on Miriam's elbows and knees, examined her eyes, and then turned abruptly. "And you folks are…?"

Lincoln looked down at the little man. "I'm Lincoln Friday. This is my mom." He pushed past the doctor and took Miriam's skeletal hand. Her eyes shifted toward his face, but they stared straight through him. He whispered to her. She did not respond.

The neurologist waited for a moment then spoke directly. "I don't think she can hear you. She's had a pretty serious stroke.

Why don't we go to one of the family rooms, and I can explain your options."

The man began before they had dropped all the way into the Naugahyde armchairs. "Like I said, she's suffered global ischemia. That means a large portion of the brain is no longer functional. It was probably due, in some way, to her cirrhosis, you know, destruction of the liver. All sorts of coagulation problems when the liver is completely gone. She lived a lot longer than one would expect, given her liver disease. Good genes, I guess."

Lincoln was blank-expressioned. Isabelle leaned forward. "You make it sound as if she's already gone."

"Well, I'm sorry to say, that is essentially the case. Her liver *is* gone, and now most of the brain is as well. She has a fractured hip, but there is no reason to operate. She would never make it through the surgery, and even if she did, she would never be able to stand again, even if she wakes up, which, I'm afraid, is impossible."

Lincoln asked in a broken voice, "How long, Doc?"

"Can't say. Never can, but usually, these folks get pneumonia and pass quietly after a few days."

Lincoln probed, "Can't you treat pneumonia?" "Is it Mr. Friday?"

Lincoln nodded.

"Well, sir, we will do whatever you want, but please be advised, your mother is, to a degree, suffering. She may have *some* level of consciousness. We simply do not know what she perceives in her environment. In fact, she may be tortured inside, trying to tell you why things turned out the way they did, wanting to apologize for the pain she caused. That's often the case with alcoholics."

Lincoln's chest clamped. He wanted to spring toward this stranger who had taken the liberty of reckoning what had gone before in his family's chronicle. But he thought quickly and understood the man was right, which, for a moment, infuriated him even more. Isabelle saw his face harden, and she reached over to touch his arm. "Then what do you think we should do, Doctor?"

"I wish I could give you a definite answer, but please think about the fact that your mother will *never* regain a level of consciousness to recognize you or Mrs. Friday." He looked at her, and Isabelle nodded. "I know you hear about people waking up from comas, but, please believe me, this is different—very different."

Sabrina and Mike wanted to come east, but neither Isabelle nor Lincoln would hear of it. Even Nhu called and asked if he could help.

By the next morning, Miriam's eyes were glued to the ceiling. He skin was sallow and her eyes orange. When Lincoln ran his hand over Miriam's arm, he sensed a roughness that made him bend forward and check her skin. It was covered in fine, white crystals that had the fetid odor of urine. An internist on rounds stopped to sit with Lincoln for a few moments. He explained the powder was referred to as uremic frost, for the kidneys had shut down, and the uric acid the body normally sent into the kidneys for disposal no longer had a way to escape, other than through the skin.

Lincoln asked, "That means it's close to the end, isn't it?" The man took Lincoln's arm in his hand and nodded.

Miriam passed the next morning. Lincoln had the original document that was presented with his Medal of Honor rolled, tied with a golden ribbon, and placed into her hand.

It did not take very long to settle Miriam's affairs. When they cleaned out her apartment, they found liquor bottles, mostly empty, hidden in crevices in the couch, under it, under the cushion of her easy chair, under the immovable mahogany dresser, and in the freezer. The only thing Lincoln kept of her things was the pin.

The woman at the funeral home discussed final arrangements, and she suggested cremation. “Seems everyone’s going that way.”

Lincoln bolted upright in his chair and hissed, “I won’t have it. My mother’s not some concentration camp victim.” He was so strident, Isabelle flinched, and her eyes widened in puzzlement.

On the way home, Isabelle waited for a couple of miles, until they stopped for a light. She mentioned casually, “Sweetheart, by the way, I agree with you completely about the burial.”

When the light became green, he shot forward, but halfway down the next block jammed the brakes and turned to Isabelle. “You ever seen a man die in a fire? I won’t have it for my family.”

CHAPTER FIFTY-SEVEN

When the funeral was over, Lincoln went back fulltime to the business. With the slew of backed up requests for lifts, he became so busy, he had to put the restoration of the helicopters on the back burner. When he finally had a weekend to open more of the crates, his two friends were not immediately available, and he undertook the business of inventorying the parts on his own. He had to climb up and over the heaps, cutting himself on the cheap metal banding. His arms and legs were covered with splinters from the roughhewn wood.

He awoke early Sunday morning with pain in his left lower back. He was sure, once again, it was a function of the physically most demanding week he'd put in over the past twenty years. Isabelle did not agree, though it turned out he was right—his UA was pristine. He expected the nurse practitioner at the walk-in clinic to congratulate him, but she returned to the room with the doctor in tow. He chuckled humorlessly, "Well, I see my star patient still enjoys his Superman complex. My friend, you need to get yourself in to see a urologist, and before the end of the week."

Lincoln answered seriously. "Doctor, please understand that the life of my business has been hanging in the balance for the past few months."

"Yeah, well, the life of your *body* is hanging in the balance this very moment, whether you know or accept it or not. Mr. Friday, I'm not trying to scare you, or maybe I am, but you're flirting with danger. We need to find out what's going on. Yes, it's probably just a big prostate due to age, but what if an oil pressure warning light came on in your cockpit? Probably just a malfunction of the sensor, right?"

"Usually, that's the case."

"Good, usually. You continue flying, or do you land," he chuckled, "as soon as practicable?'"

Lincoln asked, "Doctor, are you a pilot?"

"I am. Navy. A-10s. Warthog. The Double Ugly."

Lincoln shook his head. "Why didn't you tell me?"

"Would it have made a difference?"

"In fact, it would have."

"Well, that's something you're going to have to get over. There are some good people out there who aren't pilots. Even a few who haven't been in the military. I will admit, though, it took me years to figure it out."

"I'm sorry, Doctor, but that's hard for me to accept. The military sucked, but have you seen what our society is made up of these days?"

"I see it every day, and I've learned to live with it. And you need to bury your skepticism for a while, at least until we get you back on the right medical track. You're going to be faced with doctors and nurses who wouldn't last twelve hours in a truly stressful situation. And you're going to need to say, 'Yes, ma'am, no, ma'am, three bags full, ma'am.' Sorry, but it's just the way it is."

Isabelle explained that, in fact, Lincoln had already scheduled an appointment at the VA, and it was only a couple of weeks away.

The doctor nodded. "Only a couple of weeks isn't good enough. You need to call them back and tell them that's ridiculous. A man with your husband's history should be seen in a couple of days."

"Doctor, I hate to tell you this, but we made the appointment nearly four months ago."

"What's the problem? They claim to get vets in within two weeks."

Isabelle rolled her eyes. "I wish we knew. We started the process the day we saw you last. Took three weeks for Lincoln to get his benefits approved. Then they scheduled him for four months out to see a urologist."

The doctor looked at her skeptically. He pulled a pamphlet from the drawer under the sink. "Here it is. Like I said, VA claims they get people in for a first visit within fourteen days. Right here in red, white, and blue."

"Not in our case, Doctor. I told them he had the Medal of Honor, but that just seemed to delay things."

The doctor's jaw dropped. "Medal of Honor? It that true, Mr. Friday?"

"So they tell me."

The doctor slumped forward. "I didn't know. I don't know what to say. Well, VA still has its head up its butt. Excuse me, Mrs. Friday. I'll call in the morning. I'll drive over there if I have to. This is an outrage."

The VA called Lincoln's home two days later. There was an opening at the end of the week. They drove to Philadelphia and stayed in a hotel the night before the appointment, took a cab to South Philly for a cheese steak and a pitcher of beer, then went back to their room to polish off a bottle of good wine.

In the morning, they drove up to the front of the hospital and looked for parking, but were stopped by a man from somewhere in Africa who smiled and explained that he would park their car, and for no charge.

Lincoln turned to Isabelle and laughed. "Yeah, right. Lemme just give this dude my keys, and we'll stroll back in an hour, and I'm sure we'll find this fine gentleman waiting for us, washing the windows."

Isabelle pointed to a sign directly in front of them. "Welcome to the Philadelphia Veterans Administration Hospital. We provide free valet parking for out honored servicemen and women." Lincoln handed the keys through the window with a wheezed, "Thank you." Another man popped from a tiny shack to open Isabelle's door and extend a hand to help her out.

Isabelle and Lincoln walked through the front doors holding hands. He whispered to her, "Another sure sign the world is coming to an end. Lincoln Friday turns his car over to a valet parking service."

They were greeted by an older man wearing a Korean War cap. He guided them through the process, carrying Lincoln's chart, stepping in front of them to push elevator buttons, then placing himself just inside the doors to keep them from closing on his wards. As he dropped them off at the Urology Department, they thanked the man warmly. He faced them fully and came to attention. "It is my honor, sir, to assist an American hero. Ma'am, you must be so proud of your husband." They turned to each other and smiled in disbelief.

The waiting area was standing room only. An old man wearing a World War Two, U.S. Navy baseball cap looked up at Isabelle and worked his arms to come to his feet. "For you, ma'am."

She took a breath to demur, but Lincoln nodded subtly for her to take the seat. She patted the man on the forearm and smiled, "What a gentleman! Thank you, sir." His ancient eyes sparkled as he half-bowed to Isabelle.

Eventually, they were shown to an exam room. Ten minutes later, a doctor vaulted into the room, dropped onto his stool, picked up Lincoln's chart, and perused it fleetingly. He spoke without looking up. "Glad you rushed right down to see us. What's it been, looks like five years?"

Lincoln paused to formulate an answer, but Isabelle interjected, her voice irritated, "Well, Doctor, we tried to get an appointment, what, four, five months ago. There were so many hoops to jump through, what with my husband's *special* circumstances."

"Well, madam, you sound angry at *me*. Let me assure you that is not the fault of this office. Those decisions are made at a level far above my pay grade. You need to contact the scheduling supervisor if you have a concern. As far as I'm aware, though, our policy is that no veteran will wait more than fourteen days for an appointment."

"I'm sorry, Dr. Render," she grimaced, "It was more like fourteen weeks."

"Well, I'm sure it wasn't that long. But we mustn't get off on the wrong foot." He cleared his throat loudly. "Now, looking at your chart, Lincoln, it seems you're nocturia is getting worse." Lincoln looked at him curiously. "Having to pee at night. So, where are we right now?"

"Back up two or three times, a little better than for the last couple of years, except when I had that infection half-a-year ago. Then it was every hour."

"I guess we should have seen you then." He sighed disappointingly. "But here we are. So this is what we need to do. First, let me warn you, this whole thing is a process. We go step by step. And each step takes time. Please don't forget that as we start down the road. I'm afraid it's a long one.

"Okay, first, we need to recheck your PSA. Do you remember your last PSA value?"

"Well, Doc, to be honest, I've never had one. You know, every guy my age has trouble going. All of us get up four times a night. Couple of my friends had that PSA test you're talking about. Doctor couldn't tell if it meant cancer or not. So, then they had more tests, and most of them wound up getting a prostate biopsy. One of 'em got an infection. Was in the hospital for three weeks. Nearly died. Cost him tens of thousands of dollars he didn't have, and then it turns out it wasn't cancer after all. Cure's worse than the disease."

"Well, the PSA's not perfect, but it is what we do to narrow down the differential diagnosis. And we won't do anything to you unless you agree."

Isabelle interrupted. "Doctor, if you say we need to do the next step, how in the world are we going to argue with you?"

"I hope you won't. I've been doing this for a while." Both Isabelle and Lincoln looked up at the man, who couldn't have been thirty-two, from what they could see of a face that had barely glanced up from Lincoln's chart. "In your case, things seem a little different than the usual. You've had a kidney infection along the way. It's my job to find out if something bad's going on." Lincoln's chest clutched. "And you were exposed to Agent Orange, it says here."

"I was, but I have to warn you that there are no official records to prove it."

"Well, that may be a problem later on, but you're entitled to care at this VA hospital based on your service, Agent Orange or not."

"Well, I can assure you I was exposed. Got a letter from an old crew chief who made a statement that we sprayed the stuff all over God's creation."

"Good. Again, that's going to be important later when it comes time to determine if you qualify for disability, based on *if* it's cancer and what kind of cancer. Oh, and let me ask if you've had a vasectomy."

"I did. Our daughter was born with a neural tube defect from Agent Orange. We weren't going to chance it again. Why do you ask?"

"Well, there are studies that suggest men with vasectomies have a higher chance of getting prostate cancer, but not the slow growing kind. It's all very complex."

Lincoln's chest grabbed again, and Isabelle's face drained of color. She pulled herself straighter in the chair and asked, "Doctor, it sounds like you think this *is* cancer."

"Isabelle, is it? I can't tell you if it is or it is not. We haven't done a single diagnostic test yet. Like I said, step by step. So, first, we need to do a rectal exam." He turned to Lincoln. "You remember that from the Army, don't you?"

"One of my favorite memories."

"But, we also need a PSA, which means we have to do a blood draw. The catch is, if I do the rectal exam today, it will massage the prostate, where the PSA is made, and that will squeeze extra PSA into the blood circulation and make the PSA look higher than it really is. So, let's get you down to the lab for a blood draw. When you come back to discuss the result, we'll do the rectal, put all the information together, and decide on the next step."

Isabelle queried, "So, after we get the blood drawn, we come back upstairs and do the rectal. Then you'll tell us what's going on?"

He hid a supercilious smile. "I thought you were a nurse. Says here that's what you do."

"Nursing assistant."

"Oh. Well, we can't do the rectal today. I'm sure you read on the internet, patients do that these days, that there's controversy over whether you can do the rectal first, but I come from the old school. I was taught to do it this way, and until I'm shown my professors were wrong, that's the way we are going to proceed. You come back, which you have to anyway to get the PSA result, and we'll do it next time. Won't change anything."

She added, "How long will that be, Doctor?"

"Well, again, that's up to scheduling. We've been really busy since the scare about prostate cancer and Agent Orange hit the papers, and then there's all the patients coming back from Afghanistan with trauma to their genitals. It may take a while, but with the prostate, weeks are not critical."

Lincoln asked, "Dr. Render, if you don't mind, what's your opinion about exposure to Agent Orange?"

"That's a good question. Right now, while I believe there appears to be an association with the neural tube defect you mentioned and exposure to Agent Orange, the connection with prostate cancer is not clear at all. And I learned a long time ago, in medicine, you don't draw conclusions based on guesses and who yells the loudest in anti-government rallies.

"And in looking into your medical history, you have a strong family history of prostate cancer—your father, who had it at a young age."

Lincoln stiffened. "But his cancer was caused by exposure to radiation in Japan. He was one of the soldiers they made go to Hiroshima to count bodies or something. It was right after the bomb."

Isabelle's face reddened. She muttered, "And the VA denied his father benefits back then, too. Said there was no scientific proof. So, here we go again."

"I did not say that the book is closed on the subject. All I am trying to get across is that we're not politicians here. We're scientists. When all the facts are in, I'll form an opinion. And it doesn't matter for you, anyway. As I mentioned, you get care for anything that befalls you, whether it is service connected or not. You may have a co-pay for non-service related diseases, but there's no free lunch, and it isn't all that much."

He scribbled on Lincoln's visit sheet and handed it to him. Lincoln turned and passed it to Isabelle. The doctor snorted, "I see, you're the captain, but she's apparently a major in the same unit." He laughed dully, stood, and left the room.

The first available appointment was six weeks hence. They asked to be put on a list in case of a cancellation, but the clerk laughed. "We don't do waiting lists. We never know who's going to show up. I don't think most of these guys know if they're coming or going."

A month-and-a-half later, they did receive a call from the VA the day before their appointment, but it was to postpone the visit for a week, as the doctor was ill.

When they sat down with Dr. Render, Isabelle asked if he felt better. He mumbled, "Just a touch of the flu."

Isabelle asked nervously, "We always get our flu shots. Is this year's not that effective?"

"No, that's not it. I simply have not seen conclusive proof that a flu vaccine is worth the risk of challenging the immune system with foreign protein from a known pathogen. But, as patients, you were right to follow the AMA guidelines and get your shots. Now, let's do this. Isabelle, why don't you excuse yourself, and I'll perform the rectal examination. As soon as we're done, you'll come back in, and we'll discuss the results."

She nodded and left the room. The door opened thirty seconds later as Lincoln was buckling his belt.

"Okay, this is what we've found. Prostate starts off the size of a walnut in your twenties. Grows some over the years. Yours is the size of a small lemon, at least. That's concerning, but on the other hand, it's possible that in your case, size doesn't matter."

He grunted a laugh. "It can just be a big prostate. That's called BPH—benign prostatic hypertrophy—not cancer.

"Right now, your PSA is 13.2. Normal is under 4. That can be a few things: BPH, just a big prostate, like I said; it can mean an infection; or cancer; or any combination of the three. Now, 13 is higher than I'd like to see. Anything over 4 is a red flag for cancer. Cancer makes a lot of PSA, even in a very small prostate. Your prostate is big, and a big prostate makes more PSA than a small one. Your prostate's also a little boggy. That's a sign of infection. And it seemed to give you some discomfort when I massaged it. Infections hurt."

Lincoln laughed, "Hurt like hell."

"Okay, so the extra PSA may only be due to size, or maybe you have an infection in the prostate, which is irritating the gland and causing it to make more PSA. If you're younger than thirty-five, an infection is usually an STD, you know, venereal disease. At your age, it's usually just some local bacteria that swam up the penis into the gland."

Lincoln laughed again. "You caught me, Doc." Isabelle rolled her eyes.

The man did not smile. "Well, then, I have to ask. I'm sorry, do want your wife to leave the room?"

"No, doctor. I haven't made any stupid mistakes."

"Okay, but we should know so we can treat it properly."

Lincoln's face tightened. "Time to move on, Doctor."

The man's face remained fixed. "Then you need to take antibiotics for six weeks to see if an infection's growing in the prostate. You come back a week after you've finished the whole prescription, and we'll get another PSA. Then, you can make an appointment to see me, and we'll go over the results. Now, I doubt very much that the antibiotics will make any difference, but that's what we're going to do." He considered the looks of concern on both of their faces. "This antibiotic is safe—not a lot of scary side effects."

Isabelle interrupted. "What *are* the side effects?"

"Well, we'll probably use ciprofloxacin, unless your husband is allergic to it." Lincoln shook his head. "There are some side effects to think about, but they're rare. For instance, if you get dizzy, have changes in vision, abdominal problems, diarrhea, you must let me know me know right away."

Isabelle stopped him. "Doctor, my husband is a pilot. If he gets dizzy from a medication, that's a real problem."

"Well, if that's the case, you need to contact the FAA and find out if he's allowed to fly while taking this particular medicine. They make those decisions. But it's not that long."

Lincoln frowned. "Month-and-a-half's a lot of time off when you own a business."

"Can't you find something to keep you busy for the six weeks?"

Isabelle pursed her lips. "Doctor, we'll do what we have to do to get my husband better. But you said you didn't think the antibiotic was going work, so why are we wasting our time and yours?"

"I also said," he looked down at the chart, "Isabelle, that this whole exercise is a process. This is what my colleagues do. I can't take a step off the path. First time I do, you will bring a lawsuit."

Isabelle queried, "Is that what you're worried about, Doctor?"

"No, Isabelle, I'm worried about making a mistake and harming your husband. So, I don't skip steps. Now, let's get you back here in seven weeks for a blood draw, and then, after that, when there's an opening."

Lincoln asked, "Is there a place to have the blood drawn in Wilkes Barre? It takes us three hours in each direction to get to Philly, and that's if the traffic isn't bad. Can be closer to four."

"Why don't you just fly into Philly?" When Isabelle and Lincoln stared at him without expression, he added quickly, "Just kidding. Look, the way the VA is set up, you have to get your care here. You can have the blood drawn in Wilkes Barre, but you'd have to pay for it. And, when you start to use other labs, there's always the problem of different techniques and results that are not exactly transferrable. It's inconvenient, but it is free care."

When Isabelle called the next morning, the VA granted Lincoln an appointment only for the blood draw. The woman explained in monotone that if the veteran actually presented for the test, she would authorize an appointment with a doctor. "You know, so many of you make an appointment and then never show up. Call us after the blood's drawn."

Lincoln phoned the FAA in Washington. He made up a name and asked if he could take ciprofloxacin and fly. They wanted his pilot's certificate number, so he hung up. He called the local doctor who did his yearly flight physical and told him he was thinking of taking an antibiotic but had not started. The man did not know what specific medications were banned. "It changes every day. Don't want to give you the wrong advice and have the FAA pull your certificate. Why don't you call them directly."

Lincoln waited a few days after starting the medication, and when there was no dizziness, he went back to flying. Altogether, he had grounded himself for six work days. Lincoln laughed gloomily, "We could have paid for a private doctor with what I lost in income, especially that job dropping the antenna on the top of City Hall in Philly. That would have been a full morning of free commercials for Friday Lift—TV stations, newspapers, the whole shebang."

Isabelle thought for a moment. "You know, Sweetheart, maybe we should look into private care. If this is what they do to a man with the Purple Heart and the Medal…I know, special privileges and all that…but if what you're getting is preferential treatment, how are they treating the average Joe? Scares me to think."

They sat in front of the fireplace that night, feet up, enjoying the cocktail hour. Isabelle poured two glasses of wine, took a long swallow from hers, refilled it, then brought both glasses to the sofa. "Sweetheart, we need to go over what that doctor said last week. I don't know how much of it I remember, do you?"

"Some. But sounds like a good idea to try and put it together. Okay, first, I have a huge prostate. May be nothing, but even if it is, I'm peeing around the clock again, and he didn't give us anything to help that except antibiotics, which haven't changed anything, just like he said they wouldn't. And how could I have gotten an infection down there?"

"You tell me. You heard what he said, VD and all that."

"Very funny. So I have to take this antibiotic for five more weeks, wait a week, and get another blood test. Then, as usual, we wait six more weeks before we find out if it's a just a giant prostate or a tumor, and in the meantime, I'm a dead man."

"Stop it!"

"Okay, let's see. That's three months from now. Add to that the past four or so months. That's six months plus gone by. Then, if the PSA is still high, I have to get a biopsy. That's six more weeks to get it scheduled, if we're lucky, and I imagine an operation'll take a lot longer to get done than a doctor's appointment, so it'll probably be two months. That means we've wasted around eight months to get a biopsy, then another six weeks to get the results, and we're working on nine or ten months, *if* everything goes normally, and don't forget who we're dealing with. We'd be better off going to Canada, becoming citizens, and using their national health system that everybody up there hates and comes to the States to avoid, and..."

Isabelle interrupted. "I want to find a private doctor around here. A good one. You're not the only man in the neighborhood with prostate problems. Let's ask around. Who cares what it costs?"

Lincoln thought for a moment. "If we do that, it'll break the bank. And if something happens to me, there'll be nothing left for you. Look, let's not make that doctor mad just yet. He'll lose the paperwork—send me 'round the hospital to every quack in the place just to piss me off. He'll show me—old fart challenging a *doctor.* My whole case'll get screwed up. He can make trouble for us. Remember, it's the Army."

"We'll worry about all that later. I'm going to ask around."

Lincoln started to answer but looked away and belted down his glass of wine.

CHAPTER FIFTY-EIGHT

Isabelle's gynecologist suggested a local urologist, one her own husband had been seeing for years for prostate cancer.

Dr. Hanem shook both their hands and thanked them for coming in. He asked, "Mr. Friday, what was your most recent PSA level?"

"Thirteen point two."

"Do you have any previous PSAs?"

"I don't."

"Well, did the VA do a biopsy?"

"Not yet. They sent me home on an antibiotic for six weeks. Stuff's horrible. I spent the weekend on the can."

"Okay. So, did they schedule a biopsy for when you were done with the antibiotics?"

Isabelle answered. "First, we have to go back and get another PSA, then go back again six weeks later to see the doctor, then probably wait another six weeks for the biopsy, and then six weeks for the answer. We'll all be dead and buried from old age by then. And, Doctor, can I ask, what is so important about the PSA?"

"Did he not explain it to you?"

"Not really. He was pretty busy."

"Well, you need to understand what's going on, so let me start from the beginning. The prostate is about the size of a walnut when you're in your twenties." They nodded. Hanem smiled. "Stop me if you know all this."

Isabelle shook her head. "We know nothing."

"Okay, the prostate grows a bit each year. No one is absolutely sure why, but it appears that prostate cells live, die, and are replaced, just like the cells of every other organ. Basically, testosterone drives the growth by stimulating the cells to divide. But it seems, as a male ages, the prostate cells don't die as fast as new ones are born. Though a man's testosterone level goes down as he ages, there is still far more than enough around to fuel the prostate to make new cells.

"Okay, next, so what is testosterone? I'm sure you know that is the major hormone that makes a man different from a woman. By the way, women have testosterone, too, but the levels are much lower than in the male. Testosterone is made in the testicles, and a little in the adrenals. When you're a kid, that's what grows muscle, lowers your voice, grows facial hair, on and on. Even though the testosterone levels go down, and men become flabby, some organs, like the prostate and the hair follicles on the scalp, take what little testosterone is still being produced and convert it into DHT. And this stuff really stimulates the prostate to make new cells, and since fewer cells are dying as you age, the net effect is for the prostate to get much bigger. DHT also shrinks the cells that grow hair on the head, and men go bald. We call that male pattern baldness. This is our present understanding, but it changes with the wind."

"Anyway, for our discussion here today, bottom line is, the prostate gets bigger and bigger. As you know, yours is, shall we say, generous. By itself, that's not a major problem, except for the fact that the urethra, the tube that carries pee from the bladder out of the body, travels right through the middle of the prostate. As the prostate grows, it puts more and more pressure on the tube, and the stream gets weak, like a pinched garden hose. When that happens, your water backs up in the bladder, which is just a storage bag, no more than a balloon that holds urine until you pee. Slowly, over the years, the bladder gets bigger and bigger from the pressure, then gets stretched so thin, it's not strong enough to push the pee out with any force, so you can only squeeze out a little before the overgrown prostate pinches off even those few drops. Bladder never completely empties, and in an hour or so, since the kidneys are making urine around the clock, and the only place they can send it is the already mostly-full bladder, it doesn't take much to overfill it again, which is the signal to pee, and off you go to dribble out a few more drops. The cycle never ends, day or night.

"So, this is what we usually do. First, a rectal exam, the old finger wave, to see how big the prostate is and feel for any lumps that don't belong there. To be frank, I almost never detect those lumps, the ones that usually mean cancer, because most prostate cancer forms in the part of the gland that's so far up the rectum, you can't get your finger that high, though I sure try, let me tell you."

They laughed nervously, and he went on. "Now, your situation is that you have had this problem for years, but, clearly, it's getting worse. We need to get a diagnosis, or as close as we can to one. I'm sorry our present method of figuring out problems in the prostate is still pretty rudimentary, but like I said, it's what we're stuck with. On the other hand, new stuff's coming out all the time. We just have to wait until it's approved by the FDA.

"My recommendation is we redo the rectal today, and then you go over to the lab for a PSA. If I feel anything in the gland, we'll make immediate plans, but if the rectal is normal, and the PSA hasn't gone up, you go back to the VA for follow-up care. Is that satisfactory?" Lincoln nodded.

Isabelle's lips tightened. Hanem asked, "Is that okay with you, Mrs. Friday?"

"I thought you had to do the PSA first and the rectal after that."

"That's the old rub. Turns out, it doesn't matter which order you do them in." Isabelle and Lincoln eyed each other and shook their heads. Hanem went on. "What does matter, though, is if, and I'm not trying to be nosey, but I have to know, have you had an orgasm in the past three days?"

"Nope, that's another problem."

"Very common with an enlarged prostate. Do you remember if you'd had an orgasm before the last PSA test at the VA?"

"I don't remember for sure, but I can almost guarantee I didn't." He turned toward Isabelle, and his head wilted. She scooted closer and took his hand.

"No matter. I only ask because the prostate contracts pretty hard during an orgasm to add its fluid to the semen. That squeezes some extra PSA into the blood, just as we used to think the rectal exam did. An orgasm makes the PSA in the blood look falsely high, but the latest is that a rectal exam doesn't. Okay, you ready?"

Both Isabelle and Lincoln nodded with easy smiles. "Ma'am, you're welcome to stay or wait outside for a moment."

"Oh, yes, that. Well, I know the drill. I think I'll excuse myself."

The doctor stood and opened the door for her. He touched her shoulder as she stepped out and whispered gently, "Everything's going to be fine."

When Isabelle was back in the room, the doctor began. "Wasn't so bad, was it?"

Lincoln nodded. "Not at all. Just makes you feel like you need to urinate really bad. I was afraid I was going to pee on your floor."

"That's normal, and no one ever does shower my room. Just the body's signal to find a bathroom, when there's pressure down there from a full bladder, and my finger acted like a full bladder. Nature's amazing. So, you didn't have any real pain when I pressed. Is that right?"

"No, not pain like the last time."

"You had pain when the urologist at the VA did a digital rectal exam?"

"Well, it wasn't when he was pushing on the prostate. It was as he was just going in. He didn't warn me like you did, and he was so fast. Wham, bam, thank you ma'am."

The doctor laughed. "Well, we all have own techniques. Each has its good points—and bad ones. At least his is over quick, not like mine that goes on and on."

"Didn't bother me. I kinda liked it. It's really why I came in to see ya."

Isabelle slapped his arm, and the three laughed. Hanem went on. "Okay, let's put this together, folks. First, you have a large prostate. No question about that. But so do half the men your age. By itself, that only means problems with frequent urination. Next, you have an elevated PSA. As the VA doctor told you, that can be from the prostate just being big, or maybe from an infection, or, let's get it out on the table, cancer. I'll be honest with you, if I may."

His two new patients nodded seriously, but more with attention than fear. "I felt a couple of areas of the prostate that were a bit harder than the rest. If I had to guess, I'd say that was probably something *someone* needs to take a piece of and look at under the microscope—i.e., a biopsy." He watched their eyes closely.

The two remained stoic. Though Isabelle squeezed Lincoln's hand and took a breath to speak, she stopped and looked at him. He nodded for her to continue. "Doctor, that's not a problem, but we want you to do it."

"I would be happy to do so, but there is something else to discuss. Let's be honest. Medical care is ridiculously expensive these days. We doctors do not set the prices. In fact, the cheapest part of going to see the doctor is seeing the doctor. Things like biopsies are pricey when you're paying for them out of pocket. There's the actual surgery, which really isn't surgery, as such. It's just a hollow needle that we poke into the prostate a couple dozen times to get small pieces of the gland to look at under the microscope. It's not bad at all. But then there's the facility fee, i.e., the use of the room, time on the ultrasound machine we use to help guide where we aim the needle, the packaging of the samples, etcetera. Then there's a lab fee for the pathologist to examine the tissue samples, and those guys don't work cheap like us down here in the trenches. Then you have to come back for another visit. It never ends.

"You see, *if* you have private medical insurance, which is unreasonably expensive for the self-employed, you get special low prices because the insurance companies set the fees for all these procedures. What they allow us to charge is a fraction of what a patient pays when they don't have insurance. The insurance companies are in control. If doctors don't go along with their fixed prices, we don't get to see the hundred thousand or more patients they have under contract. We take the hit in how much we can charge for each procedure in trade for volume. I'm being honest with you because I think you need to hear this.

"Now, you can do the biopsy with my practice, and maybe you can afford it, but what happens if it's positive? I mean, you have a tumor and it needs to come out, and then you have to be admitted to the hospital for a couple of nights if there's a lot of bleeding. Well, you'll say, 'Doctor, please make sure there isn't too much bleeding,' and I will tell you, I'll do my best, but let me assure you, the truth is there's *always* something. You own a business, Mr. Friday. That sound familiar?"

Lincoln smiled. "If you only knew."

"Okay, after you cancel the next three years of vacations to pay for the procedure, then it's two days in the hospital. Maybe you can even handle that financially. Then what about radiation therapy and the years of follow-up tests and bone scans? I suppose, if you're Bill Gates, it's not a concern, though I bet even he'd gasp when he saw the bill."

Isabelle spoke softly. "Doctor, is it too late to get private insurance? What if we pay a premium for it?"

"No chance. And, let's face it, they're running a business. You can understand why they won't take on a patient who's already guaranteed to cost them a hundred thousand dollars before the first doctor weighs in on the problem. I will give you my medical opinion, and my opinion as friend and neighbor in this beautiful town. Go back to the VA. It's a pain in the neck, to say it politely, but it's the best option for you right now. Their doctors and nurses have to meet the same standards as every other doctor in the country.

"Look, I don't want to lose you guys as patients. You're the folks every doctor dreams about filling his practice with. Non-complainers, honest people with a challenge who want to get better and aren't asking for pain medication or for me to write letter after letter to those rip-off disability insurance companies that promise to pay if you miss a few days of work, or cover your car payment if you're under the weather, but never do because they always find a loophole. That's after I've spent months filling out their questionnaires, for free, and listening to them essentially call me a liar."

Lincoln laughed. "Hey, Doc, so how do you really feel about the insurance industry?"

The man spoke gently. "Folks, I'll do whatever you want. Why don't you go home, have a glass of wine, or two, and let me know. It's not my feelings that count. It's what's good for you, Mr. Friday. Of all people, you deserve the best."

Lincoln thought for a moment. "Let's take the next step with you, Doc. What's it going to be?"

"Well, it's to wait for the PSA. We never make important decisions based on a single blood test, i.e., the one you did at the VA. I'll get the result back in two days, max. I'll give you a call. We can discuss it over the phone. Save you a trip to the office *and* a charge for the visit. How's that?"

At the cocktail hour that evening, they sat at the fireplace holding hands. Isabelle asked softly, "Sweetheart, how do you feel?"

"Actually, pretty good. I think I understand what's going on. All of a sudden, it's not as scary."

She squeezed his hand. "He seems to care. I really liked him. Mountain doesn't seem as high, does it?"

"Guy's doing his best. I guess that's all we can ask. Sweetheart, if you don't mind, I want to go back to him. I think we can afford the biopsy. Is that okay?"

"Sweet Lincoln, we will pay every cent in the bank if that's what it takes. Who cares? We're going to make you better."

Dr. Hanem called the next evening at eight. The PSA was 13.1, just a tenth lower than at the VA. They asked him to do the biopsy. He gave Lincoln a local anesthetic through the anus into the prostate itself. It stung. Then the doctor put an ultrasound probe in the rectum, found the areas he wanted to biopsy, slid a thin, spring-loaded device through the anus, and pulled the trigger. Lincoln felt a snap, but no pain. The doctor took twenty-four samples. It was over in fifteen minutes. When Lincoln sat up, he laughed. "My butt hurts less than if I'd been stuck in the helicopter for an afternoon."

The doctor walked him to a meeting room. He told Isabelle and Lincoln that it all went very smoothly. "These will go out today, probably'll get read before sundown. Usually in urologists' offices, they have you back in a week or ten days for the results. That's cruel and unjust punishment. I'll have my receptionist call you as soon as I've seen the pathology report. We'll get you in the next day, or that day, whatever. Are you available at a couple of hours' notice?"

Lincoln laughed. "Can I land on your roof? Give you a ride."

"That's kind of you, and your doctor is flattered, but helicopters give me the heebie-jeebies. They got no business in the air. The truth is, they can't fly. It's been scientifically proven."

"Who told you those lies, Doctor?"

"My brother. He flew Blackhawks in Iraq. You people and your autorotations and pinnacles. Madness. I'll take too much exposure to x-rays as an occupational hazard any day over climbing into a flying machine that can't. No insult intended, I guess."

Isabelle and Lincoln were back in the office at seven-thirty the next morning. She brought a bouquet of flowers and blushed as she handed it to Dr. Hanem. He sat them down. "Folks, no beating around the bush. Bottom line, we found some abnormal cells in the prostate." Isabelle and Lincoln blanched. Hanem waited until the color seeped back into their faces. "I can see you understand that means there's cancer in the gland.

"So, now, we're going to muster the troops and come up with a plan to confront this head on. But first, you're going to have to learn all about the next level of prostate science—Gleason Scores. That's how we tell just how aggressive a tumor is. That means how fast it's growing." He watched the blood drain from their faces again then nodded as they recovered. "Okay, now that we've got the bad news out of the way, here's the good news. Let me assure you, most prostate cancer is treatable, so the odds are with you.

"Let's get started. There are two things we measure to come up with a Gleason Score. And, by the way, it's named for Donald Gleason, who was, of all things, a urologist at the Minneapolis VA Hospital back in the 1960s. There have been some improvements over the years, but it's basically the same, at least for our purposes.

"First, the pathologist who read your biopsy under the microscope found cancer cells. Normal cells that come from the prostate look different than normal cells from any other organ. And prostate cancer cells look different under the microscope than cancer cells from any other organ, say, the lung. Now, basically, cancer cells are more or less primitive forms of the cells of the organs they grow in. So, mild prostate cancer cells look fairly much like normal prostate cells. Aggressive prostate cancer cells are the most primitive, and you can barely tell they're from the prostate, if at all. That's why, sometimes, we can't tell a patient where their cancer is coming from. And because they are so primitive, they have the power to divide and grow much faster than normal prostate cells. That's because primitive cells are designed by nature to divide quickly in the womb and become the organ they're supposed to be. Only difference, the normal cells in the womb are programmed to stop growing when their organs are fully formed. In cancer cells, the program is corrupted, and they don't get the message to stop growing. Have I completely screwed this up so far?"

Isabelle smiled weakly. "We're with you."

"So, the first thing to look at is the 'pattern' of those bad cells, that is, how primitive they look. We rate them from one to five. One is the best. These cells look almost normal. Five's not so hot. The cells don't look anything like normal cells. Have to tell you.

we rarely see one or two. By the time there are symptoms, and a man comes to the doctor, three or four is the tamest we run into.

"After we decide on how primitive the cells are, we go to the next step. The pathologist 'grades' those collections of bad cells. That just means figuring out what percent of the bad cells under the microscope are what number. Say sixty percent of the abnormal cells are grade three and forty percent are grade four. The type that is the highest by percent is rated by the pathologist as 'primary.' That's grade three in our example, and grade four is 'secondary.' Sometimes, we even go to tertiary, but let's not muddy the waters. So now, we have two numbers: how bad the cells are, and how many of them are there. Think of a bushel of apples you buy but forget about and leave out in the garage. A month later, you smell something—a 'symptom', and you investigate. Some of the apples are bruised. Of those that are bad, sixty percent are damaged to the point they still look like apples but have begun to rot. The other forty percent are so far gone, you can barely tell they're apples—could be pears, for all you can figure out. So sixty percent of the apples are grade three and forty percent are grade four. The pathologist then simply adds the pattern number of the primary and secondary grades. Just adds them up. In our example, here, three plus four is seven, so the final Gleason score is seven. Now, when doctors get their hands on anything, they don't rest until they've made it so complicated, only a helicopter pilot could understand."

Lincoln laughed. "That's not sayin' a lot for doctors."

"My point exactly. So, naturally, there a million different side tracks, like if only two patterns are seen you just add the two scores. But if the pathologist sees three grades, he adds the primary score to the highest grade. Let me give you an example. If the primary tumor grade was three and the secondary tumor grade was four, but some cells were found to be grade five, the

Gleason score would be three plus five, or eight. Sadly, we have to define the worst scenario.

"Your Gleason score, Mr. Friday, is seven. Now, I have to tell you what that final score predicts. And these numbers are not fixed in stone. Less than six has a very good prognosis, but not perfect, and there will be some men with as low as four or five whose cancer will progress real fast. Six and seven are in the middle—okay, but not the best prognosis. Again, some of these guys live for another thirty years with those numbers. Then, there's eight to ten. Generally, these are not curable.

"So, you are still in the treatable range. And that's the rub. You *will* have to have some sort of treatment. And no matter what it is, it's going to cost a mint. And also, there's another consideration. I looked into the whole Agent Orange mess. The VA now accepts—very, very, grudgingly—that there *may* be some association between Agent Orange exposure and aggressive prostate cancer. And I have to tell you, yours is, though treatable, fairly aggressive. If you go through a private doctor, you may have a big problem paying for the treatment *and* claiming benefits.

"Let's be up front again. If something happens to you, Mrs. Friday may not get your benefits if the diagnosis and treatment were done elsewhere, that is, with a doctor not approved by the VA system to make those determinations.

"So, here we are, back to square one. Again, I'll do whatever you folks desire, but you can tell where my advice is going."

Lincoln asked, "If we go back to the VA, will they at least accept your diagnosis and just get on with the surgery?"

"To be honest, if you came to me with VA results, I would be hard pressed to take their data at face value. I mean, I don't know who did the biopsy, if he was seventy-five years old, or worse, maybe a second year resident, or maybe an intern, God forbid. It's not brain surgery, but there is a learning curve. Then, I don't know the lab that looked at the tissue under the microscope.

There are some less-than-superior labs out there who survive by working cheap. Government likes to contract with the lowest bidder. Then the lowest bidder *always* finds ways to make a profit, usually by skimping and putting out shoddy work. It's a law of nature. And what if the urologist or the lab switched samples, or lost them, and neither one of them wants to lose face, so they just make up the results? Happens."

Isabelle and Lincoln looked at him with dropped jaws and disbelieving smiles. "Laugh if you like. But it's a human endeavor. Mr. Friday, did you ever see any mistakes in the military?"

Lincoln smiled. "Not that I recall."

"The doctor rolled his chair to Lincoln's side. He put his hand on Lincoln's shoulder. "I had a doctor in my residency who told me that if he never received a note from a lab that a specimen was lost, he fired the lab. It's a human endeavor.

"So, that's my best advice. Please keep me informed. I want to help."

Isabelle called the Philadelphia VA the next day to explain that her husband already had had a biopsy and needed to see the urologist as soon as he could. The scheduler listened and said she'd discuss the matter with her supervisor. She called back in an hour and reported that Dr. Render would not see him until another PSA was done. They drove to Philly, and Lincoln's blood was drawn. It was weeks before the doctor's next available opening.

When they finally sat down with Dr. Render, he opened the medical record. His face curled in shock. "Your PSA is off the chart. There's something wrong."

Isabelle caught the doctor up on the past weeks and the biopsy that had just been done. The man snapped, "Why didn't you tell me? This PSA is worthless. You never do a PSA right after a biopsy. It's stupid." Lincoln stood and turned to Isabelle to take her hand and leave, but the doctor stammered, "Well, it's not your fault, really. It's the system. Let's just move forward."

Isabelle handed him the pathology results and the Wilkes Barre doctor's typed chart notes. He glanced at them then flipped them on the sink top. "That's helpful, but we are going to need to repeat the whole thing."

He started to justify his decision, but Isabelle interrupted. "We understand that you can't simply accept records from somewhere else. So let's just cut to the chase and get it all done here. We'll do whatever you tell us to do."

A biopsy was scheduled for two weeks.

A few days later, when Lincoln got out of bed in the morning, the first thing that he noticed was not the cancer, but an ache in his back and a remote discomfort in his belly. By reflex, he blamed the pain on the three-hour lift he'd flown the afternoon before, comforting himself with the fact that it did not hurt to urinate. So he didn't tell Isabelle. He started taking ibuprofen around the clock, and for a while it helped, but after a few weeks, the pain was with him all the time, especially in his gut. Still, he said nothing.

Their lives swung from days underpinned by dread back to the mundane, but each cocktail hour, they held each other more closely than they had the night before. And there seemed to be less and less to say. As they lay in bed, before falling to sleep, Isabelle always placed her hands on his lower back and whispered, "I'll love you forever."

Friday Lift had backed up with missions during Lincoln's absences. He started flying fifteen and twenty hours a week, and as the appointment for the biopsy with the VA doctor neared, he squeezed in even more. Soon, his back had begun to ache so while flying, he could not find a comfortable sitting position, and his ability to drop loads on tiny targets suffered. He finally gave in and had his pilots fly the sorties he had assigned himself. Still, the pain worsened, and a few nights later it woke him from sleep. He hurt so badly, he could not stop the shaking in his legs. Isabelle forced him to the emergency room. They found nothing but gave him a few pain pills, only because he was to see his doctor at the VA before the end of the week.

When they arrived at the hospital, Lincoln was given two Valium tablets to take twenty minutes before the biopsy. He was helped into the procedure room and tried to tell the doctor of his back pain, but he couldn't form the words through the haze of the Valium. He did not remember much of the process, except that there was painful throbbing deep inside him each time the biopsy tool snapped.

When it was over, Dr. Render took off his gloves and warned, "There might be blood in the semen for several weeks, but it really doesn't mean anything. It's not dangerous, and it always goes away, eventually. And there's always the chance of infection, but you look pretty healthy."

Lincoln mumbled cheerlessly, "If I was so healthy, I wouldn't be sitting here." He began to mention his back, but he was curiously pain free, and his mind was in such a muddle, it was never brought up.

The nurse who walked Lincoln to the waiting room handed Isabelle a paper that she was told to take to the appointment desk. Isabelle gave Lincoln her seat. He fell asleep. Isabelle listened to the appointment clerk hem and haw that the soonest appointment was four weeks hence. She opened her mouth to assail the woman but just glared for a moment, spun around, and bristled back into the urology waiting room. She asked the receptionist if she could have a moment with the doctor. After several calls to the nurse, Isabelle was told it would be half-an-hour. She waited forty-five minutes, looked at Lincoln, who was slumped to the side, asleep, patted his arm, and stomped into the treatment area. A nurse doing her nails looked up. Isabelle spit, "I want to see the doctor, *now*!"

The nurse picked up the phone and pushed a red button. She spoke in an excited whisper then rolled herself off the high stool and moved slowly toward an exam room. The doctor charged out with an air of exasperation that stole Isabelle's breath. He pulled up in front of her holding a chart. One leg began to pulse rapidly as he waited for her to speak.

"Dr. Render, they're telling me it's going to be *another* month before we can get in to see you for the biopsy results."

"Well, Miss, I want you to know there are a million old guys from Viet Nam with the same problem as your husband. All of them have cancer. It is an epidemic. Don't blame the VA. And we just got yet another new load from…"

Two enormous men in blue uniforms jumped out of the elevator and shot to the medical assistant's side. She jerked her head toward Isabelle. They puffed their chests and took aggressive steps toward her, but Render looked up and shook his head. "I am taking care of this."

"Are you sure, Doctor?"

"Yes. Please go away." Render waited until he could no longer hear their grumbling. "As I was saying, there are men lined up to see me from Afghanistan, and then there's the old guys from Viet Nam like your husband. To be honest, the young ones come first. They have urological trauma on top of their closed head trauma, on top of their amputations. *Your* Veterans Administration has chosen to hire but two urologists. And you need to know that prostate cancer is not like the breast cancer you women get. It's very slow moving. We can wait for a lot longer without treatment than with the serious cancers. And, if I remember correctly, your husband has already been out there for years with the problem. It would have been a lot easier to treat had he come right in."

"Are you saying it's going to be hard to treat?"

"All I'm saying is that we have a higher wall to climb because of the delay. Please calm down. It is just prostate cancer." The nurse glared impatiently, prodding the doctor with her eyes and twisted mouth to terminate the interruption, get back to his patients, and make up the time, so they would not finish late again. He nodded tersely to Isabelle, "Step by step," then barged back into the exam room.

CHAPTER FIFTY-NINE

Lincoln returned to work, though his chest was never free of foreboding. He often took off saying he was going on a test flight, but landed in tiny clearings deep in the Poconos, where he shut down and played music from the Sixties on his Walk Man—*Galveston, The Boxer, If You're Going to San Francisco.*

He thought back to the soldiers he'd stood over in Viet Nam, bodies twisted, eyes open, staring into the sky at nothing. Though he envied them their final freedom, the madness finally vanished, he often thought about the moments before they died, curled in mud, shaking with pain. He remembered watching their fatigues soak up blood faster than he could tie off wounds, consciousness ebbing, their last moments consumed with the need to be valiant, to die alone, but quietly, so they would be remembered in the eyes of their teenaged peers as fearless. How horrible he thought, to have had only the gloomy years of adolescence to contemplate the meaning of their lives. He had seen so many cross over, yet he still understood nothing of the journey.

And now, it was his turn. He pondered what would happen to Isabelle. He doubted she would ever smile again. He knew he wouldn't, if it was she who would soon fade.

Kerrith hadn't remarried. She hadn't even had a single date since Bob passed, for she had never, for one moment, thought she could fill the desperate loneliness by touching another man. Lincoln did not want that for Isabelle, for her dear spirit and love to simply wither. But how could he tell her that? How could he touch her and whisper the words that he would not die in peace knowing she'd remain alone for the balance of her life?

He reached down to start the engine. He would fly straight back to the airport, speak to no one, just drive home, dry his tears, and walk into the house in the middle of the afternoon. He would tell Isabelle straight out that when the time came, he would not be able to rest unless she promised to find someone to share the rest of her precious years.

But he withdrew his hand from the throttle. He knew it would cause her such pain, to ask her to share herself with someone other than the only man she had ever known. He wiped his eyes and accepted that, while neither of them could ever replace the other, there were still warm seasons ahead for her. It was not necessary to say the words. The blessing of time would open the door.

When he got home that night, Isabelle was sitting at her desk, eyes frozen to her computer. She jumped in surprise when he walked up behind her and put his hands on her shoulder.

He laughed. "You writing a novel?" When she didn't turn around, he asked gently, "You okay?"

"Sweetheart, I'm not going to stand for their crap anymore."

"Whose crap, the kids next door?"

"Very funny. No, your damn VA."

"I know. But they're pulling all the levers. Nothing we can do—federal government. You make waves, and they can bury you, they will bury you, and we can't afford opening another front right now."

"I'm sorry. I am opening one. May turn out to be the Russian Front, and I may get my head handed to me like Hitler, but I'm not sitting on my thumbs anymore. You won the Medal of Honor, for God's sakes. I'll write to our senators and our congresswoman. The VA works for them."

"Sweetheart, they work for nobody but themselves, and do you think the senators know or care about what's happening at the VA? Old soldiers have no voice. Troops we saw at the VA aren't the movers and shakers. Guys we ran into ain't got no money, honey. If a vet did well in life, do you think he'd use the VA?"

"*You* did great."

"Yeah, well, Sweet Pea, I'm not the usual vet. I got lucky and married you. I'm tellin' ya, no one cares, no one listens. The guy running the show is some high general. I never told you, but I heard him on the radio, right around the time the Nhus were here. NPR. Said the psychological problems in the vets coming back from the Middle East were temporary, just another adjustment reaction, and that the cost of granting these guys a pension for a simple, passing period of confusion would break the bank. It was just like they told Huber a thousand years ago. They don't learn. And do you know why they don't learn?"

"Let me guess. Because they don't have to."

"Yes, Sweetheart, no one's gonna make 'em learn. Not sexy. Just working stiffs who had their butts handed to them in a war that everyone still wants to pretend didn't happen, and again and again in Iraq and Afghanistan. Not worth an ounce of a politician's sweat, the guys we saw lined up at the VA. And that general, he didn't get four stars caring about his privates and corporals. He got to where he is kissing ass, colonel and above, and you can be sure they ain't the ones using the VA now.

"And I looked him up on Wikipedia. A real soldier, that one. Wounded a few times and still volunteered to go back. Probably just to build credentials for his career. You know, some guys, that crap over there didn't affect them. Maybe the way they were raised. Parents from a warrior culture or something. Hard for them to understand wholesale murder's not so easy to forget for some of us."

Isabelle grunted. "Sweetheart, I'm just so tired of it all. Taxes spent on fancy VA brochures, on beautiful websites, and on the GS-15s and 18s. That's where the money's going, to the ones running the show. I can't stand it anymore."

Lincoln bent forward and kissed the top of Isabelle's head. Her scent soothed him. "I'm still the luckiest man that ever lived. 'Cause of you."

She turned and kissed him then swung around back to the computer. "But I am gonna rattle their little cages." She finished the first e-mail, the one to their senator, that evening, but decided to wait until morning to push the send button.

Dear Senator Kozub,

I am sorry to bother you, but I am writing to ask for your help. My husband is a Viet Nam veteran and has prostate cancer. The VA says it could be two months before they can even give us the results of his biopsy. His doctor told us it doesn't matter because prostate cancer is not serious, and we can safely wait for a long time.

He was a helicopter pilot in Vietnam and sprayed Agent Orange. The VA doesn't think that caused his cancer. That is what his VA doctor told us, but I read on your website that you have been fighting to take care of the men who were exposed.

I must tell you that he earned the Medal of Honor. I know that doesn't mean he should get special treatment, but what kind of care are the privates and corporals getting?

Please help us. We have been married for 47 years. I love him so much.

Thank you.

Isabelle Friday

A week later, Isabelle received an e-mail from Senator Kozub's office.

Dear Ms. Friday,

Thank you for contacting my Philadelphia office regarding the difficulties you are experiencing with your combat-related claim. I am happy to look into this matter for you.

A member of my staff has forwarded your letter to the Department of Veterans Affairs seeking further information regarding the issue at hand, and she will notify you as soon as a response is received. If you have any questions or concerns in the meantime, please do not hesitate to contact Cindy Startup in my Philadelphia office.

Sincerely,

Francie

Francine Kozub,

United States Senator

Three weeks later, a final e-mail arrived.

Dear Ms. Friday,

I have now heard back from the Veterans Administration regarding the request for treatment of prostate cancer. They remind us that there are many men being treated for acute wounds received in Iraq and Afghanistan. We must wait our turn.

If the subject is terminal, please let me know, and I will see what I can do to help you expedite the process. In the meantime, please follow up with the Veterans Administration directly. Their hotline number is 542-569-2548

Sincerely,

Francie

Francine Kozub,

United States Senator

Isabelle read the words, "If the subject is terminal…" over and over, crying harder with each echo. Finally, her tears stopped, and she slammed her palm onto the desk. She called Kozub's office and screeched until they put Cindy Startup on the phone. Isabelle hissed, "I want to come in and see Senator Kozub. I want to know why she wrote back to me as if I was the patient. Did she even read the letter?"

"I can assure you she did."

"Then it was a United States Senator who thought Isabelle was a man's name? And that an Isabelle could have *prostate cancer,* even after I said it was my husband who's sick, not me. And how dare she ask out of hand if 'the subject is terminal'? Is that how you people speak to your constituents?"

"Mrs. Friday, I apologize if there was any confusion or distress."

"Confusion? You mean you apologize for not giving a damn. Do you even know what a Medal of Honor is? How about a Purple Heart?"

There was a fuming silence on the other end, and Isabelle could hear the woman take a very deep breath. "I know very well about both. I lost my right leg and half my pelvic organs to an IED in Iraq. Do you *even know* what an IED is?" She gave Isabelle a few seconds then spit, "An improvised explosive device? I was the only one on the Humvee who lived." She was silent for a long time, and Isabelle did not dare speak. "I will be happy to meet with you here in the Philadelphia office, but I will not discuss VA policy."

Isabelle was about to demand to know why not, but her spirit ebbed and she quietly finished the call.

CHAPTER SIXTY

Weeks after the biopsy at the VA, they received a call from Render's office. They were to appear at the Urology Clinic office the next morning. The doctor glanced at the chart as he spoke. "Well, the Gleason score on your biopsy was eight."

Isabelle asked if the worsening was due to the delay. Render still did not raise his eyes. "To be honest, it is hard to predict if… no, it's just a different set of biopsy samples and a different pathologist's eyes." His face hardened. "With a Gleason score this high, we are going to have to think very hard about treatment."

Isabelle whimpered, "There is going to be treatment, isn't there?"

"I'm afraid there is little we have to offer in the way of curative treatment."

Isabelle took Lincoln's hand. Her voice rose an octave. "What does that mean, 'curative'?" Render's leg started shaking. "Surely there's something you can do to get the tumor out of him, Doctor. We hear about all sorts of surgery and seeds that kill the cancer."

"Now, Isabelle, isn't it? I'm sorry, but this is not simply my opinion. It is what the science shows. Naturally, we will treat your husband, and, who knows, he may survive for ten or twelve years. Many men do. All I am saying is that there is a likelihood that this cancer has spread out of the prostate itself, and that means even if we remove the whole gland, there are bad cells already on the loose in other parts of the body. We can't find every single one of them."

Isabelle's voice was tremulous, "The other biopsy was only a seven. Is that helpful?"

"Though seven or eight sound so close, the science shows there is a statistical difference. And we have to be rational, not emotional, in deciding what the level of care is going to be. When the number is eight, we must follow a certain protocol. It is the rule here. It is not my decision. *Our* pathologist said eight. We have no other choice."

Her voice hardened. "Dr. Render, you just told us that eight can't be treated but seven can. If there is any question, we want to go with the treatment that gives the best chance to cure the problem."

"It is not just the Gleason score." He opened Lincoln's chart and flipped through several pages. His lips tensed. "When we took the blood, I had them also check a general panel of tests. It looks like your husband's calcium is up near the top limit. Not over, mind you, but it is a bit concerning."

Lincoln interjected, "I think that's because I've been taking so many TUMS lately. My stomach has really been bothering me."

Render stifled a smile. "No, I'm sure not. Elevated calcium is not from the diet. It usually means there's a problem with the bones. If cancer invades the skeleton, it consumes it, kills the cells. The bone dissolves, the calcium that was once stored there is released into the bloodstream, and your calcium level goes up on our tests. Let me ask, do you have any bony pain?"

Lincoln answered tautly. “I don’t know what you mean.”

“Any pain in your arms, legs, your back?”

“Actually, my back has been killing me, and it’s…”

The doctor interrupted. His eyes bore into Lincoln’s. “I want to know if your back pain keeps you awake or wakes you up from sleep.”

“Yes, it does, recently. What does that mean?”

“Do you sweat at night?”

“Yes, but I’ve been working so…”

The man stared at the door for several seconds and spoke as if to himself. “We need to get a bone scan before we go any further.” He stood abruptly and left the room. Isabelle and Lincoln did not speak while he was gone. When he came back, he handed Isabelle a sheet of paper. “I’ve ordered a bone scan for your husband. Please go to the nuclear radiology department in the basement before you leave and schedule the appointment. I’ll know more when we get the results. It sounds like the cancer may have gotten into the bones of the lower back. That’s where prostate cancer often spreads. I’m not sure, because the PSA isn’t *that* high, but we need to rule it out right away.”

Isabelle clutched Lincoln’s hand. She asked in a deflated whisper. “What is a bone scan? Can we do it today?”

The man nodded. “I’m not trying to alarm you, but I’m concerned. A bone scan tells us if there is cancer in the bones. We inject a small amount of radioactive chemical into the blood. It is designed to circulate until it finds a bone that is trying to heal itself, like a broken bone, *or,* where a cancer has eaten into the bone and the bone is reacting and trying to fight back. The chemical stops there, and because it is radioactive, it shows up on an x-ray.”

Isabelle was numb, the world around her eyes hazy, but she managed to mumble, “I don’t like the radioactivity part.”

"Let me assure you, it is a small dose, and nearly ninety-five percent of it decays into a harmless chemical in one day and then exits the body in the urine. We have no choice. We have to know if there are tumor cells in the lower back because that will change everything."

"Everything?"

"Yes. That would mean, even if the Gleason score was seven, or six, or five, the cancer is already growing outside the prostate gland itself. And we might not consider surgery to remove the prostate because the cancer is essentially everywhere." Both Isabelle and Lincoln flushed, and Render exhaled deeply. "Don't you see? If that's the case, there may not any point in doing a major operation to remove the prostate gland, because that doesn't get rid of the cancer."

Lincoln put up his hand. "Doctor, let me try to understand. This is prostate cancer, yes?"

"Yes."

"If the cancer is in the prostate, you remove it, and there is no more cancer left to spread."

"No, that is incorrect. Once even a few microscopic cells leave the prostate, or the breast, or the lung, whatever kind of cancer you have, wherever these breakaway cells finally get lodged, perhaps in a tiny blood vessel or a lymph node, they start a new tumor. By then, prostate cancer has nothing to do with the prostate, breast cancer has nothing to do with the breast, and the same for lung cancer.

"You must understand; cancer cells do not have normal genes. Normal cells are programmed by their genes to divide only when needed to repair damage. They stop splitting when the wound is mended because a special gene tells them to stop. But in cancer cells, that gene has been damaged by cigarette smoke, by x-rays, maybe from chemicals in the environment."

Lincoln interjected, "You mean like Agent Orange?"

"I'm sorry. As I said before, we just do not know that. Sometimes, it's just by chance." He looked surreptitiously at his watch. "Anyway, the damaged cells travel to other parts of the body, and they form new tumors that are as just as bad or, perhaps, grow even faster than the original tumor. There are a few not-so-perfect studies that say taking the prostate out even after the cancer has spread is helpful, but they are just studies. As I have told you in the past, I rely on proven science. I will not experiment with my patients. So, taking out the prostate, which is a major operation that weakens the patient and makes you less able to fight the cancer, is off the table, as far as I am concerned. My opinion is it would be of no use. In fact, it would cause undue harm.

"Eventually, cells from the new tumors around the body break off and start more and more new tumors. It's endless, well, until they take over and block tubes and arteries, or they take so much nutrition, they consume the body. That is why it is called cancer."

Isabelle shook her head. "I don't understand."

"Cancer is the crab in Greek mythology. A crab gnaws and gnaws away, just like cancer does. Okay, but back to why I want you to understand all of this. You see, when the cancer has spread, we switch from trying to remove it from the body to trying to slow it down. And we do a pretty good job.

"First, we can treat with emission energy. That means pointing the barrel of a radiation gun right at the bigger tumors. We focus the waves to go through the skin and come together at a point right on the cancer. Radiation kills fast-growing cells really well, though, unfortunately, it can never get all of them.

"So there is another step we take. But let me warn you, this is a treatment most men of your generation rebel against, though, I must say, it is effective." Isabelle took a breath, but Render went on quickly before she could ask. "You must understand that testosterone acts as fertilizer for prostate cancer cells. Since we cannot kill all the cancer cells, our goal becomes to slow the growth of the cancer cells that have escaped to other parts of the body. To do that, we need to get rid of the testosterone, so those cells that survive radiation don't have testosterone to thrive on.

"We do that by, and here's where I want us all to be strong, by removing everything that makes testosterone. We can use medicine that stops the testicles from making testosterone, or we can just remove the testicles themselves. Or we can do both." He leaned back to let his patients absorb the news.

Lincoln looked up. "Oh, Jesus Christ. You mean cut off my balls?"

"Well, I would not put it in quite those terms. But, yes, if you choose to use the vernacular. There are some who say you can do one or the other, medicine or surgery, that the combination is not necessary. But, you see, if you just remove the testicles, there is still some testosterone made in the adrenal glands. That's why we use medicines to stop that. On the other hand, the medications are unpleasant. They cause feminization—hot flashes, loss of a lot of muscle, loss of libido and the ability to get an erection. I've seen a good deal of depression with it, but we can treat that.

"On the other hand, we have people who live for years and years after the procedure. Not going to be playing NFL football, but it is a relatively pain free life."

Isabelle blurted, "*Relatively* pain free?"

"Yes, and we can treat pain. And I must warn you, if the cancer comes back in cells that have mutated and no longer need testosterone to grow, we use chemotherapy. Many new medications are available. They go to every corner of the body through the bloodstream and find most of the tiny collections of tumor cells that escaped the radiation gun, but are too small to be seen on bone scans, CT scans, and MRIs. Therefore, they can't be treated by the radiation gun because we don't know where to point it. The chemotherapy is very effective, but the cancer cells are very smart. A tiny percentage of them are not killed by the chemotherapy because their genes suddenly mutate and become resistant to the medicine. Eventually, these extra strong cells form new tumors that have the same mutation, so they don't respond to chemotherapy anymore.

"But you must understand, all of these processes take years and years. A lot of annoyance, more visits to doctors, hospitals, but the reward is you can spend the time together. This is not a bad thing. My patients tell me these are the best years of their lives, because, finally, you've become smart enough to realize you do not have to do anything you do not want to. You are finally your own boss. Most of my patients say they don't care what people think of them anymore. They find it very liberating.

"But back to the bone scan. The reason we cannot do it today is because we have to order the isotope, I mean the radioactive tracer, the chemical. They have to make it right before we use it because, as I mentioned, it lasts such a short time. They deliver it in a big flurry in the morning. The nurses become quite unbalanced when it arrives. Young ones won't go near it. Only the post-menopausal girls will come in the same room, and even then, there is such a level of static. Very unpleasant to be around them. Silly, really. Harmless in the container, but you know people these days."

When they were finished, Isabelle went to the basement to schedule the bone scan. They were closed for lunch, and the sign said it would be an hour before they reopened, so Isabelle told Lincoln she'd call in the morning, and they went to a movie. As they walked to their car late in the afternoon, a soaking rain caught them, and they decided not to drive home until morning. They checked into the Sofitel Philadelphia. After dinner and two bottles of wine at Bistro La Minette, they walked, hand in hand, back to their extravagant hotel. Lincoln carried a doggie bag. He laughed that he would heat the leftovers in the microwave and serve her breakfast in bed. She rolled her eyes.

As he gave her a peck on the cheek, a white-bearded creature appeared in front of them, palm extended. "Hey, kissin' man, you got somethin' for someone who ain't got nothin'?" Lincoln handed him the food, and Isabelle poked around in her purse for ten dollars.

Isabelle got into bed and slipped out of her robe. Lincoln took off his pajamas. They draped their bodies over each other and fell asleep. When they woke in the morning, Lincoln whispered, "That was better than the first night, huh?"

Isabelle huffed, "I beg your pardon, good sir!" then giggled and cooed, "Best ever."

They drove home slowly that day, silently, pondering the fields and forests, not a word passing between them. That night, they went to bed early and sat reading, shoulders touching.

CHAPTER SIXTY-ONE

Isabelle slept in the next morning while Lincoln went to the hangar and made arrangements for the company's work to be carried out by his stand-by pilots. She made a cup of coffee and sat down at her desk to call and schedule the bone scan. She turned on her computer and gazed at her e-mails as she rummaged through the drawer for the card with the VA number. There were the usual notes from friends and solicitors, and one hidden in the middle from a name she did not recognize. The subject line had three words: "Searching For You." It contained an attachment, and that convinced her to erase it out of hand. She and Lincoln had long since sworn to each other that they would not open strange e-mails, and certainly not ones with attachments, no matter how seductive.

As Isabelle prepared to click delete, the phone rang. It was the VA Hospital. A woman stated she had called to schedule a bone scan. The first appointment was two weeks off. Isabelle raised her voice, and the woman growled, "Who the hell you think you yellin' at?" She hung up. Isabelle called back, but the next clerk droned the doctor had not labeled the test urgent, and even if he had, it would still be a week.

Isabelle called the urology department and demanded to speak to Render. His medical assistant phoned back at the end of the afternoon. Isabelle refused to talk to her. The woman hissed, "Wait," and dropped the phone with a thud. Three minutes later, the doctor took the phone. He remained calm until Isabelle accused him of not caring about his patients because he hadn't made her husband's test a priority.

"We've been through this before, Madam. I told you that the men from Iraq and Afghanistan come first. Half of them have been blown up. Some are paralyzed below the waist. I spend my life doing surgery on them, mostly ineffective. Few of them will ever get an erection again. None of them are going to father children.

"And I told you, your spouse's prostate cancer is far advanced, so the delay is not critical. It's no big deal."

She was silent, overwhelmed that her husband's life had boiled down to "no big deal." It was her turn to slam the phone down.

She made an appointment with Dr. Hanem, who agreed to see them that day.

He smiled warmly but curiously. "Well, how are the treatments going? You must be getting pretty close to the end. You look great. They don't seem to have harmed you at all. You've got more hair than me."

Lincoln looked to Isabelle and nodded. "Dr. Hanem, that's why we're here. They haven't started yet. We haven't even gotten a bone scan yet. It's been one delay after another."

Hanem shook his head subtly and was about to speak but stopped himself. His expression hardened. "Tell me what's going on."

Lincoln turned to Isabelle. "Well, the biopsy at the VA showed an eight, the Gleason score." Hanem nodded comfortably, as if he was not surprised. She waited for a comment, but he was silent, so she continued. "They said his calcium was high, well, not high, but near the top limit." He nodded again. "So, the doctor there said the cancer had probably spread to his bones. They want him to get a bone scan, but they want us to wait for a few more weeks. His back and stomach are really hurting. Supposedly, if the cancer has gone to the lower back, they can treat that with radiation, and the pain will be relieved. Is that true?"

Hanem sat quietly for a moment, thinking. "Okay. I understand. It is possible that the Gleason score is eight. May really be seven, but to be honest, there is no concrete barrier between the two numbers. I would imagine there is some spread, but the tumor hasn't been staged yet. Yet another step, I'm afraid."

Isabelle's head drooped. "You mean *another* part of the Gleason score?"

"No, this is something different, Mrs. Friday. Nothing to be fearful of. It just means another piece of information, the TNM. That's how we stage how far the cancer has spread from the prostate. It's not complicated, just a matter of gathering the final bit of information, crunching the numbers, and coming up with the best prognosis we can. You need every bit of information we can give you, but let me remind you, even with all the numbers, we're only right some of the time. It's the best we can do at the moment.

"So, let's go over the TNM score. The T stands for tumor—that is, has the tumor spread *locally* from the prostate and crept its way directly into the organs next to it? That gets a number from T1 to T4. Basically, T1 is the doctor doesn't feel the tumor when you do a rectal exam, and T4 is that it has grown big enough to include organs next door, for example, the bladder.

"Then there's the N number. It stands for nodes. Only two choices: has the tumor spread to the lymph nodes near the prostate? It's either N zero, no spread to the nodes, or N1, yes, spread to the nodes.

"Finally, there's the M number, and that stands for metastases. It's different than the T score, which measures if the original tumor has grown big enough to get out of the prostate. Metastases, on the other hand, are bits of tumor that have broken off and are growing in organs far from the prostate. That's also two choices, M zero, or M1, in other words, yes or no.

"So, we can't stage the tumor until we know a lot more information. The next step, with your back pain, is the bone scan. And, yes, radiation treatment can really decrease the pain.

Isabelle raised her hand. "So what is the Gleason score for, then?"

"Well, let's backtrack for a second. The Gleason score tells us how aggressive the cells are that have become cancerous, *and* how many of those cells there are. The TNM tells us if those cells have gotten out of the prostate, and if they have, how far they have travelled."

Isabelle's shoulders sagged farther. "It's just too much to absorb. So, what do we do, Doctor?"

"If you want to have a bone scan done here, I'm sure we can accommodate you. I have to tell you, though, I am not comfortable with the thought that your care is becoming piecemeal. We need to do what will be best for you in the long run. Think of it like this, Mr. Friday. You went to flight school at Fort Rucker, but, say, you didn't care for your instructor because he was Government Issue, so you went off to get private lessons at the same time. One guy is telling you to do autorotations this way, the other has a different system. Both work, but as a student pilot, you have created a wasp's nest of not-so-good possibilities. You see my point?"

Lincoln nodded.

"Again, I'll help you any way I can, but my recommendation is to follow up with the VA. Yes, it's taking a long time, but I am not convinced it's terribly dangerous to wait a few more weeks.

"And, just how bad is your back?"

"I can live with it. Ibuprofen seems to help."

"Yeah, but the medicine may also be the source of your stomach pain. That stuff can cause an ulcer, and if you take it for a long period, maybe over eight months, there is a risk of heart problems. Always better to get to the source of a problem and treat that, rather than the symptoms."

Lincoln nodded again and stood. "Doctor, we won't take any more of your time. You've been wonderful."

The doctor put his arm around Isabelle's shoulder. "And you are wonderful people. Keep me in the loop."

They went out for dinner, and when they got home, it was too late to check for e-mails or browse the news. Isabelle promised to call the VA again in the morning and push for a sooner appointment. Lincoln skipped his evening dose of ibuprofen.

CHAPTER SIXTY-TWO

When Isabelle went to her desk in the morning, her mind miles from the computer, the e-mail entitled "Searching For You" was still sitting in her inbox. She glanced at it briefly, and, without thinking, her hand reached for the mouse. She glanced disinterestedly at the first lines until the meaning of the words broke through her near trance. Her throat clutched, and, as in the doctor's office when Lincoln's cancer was confirmed, her peripheral vision began to collapse inward. Her hand moved so suddenly, the mouse tumbled to the floor and shot across the room. As she sprang to her feet in reflex to retrieve it, the room blackened, and she dropped to her knees, but was able to settle onto the floor before all consciousness had ebbed. She was not sure how long it was until her mind cleared, but the next thing she realized was her wobble back to the computer. As if driven by a force outside herself, she was captured by the rest of the message. With the last words, her thoughts became so tangled, she stumbled out of the office to the bedroom and dropped onto the bed. As she calmed, it began to crystallize just how dramatically their lives were about to change.

For a few moments, she told herself it was part of God's plan, and she had to accept His will. With faith, she and Lincoln would rise above this latest challenge, as they had all the others. As time slowed, her eyes closed, and she may even have fallen off for a few seconds, but the enormity of what had just emerged from the ether shocked her awake, and tears shot from her eyes. Her chest seized to the point it hurt, and with pain radiating into both arms, she feared she was having a heart attack. When the pain did not release, she reached for the phone to call 911, but in her panic, she could not fix on the buttons.

After another minute, the harshest of the throbbing faded, and she sat up suddenly but was so light-headed, she dropped back. First, a wave of nausea rolled over her, then a sense of doom. She could not imagine their lives recovering and, for a moment, felt there was nothing left to live for.

A few minutes later, the phone rang. She dug her nails into her palm until the pain brought her back. She picked up the phone and spoke with a ring in her voice. It was Lincoln, just calling to say hello.

He asked, "Are you okay? You sound funny."

"Nope, I'm fine. Just thinking."

"Don't you worry, Sweet Pea. Everything's gonna be just fine. About every guy I know has gone through this, or something like it. Soon all the waiting will be over, and I'll be on the mend. You'll see." They spoke for a few moments, and he asked again, "You sure you're okay?"

At the cocktail hour, she sat a bit more edgily than usual. Lincoln was about to question her once more but decided to leave her the privacy of her thoughts. There was, he accepted, so much on everyone's plate.

Lincoln woke in the middle of the night. He did not have to go and was surprised, for he usually slept so well in between bathroom runs. As his consciousness cleared, though, he realized Isabelle was crying in her sleep. He dared not rouse her and simply kissed her cheek. He lay awake for an hour and made the decision to ask Isabelle in the morning to get whatever it was out of her and into the open.

She was up before dawn. Lincoln stirred, and she kissed his forehead. She went straight to her little office, turned on the computer, changed her password, duplicated the e-mail, erased her inbox, and saved the copy to an obscure folder deep within her personal files.

Lincoln was surprised she was already up, and he walked down the hall. The door to her office was shut, the first time he'd ever seen it closed. He knocked and waited for her answer. She hesitated for a moment then invited him in, though as he looked at the computer, the Welcome Screen blinked on.

Lincoln stood in the entry looking at his wife's back. "You okay? What's so interesting on the computer?"

"Nothing," she grunted more coarsely than intended. "Just, ah, answering some e-mails from my old friends, you know, the girls back at school." She drew in a deep breath and turned toward Lincoln but did not engage his eyes. "We were carrying on about the trick we pulled on that stupid lab instructor. Do you remember that?"

"Yeah, I remember. I was still in Viet Nam. You kept it to yourself until I got home, which was probably a good thing. Wish I'd been here, though. I would have taken care of the problem in about three seconds."

"I don't know. Don't you think we did a good job, me and my pals?" Isabelle seemed to relax a bit and even laughed, though Lincoln could feel her joy was hollow. "One of the girls was saying that she was going to look that jerk up on a people finder.

Threaten to put copies of the picture on the internet. That would be a hoot."

"Serve him right, but maybe he learned his lesson. We all make mistakes when we're young—and when we're old. You want some coffee?"

"No, thanks."

Lincoln shook his head subtly and left for the kitchen. Isabelle waited until she heard him bustling about with the coffee maker before reopening the file with the e-mail.

Lincoln met with his aircraft mechanic friends over lunch that day. He came clean that a long period of treatment was ahead. They sat quietly, and finally one of the men asked, "Do you want us to go ahead without you? We can still get a lot done, just the two of us. Love to help out."

Lincoln shook his head. "Guys, let's wait until I'm back. There'll be plenty of time. I've been cogitating about it a lot."

One of the men interjected, "Please, Linc, don't have to waste brain cells worrying. We're here to help."

"No, I mean, I've made the decision to fight this thing, the cancer. I'll go to the VA and wait my turn. I don't know who the hell I thought I was. I got too much to live for to just give up."

Though the pain in Lincoln's back and belly continued over the next weeks, he began spending the days from just past dawn to after dark at the hangar, opening and picking through the crates. At home, while there were never harsh words, Lincoln felt a rift had opened with Isabelle. She'd become very quiet, and while not unaffectionate, she spent more and more time sitting quietly. Occasionally, though, she'd call out from her office, "I love you, Sweetheart."

He'd answer and start to get up from his computer to go see her, to touch her shoulders and kiss her hair, to ask what she was working on, but an uneasy sensation would grip him, for he could not miss the change in the timbre of her declaration, and he'd drop back into his chair to stare at nothing.

He was surprised at how he had begun to reflect less and less on the thought that he would soon be gone. The specter had lost its strident echo, and he began to feel periods of calm during the day that he had never before experienced. Perhaps this was what Dr. Render had meant, that his patients reported their lives softened as the final chapter unfolded.

CHAPTER SIXTY-THREE

Isabelle and Lincoln left for Maui to spend ten days away from the unceasing, gray Pennsylvania winter. They stopped in Oregon to see Sabrina and Mike. Sabrina had been chosen by a start-up to participate in a trial of FES, Functional Electrical Stimulation. She pushed up her sleeve and showed them the series of electrodes that had been implanted along her upper arm. There were also wires and a small computer. When the sensors picked up a faint message from her brain, one not strong enough to cause a muscle to contract, the computer amplified it and stimulated the muscle to move. She was able to shift her hands freely, and even her forearms, though jerky, moved with a greater range of motion than they had since the accident at the hospital. Isabelle stood next to Lincoln and held his arm. When Sabrina extended her hand toward her mother's, Isabelle reached forward. The instant their fingers touched, Isabelle broke into sobs and collapsed into a fetal ball at Lincoln's feet.

Sabrina and Lincoln were motionless as Isabelle moaned, "I can't do it any more, not for one more minute. I can't do it; I can't do it."

Mike ran into the room. He and Lincoln helped her onto the couch. Even Mike's eyes reddened as they stood and waited.

Lincoln knelt in front of her. "Please, Isabelle. Everybody here loves you. Please, Sweetheart. *What is eating at you?*"

"I want a glass of wine. Everyone will drink wine."

Ten minutes passed before the alcohol had been absorbed. Lincoln sat next to Isabelle on the couch and held her hand. Mike pushed Sabrina's chair to her mother's side, and she took Isabelle's other hand. Mike stood in front of them, a lost puppy. "What am I supposed to hold, Mom, your foot?"

Isabelle choked on her wine, and some of it dripped out of her nose. She bellowed with laughter, and soon the others did as well, and then the room became tranquil. "Lincoln, I'm sorry for what I have been over the past weeks. It is not you, or Sabrina, or Mike."

Mike piped, "You sure about that? That it's not me?"

"Please, I need you to be serious for just the next sixty seconds."

Sabrina rolled her eyes. "Good luck, Mom."

Isabelle giggled. "God, I love you, Mike. You are a blessing in our life." He leaned forward and kissed her cheek. "Okay, here goes. Sabrina, you have a sister. Lincoln, you have another daughter." Mike's jaw might have hung lower than his wife's. "Sweetheart," she turned to Sabrina, "you didn't know this, but I got pregnant when your poppy and I were in high school."

Mike whispered, "No problem. You're Catholic. Immaculate Conception. Nothing to be ashamed of."

Sabrina snapped her head at him. "Will you please?"

"What, it was after sixty seconds."

"I went off and told everybody that I was going to study for nursing school in Florida. I went to Florida, all right, but stayed in a Catholic home. They were wonderful, considering everything."

Lincoln looked so small sitting next to her. He squeaked, "Sweetheart, I thought you said you had a miscarriage, that… that I didn't have to worry, that, 'God had shined on us.'"

"I told you that. I had to. Helicopter school was going to be hard enough. You'd been screwed by the Air Force and by those idiots in the hospital in Wilkes Barre. Enough was enough. When we were kids, you should have seen your face when my poppy told you about flying. It seemed the only time that precious spark in you gleamed. Fate took away the Academy. I wasn't about to rip helicopters out of your arms. I just couldn't.

"Couple of weeks ago, I got an e-mail from a private detective agency. Our little girl hired them to find us. At first, I didn't answer it. Then I wrote a dozen replies and erased them. When that doctor at the VA kept saying Gleason eight, Gleason eight, it just became too much. I wrote back. I told them I would like to e-mail our daughter first, and the detective was very kind. That was fine. Then I couldn't stand it, and I called her. You were at the hangar. We talked and bawled for six hours. The battery ran out on the phone. I borrowed Connie's next door. I think she was afraid to ask what was wrong. I was such a mess.

"But then it was done, and now it's done. Mike, would you mind bringing my carry-on over here?" She pulled out a picture of a regal, slender, raven-haired woman with black eyes. She turned to Lincoln and presented the image. He could not take his eyes off her but finally handed it to Sabrina.

Then Sabrina's eyes bore into the photo, unable to look away. Finally, she mumbled, "We are like total opposites except that we're identical. Mom, what's her name?"

"Gina. Her parents thought she looked Italian. She does, doesn't she?"

Sabrina handed the picture to Mike. He studied for a minute then handed it back. Sabrina remarked quite seriously, "Nothing to say?"

"Well, now that you mentioned it…"

"Don't you dare. Mom, do you know if she works?"

"Yep. Are you sitting down?" There were chuckles. "She's a clinical psychologist. PhD from the University of Florida. I'm not making this up. Gina and I have decided that it should happen, I mean, that we meet. This was what we came up with. When your dad and I return from Maui, she'd like to come out here, and we all could get together. Her husband is a teacher—yep, math. I know, I know, it's all too hard to believe, but there's no way I could make this up. So, if that's okay with everyone, most important, you, Lincoln?"

"More than anything on Earth. But, you know, I'd like to talk to her first. I think I really need to do that, Sweetheart."

They spoke that night.

CHAPTER SIXTY-FOUR

Isabelle and Lincoln stayed in Lahaina, the quaint, former capital of the Hawaiian Islands during the epoch of the kings. Mike told them there was an Elvis impersonator, one he and Sabrina had seen in Vegas. The man had been baptized the king of all impressionists, so Mike and Sabrina had made reservations for Isabelle and Lincoln to see his show.

The night they went, the clerk at the will-call desk nodded to the woman next to her when Isabelle showed her ID. A man came out of the theater and asked them to follow him. They were seated front-row center. They turned to each other, and Isabelle whispered to Lincoln, "We are the most blessed people that have ever lived." He squeezed her hand, and they hugged.

The show was as magical as when they had seen The King four decades before. Darren Lee made the audience feel as though they were actually just feet from Elvis. He engaged older women in the front rows, holding their hands, serenading them to *The Hawaiian Wedding Song* and *Love Me Tender.*

Halfway through the performance, he stopped dead, came down from the stage, walked to Isabelle's side, and took her hand. "Ladies and Gentlemen. We have a special treat tonight. This is Isabelle Friday and her husband, Lincoln. The Fridays had the thrill of seeing the real King in concert, what, forty years ago?" Isabelle nodded. "They were so special, these two. You see, Mr. Friday was just leaving for Viet Nam to be a helicopter pilot, and they had just gotten hitched, so The King introduced them to the audience in Vegas. And do you know what? Mr. Friday went to Viet Nam. Yes, indeed, he did. And he flew those helicopters, and he was wounded. And listen to this, Ladies and Gentlemen, Mr. Friday was awarded our nation's highest ribbon for bravery, the Medal of Honor. That's who we have here tonight."

And, once again, Lincoln Friday stood before an audience that had come to its feet to honor him.

The next morning, they had breakfast at Betty's, a restaurant just feet from the ocean. They sat over coffee, staring across the strait at the island of Lanai. Lincoln took Isabelle's hands. "I feel like Forrest Gump. Elvis, the President, the President, *again*, and Elvis, *again*. And now I have two beautiful, successful daughters, and the loveliest wife in the history of the world. I don't care about the future. I've already reached nirvana."

"Don't say that. Don't tempt the fates." She leaned over and kissed him.

Toward the end of breakfast, Lincoln went to the men's room. When he came back, he mumbled, "Sweetheart, I think I had too much coffee. Stomach's acting up again. Do you mind if I go back to the room and lay down for a few minutes?"

She studied his face and shook her head. "I'm going with you."

She expected him to scoff, to urge her not to become hysterical, but he nodded, and they walked slowly back to the hotel. By the time they got to the elevator, he was hunched forward. "What is it, Sweetheart?"

"My back and my stomach." He exhaled loudly through his mouth and gnashed his teeth. "Whoa! I need to lay down."

In the room, he crawled into a ball on the bed. "Sweetheart, I think I need to see a doctor."

She went to the desk. They called a taxi, which took them to a clinic in Lahaina. The doctor saw him immediately. Lincoln's vital signs concerned the man. "Does your husband normally have blood pressure on the low side?"

"No. Recently, pretty high."

"Tell me about his medical history."

She related the cancer and the history of a kidney infection, so the doctor took a urine sample and did a rectal exam to see if there was bleeding in his digestive track. All was normal. Lincoln sat up and smiled that he was feeling better. The doctor seemed pleased because the deep pain had resolved as fast as it had begun, and he had not discovered anything on his physical exam.

"Okay, Mr. Friday. We can chalk this up to something you ate, probably last night, or maybe just a viral stomach infection. Anything's possible. My suggestion is that if you're not darn near all better by noon, you get on an inter-island flight and be seen at Queen's Hospital in Honolulu. They're much better equipped than we are on Maui. You call me, and I'll make sure you get seen right away."

They stayed in that afternoon, and by evening, he was well enough to have some ginger ale, but early in the morning, the pain returned, and they took a cab to the airport. While sitting in the waiting area for the first flight to Honolulu, the cramping worsened, and a few tears dropped from his eyes.

A man approached him slowly. "I'm sorry, sir. Are you okay? I'm a doctor. Can I help you?"

Isabelle explained the situation, and the man asked Lincoln to point to the worst pain. It was right below the belly button. He asked Lincoln to follow him to a corner of the room, where he did a cursory exam. His face tightened when he pushed on Lincoln's abdomen. It was as hard as a board, yet he thought his fingers detected a pulsing mass. The doctor frowned. "You need to get to the hospital."

He went to the gate agent, who told him there was no room on the next flight, so he pulled his medical license from his wallet and insisted that if Lincoln wasn't in Queen's Hospital within the next two hours, he would hold the gate agent and the airline responsible for the bad outcome he warned was inevitable. The doctor stared at the man's name tag, and the agent puffed his chest to make sure the doctor could see it.

The doctor gave up his seat, but no other passenger was willing to wait an hour. The last two passengers to walk up to the jetway were elderly, Japanese men, and, though the doctor tried to explain the situation, the men understood not a word of English. The gate agent refused to call an interpreter, and the ancient men toddled through the door unawares.

The doctor stayed with them until the next flight and talked with Isabelle during the forty-five-minute trip. She told him Lincoln was being seen at the VA Hospital in Philadelphia, and the doctor brightened. "You know, there's a VA hospital, or I should say, a military hospital, in Honolulu. It's called Tripler Army Medical Center. It's not far from the airport. Let's head there when we land."

He told them to leave their luggage and tugged at Lincoln until they reached the interminable line at the taxi stand. The doctor shouted, "We have a medical emergency here, medical emergency. Step aside, please."

He pushed the driver to speed out of the airport, up the hill toward the hospital. As they pulled into the mammoth complex, the doctor sprang from the car, ran into the emergency room, and through the doors into the treatment area. He shouted, "Surgical abdomen. Possible rupturing triple A."

Lincoln was on a gurney and in a procedure bay with a large bore IV in his neck in less than a minute. A portable x-ray machine was wheeled in and a "poor man's cross table lateral" was performed. The doctor had called the diagnosis correctly. Lincoln had an abdominal aortic aneurism, and it was leaking, ready to rupture at any moment. The chances of his survival, if it actually burst, were essentially zero, for the blood would gush out of the aorta into the abdomen in a cloudburst, leaving none left to feed the heart and the brain.

A vascular surgeon was summoned. Lincoln was prepped for immediate surgery, but as they wheeled him to the OR, he screamed in pain, then became deathly quiet as his face drained of color. The anesthesiologist jammed chemicals into the IV, and the surgeon began the operation before Lincoln's eyes had closed. Lincoln arched his back at the first plunge of the scalpel, but then collapsed against the operating table and went limp. The nurses pumped blood and saline into him, but his blood pressure ebbed until the surgeon finally just reached through the pooling blood in Lincoln's abdomen and pinched off the ruptured aorta with his fingers.

The man worked as if the future of civilization lay in his hands. The nurses worked as if the future of civilization lay in their hands. Eventually, enough of a repair had been accomplished to allow some continuity of blood flow, a chance for the body to catch up. The surgeon leaned back and stretched, drenched in sweat, as were the nurses. He took a very deep breath, gazed toward the heavens, and set back to work fashioning a permanent repair.

It was hours before the graft was in place and all the layers of the aorta sewn meticulously, to preclude even the slightest leak. The surgeon had asked one of the nurses to go out and speak with the patient's family. She came back and told them it was only his wife. They were on vacation, resting up before treatment for prostate cancer. She had also checked his records on the VA's master computer and come to the Medal of Honor. She looked that up on the internet and found Lincoln's name and the actual document honoring the award. She printed a copy and brought it back to the OR. The surgeon asked her to read it aloud.

As they began the protocol to wake Lincoln up, his blood pressure drifted down to the point it might not sustain consciousness. When the systolic pressure dipped to eighty, the surgeon called for the heart-lung bypass team.

Within minutes, Lincoln's life was sustained solely by the wheels and cogs and plastic tubes of the heart-lung machine that drained spent blood from his veins and pumped fresh blood back into his arteries. But there was only so long he could be supported by the machine, and when his heart rhythm deteriorated into ventricular tachycardia, the surgeon prepared himself for the inevitable. They shocked Lincoln several times, each jolt with increased voltage, but they were soon at the limit of what the device offered. There were a few beats, but the heart stopped again in seconds.

With the team ready to cease and accept they had lost their patient, a sad calm replaced the frantic crusade. The surgeon looked at the anesthesiologist and mumbled, "You did good, Jack. Thank you."

Jack nodded and sighed loudly, "I hope I have a team like this working on me at the end. Thank you, everybody."

The surgeon took a step toward the door, removed his gloves, and started to wiggle out of his gown. "I'll go talk to the family."

As he pushed on the door absently, a beep from the cardiac monitor interrupted his reverie. He turned back. Everyone turned to the monitor. There was another beep, a pair, and then four in a row. The electrical spikes on the screen became regular, and some even relatively normal. Lincoln's heart began a gentle quickening. It steadied at fifty-six, and his blood pressure was ninety over forty. His head lolled, and he tried to speak around his breathing tube.

The surgeon whispered through tears, "Tough son of a bitch. Thank you, God."

The man sat with Isabelle. He took her hand. "Mrs. Friday, your husband is waking up. It was a tough procedure, but he's still with us, and that is fairly rare in these cases. He's got a long road ahead of him, though."

"Do you think he'll make it, Doctor?"

"I'm afraid only the Creator knows, but we will spare nothing to make him comfortable and to support whatever his body does to get over this." He waited for her to absorb what he'd said, then went on, "Oh, and by the way, let me ask, was Mr. Friday ever a smoker?"

"Not really. He'd puff on an occasional cigarette when he was in the Army, sitting around with the guys. You know, I don't think he ever bought a pack. Why do you ask? Could you tell from something inside him?"

"Believe it or not, smoking as few as one hundred cigarettes, not one hundred packs, is enough to cause the aorta to fail. Hard to believe just how dangerous smoking is. Every day, we find out something else. And, let me ask, did this pain just begin today, I mean, the abdominal pain?"

"Yesterday, but he's really had a bad stomach for months. His low back, too."

The surgeon shook his head. "Probably been building for some time. No way to tell, though, what the pain was all about. Probably a combination. By the way, Mr. Friday is in good company. This is what Albert Einstein had, Lucille Ball, and George C.

Scott. And thank you for his exceptional service to our country. You must be very proud."

Lincoln was wheeled to the Intensive Care Unit. The hospital was situated on a rise facing the mountains on one side and the Pacific Ocean on the other. The view was humbling. He was sedated to keep his blood pressure just low enough to sustain life, but not put too much pressure on the freshly sewn aorta. He was unconscious, and the hospitalist told Isabelle he might be for days.

She sat there for a while then asked a nurse for the nearest hotel. The woman looked surprised. "Hon, we'll put you up. I guess your husband is quite the VIP." Isabelle stayed at the bedside for an hour then took a cab to the airport to pick up the luggage. She was shown a room in the women officers' quarters. As she sat in the hospital cafeteria, barely touching her meal, she realized she hadn't told Sabrina where she was and what had happened.

Despite her insistence they not leave home, Sabrina and Mike declared they were on the way. Mike called ahead to rent a wheelchair van in Honolulu, and the company arranged to meet him at the terminal. He called for emergency leave from school. Sabrina rescheduled her patients.

They arrived the next afternoon and met Isabelle in the cafeteria. Before going to Lincoln's room, Isabelle spoke so faintly, they could barely hear her. She mumbled that she'd overheard the nurses during the change of shift. It was unlikely Lincoln would wake up. The goal for his care was to insure he suffered no pain.

The three said nothing as they walked from the elevator to Lincoln's room.

Sabrina gasped when she saw her father. "Poppy!" She worked her way out of the wheelchair, sat on the edge of the bed, then leaned down to hold him. Mike began to cry and left the room.

Isabelle hovered over Sabrina, and the three were soon breathing in cadence.

Lincoln's head moved. His eyes fluttered. Isabelle gulped, "I think we're squashing him."

She helped Sabrina back into the chair and called Mike into the room. Mike went to the bedside and took Lincoln's hand, very softly, but then squeezed it in his grief. Lincoln's eyes fluttered again. He squeezed harder, and Lincoln's eyes unlocked into narrow slits and stared at Mike. Slowly, Lincoln rolled his head toward Isabelle and tried to speak.

She smiled through her tears. "Sweetheart, don't try to talk. There's a tube in your throat to help you breathe. It's going to come out real soon."

He nodded slightly and turned toward Sabrina. She reached forward and stroked his arm. The nurse brought orange juice for the visitors, and Lincoln looked at the container and feebly lifted his hand and pointed to himself. Mike went out and told the nurse.

She chuckled softly. "He's not going to be taking anything by mouth for a while. But what we can do is rub his lips with a damp washcloth, and I'll put some lip balm on when you're done. We're gonna keep Mr. Friday feeling good. I promise."

An hour later, after Lincoln had fallen asleep and awoken several times, he moved a finger weakly toward his mouth then turned it and pointed at each of his guests, one by one. He was dismissing them to the cafeteria.

They sat silently, and after just a few minutes, left their meals uneaten. As they walked back through the main lobby, Isabelle paused and her ears perked. She scanned left and right but shook her head and continued behind Sabrina and Mike toward the elevator. When she halted abruptly a second time, Mike sensed it and twisted around to see Isabelle moving toward the information desk. She stopped behind a couple talking with the receptionist. Mike spun the wheelchair about.

Sabrina was startled and opened her mouth, but when she saw her mother, she bolted upright in the chair, frozen, staring. Mike took her hand.

Isabelle gasped, "Gina?"

A tall, dark woman with black, silken hair spun around, though, in a trice, her legs faltered. She grabbed for Isabelle, and the two held each other unsteadily until Mike and the other man led them to a couch in the admissions area. Still, they hadn't spoken, but Gina's eyes shifted suddenly to Sabrina, and she darted toward her sister, bent forward, and wouldn't let go.

Gina's husband took a step back and laughed through his tears, "What am I, chopped liver?"

Isabelle and Sabrina looked up in disbelief. "Oh, my God, another one!"

They barely left Lincoln's side that day and night. Early the next morning, he had more and more trouble keeping his eyes open. The nurse said he had a bit of a fever, but not to worry, though she called the hospitalist. Lincoln's temperature spiked an hour later, and the doctor put him on strong antibiotics. They wrapped him in a cooling blanket.

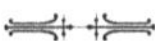

Lincoln Friday passed late that day, just as dusk consumed the islands. His family watched the last bit of light and, finally, the green flash on the horizon of a sun that was now shining on Asia.

He was buried at Arlington National Cemetery.

EPILOGUE

Dr. Render seemed relieved when Isabelle contacted him to let him know Lincoln had died of an aneurism rather than the cancer. She was not sure if it was because he'd dodged the bullet, the delay in treatment had not contributed to his patient's demise, and he, thus, could not be sued, or because he knew Lincoln's cancer would not have been cured and his patient would have withered painfully before their eyes. She did not, though, care, for she knew that even if the interval had not killed him, it had robbed them of any semblance of peace during their last year. How, she wondered, could Render, the VA administrators, or the senators—how could any of them—live with themselves? What if it had been their fathers or brothers?

Isabelle had the helicopter parts re-crated and advertised in *Trade A Plane.* She received an offer from a man in Khartoum, Sudan. It was for ten thousand dollars, but he'd pay for shipping at both ends, and even make arrangements for the freight to be hauled out of the hanger in Wilkes Barre and loaded on trucks. All she'd have to do was push the button to open the hangar doors. She wrote on one of the boxes, "Sure hope these ships do some good."

When the scandal of lies, corruption, and incompetence at VA hospitals throughout the nation was exposed in 2013, Isabelle thought about joining the movement for accountability and professional care for veterans. After all, her senator, Francie Kozub, was now the most vocal of the lot screaming for heads to roll. But Isabelle thought about Kozub's office, the lack of caring and the insensitivity, and she reminded herself that everything in an organization came from the top. She knew Senator Kozub's fervor would last only as long as it was politically expedient, as long as there were photo-ops, and then she would move on to another cause and draft unsuspecting constituents into keeping her in the Senate. Lincoln had taught her that much; it was all just a well-oiled ruse, smoke and mirrors, driven by the greed that swathed the country's leadership.

She sat at the window in her little office and was honest with herself, admitting that she no longer possessed the spirit to pound sand. She had two beautiful daughters, two grandchildren, her mother, and a peaceful city in which to spend the rest of her years.

It was enough.

OTHER TITLES BY WILLIAM S. GOULD, MD

AT YONAH MOUNTAIN

Brand new Second Lieutenant J.W. Weathersby is on orders to depart for a combat tour in Viet Nam. At a West Point wedding, though, he commits a very public faux pas and is thrust as punishment into a class of 160 select young officers who sweat and freeze through months of brutal training at the United States Army Ranger School. J.W. joins an African American PhD candidate and a Rose Bud Sioux Harvard graduate, the three pushed together to trudge the mountains, forests, and deserts as Ranger buddies. As half the class is weeded out, they share their disparate lives and dreams. J.W. struggles to be cut from the program, and at the same time fights desperately to remain.

At Yonah Mountain is a coming of age adventure, an examination of race relations in the military, and an authentic tale of Army Ranger training.

CAPTAIN IRON MUSTACHE

Captain Iron Mustache takes place in 1968 and 1969. United States Army lieutenant, J.W. Weathersby, just out of Ranger School, volunteers for duty in Viet Nam. It is not long before he changes from naïve youngster to hardened soldier.

Something about rural Viet Nam, though, captivates him, and he convinces his commanding officer to allow him to live as the sole American in a remote rice-farming hamlet. His mission is to win the hearts and the minds of the peasants. J.W. forms a deep friendship with the village chief, and falls in love with the schoolteacher, Miss Lin.

During a mid-night battle, Miss Lin is arrested and tortured as a communist agent. At the same time, the chief is critically wounded, and disappears after being flown out of the village by an American medevac helicopter. J.W. and the chief's wife spend the last month of his tour driving the deadly roads of Viet Nam searching hospital after hospital for the man.

Nearly half a century later, J.W. and his wife return to Viet Nam in a surreal effort to find the chief. He also wants to see Miss Lin, but the Vietnamese government is suspicious of his motives, and the days of his sojourn are fraught with struggle and frustration until a simple act of kindness changes his life.

IN BLACK GRANITE

In Black Granite is set in the decade after J.W. Weathersby returns from the war in Viet Nam. He eventually accepts the assessment of family, friends, and medical school deans that he will never become a doctor. He drifts without focus until the miracle of his first child's birth rekindles the craving to study medicine. This is a narrative of his dogged struggle to beat the overwhelming odds against a man in his mid-thirties gaining admission to an American college of medicine.

In Black Granite scrutinizes the ruthless battle for places in medical school, and how the psyches of the chosen are sieved as they are herded through the decade as students and residents. The strain of endless days and nights away from family, of sleepless months, and of pervasive arrogance, distorts the souls of even the strongest. Some find the path more treacherous than surviving a war.

C.O.L.A.

The day his father died, Dr. Solomon Forte promised his mother he would honor him by dedicating his years as a doctor to the treatment of injured workers. It seemed so clear a decision—his patients would be like his dad, stoic, honest, working class stiffs who sought nothing more from a doctor than an arm around the shoulder, a word of reassurance, and an ally in dealing with the state industrial insurance system.

His life at the Whitaker Hospital and Medical Center is, though, the antithesis of his dream. He can't tell which of the roadblocks is most daunting: that posed by his medical colleagues, the threats of S.M.A.C., the State Medical Abuse Commission, the bureaucracy at C.O.L.A., the state's Commission on Labor Affairs, or the duplicitous patients, some of whom spend every waking moment trying to dupe him out of drugs and government benefits.

Occasionally, a case is obvious–the worker really was devastated by an industrial accident. It seems to Sol, though, that those are the very patients C.O.L.A. torments. On the other hand, claimants skilled at ripping off the Commission run free for decades.

C.O.L.A. also examines the specter of serious medical errors, and how they are so much easier to make on patients whose care is mired in the aggravation of government-sponsored insurance plans. Questions are also raised about the state-appointed morality commissions that determine which doctors relinquish their licenses for treating pain. Finally, it is a disturbing look behind the scenes of a modern, multi-specialty medical clinic.

A HEART WIND FROM THE DESERT

Dr. Solomon Forte has lost everything. There is little left but to offer himself to the wretched in war-torn Sudan. Arriving in the desert, heart brimming with hope, it does not take long to recognize that the social and political beliefs that have spawned the war and famine are the very forces that prevent him from carrying out his dream of caring for the dispossessed.

At first, despite the warnings of the tiny European medical team left at the refugee camp in Darfur Province, he fights back with typical, strident, American resolve to save the entire population of refugees. The obstacles of central African life, however, soon draw the spirit from him, and he turns his efforts to preserving the lives of his Western companions.

He falls deeply for a gorgeous, but outwardly hardened, British nurse. When she disappears from camp, he spends what strength is left searching for her.

A Heart Wind from the Desert examines the need in all of us to accomplish something meaningful in the tiny fragment of time we are allotted, and the impossible hurdles faced when trying to change the way people have thought and behaved for the millennia.

It is a tale of beautiful, warm children, but also of the stark life in the sub-Saharan Sahel.

RAPHAEL'S BLANKET

Raphael Blumenkopf is born clandestinely at the Bergen Belsen Nazi death camp on the 14th of April, 1945. His birth is an unprecedented miracle, as is the liberation of the camp by British forces that very afternoon.

He has only his mother and a few surviving villagers from their home in Checzonovska, Poland. While the majority of the refugees leave Central Europe for Israel and the West, his band travels across Russia to China. A relative has promised jobs in Shang Hai's old Jewish settlement.

The journey is fraught with threats from starving Russians, barbaric border guards, and destitute Chinese peasants.

Just as the lives of the immigrants begin to normalize in China, the victory of Mao Zedung's communist army forces them to flee, this time to Hanoi. Five years later, the communist movement in North Viet Nam topples the French government, and the Jews run again. They settle in Saigon until the unrest there compels them to emigrate to America.

Raphael's years in the U.S. are colored indelibly by the poison that follows him from the Holocaust, and he formulates a plan to extract revenge from a Federal judge with ties to the Nazis. Who could have envisaged the price he'd pay?

www.ingramcontent.com/pod-product-compliance
Lightning Source LLC
Chambersburg PA
CBHW072009020726
47501CB00006B/1747

9780991223787